RAVEN'S RESURRECTION

A CYBERTECH THRILLER

by

JOHN D. TRUDEL

Author: John D. Trudel

Cover Design and Art: Bruce DeRoos

Raven's Resurrection is available through major book distributors in paper and on all major eBook platforms.

ISBN: 978-0-9996305-0-1

PRAISE FOR JOHN D. TRUDEL
RAVEN'S RESURRECTION

"John D. Trudel is one of the best writers in the Thriller genre, with his own unique voice and style. *Raven's Resurrection*, his 6th novel, raises the bar. It's a great read. Recommended!"

– Robert Dugoni, #1 NY Times Best-Selling Author

"Raven's Resurrection is Trudel's best Thriller yet. Compelling characters, deadly weapons, Washington intrigue, ruthless jihadists, a secret Iranian Quds base, and deadly Russian spies as dubious allies. It could be real. You pray it's not."

– Paul E Vallely, MG US Army Ret.

"John D. Trudel's latest Raven book moves at a lightening pace from vividly portrayed action to well-calculated psychological tension. Tight, cinema-graphic writing put the readers in a dangerous world that much resembles a darker version of the current USA. You'll want to keep the doors locked and the shades down!"

– Anne Hillerman, Best-Selling Author, *Song of the Lion*

"Raven's Resurrection is an epic tale that is as close to reality as a thriller can be. Trudel weaves a complex series of events into a 'can't put it down' novel that will have you looking over your shoulder at every turn."

– Joseph Badal, Amazon #1 Best-Selling Author, *Sins of the Fathers*

"Trudel continues the excellent Raven's series with another powerful thriller. The character of Raven continues to evolve. This is a book that you will get totally immersed in and won't want to put down."

–Michael Connelly, Novelist and Constitutional Lawyer

DEDICATION

I dedicate this novel to Jerry Pournelle (1933-2017), the novelist, scientist, technology pundit, columnist, and blogger who mentored me and endorsed my novels.

Jerry was one of the giants of science-fiction literature with an emphasis on both the science and the literature. He was a key contributor to the Star Wars program that helped end the Cold War.

The masthead for Jerry's blog included these:

> *"Being intelligent is not a felony. But most societies evaluate it as at least a misdemeanor."* - **Robert A. Heinlein**

> *"Those who cannot remember the past are condemned to repeat it."* -**George Santayana** [Worth pondering at a time when the radical left is frantic to erase American history, culture, and monuments.]

> "Freedom is not free. Free men are not equal. Equal men are not free."

I dedicate my novel to **"We the People,"** to all Americans (regardless of gender, ethnicity, or political party) who upset the political elites, media hacks, and Washington insiders to foil a rigged election and elect an outsider to the highest office in the land.

America is coming back. It is not over of course. Good versus evil is forever.

Finally, I dedicate this novel to my wife Pat. Without her patience and bright spirit, this book would not exist. She is a saint.

ACKNOWLEDGEMENTS

Ernest Hemingway said, "There is no such thing as writing, only rewriting." He also said, "You never finish a book, you just let it go." He was right.

I could not write at the level I do without my team of critical readers, content experts, and editors who take the time to scan my drafts with eagle eyes, amazing insight, and brutally honest criticism. Each time they touch my words, my novels get better. Kay Jewett deserves special credit.

It is uplifting to get validation. One of my critical readers is an expert on Western mythology and history, which he taught for years. Part of this novel that prompted a lot of discussion was the Epilogue, where I expanded the scope to pay homage to 24/7 diversionary ranting in the fake news media about "the Russians," enemies with some common interests. Here is what he said:

> *"The bridge exchange in the fog was high art, as was your comment about Russians losing children at Beslan being far worse for them than our 9/11 for our culture, which opens a whole new direction for your next book."*
>
> Chuck Moody

My novels bring me into contact with exceptional people who have sacrificed to keep America safe from our enemies both foreign and domestic. You know who you are. I honor your service and your personal stories inspire me.

Finally, you, my readers, are most important of all. **Thank you for your support.**

ACRONYM INDEX

ADS-B: Automatic Dependent Surveillance – Broadcast

APC: Armored Personnel Carrier

ATC: Air Traffic Control

CBSA: Canada Border Services Agency

CIA: Central Intelligence Agency

COMs: Communications

COMSEC: Communications Security

Covfefe: It literally means covfefe

CSR: Counter Surveillance Route

DOD: Department of Defense

DOJ: Department of Justice

ECM: Electronic Counter Measures

EMP: Electro Magnetic Pulse

ETA: Estimated Time of Arrival

EU: European Union (NWO, writ small)

FAA: Federal Aviation Administration

FBI: Federal Bureau of Investigation

FEMA: Federal Emergency Management Agency

FSB: Replaced the KGB

GPS: Global Positioning System

HE: High Explosive

HQ: Headquarters

HVT: High Value Target

IED: Improvised Explosive Device

ISIS: Islamic State of Iraq and the Levant: Daesh

JCS: Joint Chiefs of Staff

KGB: Soviet spy and state-security machine

MI5: Counter Intelligence (British FBI)

MI6: Secret Intelligence Service (British CIA)

NRO: National Reconnaissance Office

NSA: National Security Agency

NSC: National Security Council

NVG: Night Vision Goggles

NWO: New World Order

OP: Operation, a mission, usually covert

PSD: Personal Security Detail

Quds: Special Forces unit of Iran's Revolutionary Guards

ROE: Rules of Engagement

SAM: Surface to Air Missile

SITREP: Situation Report

SOCOM: Special Operations Command

TANGO: A target

TFR: Temporary Flight Restriction

TSG: Transnational Services Group

UN: United Nations

UNCTAD: UN Conference of Trade and Development

WMD: Weapon of Mass Destruction

"We have to start with the premise that the goal is to defeat the enemy."

Jim Woolsey, former CIA Director

"People sleep peaceably in their beds at night only because rough men stand ready to do violence on their behalf."

George Orwell

"The object of war is not to die for your country but to make the other bastard die for his."

George S. Patton

"So much of left-wing thought is a kind of playing with fire by people who don't even know that fire is hot."

George Orwell

"Political Correctness Is Fascism Pretending To Be Manners."

George Carlin

"In 1940, we knew who we were, we knew who the enemy was, and we knew the dangers and the issues…. It is different today. We don't know who we are, we don't know the issues, and we still do not understand the nature of the enemy."

Bernard Lewis, Historian

CHAPTER ONE
IT'S A NEW GAME

Private House, South of Monterey, California, Late Afternoon

Josie seemed pensive. The woman was sensitive, empathetic, and usually eager to share her visions and perceptions with him. She was a bright spirit, chasing rainbows and butterflies in strange dimensions.

Not today.

It was Josie's unique perceptions that made her so valuable. She was a remote viewer, a paranormal. She sat brushing her long brown hair, silhouetted against the low sun, watching a gentle wind rustle the branches outside through the sliding patio door on the raised deck.

She had the door open and was listening to the birds. She'd put feeders out to attract them.

Raven watched her silently. Not wanting to interrupt. His world was so much darker than hers.

"You're staring at me," I said.

I had not turned my head. I didn't need to.

Raven chuckled, "Bet your ass. You brighten the entire room. You look good, Babe. Just watching the sunlight on your hair. It turns gold when you stroke it and flip it up."

He made me smile. He'd always said the safe house was too dark with its solid walls, massive rock fireplace, small windows, and the dense forest that surrounded it.

I loved forests. I drew comfort and serenity from them. It was probably my Celtic heritage. I didn't mind a bit of visual gloom. The sense of life all around me was calming.

Except for the kill teams, of course.

Raven saw the deep dark as a danger zone. Even with the sensors and security cameras, he wanted to personally see what was coming at him. He'd said, "*The problem with walls and doors is that you can't see what's on the other side.*"

It didn't matter. Our safe house was compromised. We would be leaving soon.

I said, "Are you going to tell me what's going on?"

"What's to tell? Out there in the world, President Blager is alive, recovering, doing well, and America is rejoicing. Here, in our small corner, we're on stand-down and you're safe."

"They found us here." I left the *again* unsaid. We both remembered Durham.

"Uh-Huh. They did. Incidentally."

"***Incidentally?*** What does that mean?"

He gave a short laugh. "Who knows? It's just what Goldfarb said. He's on the National Security Council now. Apparently they talk that way."

I turned and looked at him. "How is he?"

"Recovering. They kept us off the grid, thank God, but some media person noticed Goldfarb's name on logs for visiting the President in the hospital. He is staying out of Washington until things cool off."

"What things?"

"High level policy issues at the National Security Council level. President Blager wanted to give him a voting seat on NSC, but that would have to be announced. Instead, Goldfarb is to be an Ad-hoc member, like Bannon under Trump was after he was 'removed.' Powerful people oppose that."

"Can you put that in plain English?"

"Goldfarb came to us from the land of broken toys at CIA. He is a relic of the Cold War, a patriot. He has been our main support. Without him, neither of us would still be alive."

"I know."

"He's being promoted. The President wants him present at NSC. He can sit in whenever he wants as a guest. The bad news is that Goldfarb now leaves footprints. He casts a shadow, one that is about to get bigger and more noticeable. He's not happy about that."

"He exposed us, Raven."

"Yes. It wasn't poor tradecraft, it was something more subtle. There is a lot of 'shit happens' in our world. He's working to get us better protection."

"Where is he?"

"Not sure. Don't you know?"

"I know you met with him…."

Raven took a deep breath and let it out slowly. "Yeah."

"Are you going to tell me what he wants?"

"You don't know?"

"Something is wrong. I've done several remote viewings, but I can't tell. We seem to be at a nexus.

"I don't see any big threats on the horizon. From a great distance, the world seems to be healing. The Abyss is gone as if it never existed. The President is good. His lifeline is strong into the future. He's loved and respected."

"Except by our enemies," Raven said. "But…."

"I can't see the close-up details. When I try to see our future – yours and mine – the trail gets lost in a probability cloud. It's fuzzy. Not a fog exactly, but there is no clarity. Things are shifting and changing. The future is uncertain, like it's trying to figure out what it wants to be."

"That's about what Goldfarb said too. Our mission is being redefined. There will be new rules. They are trying to sort it out…."

"Is this about the Blager Codicil?"

"That's the big picture. It's stated policy. America is putting it into treaties."

"Going back to the tactics of General Blackjack Pershing? Extreme punishment for Islamic terrorism?"

"Not extreme. ***Appropriate*** would be a better word, I think. More effective."

"You need to explain that."

"Trump wanted to destroy ISIS and he pretty much did."

"Yes."

"Blager wants more. He plans to totally eradicate radical Islam. The Arab Spring rejuvenated the ancient horrors. *Hijrah.* Migration *jihad.* Blager wants to put that Genie back in the bottle and hammer the cork down before they get Nukes and other WMDs."

"By killing more Islamic terrorists." Josie shuddered. "You do know that there are millions of them? Millions! Before we met, I saved you in Iran. I had to give up those missions. It was killing me."

Raven nodded. "Reality sucks. Intelligence services estimate that 15-25% of Muslims are *jihadists*, perhaps 180 to 300 million people. The Blager Codicil is an effort to trim the percentage **without** having to kill them all.

"In any case, wars and battlefields are a job for our military. We're being tasked with key small-group strategic threats, defending the homeland. That's what we've been doing. This will just formalize it."

"What about me? They came for **me**."

"They did. Because you are a national asset. Goldfarb wants to shift us from defense to offense. He wants a narrow, focused, preemptive elimination of top-level strategic threats."

"It sounds like he is talking about playing God. Do you want any part of that?"

"I don't and he's not."

"What then?"

"He's talking about identifying and removing a few specific major cancer cells. America has done that before in wartime. We are talking about small numbers."

"How many?"

"Single digits. This is about killing Grendel, not slaughtering an endless wave of zombie armies. That's the job of our military, God bless them."

"It's still killing *jihadists* without due process...."

"Spies, saboteurs, and illegal enemy combatants have never had Geneva Convention protection, Josie. Not ever. The norms of conventional warfare or law enforcement simply don't apply."

I shook my head. "You are talking crazy."

"Islam is an ideology of conquest. The death penalty doesn't work against *jihadists* who want to kill and die for Allah. Death is not a deterrent for Islamic *jihad*. Instead, it's an incentive, an added reward.

"All Pershing did was to tailor punishment to accommodate the customs and culture of Islam in the treatment of captured terrorists. History shows that it worked for him."

"That's disputed."

"What isn't? Muslims have been killing each other for a thousand years over different interpretations of the Quran. The vast majority of them disagree with radical *jihad*, but if they dare speak out they become apostates who can be killed.

"The word Islam means, 'Those who submit.' If you don't submit, the good Muslims can murder you."

"Murder," I said. "Goldfarb wants you to kill someone, doesn't he?"

"Not yet."

"There are monsters stalking me. Please tell it to me straight. When my senses come into focus, I'll know."

"I don't want to scare you. 'Fear is the mind killer.' You know that."

"Talk to me."

"Must we? You know the threats. You know the horrors. You know my skills. You know what I do. I won't lie to you. If you insist, I'll tell you what he said, but...."

"I'm waiting."

"They are still sorting things out. There will be new rules, new policy. He doesn't know what exactly will result, but he does know what President Blager wants us to do. I think we can live with it."

"I'm listening...."

"We have support. President Blager wants to keep you alive. He said that's job number one."

I blinked. "**What?**"

"You saved the President's life. So did Goldfarb. He's grateful.

"There have been persistent efforts to kill you and one to assassinate him. He sees them as clear and present dangers to the United States, as top-level threats. Objective one is ensuring that it stops. He wants to get those involved in these operations and eliminate them. Objective two is to focus primarily on the human components of Objective number one that have touched American soil."

"There is a list of names?"

"There will be, yes. It will be short. There are constraints. Details. Rules. Limits."

"Which are?"

"I don't know yet. I expect there will be bright red lines to prevent Constitutional breaches, like killing American citizens and targeting political opponents."

"For example?"

"Goldfarb was explicit that neither he nor President Blager will tolerate a Police State. America got dangerously close to it under Obama, Susan Rice, and the rest of that gang. Blager won't."

"Do you have a list of names?" I asked again.

"I do not."

"What do you have?"

"He did ask me about a name, but it wasn't a targeting. We can discuss it if things go that way."

"No," I said. "That's bullshit and you know it."

Raven frowned.

"We're a team."

"Goldfarb **knows** that. This person might be behind the attacks on you. I would take that personally."

"I thought it might be something like that. Goldfarb sucks you in, doesn't he? You told him you were going to quit, but he talked you into getting me out of the hospital instead."

"He saved your life, Josie. He wanted to save you. I'd given up hope. I wanted to avenge you."

"You got me out. *You* saved me. I still want the name."

He frowned and shook his head. "Bad idea. Very bad idea."

"Is this person a threat or not?"

"Goldfarb asked me the same question. He could be. At present, he's just a person of interest that the FBI has flagged."

"We need to find out. This is what I do."

"Why bother? The FBI is all over it."

"So why not just do it? We'd need to research this thoroughly **ourselves** before we agree to anything. We'd need to get it right. Not just for operational reasons, for morality. For my sanity."

Raven sighed deeply. "Why don't we just let the FBI do its job? Their record is less than stellar when it comes to traitors, moles, and *jihadists*. They could use a win. They can put him on trial or something."

"Good for them. Then maybe you and I could still do an interesting and peaceful assignment together without leaving a trail of bodies. The working vacation we were promised."

Raven thought for a long moment. National Security was a harsh mistress. He started to speak, thought better of it, shook his head, and said, "You know that's not our call."

I nodded, but didn't speak, setting the silence lengthen.

Finally Raven said, "Marco Ricci."

"He was on our list to investigate. The *jihadist* you almost fed to the pigs mentioned him."

"Kamal. Yes, he did. It seems the FBI and others have noticed."

CHAPTER TWO
AMERICAN KIDON

The White House

"The President can see you now, Doctor Goldfarb," the young Secret Service agent said.

"Thank you, Sally."

I limped into the Oval Office under my own power, escorted but not supported. No cane, no walker, but still a cast on my right foot. The President stood and came around the desk to greet me. "You look better than the last time I saw you, Aaron."

"I could say the same for you, Sir. We were lucky." I extended my hand.

The President brushed it aside and gave me a hug instead. "Screw the protocols. You saved my life. Please sit down." He gestured at the chair.

"We just got some fresh New York Bagels. They are damned hard to get in Washington. Would you like one? The coffee is excellent."

"They are hard to get in New York, too." I smiled in spite of myself. "Thank you. I'd appreciate that."

They seated themselves and a burley Black porter came and served them. As he left, the President said, "No interruptions, please, David."

"I'll tell them, Mister President."

After the door closed, President Blager said, "I owe you an apology. No one broke any rules, but your name was in the logs at the hospital. It leaked."

"Yes, Sir." Our enemies had located and targeted me. Following me eventually led them to the safe house for Josie, which could have been a disaster. *Now we knew how.*

"I've started using Trump protocols. The visitor's logs for the White House are classified and sealed for at least 5 years after I leave office. Our Intel people put out smoke about the hospital leak. It may help."

I took a sip of coffee and then tasted my bagel, nodding approval. It was excellent. The President was still looking at me. Apparently he wanted a response.

Not bloody likely. I thought about spilled milk and open barn doors, trying to decide what was best to say. Finally, I just said, "I hope so, Sir."

"You don't agree...."

"Few of the hostiles survived, Sir. We won that battle, but the Clash of Cultures continues. I expect my name is out there somewhere. That compromises me, but it also exposes the assets I run."

I looked him in the eyes to make sure he got my point. He did. *Josie.*

"What do you suggest?"

"My vote would be to find and eliminate all those who were directly involved especially the controllers and those who gave the orders."

"The FBI is working on it...."

"Yes." *The FBI did justice, but I was more interested in accountability and retaliation.* "You might want to consider allowing counterterror operatives special access that isn't logged. Protecting our sources and methods is essential. We still have too many leaks."

"That's a good topic for the NSC. I will bring it up again. Did you bring the target list I wanted?"

"I have a few names. There are problems...."

"We will discuss them. What about our end of things?"

"Like I said, we need tighter operational security, Sir. Even George Washington suffered his spies and traitors. The Russians stole the Bomb in the 50s, setting off the Cold War. It went downhill from there. The early 21st century saw endless leaks and security breaches, the personnel records of all our people with clearances, all our State Department records, surveillance of political opponents...."

"We are waking up. We now name the evil. Radical Islam. Rogue States with WMDs...."

"The country is still too complacent. Americans are a compassionate and caring people. In the 1930s we tolerated Nazi's and Communists, today we face other threats. Radical Islam has killed far more people than Hitler, Mao, and Stalin combined, but the left still has fantasies about coexisting.

"During the Cold War, the left and academia favored Soviet Communism. These days, with *jihad* as a mutual threat to American and Russia, they whine if we work together.

"We're not at war, Aaron."

"No, but **they** are, Sir."

"Islamic genocide and conquest was a long time ago, Aaron. Most Muslims are not threats. They are good people. Some are allies. The Muslim conquests are ancient history."

"I agree that a formal declaration of war is unproductive. Iraq accomplished nothing. I'm not suggesting that."

"Good."

"The Arab Spring was genocide, which saw more refugees than any time since World War II. It was invasion, *migration* jihad. They tried to assassinate you last **month**, Sir.

"Last year, we thwarted an EMP attack with Iranian missiles and Nukes. How many Americans would that have killed?"

"Millions."

"We would potentially have had more dead Americans than World War II."

The President nodded. "They won't try it again. Not soon. I'm not going to start beating the war drums, Aaron."

"I don't suggest you should. Like I said, the last thing we need is another Iraq."

"What then?"

"Small focused efforts carefully targeted. You've not yet hanged any spies or traitors. We need to go on the offense, Sir."

"In general, I tend to agree. We are. I am. Investigations are pending. Action is planned. That is part of what we'll be discussing today."

"Yes, Sir."

"How did we do with getting you in to see me this time?"

"The tradecraft displayed was excellent, but it may not matter, Sir."

"Explain."

"Your security people were meticulous about sneaking me in today, but if there's any regular pattern of activity even the best operatives can get blown. That is unavoidable.

"I screwed up myself in Monterey and it put some of our most crucial assets at risk. That would have been a disaster, Mr. President."

"Your point?"

"Black assets need to stay dark. It is our only safety. There were many eyes watching who met with you in Monterey, and there are more here at the White House. All it takes is one leaker, one set of loose lips, one mole."

"I know where you are going with this. I want you on the NSC, Aaron. I need you there."

"How often does it meet?"

"Once or twice a week…."

"You see the problem?"

"Perhaps it's best if we spoke in the bubble."

"Yes, Sir."

In the Bubble

The two men walked down the hall to the bubble, entered, and sat across from each other at the small table. They didn't speak until after the door closed with a solid *thunk*.

"This room is totally secure." The President glanced to his right, assuring himself the green light over the door was on. "We can speak freely."

Goldfarb looked around at the triply shielded walls. "I believe you."

"We couldn't be more out of communication if we were on the dark side of the moon."

"People saw us enter. They will see me sitting in on the NSC meetings too."

"Then perhaps it's best if I briefed you as to why I need you there. There are two reasons, and both are crucial to National Security. I need you on board."

"Yes, Sir."

"Do you know how the National Security Council works, Aaron?"

"Not really. I do know there have been problems, Sir."

The President nodded. "I'm afraid the problems are built in. The NSC is a recent construct. It was created by Truman on September 18, 1947.

"Here is my view. Truman, bluntly, was a less-than-well-prepared President. He inherited a world with Weapons of Mass Destruction, one where the United States was a superpower and half the planet was in ruins. He'd not even been told of the Atomic Bomb, but it was he who suddenly had to first use them when FDR died.

"The notion of Nuclear War was horrific, so he set up National Security Council under the chairmanship of the President, with the Secretaries of State and Defense as its key members, to coordinate foreign policy and defense policy, and to reconcile diplomatic and military commitments and requirements.

"That was the focus. How to prevent fallible humans from turning the planet into a cinder. There were terrifying movies and novels of the day about that."

I said, "Let me summarize. The Cold War started. Truman was way over his head. He was overwhelmed and felt desperately in need of military advice. Was that it?"

"Strategic National Defense was the primary focus, but Truman was also behind setting up the UN, God help us all. A New League of Nations to prevent war."

"Didn't Truman also set up the CIA?"

The President nodded. "It was part of the same National Security Act. Truman was confused by all the conflicting advice he was getting from Congress and the various services. His notion was that the CIA was to be a body of experts to sort this, filter it, and keep the President informed."

"Expecting spies and dirty-tricks experts to serve as objective analysts and unbiased reporters may not have been his best idea."

"It was Truman's stated expectation nonetheless. We could spend days talking about it."

I nodded.

"It didn't work, of course. Immediately they were off into spying and dirty tricks and pressing for covert paramilitary ops. Eisenhower reined them in, but soon Kennedy was rolling though his own disasters. The Bay of Pigs, the Berlin Wall, etc."

"Kennedy hated the CIA," I said. "He blamed them for his problems."

"He did. But both CIA and NSC proved useful during the Cold War, and today we have seventeen separate intelligence agencies, with a funnel at the top. That's not my point."

"What is your point, Sir?"

"I have **two** points. Here is the lesser one. Whatever it was intended to be, whatever it was, whatever it is now, you need to know that the NSC **is** central to most -- if not all -- of the major policy decisions of the United States. For example, it seems that Obama primarily used his NSC for spying on his political opponents, not to focus on foreign threats."

"Shades of Big Brother, Stalin, and the Stasi. I've always wondered how Obama justified that."

"There was no need to justify it. He didn't admit it and the media covered for him. His administration saw his political enemies as the biggest threat to America. I think they sincerely believed it. Hillary had pretty much the same view. Hence, her comments about 'deplorables.' The radical left favored raw power over bipartisanship. For a time, it worked for them."

"Understood, Sir."

"Good," the President said. "Here's the big one, the main point. Know this: The NSC has only **ONE** official purpose."

"Which is?" I asked.

"The NSC exists to best serve the President of the United States. In this case, that would be me."

"What does 'best serve' mean?"

"Exactly," the President said. "You have identified the key issue. We have a Republic with a Constitution designed to be 'By and for the people,' but an NSC designed to serve the President. Are they his courtiers, his staff, or his Soviet style *apparatchiks*?

"You tell me, Sir."

"I cannot," President Blager said. "We've had instances of all three in recent history. Some truly vile personalities have been revealed and much harm has been done. There have been three basic models for the NSC. All have had problems."

"I never understood what an operationalized NSC was, Sir."

"That was Washington-speak. A better name for that model is 'President-centric.' General McMaster wrote an award-winning book about it, ***Dereliction of Duty***, back in 1997."

A long time ago. "I know McMaster. So?"

"After some problems, Trump chose General McMaster to be his National Security Adviser, to head the NSC. If nothing else, it was a clear signal he didn't want sycophants telling him what they thought he wanted. Many heads rolled, including the director and top two levels of management at CIA."

"That I recall, Sir. You said there were three models?"

"Yes. I don't think Truman had much of a clue, but there are three models that most agree have been used. Eisenhower had what most would call a 'process-centric' NSC. Such an NSC adheres to established military staff decision-making procedures. It's the one I personally prefer, but it's much too ponderous and slow for the type of things you are doing."

"Were other Presidents comfortable with such a system?"

"Eisenhower was unique. I don't think so. Not in recent times. Trump was trying, and so am I. It's not easy for me and that's one reason I need your help."

"I don't understand, Sir."

"Like Trump, I came from private industry and, worse yet, from high technology. As an executive, I grew to distrust using my staff for strategic decisions. Staff is inclined to see the world through a rearview mirror. It tends to be slow and conservative in making decisions."

"Why?"

"It's the nature of the beast. You can wind up drowning in data, but starving for information. Staff decisions tend to be conservative, too little, too late. If staff dominates, there is too much cover-your-ass and not enough vision and leadership.

"In High Tech we used to say, 'If Edison was an MBA, he would have invented a large candle.'"

"Eisenhower had his staff and process, but he also had commanders like Patton?"

"Exactly. He had them and he *supported* them. That is probably why Churchill went along with making Ike the Supreme Commander instead of Montgomery. When you fully understand that, you will understand why I need you and Raven's team."

My mind was churning. No wonder the President had been giving us so much support.

I said, "Please continue." I was learning things. It was clear the President had thought a lot about this.

"Kennedy and LBJ both had 'President-Centric" NSCs. Their NSCs were 'operationalized' and it caused them big problems that left scars on America. Reagan was as different from those two as could be imagined, but he too had an operationalized NSC – which bedeviled him in 1984-86 and resulted in Iran-Contra. Obama was up to his ears in institutional abuses, from Susan Rice's 'unmasking' to Lois Lerner using the IRS to target political enemies."

"You skipped the Clintons," I said.

"The Clintons greatly expanded the NSC. Hillary was the one who created Susan Rice and the Benghazi video. One of the innovations during Clinton's terms was the creation of a communications and press component for NSC."

"They set up a propaganda arm for a secret group advising the President? Goebbels would approve, but how in the world did they justify it?"

"The usual way. Emotionally, by hiding their actions behind good intentions. The Clinton focus was on humanitarian crises. 'Traditionally considered a function of the White House press staff, the new administration began to see the need to more effectively articulate its foreign policy in the wake of crises in Somalia and Haiti,' that's what they said.

"Brookings Institute said the Clintons made the NSC look more like a Government Agency, but most of the media gave them a pass. You can look it up."

The things we don't know. Thus, the Clinton Foundation. I shook my head. "I suppose Nixon was also a victim of an operationalized NSC?"

"Oddly, most of the experts would say no."

"Even after Watergate?"

"The public might think that, but it was an aberration. It was a squalid third-rate burglary, not policy, which ended the Nixon administration. Nixon used the third model. Effectively, he delegated his foreign policy to an unelected expert."

I blinked. "Sir?"

"The experts argue his NSC was guru-centric. Nixon depended almost entirely on Kissinger, who was an ideologically sympathetic expert whom he trusted."

"Has that ever worked?"

"In the 19th Century it worked splendidly for Britain with Disraeli, but he was a genius who had served as Prime Minister. It sort of worked for Nixon. He avoided major disasters."

"Until Watergate…."

"Yes."

I felt stunned. *What a tangled mess.* "I now begin to understand why you feel such a need to screw up my life and blow my cover by putting me on the NSC."

The President smiled. "I trust you, Aaron. I need another set of eyes and ears. I need your brain and experience. I will concoct a plausible cover story for your frequent presence.

"What specifically are you trying to do with the NSC, Sir?

"It's simple. My goal is to refocus the NSC on enemies foreign and domestic, to better target and engage the enemies who would use violent force to overthrow or destroy the United States. Do I sound like the ghost of Joe McCarthy?"

"You sound realistic. McCarthy was a tail-gunner to the core, protecting America's back. He was branded as a political nut, but there was a lot of evidence to support his views. The Rosenbergs, the Venona Intercepts, and so forth…."

"Some may choose to reflect about McCarthy, but that's politics and not my dilemma. My need is to quickly get the NSC narrowly tasked on the real and urgent threats to our National Security. As part of that, I want highly sensitive information to flow in both directions between my NSC and small teams of operatives like Raven's."

"You seem to have made your decision, Sir."

"With reservations, yes, I have. I personally don't share the confidence that Eisenhower had in staff decisions, but I reject the other two models. Therefore, I have to somehow make his model work, even though I'm not sure it can."

"What do you wish of me, Sir?"

"I wanted you formally on the NSC, but I now see that can't work. Therefore, you must be the observer and cut-out. I also need you to control Raven's team without my fingerprints being on it."

"Please say it more clearly, Mr. President."

"I want all sources of intelligence to flow through you to Raven's Team as needed. At times, I may want it to go in the reverse direction. This will be a bit tricky. The team, as in the past, will have an action role with plausible denial. I have to be distanced."

"I got that part. What else?"

"I want you present at NSC to observe and tell me the truth. I need your council."

"When asked?"

"Yes, but also to kick me in the ass if you see this going off a cliff or down a rat hole. To tell me the things I don't want to hear. Will you do that?"

"I see the need, Sir. I will have to let you know, Mr. President. You have me primarily tasked with Raven's team. I must confer with them. Is that acceptable?"

"Fair enough," the President said. "I need a decision in ten days."

"Yes, Mr. President."

"You will still be the control for Raven's team, reporting to me. Is this a good time to talk about the list I wanted?"

"I don't have a list to hand you, Sir, just issues to discuss. There are problems. I need to get some decisions before I can present this proposal to Raven and Josie."

The President looked at his watch. "How long do we need?"

"At least thirty minutes, Sir. I don't have the list you wanted, but the good news is that I've come up with a name. I have drafted a new mission for the team. It is not inconsistent with what we've been discussing."

"Good. I can give you an hour today. We'll need to break and reconvene. Can you do that?"

"I'm at your service, Sir. Just keep me out of sight. I do better in the dark."

The President smiled and stood. "Done. We've almost lost that team twice. I don't want a third time. They are not expendable."

"I know."

"What's the name you suggest for the team?"

"Kidon, Sir."

"I've never heard of it, which is probably good. Wait here. I'll be back soon. The Secret service is outside. Just ask them if you need anything."

The President left with a spring in his step. I was glad he didn't slam and latch the door. Wanting to be in the dark or not, the bubble was too much like a tomb for my tastes.

CHAPTER THREE
NEW WORLD ORDER, OR NOT…

UN Building, New York

Marco Ricci liked Ethiopian Coffee, strong and black. He took another sip and gazed out his window over the East River. Spring was gentle. The city was almost pretty in the bright sunshine, but he missed Italy a little more each year.

He'd been stationed in America too long. The halcyon years of globalization were fading in the rearview mirror. Nation States were coming back.

Rome had been spared the violence and New York was recovering. It was no longer a sanctuary city. Americans were drifting back into their attitudes of cultural arrogance and claims of exceptionalism. When he mentioned that disturbing trend to his younger colleagues at the UN, they smiled vaguely and changed the subject. It was irritating.

Ricci's career had stalled out. His power and influence had peaked.

A few good things resulted, but only a few. Crime was down. The graffiti had been cleaned up. It was safe for Ricci to stroll from his luxury apartment at One East River Place on 72nd to Central Park. Five years ago, police would not have dared, not alone, not at night.

He kept his mistress over on 61st and no longer needed a security entourage to visit her. Still, he disliked walking the streets. The flag waving and posturing of the natives was offensive to him. Limos were better.

Marco frequently reminded his visitors the UN Complex was international territory, not part of the United States. He was above U.S. law and politics. He found them bothersome.

He ran UNCTAD, the UN Council of Trade and Development, and, as such, his responsibilities were delightfully vague. He reported to the General Assembly, but also had a dotted line relationship with the UN's Economic and Social Council.

The relationship wasn't an umbilical cord, just a fuzzy liaison and coordination role without oversight or accountability. Marco attended a lot of boring meetings, but, in the end, he could do pretty much as he pleased so long as he wrapped it in high purpose and periodically bashed the selfish interests of the major nation states, especially the U.S. That was what the UN was about, after all.

Marco still had the large cartoon from one of the annual Global Economic Forum meetings hung behind his desk. It had been there for over twenty years, from the time when he had dreamed of waking up to a new world. The image predated Obama and the Arab Spring.

Matted in black and framed in chrome against a glossy white wall, it was a graphic depiction of Noah's Ark, a ship that was dangerously down by the bow, where there huddled five large, somnolent beasts – an elephant, bear, dragon, hippo, and rhino. All the large beasts had their eyes shut, while a gaggle of smaller creatures huddled in the back of the boat, looking terrified.

The large, clueless beasts depicted the Security Council, of course, but, just in case one missed that point, the cartoon was labeled. The dragon was China, the bear Russia, the hippo the UK, and the rhino was France. The biggest problem, of course, was the Elephant, the United States, a nation the Islamic world called the Great Satan. A long forgotten, politically correct, previous Secretary General, a Black from a minor nation, took the role of Noah, saying, "I told you it was unbalanced."

Marco had chosen that art for a reason. The cartoon was a near-perfect icon for the dream, for the pending dawn of a New World, one of social justice where Non-Government Agencies were increasingly ascendant over the whims and traditions of Western Nation States.

Those were good times. A President with roots from Kenya wound up running and transforming America. Marco's focus was on high level policy. He and his masters pulled the strings, and the leaders of the Western Nations complied. It had been delicious.

Then it all changed. He'd been dragged down to being a handler for messy, bloody covert operations. They gave him idiots and madmen to work with. Squalid missions had failed, blood was shed, and people in high places were looking for scapegoats. He didn't want to be one.

In twenty minutes one of the most powerful men in the world, Dr. Claas Vogel, was arriving to personally review the latest disaster. Marco had the unhappy distinction of being the highest person in the command chain still alive and within the continental United States.

Marco sighed and glanced at his watch, a mechanical Panerai Luminor, Italian made and trustworthy, from a firm established in 1860 to secretly supply the Italian Navy. These days, anything electronic could be, and probably was, bugged. Even the Russians had gone back to using the old, mechanical IBM Selectric typewriters for their secure communications. They acquired the rights and built them for their own use, of course.

No one trusted phones or computers these days, especially now. America was fully alert and probably monitoring all communications. Attempts to assassinate President Blager had failed. Blager was alive, America was angry, its policies were becoming more Draconian, and the Muslims and Globalists were ducking for cover.

Ricci blamed the Muslims. Iran had recalled their control, a Revolutionary Guard member named Firouz. Their field commander, a thug named Kamal, had resisted taking his orders.

Then he'd charged off on his own. He'd never reported back. Firouz was back in Iran, disgraced or dead. Kamal and his team had not returned from their suicide missions.

President Blager was still alive. Not just alive, but aggressive and furious about the attempt on his life. Blager was putting an anti-*jihad* clause, a codicil, a binding side agreement, into all of America's treaties. Most of the world was going along.

Italy's term on the UN Security Council had expired in 2018, but its government officially opposed *jihad* as did the Vatican. If Ricci ever left the UN or traveled privately, he would need his Italian passport. He dared not take any public position on the Blager codicil.

None of that mess was Marco's fault, none of it was anything he could have prevented, and none of it -- except for the survival of Blager and its aftermath -- seemed to be any great loss from his viewpoint.

Ricci was supposed to be serving in a diplomatic capacity at the UN, influencing policy, not out in the field with a crazy *jihadi* kill team in California who smelled like goats and could not care less about his opinions or directives. It was madness.

If you strike at a King, you must kill him. The Muslims had failed. They were fools.

The White House – In the Bubble

The President was waving his hands, symbolically brushing interruptions away, as he entered. "Sorry Aaron, I was…."

I shook my head and held up a notepad. "No need to apologize, Sir. I've been productive. Your staff trusted me with pencils and marker pens."

The President smiled and settled into the chair. "I must speak to them…."

"Where should we start?"

"We were talking about the **list**, Dr. Goldfarb. We need to discuss that, plus getting you up to speed on the National Security Council."

"Before the urgent business of the NSC consumes us, I'd like to request a few minutes of reflection, Sir."

"Why?"

"I'm going to suggest you still have a bit of swamp draining to do, Sir."

"Five minutes."

"We agree that the core assumption is our agreement that Josie and her paranormal talents are a national treasure? That she and Raven's team must be protected at all costs?

"Yes, of course. It's why we have it separate and deep black."

"Are you aware that the existence of this sensitive resource has been compromised?"

The President's eyes narrowed. "What are you talking about?"

"America's use of paranormal research as an Intelligence Asset was publicly outed."

"That is a serious allegation. When did this happen?"

"2017, Mr. President. The same day President Trump was inaugurated the CIA declassified some 13 million pages of documents, including 160,482 documents which involved remote viewing."

"Why don't I know this?"

"There has been subsequent damage control. Some documents, like the ones about Russian nuclear subs, have since been redacted or removed. Last I checked it was down to 36,894 hits for remote viewing."

The President sighed. "Brennan."

"With help." *Brennan was long gone before the inauguration.*

"Was Josie exposed?"

"No. There is a God, Mr. President, and he does protect fools and Americans."

"How did they miss her?"

"I do not know, Sir. Nor do I think we should try to find out. Better to let sleeping dogs lie."

"Say more."

"Josie did not and does not appear in any CIA records. Raven had a troubled but eventful history at the agency. He was known to them under another name, and often in trouble. They fired him with prejudice. I faked his death and gave him a new legend. They don't know Raven exists. They don't know she exists either. She is America's last paranormal so far as I can tell."

"We will keep it that way. This conversation never happened."

"It did not."

"What was leaked by CIA?"

"A lot. Some about paranormal research is still up on the CIA website in a library folder named 'reading room.' The records released discussing remote viewing spanned many administrations, both parties, and a time frame of 1941 to 2014. Activity was highest during the intense days of the Cold War, after Sputnik and the Cuban Missile Crisis. Most was removed quickly after Trump took office, but we can assume foreign intelligence sources copied it."

"What about Washington and the public?"

"The media only made a brief mention, in the context of government waste and tin hat conspiracy theories. It was quickly forgotten."

"Like flying saucers?"

"One hundred and forty-two mentions. What's still up on the CIA site is muddled, incomprehensible, and boring. I don't suggest that any action is required now."

"Why not?"

"The current site is a honeypot. It displays warnings about not being safe to visit. It archives those who visit, their location, and what they searched for. I assume it also plants spyware and that logs are kept."

"Good. People at the Agency are doing their jobs. We'll keep Josie and Raven off the grid. Does that close the matter?"

"I'd deem those actions to be necessary but not sufficient, Sir. Brennan and the top two levels were purged, but my bet is that we still have rot in the foundation and a few termites and moles burrowed down inside."

"We have good counter intelligence…."

"Which is focused on external threats, not moles or traitors."

"What do you suggest?"

"A special unit of trusted, seasoned operatives and analysts would be good. The Cold War CIA had James Jesus Angleton. He was obsessed with moles. It took decades, but he found them."

"Angleton was Chief of CIA counterintelligence from 1954 to 1975. Do you think the internal threats posed today warrant that level of attention?"

"The threats are different. I suggest something as relentless and paranoid, but less all-consuming. You want me to give **you** a list. That got me thinking. Why not have the agencies take a few trusted people and task them with preparing and maintaining an actionable list of suspected internal threats?"

"It is wise to divert scarce resource from external threats?"

"Is it safe not to? We've had radical Islamists inside both the White House and the Intelligence community. "

"Examples?"

"I don't have that data at my fingertips, Sir. The FBI…."

"I concede that from the Towers to Boston to Fort Hood to San Bernardino and beyond, the FBI has vetted and cleared a long list of domestic terrorists. Just name a few off the top of your head…."

I shrugged. "Valarie Jarrett was effectively Obama's handler, born in Iran to American Communists. She is a red diaper baby and an Iranian citizen. She had high level Muslim Brotherhood connections, specifically her mother and brother. John Brennan was an admitted Communist when he joined the CIA. He allegedly converted to Islam after he was Director. Obama had Muslim Brotherhood members in Homeland Security.

"Who was the Black guy from Oakland in Obama's cabinet, the one who advocated riots and violence? The one he had to drop?"

"Van Jones. He wasn't a Muslim. He wasn't in the cabinet. He was green jobs Czar."

"Okay, scratch that one. We've had a few Muslims in Congress. One became Deputy Chair of the DNC. ISIS reportedly threatened to kill him, but he had Hamas connections…."

The President held up one hand. "I've been briefed on that one. Muslims practice *Taqiyya* and have been killing each other for a thousand years. You made your point. Moles. Termites."

"We could start the staffing with agents about to retire or younger ones who've been wounded in the field."

The President gave me an intense look. "People like you, Aaron?"

"No, Sir. I have a job."

"You do. You are needed here, but that was a good idea. I will make sure it gets attention. Now what about that list I want today?"

I passed him seven names. Two were highlighted in purple, two in red, two in yellow, and only one was green.

He studied it, frowning. "I assume the one green-lighted is a possible target. What do the other colors mean?"

"Purple is hard-core untouchable."

"I should think so. The top name is Vice President Dunbar. Why?"

"You see the name in Green?"

"Ricci?"

"Ricci is a possible. We can hit him, but may not want to. He was in the command chain for the attacks on Josie in both Durham and Monterey, and for the two attempts on your life. He has had multiple contacts with VP Dunbar. That alone makes Dunbar a person of interest."

"What about the other colors?"

"Red is untouchable for now. Yellow indicates that we could hit them, but probably should not. It would be an act of war in an area where we have larger issues. Both of the yellow highlighted tangos are in Iran. They are presumably well protected."

"The attacks on you, me, and Raven's people involved several teams. Why do you only have one name for action?"

"We are fighting terrorist cells, not nation states. There were few survivors. Only one person at the command level was captured alive, a *jihadist* named Kamal. He is in custody."

"The one Raven left for the pigs?"

"Correct. Ricci was two levels up his command chain. Kamal reported to one of the yellow highlighted names, a Mr. Firouz."

"Now in Iran?"

"Recalled in disgrace. Shipped out on Aeroflot in the dead of night."

"This leaves us Ricci. What are the problems with him?"

"He's an Italian citizen who works for the U.N. as a senior official with diplomatic immunity and a diplomatic passport. His brother is a Senator in the Italian Parliament. His mother was President of their Chamber of Deputies, the equivalent of our Speaker of the House…."

The President nodded. "I get it…."

"It is the nature of terrorism. During the Cold War, enemies were easy to find, but hard to kill. Now they are easy to kill, but hard to identify. Do you think we could convince the UN or Italy – or even our own courts and Congress -- to arrest and prosecute Mr. Ricci?"

"Not easily. What do you recommend?"

"Two things, the first of which I will suggest as a policy. I think it is best for us to give general suggestions, not orders, to Raven and Josie, especially if extreme action is indicated."

"Why?"

"We are blessed to have exceptional talent with conflicting inclinations. As a team, I think they can make better decisions on the ground than we can in Washington. We should use that, not resist it, Sir."

"I don't understand you. Raven would kill Ricci in a New York minute, would he not? "

"Yes. He would see Ricci as a clear and present danger, both to Josie and to the United States."

"So I'd be giving him a kill order no matter how I worded it. Why not just…?"

I shook my head. "No, you would not, Mr. President. Worded correctly, he and Josie would *jointly* decide. She would not harm a fly. She detests violence. She more than detests it, it literally traumatizes her. Proximity to violence has almost destroyed her in the past."

The President nodded slowly. "She's a sensitive, a healer, not a killer."

"Raven would never knowingly let anything harm her. Surely you know that?"

"I do."

"That's the tension, Sir. Leaving Ricci alive is a clear and present danger to Josie. Raven knows it. So will Josie when she researches the threat. Let's see what they come up with."

"You said **two** things. What's the second?"

"Action, Mr. President. We need to go on offense. Unleash the hounds. I've already given them Ricci's name to research. They are on it. They **know** he's a threat."

"What specific action should I take?"

"Issue a vague but aggressive directive. I suggest that we say that Ricci is green-lighted for action however they deem appropriate, **provided that** it leaves no tracks and America has plausible denial. Unleash them, have them tell me if they need any resources, and then wait."

"Wait?"

"Sure. Why not? We'll see what they do. If they need anything, I'll provide it to them in a timely manner."

"What do you think they will do?"

"I don't know. If you authorize action, we will find out."

"What if they can't solve this?"

"Possibly they can't. If so, they will tell us that. We'll either abort or figure out something else."

"We don't seem to have much to lose."

"I agree. Do we have a green light for Mr. Ricci?"

"Action including lethal force is authorized. I want you to personally tell them, face to face, including briefing them fully on the details of what we have discussed off the record."

"Roger that, Sir."

"Clearly understand that the office of the President did not give you a kill order. We do not need another Watergate or Iran Contra. If this works, we will both thank God, but any blowback from it is on your head, Doctor Goldfarb."

"I would not have it any other way. I will tell them that too."

"Good. I will see you at the NSC next week."

Our meeting wrapped up. I left feeling optimistic, thinking that it had gone well.

CHAPTER FOUR
GOLDFARB'S GAMBIT

Private House, South of Monterey, California, Midmorning, two days later

Josie watched as Doctor Goldfarb's SUV disappeared down the driveway into the fog. It had been an unusual meeting.

"Did you take notes? I've had my head off into trying to make any sense of the remote viewings we've been doing, but he tabled that discussion."

Raven gave a short laugh. "He sure as Hell did. We're stuck out here in the cold, sitting in a safe house that he **knows** has been blown. He wants us to stand down until he and the President can get their shit together at the NSC. He leaves us an old book about Vietnam for homework.

"We have no direction, no mission, nothing actionable, and our control seems to have been dragged off into some Washington swamp draining exercise. Freaking marvelous...."

Easy, I thought. *Raven distrusted Langley, and, next to that, anything inside the beltway.*

"He did say they are extracting us. He said he has a meeting being scheduled with people he says will help us. Do you know this Twenty Mike guy?"

"Mostly by reputation, but I have met him twice. First time was a long time ago at the Agency. Back in the day, he led a secret raid deep into Bukhari. It has since become the stuff of legends they whisper about at the war colleges. Mike is a good guy. Unconventional."

"We invaded Bukhari?"

"Lord, no. Unofficial, deep black, plausible denial, one of those 'it never happened' deals. Whatever went down was need to know stuff, but the rumor was a mixed force of Saudis, Israelis, and a few Marines on a smash and grab. They went way deep and got blown."

"How far into Bukhari?"

"The rumor was several hundred miles. They somehow shot their way out with President Nassid's forces hot on their heels and no U.S. military support. Word was they all made it back. Mike retired out not long after."

"Any idea what prompted the raid?"

"Not a clue. You're the paranormal...."

"You met Mike twice?"

"I told you. He is now a civilian running TSG. I met him at the Presidio in Monterey last month. We had a meeting. John Black was going to quit, but we talked him out of it."

"Transnational Security Group? The company that is supposed to be our operational support?"

"Uh-huh. Goldfarb was still in the hospital, so he roped me in as a proxy."

"What exactly is TSG going to do for us?"

"I don't think it's been determined yet."

"You had a meeting to talk Black into staying around?"

"It was Mike's meeting, not mine. He had the other side of that problem, and it was a show stopper. His number two is some kind of a financial genius who goes by the name of George Washington Jones. He looks like Einstein, hair and all, except for the black skin and glasses."

"I don't understand."

"Mike told me Jones was the key to putting TSG together and getting it running. If he dropped out, we were all screwed. Mike was trying to prevent that."

"You need to talk to me, damn it. How do Jones and Black intersect?"

"Moira. Her death screwed them **both** up."

I winced, remembering the savvy young Black woman we'd failed. "Black blamed himself for Moira's death and wanted to quit."

"Correct," Raven said. "Turns out George Washington Jones was Moira's cousin, and he blamed Black for her death too."

"Why?"

"Jones thought – with some justification – that our whole OP was a cluster fuck. He wanted Black prosecuted for Moira's murder."

"That makes no sense."

"Doesn't have to," Raven said. "It was about emotion and feelings of betrayal. Black *already* blamed himself. I think he was falling in love with the girl. He was holding her when I found him that night. He carried her body out."

I remembered that night too well myself. "Why does Jones…?"

"Jones and Moira were close. Her parents both died in an accident. She was raised by his mother, her aunt. Moira was like his little sister."

"Shit."

We sat in silence for several minutes. I took deep breaths, determined not to cry. Finally I said, "So how did you and Mike convince them…."

Raven said, "No idea. Maybe it was God. Sometimes miracles happen…."

"Keep talking. I need to know what happened."

"That *is* what happened. Black talked. Jones talked. There were a lot of words. Too many words. Mike and I didn't say much. Jones said Black was responsible. Black agreed with him. Eventually, they both got quiet…."

Raven trailed off. He seemed to be lost in thought. That wasn't like him.

I waited. Several minutes passed. "Talk to me. Please."

"I just figured out what really sucks about what we've been doing. We need to change things. There is no closure. No post OP debriefings. No grieving over losses."

"I used to do that." *It all seemed so long ago.*

He met my eyes. "When was that?"

"Before I met you, back when I worked for Rhine Institute, I had a shrink as my handler, Doctor Niles Lundgren. He handled my mission prep and debriefings. He was a gentle man. Did you ever meet him?"

Raven gave me a strange look. "Not really…."

"What does that mean?"

"I saw him in your hospital room in Portland. You were gone. Black had extracted you."

"Lundgren was already dead."

"He was."

What a mess. We're lucky to still be sane. I sighed. "I think maybe that's enough chit chat and reminiscing."

"Roger that. I'm going to bring mission support up with Goldfarb though, if you agree."

"I do." I leaned over and kissed his forehead. It was not often that Raven showed his soft side.

"Please finish telling me about Mike's meeting. About Black."

"There's not much more to tell. Jones said he wanted the person who'd killed his cousin. Black said he understood and that he did too, but that it wasn't possible."

"Why not?"

"Because I'd already blown the bastard's head off...."

"Oh. That." *I'd had to back out of the viewing that night. Once they were in contact it got messy.*

"Yes, that. The two of them talked a bit more. I thought they were **both** going to quit. I think Mike thought so too."

"But they didn't...."

"Black had missed Moira's funeral because he was still in the hospital. Jones invited Black to meet her 'Aunt Alveda,' to visit and tell her how Moira died. Black accepted.

"They went off to talk privately. Mike and I discussed operational stuff. Afterwards, I told Black to do what he needed to do and to take some time off, as long as he needed."

"He's not quitting...?"

"I don't think so. Not yet, but you never get over the losses."

I said, "I think we need to stop now. I need to take a break."

"Yes." Raven was looking out the window. The fog was evaporating and a bright sun was peeking through. "How about coffee and rolls on the patio?"

I met his eyes. "I can't keep doing this...."

"I know. I'm getting there myself. We'll discuss it with Goldfarb. I'll support you, no matter what you decide."

I leaned over and kissed him again, this time on the lips. "Thank you."

It took over an hour of sipping coffee and nibbling rolls before Josie managed to regain her center, her calm. The breezes were soft, only a slight rustling of leaves in the woods around the house. She thought she could almost hear the distant surf, but it might have been her imagination.

"I want your reactions to Goldfarb's visit. Do you want to go inside?"

Raven glanced over at his laptop on the small side table monitoring his security systems. Everything was green. "We're good. Inside is good, or right here. Your choice…."

"Let's start here. We were almost done."

"Are you sure?"

She nodded.

"Tell me if we need to stop. I don't want you to get tense. I'm hoping you can maybe do a short viewing later, before we relocate."

"I've been doing viewings every day. Goldfarb never asked me for a briefing about them, not even a summary. Did you find that odd?"

Raven shrugged. "Odd. Not odd. I don't think it matters. Goldfarb's on fire. All full of piss and vinegar. The President is back in the saddle, and I'm past ready to blow this place."

"On fire? He's all bruised up limping around with a cast on his foot."

"Both his arms are working and he's getting around. When I saw him in the hospital, the little guy had been beaten half to death. He had casts on most of his limbs.

"What is he, maybe five foot eight, overweight, and seventy two years old? The crazy bastard put his body in front of a muscled up badass who'd recently qualified in U.S. combat training, one Abdul Baari Mubarak."

"Hopping around. And he used a weapon…."

"OK, hopping. If I can do all that in my 70s, make sure I get a medal and a public ceremony, Babe. I want bragging rights."

"Goldfarb can't even talk about it, much less take credit. It never happened. And you can't ever talk about anything. Me either. That part of his message was real clear."

Raven grinned. "Crystal. But seriously, the man is happy, and the President just put him on the National Security Council. We not only have support, we have friends in high places to give us cover. For the first time since I met you, we're not on defense."

Maybe.

"Do you sense any threats directed at you, at us?"

"Not at present. I told you, our personal lines are still fuzzy. Like the future is trying to decide itself. Let's go inside and sit down. I want to read your notes. It might trigger something."

Raven passed her a spiral bound notepad and they went inside. He pulled the shades and turned on some lights.

I was coming to know his habits. *Never backlight yourself. He has weapons around. She could feel them, but she was getting used to it. They were protective, not threatening.*

I said, "He gave us seven names, with a color key. They have expanded our mission. Up from the three names we had: Vogel, Firouz and Akbar Safdari."

"Maybe he *reduced* it. The only name on the list we had that he said might be actionable was Marco Ricci. Today he said even that name is doubtful. Two of the new names are hard core untouchable, the PURPLE ones -- VP Dunbar and our elusive Mr. Smith."

I shrugged. "Dunbar resigned. Smith is supposed to have flipped over to our side."

"So they say, but I want you to check it out. The next two are harsh RED. Dr. Claas Vogel, the super-rich New World Order ex-Nazi. High profile. Connected. Stratospheric. Untouchable."

"Vogel is pure evil. He gets his wealth and power from war and genocide. I've viewed him meeting with Dunbar regularly and with Ricci and Firouz too. He's dangerous, Raven. I was feeling his presence before I even met you, back when I was covering you in Iran."

"I know his history." Raven jotted notes. "The other code RED is our old friend Reverend Dilbert Jones, right here in Monterey. Firouz and Safdari are both coded YELLOW."

"Jones wanted no part of the Muslims, or they with him. The YELLOW two are last known to be in Iran. As was Smith, our other PURPLE person. It's a good place to avoid."

"They wanted to send me there. I went for you instead."

"A wise decision. So what should we do now?"

"Sex?"

"Um," I said. "Is that all you ever think of?"

"I can multitask if you press me. Lunch? Clean the guns? Raucous sex? Another viewing? Pack to leave?"

I rolled my eyes. "Food, weapons, and sex. Why do I bother?"

"The mission too. Don't forget that."

"Mostly sex."

"Would you seduce a starving, helpless man?"

I flashed a smile. "In a heartbeat. The day is ours!"

"We're to be at the airport early. We're probably not coming back. This safe house was almost hit. It's best if we fit a viewing in soon."

"My viewings have not been showing any threats."

"You said they were fuzzy, that things were uncertain and changing. We have specific direction now. We've been re-tasked."

"True."

"How about I make you a deal? You take a shower, relax, and get ready to meditate. I'll get lunch together. We have that container of barbecued Cajun shrimp from Pascal's Manale in New Orleans in the freezer and a loaf of fantastic French bread."

"We were saving those for a special occasion."

"This is it. World famous and special since 1913, use it or lose it, Babe."

"Don't get your hopes up. My remote viewings have been odd lately. I got hits all over the place when I was looking into Ricci, but I couldn't keep a focus. Then, when I looked close in, at the here and now, it got blurry. What do you want me to do differently?"

"Can you focus on the intersections of Ricci with the other six on the new list? Ricci's GREEN, the only one Goldfarb thinks we can touch. Go in soft. Back off if you run into anything scary. Then recheck to see if we're safe here. Just a quick look…."

I sighed. *He was right.* "If you insist. Feed me first, though."

"Deal."

I stood and grinned at him. Then I turned away and headed for the shower, shedding my clothes gracefully. As I vanished down the hall, I gave him my best sensuous wiggle.

UN Building, New York

Ricci shook his head. "This was an impossible assignment."

"Nein. Iss normal."

"Why would anyone think that getting Muslim *jihadists* and Black Lives Matter to work together was workable? They distrusted each other, the leaders fought, and neither group was willing to accept orders, not from me, not from anyone. They were thugs."

"Ja," Vogel said. "Iss the situation all over. Muslims, Antifa, Ecoterrorism, Nazis, Communists and New World Order only agree on destroying Western Capitalism. Hass been that vay for many years. Vee come together for power, but then vee fight each other."

I said, "World War II. Russia and Germany fought. America and Britain won. My country was ruined along with most of Europe."

"You know diss Mr. Ricci. The UN is vhere it musst come together. Global Governance and an end to nation states. No borders. No national armies. World peace at last."

That was the dream.

"I have nothing to report, Sir. They are all gone. It's over. President Blager lives. He's taken a hard line against radical Islam, against *jihad*."

"Ja, I vatch the tvee. I haff news to tell you. There is no hard line against us. Americans are soft. They do not vant to kill their enemies."

"What are you saying, Sir?"

"It doss not matter that Blager lives, it matters that hiss replacement is alive. The plan is alive. Vee can still win. Vee must not let this pass. Vee must rebuild"

Rebuild how? "Vice President Dunbar resigned."

"Ja. Of course. They force him out. That or prison. Gott villing, vee can reverse this. I come to tell you to vait while vee rebuild. I haff resources coming, but you musst be patient."

"Is there a plan? Where is Dunbar?"

"I come to share that. Iss important, you know. You know of the old Gehlen organization? After Hitler, he vorked for the Vest."

I racked my brain, thinking. *Finally it came.*

"Major General Reinhard Gehlen, chief of the Wehrmacht Foreign Armies East military-intelligence unit, during World War II. The Russian Front. He was a Nazi spymaster."

"Ja. Good one. He knew the Russians and the Germans. Turned it to good use. After the war, he worked for the CIA. The Gehlen Organization was an intelligence agency established in June 1946 by U.S. occupation authorities in the United States Zone of Germany. It consisted of former members of the 12th Department of the German Army General Staff, Hitler's best."

Where was he going with this? I had no idea.

I said, "Old history. Dusty books."

"Nein. Not so old. Reinhard Gehlen acted under the tutelage of US Army G-2 (intelligence), but he vanted an association with the Central Intelligence Agency. In 1947, in alliance with the CIA, the military orientation of his organization turned increasingly toward political, economic and technical espionage against the Eastern bloc. His CIA base, Pullach, became synonymous with secret service intrigues."

"Is this like the old James Bond stories?

"More crazy. The Gehlen Organization was for many years the *only* eyes and ears of the CIA on the ground in the Soviet Bloc nations during the Cold War. Then Gehlen vass blown by the Russians."

"How?"

"Vass funny. The Gehlen Organization had East German Communist moles within the organization itself and vass intensely watched by communist spies and their sympathizers within the CIA and the British MI6, particularly by Kim Philby.

"Gehlen had hundreds, maybe thousands, of hard core Nazis, and MI6 made sure it was all leaked to the press. KGB helped. Philby defected. It vass a huge embarrassment for CIA."

"I can imagine."

Vogel actually smiled. "It got worse. There was also Alois Brunner in Syria, alleged to be a Gehlen operative, who was responsible for the Drancy internment camp near Paris and for the death of 140,000 Jews. That was the end. CIA had to drop Gehlen."

"So Gehlen was arrested and tried as a war criminal. End of story."

"You haff much to learn, Mr. Ricci. He vass not tried by the Americans, not by the British, and not even by the Germans. He knew too much. Vass too valuable."

"Why would the Germans want to try him?"

"High treason. He knew of the plot to kill Hitler for years and did nothing to stop it. Rommel and others died, but Gehlen survived."

"So what happened to him?"

"Vass fitting. On April fool's day 1956, the Gehlen Organization was formally established as the Federal Intelligence Agency of the Federal Republic of Germany, vich still exists. He almost went down when the Jews caught Eichmann, but Gehlen wasn't implicated."

"Why not?"

"Jews wanted revenge, not intelligence. They hanged Eichmann in 62. Gehlen stepped down as President of the Federal Intelligence Agency in 1968 after reaching retirement age. He died in his bed in 1979."

Why is he telling me this? Vogel was watching me intently, still smiling.

"You musst haff courage, my friend. You are one of us. Nothing will happen to us. Vee will run the world."

"Where is VP Dunbar?"

"Ja, I come to tell you. He is safe at a UN facility in San Luis Obispo County. In America. Gehlen himself set it up using the NAZI model of internment camps. Originally, it was called the 'California Specialized Training Institute' for foreign security forces. Later it became a FEMA agency facility. Iss still there. Mostly underground."

A UN facility? "How large is this?"

"Vass a small one, designed for company strength, about 160-200. More than enough to overwhelm a President and his Secret Service detail."

"Why didn't we didn't use it...."

"Vass a mistake. Dunbar said no. The President was dying. There were backup plans to kill him twice over. He did not die. The Arabs bungled. Vass not your fault, Mr. Ricci."

"So what do I do now?"

"Vee wait. Help is coming."

"Not more Arabs or Black thugs, I hope? We lost them all."

"Vass a few small chess pieces and of no matter. Now we get serious. Persian warriors. Military professionals.

He meant Iran.

"What do you want me to do, Sir?"

"Vait. I vill get you money and weapons. We need to restock that camp, to provision it with weapons and vehicles, but slowly, without attracting notice. You vill do this as an UN humanitarian program, to support the collapsing state of California in case of an emergency. They are bankrupt. There are local officials, Americans, useful idiots who will gladly help."

"Then what?"

"Iss simple. California has many votes. We vait for opportunity. President Blager will return. Then comes the coup and this time he dies."

"Thank you, Sir. Is there anything else?"

Vogel looked at his watch. "Vait. Stay calm. Do nott use computers or phones. If you musst communicate send a trusted messenger. I vill be in touch."

"Thank you, Sir. I will escort you out."

Private House, South of Monterey, California, Afternoon, Same Day.

Raven was frowning, looking down at Josie. He checked his watch. She'd been deep in her viewing for over two hours.

Josie was convinced she'd long ago been a High Druid Princess and that they'd met in previous lives. According to her, she and Raven had died together in 56 BC when Roman soldiers under Gaius Julius Caesar had destroyed her temple.

He had asked her when they first met if that was where her psychic powers came from. Josie's answer, like so much about her, was unexpected.

"I like to think so," Josie said, "but I fear the dark side."

It was a core truth, one they fully agreed on. The dark side was much to be feared. The battle between good and evil was eternal.

Raven worked in the deep dark of night, killing monsters. It had made him enemies in high places. Josie could find evil across time and space, but was powerless to thwart it if it came for her. The least hint of violence shut down her paranormal senses.

It was his job to keep her safe and alive, but their worlds were vastly different. At times he'd almost destroyed her. His world was one of violence and betrayal, one where the good guys all too often lost, sometimes betrayed by their own leadership. Over the years he'd lost too many friends.

She was a bright spirit. Her powers allowed her to sense realities far beyond what most mortals could perceive. Many were places of beauty, but some were dangerous.

It was on the sharp edges of reality where their worlds overlapped, a place where beauty sometimes met unimaginable horrors. Josie shared Raven's sense of loss. She'd once told him, speaking of the Celts, "In the end, our entire culture was lost except to myth."

Civilization was fragile. No matter how many times you won, if evil prevailed the darkness on the land lasted for centuries, perhaps forever.

America's exceptional culture could vanish as quickly as had that of the Celts when it was crushed by the Romans. It was another point on which they agreed.

Josie was still deep in her trance. Her face was relaxed and peaceful, her brown hair shiny in the afternoon sunlight. She preferred to do her viewings naked. He could see the curves of her body under the thin sheet.

She was fine, even though the viewing seemed to be taking a long time. He knew better than to interrupt her during a viewing. That was a cardinal rule.

They had time. His security systems were active and his weapons were just outside the room. Far enough away that their presence wouldn't interfere with her viewing, but close enough that he could reach and deploy them quickly.

Raven kept his thoughts peaceful and reached for the book Goldfarb had given them. He settled into the chair where he could see the main approach to the house and started reading.

CHAPTER FIVE
OFF THE RAILS

Unknown Location, Washington DC

Goldfarb was standing at the end of the tunnel with the President having a few private words when his secure phone gave a raucous buzz. It got him a sharp look.

He pulled it out, looked at the ID, and said, "Sir. I need to take this."

"Pardon me all to Hell, Aaron. We're scheduled tight. I need you in the room. You were directed to clear your schedule for the week."

"I did, Mr. President. I still have a running OP. We put it on stand down, but this is an emergency signal. I need to take it…."

"Oh." Their eyes met. He got it. *Josie.*

"Five minutes. I'll get the meeting protocols started. Get a time slot with me tonight. I want to know what the Hell is going on…."

"Yes, Sir."

Goldfarb punched the button, waiting for the secure light to illuminate while the President and his security detail cleared the area. It went green and he said, "Stand by."

He knew who it was. Only one person had that access.

When the nearest secret service agent was out of hearing range, he said, "What the fuck, Raven? I have three minutes max. Are you declaring an emergency?"

"Not yet. Incoming hostiles."

"Details?"

"Iranian Quds force. The two we know about are high level. Josie is sketching them. I'll text pictures. They will likely have assault teams and watchers."

"What are your intentions?"

"I need backup like we had in Durham." *Military support, constrained by dysfunctional rules of engagement, got there just short of too late and left a high end neighborhood in flames….*

"Negative. You're on your own until I can get you extracted."

"That sucks."

"I agree and will pass that along. What are your intentions?"

"Plan A, we get clear with no ticks and run like Hell. Plan B, preemptive lethal force. I'll leave the bodies for the wild pigs. Clean up is your problem."

"All of them?"

The kill teams they'd encountered a few weeks back in Monterey consisted of two-vehicle teams, four to a car, all heavily armed.

"There's no one to cover my back. I'm taking no chances with Josie. Gloves are off. We'll try to get clear of the house by 06:00. Local Sunrise is 06:32."

"Do what you need to do."

"Sir?"

"I'm late to a meeting with the FBI director. Maybe we can make this his problem. I'll try to get you help."

"Authorization received. Extraction is 08:00 and we'll try to get there early. Raven out."

The phone went dead. *Too many maybes*, Goldfarb thought. *What a mess.*

Goldfarb limped down the hall at his best speed, heading for the meeting room. The lead Secret Service agent saw him coming. When he was ten feet away, she rapped twice on the door and held it open for him.

What got my attention as I entered the room were the eyes. Four intense gazes, focused on him like laser beams. Only President Blager's were friendly.

The President was seated at the head of the rosewood table. The others were lined up along the side to the President's left, so he took the middle seat on the other side, leaving one empty chair between them.

"Aaron, you can catch your breath while I do the introductions."

"Thank you, Mr. President."

"We've been discussing you. Drop your phone in the secure container and make sure it's turned off. No electronic devices. Everything here is off the record."

Seated next to the President on his left was General Peter Neumann, his National Security Advisor. He had written several military histories and taught at both West Point and the War College.

I had read his books and recognized him from the cover photos. Neumann was meticulous, both in theory and practice. His books spanned history from ancient Rome to the present day, though for some reason he'd skipped the Civil War and World War One. He had commanded a tank brigade in Iraq, but retired when Obama took office.

Roger Johnson, the FBI Director, was thin and new to that post. He looked fit. Light brown hair, no glasses. He was impeccably dressed in a dark suit that presumably covered his shoulder holster. His reputation was low profile, apolitical, and no bullshit. Career FBI and a lawyer, he'd focused on counterterrorism and secure borders. Homeland Security and the Border Patrol loved him, but Washington DC was mostly noncommittal. Except for his confirmation hearing, he'd avoided Congress.

Admiral Brandon Quigley was old-school Blue Water Navy. Before the Pentagon, he'd commanded Carrier Attack Groups in a career that included a slap down of North Korea and several skirmishes with Iran. He'd been a surprise pick for the Joint Chiefs. His focus was on war fighting, not asymmetrical war or resisting migration jihad, but being ready for the big one if it came.

The others, including the President, had shed their coats and loosened their ties. Presumably that signaled that this was a working meeting. Goldfarb took the cue. He draped his coat on one of the empty chairs and loosened his tie.

"I'm going to restate the guidelines before I turn the meeting over to Peter," the President said. "First, my decision is final that I'm putting Aaron on the NSC as an Ad Hoc member. He may have active roles from time to time at my option, but mostly he is there to listen, to be informed and be aware. He has an all-sources clearance. I will be using him as my private advisor."

No one spoke.

"Is that understood? We need to be clear on that one. I'd like verbal responses."

"We understand, Mr. President," they chorused, except for Admiral Quigley, who added, "but...."

The President looked at him. "Do you have a problem?"

"I wanted to note for the record that this is unconventional."

"It is unconventional, but not unprecedented. President Trump had exactly such a role for Bannon."

"One minor point," NSC Director Neumann said. "There is no 'on the record' for these meetings. They will be informal and strictly off the record. No leaks. No discussing our talks here with your staffs. Understood?"

Everyone nodded, and the President added, "That is not a minor point. It's paramount. We are required to document all NSC meetings under the presumption that putting high level classifications on the records will keep them secret and protect our National Security. In my view, too many eyes see those documents. I will not tolerate any leaks about what we discuss here. My policy is zero tolerance. Understood?"

There was a chorus of, "Understood."

"One more thing. The law that established the National Security Council in 1947 gave the Joint Chiefs of Staff the paramount role. The assumption was that the NSC was to focus on avoiding wars if we could and winning them if we had to fight.

"I want it clear that this is again our primary purpose. Not our *only* purpose, but our overriding purpose. Is that clear?"

"It is, Mr. President. Thank you." Admiral Quigley seemed to relax a bit.

"With that I'll turn it over to my NSC Advisor. Your meeting, Peter."

"Good." Neumann pointed at Goldfarb. "Two questions. Why are we here, and what, exactly, do you do?"

I blinked. *So much for the quiet professor.* "I've read your books, Sir. Most impressive."

Neumann nodded.

"You didn't write about the Celts, General. Are you familiar with them?"

"Why should I write about them?" He raised an eyebrow. "No one writes about the Celts. The Celts didn't even write about themselves. They were brutish savages. The myths claim the severed head of an enemy killed in battle was considered a priceless trophy, one proudly shown to guests."

"By the end, yes, after their culture was crushed by Imperial Rome, what few remained were savages. Initially, they were sophisticated. For example, they had better communications technology than the Romans. The Celts were successful at migration-based invasions almost a thousand years before the Muslims started their own *Hijrah*, migration *jihad*."

"Even if so, why does that matter?"

"Because we, not just America, but all the Western Democracies and most of the Muslim countries, are losing to *Hijrah*. Radical Islamic terrorism is ascendant. Did you ever consider that our Western Civilization could go down the same way as the Celts if radical Islam prevails with a Global Caliphate and Sharia Law?"

Neumann was scowling. "I don't agree we are losing, but even if that were true, there is no need to discuss the Celts. I didn't feel a need to go that far back in history in my writings to frame the current threat from radical Islam."

"Why not? The Celts *invented* migration-based invasion. Mighty Rome was *terrified* of them. The Celts were highly literate. Writing implements have been found all over the Celtic world. Inscriptions on plates, pots, coins, and curse-tablets have been unearthed."

"Curse tablets?"

I smiled. "Remarkable, isn't it? *Two thousand years before tweets.*

"Their Druids had a record of resolving disputes that would put the UN to shame. The UN has never resolved a conflict. The Druids did it routinely for centuries."

"So why no recorded history?"

"Celtic writings were not published in Rome or catalogued in the Library of Alexandria. Their culture is not prehistoric, but it is protohistoric. All we know about them is what little was published by ancient Greek and Roman travelers, or what was preserved in verse and memorized by bards.

"More important, the Celt leaders, the Druids, *banned* all written expression of their wisdom, just as President Blager has directed us to do for these private meetings. Personally, I resonate with such a viewpoint."

Blager and Neumann exchanged a look.

The President said, "Some on Aaron's team are fascinated by Celtic mythology. Aaron gave me a tablet that bears the inscription: *'I'll tell you what's wrong with society. We no longer drink from the skulls of our enemies.'* I deemed it best not to display it in the White House."

Director Johnson smiled. Admiral Quigley laughed.

"My presence at this meeting and your reactions when I entered triggers a darker reflection."

They all looked at me.

"At Celtic war councils, punctuality was encouraged by the custom of torturing the last man to arrive and then putting him to death in sight of the whole assembly. That would be **me.**"

There was general laughter. Even Neumann joined in.

"Should I be worried?"

The President smiled. "I think you get a pass this time. Your tardiness and infirmity was incurred in a good cause. He put his body between me and an assassin, Gentlemen."

Neumann was smiling too. "It's clear the good doctor doesn't wish to discuss his sources and methods. His team was crucial to thwarting the recent attacks on the President. They've done other unconventional things that made a difference."

Admiral Quigley had an odd look on his face. "That Russian Icebreaker with the Iranian Nukes...."

"*Krasivi Oblako,*" Goldfarb murmured. "A most unfortunate accident in the far South Atlantic with no survivors...."

"Right," Quigley said. "My command had purview. Tragic, it was. Someday we may want to salvage and study those nukes."

Neumann threw up his hands. "Okay, enough. Let's skip the first part of my question. Doctor Goldfarb's job content is off the table. We can reflect on lost civilizations and ships later."

He pointed at me. "*Why are we here?* What is the purpose of this meeting, Doctor?"

"There will be times, not often I hope, when I need timely, low-profile assistance for my teams. A larger problem is that we will need to constantly de-conflict our battle space to prevent embarrassments. That's why it was imperative that we got acquainted."

"De-conflict? Does anyone know what the Hell he's talking about?" Quigley said.

"Durham," the President said. "Tell them about Durham."

I nodded. "Durham was bad. Do you recall the incident? It made the news."

Heads nodded.

"We try to run deep black, but one of our teams was stalked and trapped by *jihadists.* It got messy."

"Most of a neighborhood was left in flames," Neumann said. "Local police officers died. There was political upset."

"Correct. My team was lucky to get out alive. Everyone was wounded. The military finally did arrive with heavy firepower, just short of too late. And that was only because a promising young Army Major took some initiative."

Quigley was nodding. "I'm familiar with the case. Major Kincaid, 101st Airborne. He was passed over for a promotion. Some want that decision revisited. He's about to be retired."

 John D. Trudel

"Kincaid was one reason why I gave the President the tablet he refuses to display in public. Political Correctness is a dangerous disease."

"Do you want to say anything more?"

"Simply that my people would not be alive without Major Kincaid. Regretfully, they will not be available to testify in his defense."

"Thank you." Both the Admiral and the President were taking notes. *A good sign.*

"How can we provide you with better support?" Quigley asked.

Director Johnson spoke for the first time. "Before he answers I have a question."

"Yes?"

"Why isn't the CIA represented here? They do covert OPs."

I answered before anyone could speak. "Because they were not invited is the short version."

He frowned. "That is an insufficient answer."

"I have no need to de-conflict with CIA for domestic OPs, Director. The agency is prohibited by law from operating in the United States. No matter how often they cross it, that's a bright line in the sand legally."

Johnson's frown deepened. "I have a close personal working relationship with the existing Director...."

"We do not," I said.

The President interrupted. "He's correct about the legal basis, Roger."

"It's his attitude that bothers me, Sir."

I said, "That's the second reason for my objection. Attitude. I have no issue with your close relationship with the agency, though I don't personally share it. I am simply not willing to put my team at risk."

"What risk?"

"Leaks. Moles. Traitors lurking in the basement."

"That's absurd...."

The President said. "The issue is one of ghosts and shadows, Roger. I can assure you that others, including some of our best allies, share Doctor Goldfarb's concerns. Brennan and those like him poisoned our Intel community. We're still recovering."

Johnson said, "Brennan and his top two levels of management were wiped clean in 2017, Mr. President. How long do we hold grudges...?"

I said, "There are some really great people at CIA, but nowhere near the numbers needed to reverse the broken culture. That will take years."

I looked around the table and saw heads nodding. I took it as a good sign.

"It's not about grudges, Director Johnson. It is about moles and termites. During the Cold War our best counterterrorism people and decades of intense work never found them all. The Brits had problems as bad or worse...."

Johnson said, "Just because you fear ghosts and shadows is no reason...."

The President held up a hand. "We will not resolve that issue here, Roger, nor do we have to. The issue we need to address is a simple one. How can we -- *this small working group, not the entire NSC* -- best support Doctor Goldfarb's teams. It's clear that they do not want and will not accept support from the CIA."

"Exactly correct," I said. "My assets are fragile and irreplaceable. They are being targeted. I dare not take any chances.

"If CIA is in, I am out. I'm here because the President insisted, because he assured me that anything we discuss here will be closely held and strictly compartmentalized, and also because, on occasion, we do need limited external support to survive.

"You asked me what I do, why I am here, and why we are having this meeting. It is to provide a Special Operations Group for NSC. I am the liaison to that group and the cutout."

"Support for situations like Durham and the issue of the *Krasivi Oblako*," Admiral Quigley said.

"You need support without visibility or oversight," Neumann said. "History might not judge that favorably. There are unhappy precedents. Ollie North comes to mind. So does waterboarding."

"Those are valid concerns." I said. "I will quote my team leader. He says, 'The best way to avoid being judged by history is not be a part of it to begin with.' As I said, I am the cutout. The NSC has no responsibility for what my group does or does not do. I am not here to discuss our operations or to seek approval."

"I am the visibility and oversight," the President said. "Hence these meetings."

"Yes. That's the meat of it. Our operational dilemma is that sometimes we do need support, but bureaucratic delays or being exposed could lead down the road to a worse fate than our not having any support at all."

"You don't trust much, do you Doctor?" Johnson said.

I met his eyes. "I trust God, my team, and our President. That's why I'm here, Sir."

Admiral Quigley nodded. "It was simpler when I was at sea, Doctor. How can we help you?"

"I was wondering how to frame that," I said. "We now seem to have a practical example."

I looked at the President. "Mr. President that is the call I had to take. We have a situation. I need a decision, but I've not had a chance to brief you. Do you want to break to discuss it privately, or do you want to deal with it here?"

"It is time urgent?"

"Affirmative."

"Your call, Aaron."

"I have two assets stranded in Monterey. I left them in a compromised safe house with an extraction planned for tomorrow. It's gone off the rails, Sir. Hostiles are inbound.

"It is the same location that was attacked concurrent with the attacks on you at the hospital."

The President said, "Your team killed them all, save one *jihadi* who is now proving useful to us."

"It seems they had friends. We have detected a new threat. This time it is Iranian Quds force, not ragtag *jihadists*."

"Quds is here?" Director Johnson said. "On American soil?

I shrugged. "Here or inbound. I should have names and images of the leaders in a few minutes."

"What support do you need?" Neumann asked.

"I'm not sure yet. My team leader has two plans, both of which I have authorized. Plan A requires no help at all. If he can get clear – clear meaning no ticks, no surveillance – with the asset he is protecting, he will run. He'll be out of the safe house by 0600, before sunrise, and ready for a pick up at the airport by 0800. I will have a plane waiting. That could happen."

"What's Plan B?"

"That one is messy. He will kill them if he can and leave their bodies for the local feral pigs. Clean up is my problem."

They all looked at each other. Admiral Quigley said, "How many?"

"We don't know. My best guess is two vehicles, each with a team of four. Eight tangos. Like what hit us before."

"Possibly more?" Neumann asked.

"Possibly. We don't know. This is new."

"They typically used larger teams in Iraq," Admiral Quigley said. "Quds had good communications security. They used couriers, not electronics."

"Yes," I said.

"How will they be armed?"

"Again, we don't know. The last batch we encountered had AKs and grenades. Quds may have different preferences for weapons."

"Your guy is going to take on two heavily armed kill teams by himself?" Neumann said.

"He's going to protect our researcher. He won't leave her."

"A SEAL or DELTA team with a couple of Apaches should be able to handle things," Quigley said.

"I agree. Can you get those resources there, hot, and ready by 0600 without attracting a lot of attention like Durham?"

The Admiral frowned. "I'm not sure."

"Welcome to my world, Gentlemen. Now you see the problem."

Johnson said, "The FBI does counterterrorism. It's our job."

I looked at him. "So?"

"We have resources in LA. I can have twenty or more people in Monterey by 0600."

"To do what?"

"Whatever I decide. We'll help you get your people clear. Then we'll deal with Quds if they show up."

"**When** they show up," I said. "How?"

"I don't know yet. We can shoot them, we can arrest them, or we can assign watchers to see where they go. You say 'yes' and this becomes an FBI OP."

"After my people are safe and clear?"

"Yes."

"That works. Thank you, Director Johnson."

"This committee gets a full report after you wrap this up?" Neumann asked.

"Of course," Johnson said. "But if we choose to prosecute, you might read it in the papers first."

"I'm good with that. Are we all in agreement?"

Heads nodded.

I said, "Thank you, Gentlemen. I will get Mr. Neumann sketches of the tangos we've identified. They are now an FBI problem, but that's our data and, dead or alive, I want to know all about them."

"No problem, Johnson said. "Is there anything else I should know?"

"The house is a rental. There are sensors on the grounds. My team will get you keys and passwords for the security system and the wireless network."

"Thank you."

"It could get ugly. I suggest you gun up and go in hot. The previous groups we've encountered have been lethal."

"Right."

Everyone stood up and I limped around the table to shake hands. The President walked me out. His staff had set me up with an office for when I attended NSC meetings. I supposed it was best if I learned where it was.

CHAPTER SIX
INTRUDER

Private House, South of Monterey, California, 4 AM, Next Day

I came out of a deep sleep with Josie shaking me. The security monitor was green. The house had a laser display that put the time and temperature on the ceiling: 4:13 AM, 55 degrees F. I listened for a moment, hearing nothing.

I whispered, "What?"

Josie said, "My senses just clicked in. We have an intruder."

"Stay put."

I rolled out of bed and grabbed my Sig. She'd spoken in a normal voice. Whatever was going down, it wasn't close. "Are they inside the perimeter?"

"No," she said. "Out by the highway. North of Spindrift road."

I pictured the terrain in my mind. North, toward the town. Well south of Point Lobos. Low terrain on the ocean side, higher terrain inland, the Caramel Highlands.

"East or West of the highway? How many?"

"East. I only sense one person. He's not moving at present."

The park would be on the West side and well to the North. It wouldn't be open at this hour.

"North of Peter Pan road?"

"I don't think so. Closer. This person is there to observe. He is on foot, up on a hill, and has night vision optics. That's why my senses kicked in."

"What about weapons or a vehicle?"

"I didn't detect any, but he must have driven in or been dropped off."

"Yes." I relaxed a bit and holstered my Sig. I'd already packed my CAMO gear. I turned on the closet light and got it out along with my Mini-14 and NVGs.

Josie was sitting up in bed. "Should we declare an emergency?"

I shook my head. "For one unarmed person? I'll check it out."

I snapped my new SOCOM2 Fast-Attach suppressor onto my rifle, one quarter turn and it clicked into place. I'd been waiting for months to get one, but it was worth it. My Mini-14 was *more* accurate with it attached, quieter, and it helped hide the muzzle flash at night.

Josie said, "He is not even on the property. Are you going to shoot him?"

"I'm going to check it out. It could be a friendly stupid enough to cover our egress without warning us, but I don't like it. One of the problems with this safe house, in addition to the fact that it has been compromised, is that we only have one way in and out of here by vehicle. I've never liked that. The intersection of Spindrift and the Highway is a choke point."

"What do you want me to do?"

"I say we get up and leave early. I'll be back in about 40 minutes. Then we bug out."

"I'll make you some coffee."

"Thanks."

The intruder was right where Josie said. I had made two wide circles. There was a new Lexus SUV tucked back into the brush with its engine still warm. It had custom Oregon plates, "STOP H8." It was white. I detected no one else in the area and there were few cars on the highway.

The Tango either lacked tradecraft or didn't care about being detected. He was perched at the top of the hill watching the Spindrift intersection intently, just as we'd thought, wearing a light colored jacket that showed up like a neon sign in my NVGs. I didn't see any weapons.

I crept closer. Soon I was tucked in the brush about 20 feet behind him. He never looked around. He just sat there watching the road.

To my astonishment, I heard his cellphone ring. *Who does a stakeout with their ringer turned up, sitting out in plain sight in a white jacket?*

The voice came clearly. "Yes, I'm here. It's boring as shit, I'm cold, and the ground is damp. I haven't seen a thing."

A woman's voice. Not your typical *jihadi*.

"Not a thing. I've been here since 3:30 and nothing." She paused, listening. "Okay, yes, a few cars on the highway. None slowed down. Nothing has come in or out of Spindrift."

Another pause. "Of course I'm sure. Good. Yes, I'll call or text if anything happens. See you at the Tickled Pink at 9:30."

I definitely had a Tango. The question was what to do about it.

My time to get back to Josie was running out. I gazed at the woman over my sights, thinking. I didn't have time to interrogate her and I couldn't leave her here over-watching our only egress route.

The woman was totally still, intently watching the intersection. My finger caressed the trigger, but I couldn't shoot. It would be too easy. Or too hard. Josie would not be happy.

With a silent sigh, I removed my NVGs, set down my rifle, and stood. I didn't even pull my knife. It would be too tempting. Muay Thai had an arsenal of nine weapons – the head, fists, elbows, knees, and feet. That's all I needed.

One silent step at a time, I crept closer. At ten feet, I rushed her.

She heard me coming, dropped her binoculars, and spun to the left. She was almost as tall as I was, and quick. Very quick. Her right hand darted into her jacket pocket.

A weapon. Great.

I grabbed her right wrist with my left hand, stuffing it down, controlling the weapon. Then I yanked hard, pulling her off balance, going with her motion.

When she faced me square, I punched her in the solar plexus. She went limp and sagged. I released her wrist, gave the fist-strike to her left temple, stood back, and watched her fall.

She didn't move, but was still breathing. I'd pulled my blows.

First I needed to secure her. With my gloved hands, I rolled her face down. I fished out the duct tape and bound her hands behind her. Then I did her ankles.

I didn't bother with a gag. If she wanted to scream when she woke up, I'd be long gone.

I checked her pocket, the one she was so intense about, finding a white can of pepper spray. Using my red flashlight, I checked the label. It was oleoresin capsicum, five million SHU, the good stuff, beyond high-end law enforcement grade.

A two-second spray would stop a bear. Bear Spray was much weaker and longer range, designed to repel, not harm. This was designed to disable at close range and perhaps even kill.

The lady had connections. That gave me some ideas.

Her other jacket pocket held an iPhone. I turned it off hard, total shutdown, wrapped it in foil, and dropped into one of my leg pouches. *Always be prepared.*

No matter how her phone was set up, no one could track or eavesdrop on me from a unit sealed inside a Faraday cage.

There was a backpack on the ground. I fished around inside, finding a wallet and some oily lotion that women like to use on their hands and faces to keep them soft. It wasn't an inkpad, but it was better than nothing.

I dripped a bit on her fingertips and pressed the spray can against them. It probably already held her prints but why take a chance? With that done and a zip lock baggie, the can went into the pouch on my other leg.

The clock in my head was running. *Gotta go.*

I pulled out her driver's license and credit cards, put them in another baggie, and dropped them in with the cell phone. Pocket litter is often useful.

I stood slowly, put everything back in her backpack, rolled the woman over, and checked her breathing. Still good and a strong pulse.

On the way out, I collected my rifle and did what I could to disguise my back trail. I walked to the road and followed the concrete for a few hundred yards, having to go to cover only once for a passing car.

Then I darted across into the woods, heading back to Josie at a jog. Thirty minutes later we were in the car heading for the airport. It was bug out time...

C H A P T E R   S E V E N

AN ENDLESS SEA OF DOTS

Two Days Later, The Ranch, a Private Estate near Mendocino, California

Raven was sitting on the balcony with his feet on the railing, gazing out over the sea, sipping his morning coffee. He never lost his intensity, but his face was more relaxed.

I said, "What are you thinking?"

"I like it here, Babe. This is a green zone: good security and great views. We are finally distanced from the craziness."

Raven felt it too. Monterey had bad Karma. "I didn't have anything solid from my viewings to base it on, but I was getting creeped out being stuck in that house. Violence was lurking out there, just out of sight, getting closer."

"Yes. My mission sense was sounding alarms. Goldfarb was getting weird. Our control was out of control. He was too busy to worry much about us."

True that. "Did he believe us about Iran and Quds?"

"Yeah, he did. Assholes are puckering at high levels. Goldfarb was heading into a meeting with the FBI director to get us help. It worked. We're here."

"Do you think Quds will hit the safe house?"

"They have the capability. It's a question of when. Whatever goes down in Monterey, the FBI should be able to handle it. Whoever goes in to breach that safe house now has to get through 15,000 agents, not just me and a gussied-up Mini-14."

"They won't send them all."

"Of course not, but they will send enough to assure overwhelming force. I'm glad we're not around."

I said, "Why?"

"The FBI may try to arrest them. I don't think that works well for *jihadists*."

"Are we safe here?"

Raven shrugged. "You're the psychic."

"I want to know what you think."

"We're safer for now. The Ranch is way off the grid and much more defensible. We have perimeter security, rehab, and exercise facilities. We don't have to go out for food. You can even get professional massages here to help you de-stress."

"What do you do to de-stress?"

"I watch you smile…."

"You *make* me smile. What else?"

"There's a private firing range close and a dojo here where I can hone my close combat skills. The instructor I had last time was exceptional.

"Our situation is greatly improved operationally. We don't have to seek permission from mother Washington. Instead of scrambling around trying to stay alive, we have a list of targets and orders that allow us to do whatever we deem appropriate."

"Are you sure of that?"

"I'm positive. Action including lethal force is authorized."

"By whom?"

"Action was officially authorized by Dr. Goldfarb, our control. The gloves are off. For the first time, we can do what **we** think is needed, limited to the target names on our list."

I said, "Ricci, Vogel, Firouz, Safdari, Dunbar, and Smith."

"You forgot Reverend Dilbert Jones. He makes seven."

"Only one of those names was coded GREEN. Safdari."

"That was then. We are now cleared to act on any of them as we deem appropriate. We are instructed to report back and request what resources and support we need."

"We still need approval."

"Approval for additional resources, not for taking what action we deem appropriate."

"Including lethal force?"

"Affirmative."

"What are you saying?"

"We should continue your viewings. I can scrounge up limited resources if needed. I propose we muddle ahead and see what opportunities become apparent. We get to improvise, to go on offense and stop reacting. Better to seek forgiveness than to request permission."

"You want to poke the bear, don't you?"

"Evil is out there and you are a target. Right now, we're in a research phase trying to decide what to do about it. Our operational freedom will only continue for a few weeks. We'll have a meeting with Goldfarb and others soon to plan action. Until then, we are free to improvise."

"If we both deem the action appropriate…."

"Yes."

"I have concerns."

"We'll need to discuss our options and decide actions together. For now we need to sort out the viewings you've done and do what further research is indicated. Are you okay with that?

I heard myself saying, "Sure."

"After breakfast…."

"Of course. Dead red meat and eggs."

Raven grinned and nodded.

Josie had the two sketches she'd made of the Quds operatives face up on the table. The ones I'd snapped and text messaged to Goldfarb. *No reply, so far.*

Each sketch had a name attached. The older looking of the two was named, "Nassar Fuad." He was clean shaven. She'd noted, "Brown eyes and hair, and a scar on his left temple. History unclear. This one is senior."

The other was younger and had a heavy beard. The only name listed was, "Yasir." Her notes said, "Brown eyes, black hair. Former liaison to Hamas in Palestine."

That was unusual. Hamas was Sunni, but Iran was Shiite. They'd been at each other's throats for a thousand years. You'd expect Hezbollah and field service in Syria or Lebanon for an Iranian terrorist.

To the average Westerner, Hamas and Hezbollah were indistinguishable. To Muslims they were distinctly different, except for a shared hatred of Jews, Infidels, and Western Democracies.

Josie had a spiral-bound pad of unlined white paper in front of her. She'd closed her eyes, reflecting on the recent viewings she'd done, and sketched. I'd asked her to find shared connections between those on our list of seven targets. She'd been doing it for almost two hours.

I'd been watching her silently. Right now, she was working on the last name. Her page was labeled at the top, "Reverend Jones."

Jones seemed to cross-connect only with Ricci of the names on our list. He'd also connected tightly with Kamal, the Hamas team leader who'd targeted President Blager, but that link was severed. We had Kamal in custody at an offshore black site.

As I watched, I saw her write, "Check recent contact with our two Quds leaders."

The rest of that page had dense circles of dots with labels like "leftist political leaders, media, black power groups, domestic terrorist groups, Communists, etc."

Finally Josie took a deep breath and wrote, "Validate Ricci meets with VP Dunbar several times a year. Reverend gets financial donations from Vogel, funneled through Ricci."

She put her pencil down and closed her eyes. I waited, not wanting to interrupt her. This page had the smallest footprint. Jones was the only one she had connected with the new threat from Quds.

Finally she looked at me. "What do you think?"

"I think you're wonderful. There are patterns."

She brushed her hair back. "Really? When I try to connect the dots, I get lost in an endless sea of dots. It goes on endlessly. Literally endlessly, both in time and space. If I zoom in on the dots, they lead back to others on our list, but with various degrees of separation. I wind up lost in a gray fog of dots."

"Explain, please."

She shrugged. "Suppose I follow a connection from Reverend Jones to, say, a domestic terrorist group like AntiFa or BLM. I will then find funding or support links back to Vogel or some of his organizations...."

"Or to the UN or one of its sub-organizations...."

"Exactly. We already have that via Ricci, but yes. I'd find connections to some global refugee group, or climate action group, or whatever."

"So?"

"I don't know what it means. It is a maze. I feel overwhelmed."

"It means you are glimpsing big things. We need to get technical help, people with computers to chase down connections and map all those trails by looking though databases and communications records. Your Celts didn't have that technology, but America does."

"What am I looking at?"

"I think you are getting glimpses of what people call the Deep State, the Shadow Government."

"I'm getting glimpses of Hell. Massive evil. I can see people and sketch them, but I don't know how to sketch what I'm seeing in my viewings.

"It's like I can almost see a monster under the surface. I only glimpse it vaguely, or when a tentacle pops up in the real world."

"What kind of monster?"

"A big one. Maybe like a modern version of the Lernaean Hydra of the Greek and Roman myths. The Hydra was a monster that hides under the surface, one that had tentacles and many heads. If you cut one head off, two would grow back.

"Images of the Hydra were first discovered on bronze plates in Greece that dated back to 700 BC. The beast had poisonous breath. If you even got close to it, you died."

"Were the Celt's involved?"

"Those myths long predated the Celts, but the beast was supposed to have been killed by Heracles, one of our Gods. We knew the story."

"Not a good beast to poke?"

"No."

"I expect this beast, the one we face today, is harder to find, but easier to kill than your mythical Hydra. It's just people."

"Whatever it is out there, it scares me."

"We don't have to solve this alone. This is a good topic for the meeting we'll have in a few weeks. General Mickelson, "Twenty Mike," is a good guy. Help is coming."

"How can a General help us with something like this? He can't fight shadows."

"Retired General. We talked about his role briefly, but I didn't give you the details and implications. Mike now runs Transnational Services Group. TSG's role is to give us Operational Support."

"So?"

"If you can't see the beast clearly in your metaphysical worlds, maybe they can get a view of it out in cyberspace."

"How?"

"One of TSG's subcontractors is a firm called Cybertech. They should be able to help us if you are able to tell them what to look for."

"They do data analysis?"

"They do much more. The secure phones we're using now are prototypes from Cybertech. They are the *Sine qua non* of hacking and cyber defense."

Josie blinked. "The **what**? Where did you learn Latin?"

"Andrew Jackson."

"The President? You are kidding me."

"Nope. General Andrew Jackson was pretty much an asshole, a crusty warrior. He had his troops hide behind cotton bales at the battle of New Orleans. The British kept attacking, and his troops kept shooting. They slaughtered a superior British force."

"He spoke Latin?"

"Only once that I know of, but it was a doozy. Harvard gave him an honorary Doctorate. When asked how that could be, the President responded to his listeners with a toast, "*E pluribus unum, my friends. Sine qua non.*"

"What does it mean?"

I grinned at her. "I think the literal translation is, '*without which there is nothing*' or '*the core condition.*' It's the paragon, the best there is. Cybertech is damned good at what they do."

She gave an exaggerated sigh. "Computers lack souls. All those ones and zeros…."

"True, but they watch everything these days. Big Brother lives. If it's out there, there is a good chance Cybertech can find it."

"So what do you want us to do next?"

"Given what we have to work with now, is there anyone on our list of names that I can target?"

"Maybe. What are you looking for?"

"I'm not sure, but I do know what we **need**. We need things that can empower us to act instead of always being reactive and on the defense. These bastards almost got the President. They keep targeting you. Eventually, they will succeed if we don't do something to stop them. Do you agree?"

She nodded. "That is my fear too."

"Do you want to do another viewing?"

"What kind of things am I looking for?"

"Weak links. I want to find places where we can easily remove one person and cause massive disruption to our enemies. I want to do to them what they are trying to do to us."

"I can try."

"When?"

"Today. Now."

"Let's do it."

TSG Headquarters, New York

Mike looked at the ID on his secure phone, then at his watch. *Why is Goldfarb calling me? He's all jammed up with that NSC political stuff. We're not scheduled to meet for weeks.*

"How are you this fine day, Doctor? I didn't expect to hear from you so soon."

"This day is going to have to improve a great deal just to make it to shitty. Can you get to California tomorrow?"

"Affirmative." *Thank God for Grumman Gulfstreams.*

"We just had a terrorist attack on the safe house outside of Monterey where Raven and his team were basing. This time it was not rag-tag goat humpers, it was Quds."

"Are our people all right?"

"They are fine. Raven caught wind and got clear. He saw it coming."

"No shit?"

"None whatsoever. He has more lives than a cat. After he and his team bugged out, our brothers at the Bureau staked it out. Apparently they were going to arrest the invaders and read them their rights."

I frowned into the phone. "How did that turn out?"

"Not well. The FBI has 11 people down and three wounded."

"What about Quds?"

"None captured alive. Four dead, the rest in the wind. They had heavy weapons apparently. I don't have details. I need you down there to put eyes on. Raven is at the Ranch getting ready for our meeting there, which I expect has now been delayed."

"I can be out there tomorrow."

"Thanks, Mike. You have Raven's secure phone number and code?"

"Affirmative."

"Clue him in. Find out what he thinks. He's cleared for everything. Raven's team gave the first alert about Quds and he knows the ground. He put down the last attack there."

"Understood. I'll report after we sort this out."

"You will for sure. The President will need a full briefing. Quds is Iranian. We just had a foreign state attack our homeland. Keep the lid on tight."

"Can do. Anything else?"

"Watch your ass. Do not reveal anything about Raven's team. What they do is Special Intelligence, need to know, limited to you, me, and the President."

"I can't reveal what I don't know. I don't have a clue what Raven does. Other than that a shit storm seems to follow him around."

"The shit storm itself is classified. I'll tell Raven you are cleared in. Don't trust COMSEC. If you talk, do it face-to-face and in a secure location."

"Roger that. I'll check in when I know something."

"One more thing. The FBI is in a state of shock. Officially, you have absolutely no idea why an Iranian team had a shootout at a private home in Monterey."

"I sure don't. That's God's truth."

"Good. When you head back East, I need you to stop in DC. The briefing I mentioned needs to be in-person. I expect this debacle will become an NSC matter."

"I'll plan a stop at Andrews. Can you give me 48 hours?"

"I can. Thanks, Mike."

CHAPTER EIGHT
RUNNING FROM SAFETY

Morning, Little River Airport, near Mendocino, California

I watched through binoculars as the white G5 dropped out of the sky, coming straight in for runway 29. I'd cautioned Mike that the airport was tight for a jet, but the general laughed and said, "You'd be surprised at the places we go."

The plane slowed just over the trees, full flaps deployed, gear down and spoilers out. Then came the sound of the big Rolls Royce engines spooling up. Nose high, deep in the back side of its power curve, hanging on the thrust of those turbines, it sank for the runway.

The landing was a non-event. The wheels touched hard, the spoilers popped full open, and, under maximum breaking and full reverse thrust, the plane was almost stopped when only halfway down the 5,249 foot runway. The engines went back to idle and the big jet slowly rolled to the end of the runway.

I stood where the airport manager said, on the taxiway with my hands raised. The pilots saw me, rolled up, and stopped. When I crossed my arms, the engines spooled down. The engines stopped, the door popped open, and I saw Mike gesturing.

"Nice landing," I called out.

"We're blocking their taxiway, Raven. We told them less than 30 minutes on the ground. Can we talk in here?"

"Affirm."

  John D. Trudel

It was nice inside. Soft leather seats and a conference table that folded out. Up front, we could see into the cockpit though the open door, the pilots getting set for the next leg of the trip. When Mike gestured, they closed it.

"On to Monterey?"

Mike nodded. "It's a mess down there. Goldfarb wants me in DC tonight to brief him. We're not trusting COMs. There is grave concern that our security has been compromised.

"The FBI is in meltdown. In the entire history of the Bureau, they've only lost about 70 agents, and fewer than 40 to gunfire. Goldfarb says you have unique sources and methods."

"So far I do. I need to keep them safe. They were after my team in Monterey, but hit the Bureau instead."

"I figured that. This aircraft is as secure as we can make it. It's not a bubble, but it is close. What can you tell me?"

"The INTL I can share with you has limits. I can give you indications, but not proof. You'll have to provide your own validation using conventional methods."

"I'll take what I can get."

"No attribution. No speculations about sources and methods. This is need-to-know stuff, tightly compartmentalized. If you use anything I give you, you will have to invent your own plausible sources and explanations."

"Understood."

"If you want any additional explanations or insights, you will have to get them from Goldfarb personally. I don't want you asking around. I need your word on that."

"You have it."

"I don't have much." I pulled a piece of paper out of my pocket and handed it to him. "This was their primary weapon."

He frowned. "M224A1. The 224 is a 60 MM mortar. It is typically fielded at the infantry company level. I know it."

"The A1 is the latest model. It's 20% lighter. The old one had an effective range of 2,000 meters. This one, with upgraded ammo, goes out to 3,489 meters, almost 4,000 yards."

"What more do you know?"

"They probably used M720A1 ammunition. It's performance-enhanced HE for use against personnel and light material targets."

"Like automobiles and Humvees?"

"Yes. The rounds were likely fused with M734s, a multi-option fuse. It can be set for a proximity burst, near-surface burst, impact burst, or a delay burst."

Mike had a dumbfounded look.

"The best way for you to validate what I said is to have the FBI do a forensic study of the firing position and the targets destroyed. It should be easy for experts to identify the weapon used."

"Where would *jihadists* get a weapon like that?"

"Good question. No idea. But if you can get me the weapon used we may be able to help."

Mike was taking notes on a small pad. "What else?"

"That was their heaviest weapon, but they also had a belt-fed machine gun."

"The FBI never had a chance, did they?"

"No."

"Who were these people?"

"Didn't Goldfarb tell you?"

"He said Quds force. Iranian."

"Did he give you any pictures?"

Mike shook his head. "Negative. Said talk to you."

I pulled the images of Josie's sketches out of my pocket. "We believe these are the leaders."

Mike laid them on the table. He studied them intently. "Where do you get this stuff?"

"I can't tell you. Goldfarb wants you briefed in. I expect we'll be discussing such things at the meeting he has planned."

"The meeting is delayed."

Good. I have more time. "I've given you all I have. Goldfarb said TSG would provide technical support for us."

"That's the plan. We're trying to figure out how to fund it. What do you need?"

"That's a longer discussion. Right now, I have a short time window where I can act against a few tangos on my own initiative. I have no funding. I need some operational support."

"Name it."

"Can you get me a high-level backchannel to the Russians?"

"Maybe. Can you be more specific?"

"I need a personal meet in the next week. It has to be with someone high up in the Federal Security Bureau, someone based in the United States."

"FSB? Not a diplomat?"

"I don't care what his cover is. I need someone operational who can make decisions, not an analyst or bureaucrat."

"FSB has a number of roles, from counterterrorism and border security to dealing with organized crime. I need you to be more specific."

"I need this part of our discussion – a Russia backchannel – to be totally off the record, including to Goldfarb, even if asked."

"Only until Goldfarb's pending meeting with us in a few weeks. I may need to bring that up there. Our masters are still nervous about the Russians."

"If you insist." *By then, if things went hot, he'd already know.*

Mike said, "I do insist. I need to keep Goldfarb's trust as much as you do."

"Not a word to anyone else? If you have an issue, you come to me."

"Yes, I agree."

"Accepted," I said. "As for FSB, I'll choose organized crime."

"You mean like what the FBI does?"

"In a sense. One of the names on my target list is, ah, difficult to access using our own assets. The Russians have a valid international warrant out for him. We do not. I might be able to help them."

"FSB does assassinations. The old KGB used to subcontract for plausible deniability, but FSB tends to be hands-on. Are you suggesting…?"

I shook my head. "I told you, they have a valid international arrest warrant. They are motivated to take this person alive. They want to arrest him."

"And interrogate him…."

I shrugged. "We can't touch him. They can. The target has major political cover."

"If FSB grabs him, he'd be better off dead. The Lubyanka is legendary for its gruesome ways of dealing with enemies of the state. They allegedly cremated Penkoskvy, burned him alive. Putin continued the old traditions when he created the FSB."

"I don't care, Mike. Shit happens. This target is a major threat to our own national security and to my operatives. I finally can do something about it. Look at the bright side."

"Which is?"

"If they do kill him, who cares? The world would be better off. Problem solved."

"You don't know what they will do with your tango, do you?"

I said, "Russian is a riddle wrapped in a mystery inside an enigma."

"Churchill."

"Yes. I know the Russians will take my tango off the board. That's enough for me."

Mike was looking at me strangely. "So how does this involve you?"

"That's the point. **It does not.** It must not involve the United States in any way. Given the right level of contact, I can provide information to FSB that would help them pull off a snatch and grab. It beats letting this evil bastard run free."

Mike didn't speak.

Finally I said, "If this goes to shit, it's my responsibility, not yours, not Goldfarb's, and not the President's. If it works, happy Russians will either take credit or stay silent. In either case the world will go on. Will you help me or not?"

"Do I get to know who this is?"

I shook my head. "It's best that you don't know. He's a foreign national."

"Why do they want this guy?"

"He's a major threat to them too. Their warrant says 'financial terrorism.' They may have other reasons."

"Counterterrorism it is. I can set up a meet for you. I'll do it under a false flag. Do you speak Russian?"

"No. Arabic and Farsi, some High School French…."

"Not useful. Your legend might be as a Brit or Canadian. You hate the EU and Globalization."

"That works."

"When and where?"

"On U.S. soil. A dense city where I can lose tails is best. The sooner the better."

"How about San Francisco? They have a consulate there."

I said, "Perfect."

"What else do you need?"

"Would you like to attend my meeting with your contact?"

"Absolutely not. This business is between you and Doctor Goldfarb, my friend. I want to see if he hands you your ass or gives you a medal after you run your OP, after someone says 'Russians' and the shit hits the fan. Faux Russian conspiracies are still a popular propaganda ploy."

"I was going to mention that myself. I need a bulletproof cover ID, one that leads away from me and the U.S. – along with security to get myself to and from the meet without ticks, just in case the Russians get cute."

"A Dixie cup?"

A throwaway identity, to be used only once and then discarded.

"That would be adequate. What's essential is that I do not get my cover blown by this meet. I dare not leave a trail that might compromise my sources. Worse yet would be leaving fingerprints of any U.S. involvement."

"Understood. Can you give me a week?"

"The sooner the better, but a week is OK if that includes the operational aspects of getting me in and out clean."

Mike was silent for a time. He kept staring at the images of the Quds agents that I'd given him. "You have some of the most interesting intelligence I've ever seen, but I have to tell you that one of these identities is in error."

I raised an eyebrow. *Josie often was often vague and sometimes couldn't see things clearly, but overt errors on her part were rare.*

"How so?"

"You have the older of the two Quds operatives labeled as one Nassar Fuad."

"Yes."

"That's wrong."

"Really?"

"It is one of his old cover names, a Saudi identity, but I can assure you that it is not his real name."

Mike's gaze was intense. *This was something that mattered to him.* I waited.

"His name is Ahmed Mahmoud Muhammad. He was a Colonel in Bukhari Intelligence the last time I encountered him. Before that he was running a terrorist group in Yemen."

Mike slid the picture over to me. "You see the faint scar on the man's left temple?"

I nodded.

"I put it there with my 9 millimeter in Yemen the first time we met. Since then, Ahmed has become one of the most wanted people in the world."

"Why did you do that?"

"I was aiming for his forehead. He moved."

Generals don't usually work close enough to do head shots with pistols. "I expect he did...."

Mike hesitated. Finally he said, "The Israelis and others, including my wife's family, have been hunting Ahmed for years. After all this time, it has been assumed that he was dead. It seems he is not."

"Small world...."

"Indeed. You have my full support on a personal level, Raven. I believe you."

"Thank you."

Mike glanced at his watch. "I have to go."

"Watch your ass. We have leaks and moles. Not just in DC. It is probably worse in the People's Republic of California. It remains a deep blue state. Radical left."

"Roger that. I agree. So does Goldfarb."

With that, we both stood. Our meeting was over. Mike walked me to the airstair. As I started down he said, "One more thing...."

I turned to face him, "Yes?"

"If you've actually located Ahmed, you are likely assured the full support of TSG, Cybertech and a former President. This is a big deal."

"Thanks Mike." I reached out and shook his hand. "Stay safe."

"You too."

The minute I hit the ground Mike started pulling up the airstair. By the time I got to my vehicle, the engines were spooling up. Within minutes his plane was a distant speck, running from safety, heading south to Monterey.

CHAPTER NINE
DEEP END OF THE SWAMP

Late Afternoon, Joint Base Andrews, Maryland , Two Days Later

Goldfarb watched as Mike's white G5 taxied in and parked in front of the big hanger. There was a flurry of activity as the plane shut down. It took several minutes for the Marine Guards to escort the General inside.

Mike was carrying a small bag. One of the Secret Service agents asked him to open it. They all tensed when he refused.

"Let it be," I said. "On my authority."

"We are ordered to inspect everything, Sir."

"Surely, exceptions are...."

"No exceptions," said an older agent.

"Would it be acceptable if I personally did the inspection?"

The older agent nodded. "Yes, Sir. Of course."

"Put it down, Mike. Step away. We don't want to make people nervous."

I limped over, bent, and unzipped the bag. I peered inside, and said, "It's safe. No explosives." Then I zipped it closed and handed it to Mike. *I had not lied.*

"Thank you, Sir."

"We've arranged helicopter transport. Please see that the General's and my luggage is put aboard. His aircraft will be here overnight. Local lodging has been arranged for the crew."

"Yes, Sir."

Mike frowned. He looked tired.

"It looks like you've had a rough trip," I said as I shook his hand. "We've had a change of plans. I need you to overnight here."

Mike's frown deepened. "Overnight?"

"We have been invited to a meeting at Camp David." I looked at my watch. "Dinner is at six, eighteen hundred for you military types. Attendance is not optional. Attire is informal. Come as you are."

I watched as the significance registered on him. *An unscheduled meeting with the President.*

"I'd planned to be in New York tomorrow. Should I cancel that?"

"I'm not sure. It might be best to leave yourself some flexibility. They got us Marine Two for transport. It has secure COMs if you need to speak with anyone."

"That works."

"How was California?"

"Bizarre," Mike said. "Charlie Foxtrot. The meeting with Raven went well. The rest, not so much."

"So I heard."

I liked how the General handled himself. *No bullshit. A succinct report.*

"We have the pilot's lounge all to ourselves. It's quiet. You can relax for a few minutes while they get things sorted out. For anything secure, we can call from the aircraft. Washington is plagued with leaks and moles."

"Dare we call them spies, traitors, and seditionists?"

"Not yet," I said. When we were in the lounge with the door closed, I sat down on the couch next to Mike and said softly. "How long will it take to give the President a quick SITREP on what went down in Monterey?"

"I made a list of bullet points. We can hand out copies. Maybe 30 minutes."

"Excellent," I said, glancing at my watch.

"Before we get into that, I have a few questions."

"Go ahead."

"Raven told me that if I could get one of the weapons they used to him physically, he could find out whom and where it came from. The FBI is blocked. Can your man do things that they can't?"

I looked at him, thinking. *It's called outbound remote viewing. We were about to brief him in. Why wait?*

"Your answer to this one is important, Doctor. Was Raven telling me the truth?"

Finally I said, "The short answer is, 'Yes.' Unfortunately, our enemies suspect something. It's why Raven's team has been under constant attack."

"How many people do you have doing this magic?"

"Very few. There was just Raven and a female researcher at the Monterey safe house."

"Two people. No other security?"

I shook my head. "No."

"Quds deployed that much force against two people?"

"Yes."

"It's a damned good thing they bugged out, isn't it?"

"Again, yes."

"This must be very sensitive information."

"It's why we are meeting with the President tonight, Mike. I don't feel comfortable reading you in without his explicit approval. I've probably broken the law by telling you this much."

"Then we have something in common. It's a good thing they allowed you to inspect my bag." He nudged it with his foot.

"I had no idea what I was looking at."

"Good. Stick to that story. I stole it. They don't know."

"*What?*"

"The ownership of that item is disputed. The dark side of the force is strong in California. They are an intensely blue state with aspirations of being a separate country, as I'm sure you know. The Deep State, 9th Circuit, shadow government, and all that…."

"So?"

"There's not much left of the safe house. It took several HE and incendiary shells. The property, the dead bodies, the security tapes, captured weapons, shot up vehicles and everything else is a crime scene."

"That surprises you?"

"It's not our crime scene, it's *theirs*."

"You are not making any sense."

"Federal Agencies, including the FBI, are banned from the property. There is a court order from a Federal Judge to that effect."

"The FBI allowed that?"

"No, they tried to stop it."

"And failed…?"

"Their senior agents did not survive the attack. Those who were left called in their management along with Federal Marshals and Homeland Security. It took those resources some time to get there. The result is a stand-off. California is daring them to act. They have deployed the State Police and a unit of the California National Guard."

"How can California do that? This was clearly a terrorist attack."

"Under Obama there were numerous terrorist attacks that were not so designated, from Boston to San Bernardino to Fort Hood and beyond. Those were just called gun violence, pressure cooker violence, or whatever. California is using San Bernardino as the operative precedent."

"Why isn't this on the news?"

"I have secure COM in my aircraft. I used it to pull some strings. I'm afraid that I may have exceeded my authority there as well."

"These things are part of your briefing for our meeting?"

"Not the item in my bag. The rest is."

"What did you do?"

"There is no dispute, at least not yet, that the Federal Government controls all airspace over the US of A, including California. I had the FAA put up a no-fly zone, what they call a TFR, a Temporary Flight Restriction. It goes from the surface to ten thousand feet.

"TFRs are not uncommon. Pilots are used to them for aerial fire-fighting, political events, military activities, drones, balloons, and so forth. I even saw a TFR once for a falling satellite."

"How is this one designated?"

"I had a problem deciding that. That is a line on the form you have to fill in.

"I finally decided on 'training exercises.' Any news people trying to get in to the crime scene will be turned away, but they are likely to notice the layers of people in various uniforms with weapons...."

"You plan a full briefing on all of that?"

"I do, except for the item in my bag. I suggest it is best that we do not mention that. You've convinced me that we need to get it to Raven."

"Do I get to know what the Hell that is – in case we both go to jail?

Mike smiled. "Sure. You can be my accomplice."

"I'm afraid I already am."

"Good point. You are entitled to know. It's an M64A1. It is safe to handle and it weighs 2.5 pounds. Don't tell a soul."

I sighed, looking at my watch again. *Why was the helicopter taking so long?*

Just then there was a soft rap on the door.

Mike jumped up, sparing me having to limp over there on my bad foot. When he pulled open the door, I saw a young Marine Captain with a grim look.

"They said Doctor Goldfarb was here."

"That would be me," I said.

"We have Marine 2 outside, but there has been a delay."

He stepped in, closed the door and approached me.

"How long?"

"I'm not sure, Sir. There was an incident at Camp David. They are on lockdown."

CHAPTER TEN
TEAM COVFEFE

Late Afternoon, Laurel Lodge, Camp David, Next Day

Goldfarb looked over at Mike, who rolled his eyes and said, "Major shit storm."

I nodded.

We were sitting in the smallest of the three conference rooms of cabin Laurel, cooling our heels, waiting for the President to get to us.

It was looking like we might be here overnight.

Except for FBI Director Johnson, National Security Advisor Neumann, and Joint Chief's Chairman Admiral Quigley, the other guests had left. Those three were locked in a room with the President, under orders of "no interruptions," with two Marines by the door to enforce them.

Laurel was the main cabin. It was near the helipad and field house which were now surrounded by military hardware. There were four Apache helicopters on the pads, and two big Blackhawks parked out on the grass in the skeet range.

Other than two incidents back in 2011 when small trainer planes had mistakenly violated airspace, the camp had never suffered security breaches. The old intrusions were accidents. Back then few basic trainers had the GPS equipment to warn them of TFRs.

The attack here, in addition to the problems in California, had rattled people. Whatever was happening in the President's meeting, it was clear that America would respond.

The attack yesterday was an inside job. A Secret Service agent noticed one of the groundkeepers acting suspicious. He wasn't armed, except with a cell phone. He hung around the helipads. Each time there was activity to accept an incoming helicopter he would make a call, and say a few innocuous code words to a voice mail box.

The mole was reporting to a team outside the perimeter. IR scans showed several locations in the forest that gave heat signatures.

Secret Service set a trap. They leaked that an important flight was inbound with members of the Joint Chiefs, all of them coming in on the same aircraft.

Sure enough, out went the mole with his phone.

At the designated time, an aircraft with the proper call sign, Minnow One, called inbound and the ramp crews came out to help service and park the aircraft.

The mole sent a text message. It would be his last.

The highest ranking officer on that particular copter was only a Captain, but he had over a thousand combat hours in the sandbox. He trolled past the suspect sites, a slow fly-by with his lights on and countermeasures off at 1,000 feet, a sitting duck, simulating a nervous pilot unfamiliar with the area making a cautious approach to a night landing at the Camp.

The tangos took the bait. They had surface to air missiles.

Captain Sanchez took no chances.

The post mission tapes showed that only two seconds after his ECM board lit up with a launch warning, he reacted. He activated jammers and dispensed showers of chaff and flares. Twenty-four seconds later, he called 'Minnow engaging' and fired a Hellfire missile. By then he was falling sideways, diving for the ground, turning hard to mask his engine exhaust from heat seekers.

Sanchez missed seeing the SAM go over, but the two Apaches in trail five clicks out saw it clearly. They called, "Shark flight is coming in hot," accelerated, and activated countermeasures.

Sanchez called, "Minnow is breaking right."

"Negative. Shark One has you Minnow. Stay low and on your present heading."

The Apaches came in fast, opening fire with their 30 MM chain guns about 500 yards out. One targeted the launch site, and the other a vehicle that had just started up and was attempting to flee. Their M879 HEDP rounds were equally useful against both vehicles and personnel.

There were no survivors.

The Secret Service arrested the groundskeeper, who turned out to be from California. After consultation with the President and FBI director Johnson, the Bureau took over.

They soon reported that the subject was cooperating fully. A decision was made not to report the attack until the FBI investigation was completed.

Dinner was late.

There were several toasts to the Secret Service and to the good Captain Sanchez. Meetings were postponed. Agendas for the next day were changed to focus on the terrorist attacks on Camp David and Monterey.

Director Johnson was the lead speaker in the morning, followed by Mike who reported on what he'd observed during his visit to Monterey. No notes were allowed from the group meetings, which broke up after lunch.

There was a rap on the door and President Blager entered. "Sorry to keep you waiting."

"We're the ones who should apologize, Sir," I said. "You now have me officially on the NSC as an adjunct. Did anyone have objections?"

"None stated. Due to recent events, we are going to be having two or three NSC meetings a week. I will need you at them all."

I could see that one coming. "Yes, Sir. General Mickelson has already met with Raven, but I've not briefed him in fully. May I have your authorization to do so?"

"He met just with Raven?"

"Affirmative, Sir." *Not Josie.*

"Interesting." The President looked at Mike. "You gave a good briefing this morning, General."

"I don't think your FBI Director was happy with me, Sir."

"He's not happy with reality, Mike. He lost agents, he lost friends, the State of California just pissed all over him, and none of that is your fault."

"Yes, Sir."

"Is 'Mike' okay? I prefer a first name relationship with my close staff."

"Thank you, Sir. I'd be honored."

"President Hale speaks well of you. You were the one whose picture coming out of Yemen won the Pulitzer?"

"I got shot, Sir. There was a reporter on the rescue chopper who took a picture. It won him a prize."

The President smiled. "I know your history. You saved your command in Yemen. Later you saved America from a major bioweapons attack. Your security clearances are still active and it's good to have you on the team."

"Thank you, Sir."

"Doctor Goldfarb, by all means brief him in clearly, including about Josie. Make sure he knows all this is SI level, with tightly controlled need-to-know access only. I'll give you guidance in a moment as to how limited that access must be, and how I want this to operate."

"Yes, Sir," I said.

The President looked back at Mike. "What did you leave out of that briefing?"

Mike looked at me.

"Full disclosure," I said.

"I mentioned that we had unconfirmed Intel that indicated the Monterey attack was led by Quds force and that they had heavy weapons, but I wasn't specific."

The President nodded. "Goldfarb shared the Raven's team sketches with me. I've not yet shared them with the FBI. Continue."

"Raven told me the primary weapon used in the attack was an M224A1 60 MM mortar. It's the latest version we have. They also had a belt fed machine gun."

"Why didn't you disclose that?"

"Two reasons, Sir. First, the FBI does investigations. I didn't want to bias them or interfere with their, ah, entanglements with California. That mortar was captured. The Bureau wants it and they need to get it."

"The second reason?"

"My strong suspicion is that mortar most likely came from the California National Guard. They have some in their inventory. There have been convictions where Guard members were selling weapons to drug cartels."

The President's eyes narrowed. "You suspect treason?"

"I'm not a lawyer. I don't know the difference between treason, sedition, corruption, or gross negligence, but I'd bet that's where the weapon came from. I can't prove it."

I said, "Sir, I told Mike that if the FBI could get custody of the weapons, we could help him find out where they came from."

"Yes." The President looked at Mike.

"I found an error on the sketches. The older terrorist is identified as 'Nassar Fuad.' That is an alias, a Saudi legend. His real name is Ahmed Mahmoud Muhammad.

"There is a scar on his left temple. I put it there in Yemen. Later, he was a Colonel in Bukhari Intelligence. The Israelis have a *Kidon* team looking for him. I thought he was dead."

"Welcome to the team, Mike. Good to have you aboard." The President looked at me. "What else do you need to proceed?"

"Only money, Sir. We need to beef up the security for Josie. Mike's company, TSG, does such things. I think we can fund it ourselves, but we may need some seed money to prime the pump. From time to time, we may need to tap some military assets for support. Small teams like Delta, the SEALs, etc."

"Anything else we need to cover?"

"Only the obvious, Sir. With you needing me for the NSC, I want to shift control of Raven's team to Mike. While serving you, I left footprints to Raven and Josie that caused problems. I was tracked to the safe house in Monterey."

"I support your decision, Aaron." The President pushed his chair back. "I've also made some adjustments. I'm going to give you a new code word, **Covfefe**. Remember it. It will be an off-the-books committee to run the Raven's team. The core members are the two of you, me, and my National Security Advisor.

"The Covfefe committee will have Ad Hoc members as circumstances dictate. At present, the only such members are Admiral Quigley, representing the Joint Chiefs, National Security Advisor Neumann, and Raven, representing the team. Need-to-know is limited to these people and the three of us.

"Quigley is there so he's aware of the Raven's team activities. It is his job to de-conflict your activities with DOD missions. Should you become aware of potential conflicts, he is to be informed."

"Sir?"

"I recall that one of your team stole an airplane from the Air Force. Things like that tend to upset the military."

"It was a misunderstanding, Sir."

"I don't want misunderstandings. That's one reason why Admiral Quigley is on the team. If Raven decides to invade Iran or something such, I'll have to add my Secretary of State, Aaron, so do be a bit careful where you put your feet."

"Yes, Sir."

"The last point is crucial, Aaron. Covfefe is a deep black activity. I expect to have an adequate advance warning if anything comes up that might cause, ah, embarrassment. Can you think of anything pending that might do that?"

Mike and I exchanged a look. He shook his head. I said, "There may be one thing, Sir. The Israelis *really* want Ahmed. Prime Minister Tamlon himself has authorized action."

"I'm expecting the Covfefe team will meet monthly or as needed, with me in attendance. You've just demonstrated why these periodic meetings are prudent. To discuss and decide such policy matters. Right now, Raven's team has a short list of actionable items."

"Yes, Sir."

"Stick to that list. No Israelis, Aaron, and I don't want Raven to attack California either. Is that clear?"

"Crystal, Mr. President."

He looked at Mike, who was smiling faintly. "What about you?"

"Crystal clear, Sir, but I do have a question."

"Go ahead."

"What exactly is Covfefe?"

"No one is sure. It first appeared as a typo in a tweet by President Trump. My working definition is the same that Press Secretary Spicer gave long ago. '*The President and a small group of people know exactly what he meant.*' If asked, that's the answer you need to give. No more, no less."

Mike grinned. "Roger that, Sir. Before you go, I have a Covfefe we should discuss. Would that be appropriate?"

"If it's quick."

"Doctor Goldfarb and I agree it is urgent that we enhance security for Raven's team."

"Absolutely. What do you propose?"

"Raven's number two is a fighter pilot, not a shooter or throat cutter. We need to train him. My company TSG trains and deploys security forces using the same methods as Blackwater did in Iraq. The model we use is fully lethal. I propose we put him through the training – Raven too, if he desires. I want the TSG team that Black trains with to be tasked with security for Raven's team."

The President looked at me. "What do you think, Aaron?"

"I support Mike. We'd have had a major disaster here last night if your support hadn't gone hard core. If Raven and Josie had been there alone in Monterey, they'd be dead. Raven would go down surrounded by spent shell cases and dead bodies, but we'd have lost them both."

"And have suffered a major strategic loss." The President looked at Mike. "Do you want to add anything?"

"According to Doctor Goldfarb, Raven's team is the best resource we have for locating and thwarting high-level assassinations and strategic asymmetrical attacks. Do you agree?"

"Yes. That is what this is about."

"We are at war, Sir. Warfighting is about killing your enemies. We forget that at our peril. If you want to arrest our enemies, you have the FBI."

I said, "A law enforcement approach does not work well against terrorist attacks, the type of threats that are targeting Josie."

The President said, "Our citizens and media dislike excessive violence. Blackwater had a bad rep as I recall...."

Mike said, "Not from their clients, Sir. Blackwater contractors never lost a U.S. official under their protection. Not a one and that is God's truth."

I said, "Sir, I agree that Blackwater gained a trigger-happy reputation, especially after the September 2007 shootout that left 17 civilians dead in Baghdad's Nisour Square. They got bad press due to a lack of Political Correctness and for being noticed. No one questioned their effectiveness. Our enemies feared them."

Mike said, "'*Men sleep peacefully in their beds at night because rough men stand ready to do violence on their behalf.*' If they do not, evil prospers. That is the pattern of history."

"Orwell," the President said.

I nodded. "Correct. What we are proposing is nuanced. No one does violence in the night better than Raven, or, if there is such a person, I don't want to meet him."

The President smiled thinly. "I suspect his name is Michael."

"Perhaps, Sir," but Raven is human. "All we are talking about here is adding a small protective force so that the thin black line protecting us can survive the nights themselves."

"Keep talking."

"We need to keep Raven and Josie deep black just so they can function. ***That is a given***. This just takes it one level deeper. I propose using a small force of violent people to protect them.

"We've already done that, by scrounging military assets on an Ad Hoc basis, like in Durham. We've tried to avoid it, by allowing them to run and sending the FBI to administer law and justice. Neither approach has worked very well. Adding first-rate, covert security is cleaner, less costly, and easier to keep out of the news."

"Major terrorist attacks will be noticed, sooner or later."

"They will, eventually," I said. "But the message we can respond with is different. Instead of discussing burning cities, gun control, or dead Americans, your Press Secretary can be denoting the body count of terrorists who were foolish enough to attack us."

"What about the terrorists who survive or surrender? We can't just shoot them."

"So far, we have collected exactly one of those, Sir. The one Raven left for the pigs. He flipped. He's helping us. The FBI says we may have gotten another one last night."

"There will be more. As we start winning and the word gets out, there could be a lot more."

"If that happy situation results, we'll need a policy." I shrugged. "That is up to you and Congress, Sir, or perhaps the NSC. I'd suggest military tribunals and treating them as illegal enemy combatants, but that one is over my pay grade. My interest now is keeping Raven and Josie alive."

Mike glanced at me. "Instead of de-conflicting with DOD, we could ask Admiral Quigley for a dedicated force of Marines or SEALs. There are precedents…."

The President looked at his watch, waved his hands in dismissal, and stood up. "It has been a good discussion, gentlemen. Your request is approved. Make it happen. I'll advise the Admiral at dinner that this is one thing he doesn't need to worry about. I expect he will be grateful."

"Covfefe, Sir." Mike said.

The President smiled. Then he looked at me. "You don't get off that easy, Aaron. We'll be having an NSC meeting at the White House soon. You will be there. Some troubling issues are on the plate."

"Yes, Mr. President."

CHAPTER ELEVEN
RUSSIAN ROULETTE

The Ranch, a Private Estate near Mendocino, California

Coming back from my morning workout, I found Josie on the patio gazing out over the sea, sipping coffee. No forest. Open spaces. Scenic vistas. Even the big fir that used to frame my view fifty yards out was gone, wiped out in the big storm a few years back.

I missed that tree. It was a good marker. Fifty was about the effective range for a hand gun, so I had them plant a replacement. It was about 150 across the lawn to the cliff that dropped off to the ocean beach far below. Easy range for a long gun, even my little Mini-14, and one Hell of a view.

In summer, I could leave the slider open to the cool breezes with full privacy, sit in the hot tub naked and watch the ocean. The lawn was over thirty feet down. Unless an assailant had special equipment, the only good approach was through the front door.

Our security was good and Josie seemed to be adapting well. She seemed relaxed. Monterey had started to spook her. Me too, for that matter.

I said, "Had a good workout, Babe. I think my mojo is coming back."

She turned and smiled. "Did you jog all the way back?"

"I did."

Back was the hard part. Nine hundred and thirty feet up a steep dirt path, followed by a mile run back across the grounds. When I first came here for rehab, I could barely walk that 930 vertical.

"You got a call on your secure phone. It wasn't Goldfarb."

"Mike?"

"That was the name that came up. Twenty Mike."

"Good."

"Apparently he is in our network now. He left a message."

"We talked about Mike. He is getting us upgraded security, among other things."

"When can I meet him?"

"Soon. That's probably part of what he wants to discuss. Mike and I have several mutual problems. I told him we needed to get through Goldfarb's target list before our meeting, while we are still approved to act as we deem appropriate."

"I had reservations. I told you that."

"Remember the tango that you said was pure evil?"

"Dr. Claas Vogel. He's a puppet master who is responsible for the death and suffering of millions. Entire nations are ravaged and he makes money from it."

"If Mike can help me, I know how to reach out and touch him."

"How? You need to talk to me."

"It's a long shot. We both agreed Vogel was evil and dangerous. We didn't think we could do anything about it. He's like one of those James Bond monsters. Hard to find, harder to kill. It gave me an idea. I asked Mike if he could get me a backdoor to the Russians. That has to be what he's calling about."

"You confused me with your list and all those colors: Red, Purple, and all that. What color was Vogel, and why do you think we can hit him now?"

"I have a tentative plan for the whole list. Do you want to discuss it now?"

"Your plan is to kill them all. That's always your plan…."

"Not this time."

Josie looked skeptical. "Really?"

"We have Dunbar and Smith, both with blood on their hands for crimes that can never be proven. I have them tagged as Purple. *Off limits.* We probably can't *ever* touch them.

"Dunbar resigned as President Blager's VEEP, but is still politically connected. He's the presumptive leader of his party. We can't touch a hair on his head, much less kill him."

"So what about Smith?"

"We can't touch him either. For one thing, he's supposed to be working for us now."

"So when we meet with Goldfarb we tell him 'No Action' for those two. We let them go?"

"I can accept that, providing that we also tell him Ricci is toast. Goldfarb and Blager greenlighted him. He's near the top of the ladder for the teams that have been targeting you. If we don't take him down, eventually they will succeed."

Josie didn't respond. She wasn't objecting. *I decided to call that good.*

"Who does that leave?"

"Four names. Two are coded yellow. They are high value targets, but out of our reach. It's impractical to deal with them now. Firouz and Safdari. Both are in Iran."

"What do you suggest?"

"Under the Blager codicil, America and our allies will be hitting targets in Iran from time to time. I say we don't touch either of them. We just pass along the GPS coordinates of where they will be. The military may take them out if we make it easy for them."

She was looking at me intensely. "If I count right, that leaves two, the code red ones."

"Yes. Vogel and Reverend Dilbert Jones. Hard limits. Code red, 'do not touch.' They have far too much political cover."

"You actually think the Russians would handle Vogel for us?"

"No. Not for us." I shook my head. "The Russians don't work that way. They will handle Vogel for their own reasons and in their own ways."

"Do you trust the Russians?"

"I trust them to be Russians, competent and deadly. Fear of Russia was the witch hunt that paralyzed America and set off a media feeding frenzy when Trump was elected. It was insane. They accused him of using Russian salad dressing or something and went nuts over it – special prosecutors and all.

"There was never any evidence of a Trump-Russia conspiracy. All Presidents, both parties and even at the height of the Cold War, communicated with Russia. It was a scare campaign. The tactics used were the same as those used successfully in cancer scares to shut down companies. The great Alar scare of 1989 to shut down American apple growers was a prototype. It was a hoax, but it worked."

"What are you saying?"

"The Russians can help us. They are strategic enemies, but we share common interests. We both believe in nation-states and not allowing a Caliphate or having the UN run the world.

"We **both** fight terrorism. That's the key thing. Vogel is a terrorist. They want him bad and they can do things we can't."

"Why do you feel such an urgency to act now?"

"Because once we are entangled with the NSC, they won't let us get near the Russians. Have you read the book that Goldfarb wants to discuss at our coming meeting?"

"I started it. The one by General McMaster?"

"Correct. ***Dereliction of Duty***. Its theme is that the Joint Chiefs for decades were criminally negligent because they didn't focus on warfighting, but instead let the National Security Council wander off into following the whims and political aspirations of Presidents. He argues this put America at risk and got Americans killed for no good purpose."

"Benghazi," she said.

"Sure, and Vietnam, and the Arab Spring, and all the security leaks, the targeting of political opponents and the press by our own Intel Agencies, and on and on….."

"Why does this affect us?"

"Because you saved the President's life, because we now have support at that level, because Goldfarb is on the NSC, because Trump picked McMaster as his National Security Advisor, and because Blager's NSC has the same basic world view as did Trump's."

"Is that bad?"

"No. It's good for America, but problematic for us. There would be concern about a group like us having back-channel Russian contacts. At best, we divert attention from the big picture. You and I don't do big pictures. We stay under the radar, deep black. We avoid notice. The military is focused on projecting raw power and demonstrating overwhelming superiority.

"McMaster was focused on the Soviet threat. He knew the Russian's as well as they knew themselves. He and their Russian General Gerasimov were head-to-head all through the Cold War. Their lives and careers were parallel. They were like Patton and Rommel, arch enemies who never met. Like John LeCarre's fictional Smiley and Karla. Two deadly enemies playing for the highest stakes, the preventing or winning of World War III."

"If Trump's NSC was so focused on dealing with Russian threats, why did the media paint him as being a Russian agent? That seems crazy."

"It **is** crazy. Western news is political theater. Doctor Sabastian Gorka said, 'Reality is optional for liberals.' All over the world we've had constant terrorist attacks by Muslim's shouting *Allahu Akbar*, but it is rarely called *jihad* in news reports. Most often, it's not even mentioned.

"We just had a Quds attack, an Iranian state-sponsored attack on U.S. soil. Iran has *Allahu Akbar* written on its flag. If we and Russia ever get together, it will be game over for radical Islam, the same as what happened with Hitler."

"Talking about Russian conspiracies was to divert attention from *jihad*?"

"Sure, but also to weaken and divide us. Psychological Warfare. Propaganda."

"Who else wanted to divert attention by talking about Russia?"

"About half the world. Certainly Trump's political opponents and the lunatic left. Maybe even the Russians themselves."

"Why would the Russians float rumors that they were tampering with our elections?"

"To weaken confidence in our government and cause fear. Many groups were on that wagon. China. The UN. Vogel. The Deep State. The Democrats. Communists. Socialists. The media. It's a long list."

"We must not do anything that could restart public Russian conspiracy discussions."

"Precisely. If I use the Russians to get Vogel, our action has to be completed successfully **before** Goldfarb and President Blager must support it before the NSC. It's better to ask for forgiveness than it is to ask permission."

"What do we do next?"

"Yes, that's the key question, isn't it? We must act in the next week or two or the opportunity is gone.

"I want to deal with every one of the bastards on that list while we can. To handle Vogel, I need help from the Russians. I think I may be able to get it if we approach it right. To handle Ricci, I need to kill him. You are probably not going to like such harsh options."

Josie said, "No, I do not."

"It's like that old *Terminator* movie, Babe. 'Come with me if you want to live.' We either act now, or the opportunity is gone."

Conflict and violence upset her, but she needed to hear this.

"The FBI was massacred. They are in a state of shock. The bad guys won that one. We're running out of luck. It could have been us."

"I know that," Josie said. "Did you get us help? Did you get us time?"

"Some," Raven said. "Goldfarb pushed our meeting back. He's off chasing NSC stuff. He said to work with Mike for scheduling and support in the interim. He's cut us some slack."

"Why didn't I see this coming?"

"We changed the future when we did the unexpected and bugged out. That is probably why your visions have been cloudy. The main thing is that Quds is after us, after you."

I went over and gave her a hug. She was shaking. I kissed her gently on the forehead.

"I need to take a shower. Then we can call Mike back, together. We'll make the decisions together. I feel a need to thin these bastards out a bit while we can, but you get a veto."

Josie was still sitting out on the deck, watching the sea. She'd settled in. Birdfeeders were up, and I watched for a long moment as she fed seagulls pieces of bread. She had a way with wild things. Amazingly, they lined up and took bread right out of her hand without squabbling.

I finally said, "Aren't you afraid of losing fingers?"

"Not unless you go kinky on me. How was the shower?"

"Wonderful. God Bless America. Hot water for showers, ice water to drink, and we still have borders."

"I made us some iced tea." She gestured at the table next to her. I sat down, filled a glass with ice, poured it in, and then refilled her glass.

"Thanks." She turned and met my eyes. "I've decided you're right. I hate to admit it, but you are correct."

"Thank you." I held up my glass in a toast to her and waited, wondering what I was right about.

"About our target list," she said. "I won't fight you. I want to survive this. These are things from **your** world. You understand it better than I do, better than I want to."

"Should we call Mike now?"

"If you wish. What do we discuss?"

"I don't know his agenda. Ours is three items. I need Russian support, we need operational support, and we need to schedule the team meeting with Goldfarb."

"We don't mention Ricci?"

"Absolutely not."

I kissed him gently. "Okay."

TSG Headquarters, New York

I picked up my secure phone, looked at the ID, and punched the button, waiting a few seconds for the green lock light to come on. "I hear they sent a Quds team after you, Raven. How are you doing?"

"We're good. We got lucky, Mike. I have Josie on the line." There was a click as she connected, a short pause when the lock light went red, then back to green. "How are things at your end?"

"Eventful. They hit Camp David too. There is a total blackout on that one. Need-to-know special intelligence and a very short list approved to see it. It turned out better than Monterey. No survivors from the bad guys, one traitor nabbed, and no causalities on our side. We smoked them."

I said, "You and Goldfarb were there?"

"We were. So was the President. Afterwards, we had a short meeting. That's why I'm calling."

"We're listening."

"First off, I'm now your control. Are you good with that?"

Josie and I exchanged a look. She nodded. "That works for us. Did you get the item I requested?"

Mike said, "I did. This one is just between us and it's on your head, like we discussed. Right?"

"Yes. Like we discussed."

"I've been briefed in and read your folder. Have you ever operated against the Russians?"

"Negative, but…."

"I've got the contact you want, but I need to put some conditions on your meet."

Josie nodded at me. I said, "Go ahead."

"I'll give you the short version. You are going up against the A team, at your request. You wanted a high-level back door. I got you one. High level FSB."

"Yes."

"Putin was a KGB thug and he set up the FSB. They do not screw around at that level. They are good. Their equipment is as good as ours, and they are more ruthless. They kill their enemies. They would never tolerate a Deep State working to subvert and undermine their government. They insert moles and agents into ours and laugh about it."

"Keep talking."

"I'll give you what you want, but you need to do the meet my way. I want you to have a personal security detail. We can use your guy, John Black as the team lead."

"So far, no problems."

Mike said, "There are problems and also opportunities. It seems that Black is a hotshot pilot. I'm impressed. They only used the best of the best for F-22s."

"He busted out...."

"I'm aware. Black can't take high-G. It's not a problem. We don't do acrobatics or close combat in our Gulfstream. I want to train him and get him type qualified in my plane and our fleet. Do you have a problem with that?"

"None at all, if he's okay with it."

"Excellent. I'll call Black today. There is another issue with him. Correcting it might be a bigger deal."

"Go ahead...."

"Black isn't used to running and gunning. He hesitates. He gets hurt. That's affected your operations. I want him trained up to our TSG norms for Executive Protection."

"Which are?"

"We use the same basic methods and rules of engagement that Blackwater used in Iraq. Many of our trainers used to work for them. We've improved some things. You can take the course when you get time. I welcome your opinions."

"I'd like that. Blackwater never lost a client. They are legendary."

"I'm thinking that fewer burning cities would please our masters."

"Yes, Sir. I expect so."

"I want him to have the Mad Dog Marine attitude. I want him to be respectful and polite to everyone he meets, but to have a plan to kill them if necessary."

Josie was looking at me, horrified. She mouthed the word *"Raven...."*

"Stand by one." I put my phone on mute. "I agree with Mike. It might save Black's life, Babe. And yours."

"Do you want to make Black into a killer?"

"I want to keep him alive. And us….."

She took a deep breath, looked into my eyes, and said, "Okay."

"Thanks." I hit the button. "We're good with that, Mike. It's between you and him. You may tell him that."

"Excellent."

"Here's the last problem. No matter how good you are, if I lose you or Josie – by the way, I look forward to meeting you, Ms. Lynch…."

"Thank you, General," she said. "What you are saying makes sense. It's a bit spooky, but it makes sense."

I said, "Yes, the world gets that way, doesn't it? Back to you, Raven. If I lose you or Josie, it would, ah, make me feel real bad. I'd miss you. I'd have upset people to deal with. There would be undesirable outcomes, some at high levels."

"We wouldn't like it much either, Sir."

"Good. I've got you scheduled for a meet with the Russians on Saturday in two weeks. The location will be Golden Gate Park. You will drive there, park, and walk in to the meet. In the park there is a small island with a small lake, Stow Lake. There are only two ways on and off the island, foot paths."

"This is just a meet to give them information. You don't have any reason to expect they will take offensive action, do you?"

"No, but I want you armed and ready. I expect the unexpected."

"A good policy. I'm always armed."

"I plan to have Black and the team he's training with there. They will cover your approach, meeting, and egress. Are you good with that?"

"I am. It's always nice to have friends and I trust Black."

"There is no time to put you though the course, but we do have some standards. You need a solid legend. Not one of those crappy Dixie Cup identities. I'll have a full dossier worked up for you, one that will stand up to scrutiny. We may want to use it again.

"Your legend will protect you and divert FSB in a harmless direction. Is that okay?"

Raven said, "By Jove, that's splendid, old chap…."

I smiled. "I assume you have personal weapons?"

"A Sig .45 for concealed and a Mini-14, Sir."

"The Sig is fine. We will provide you with one of our special vehicles and an M4A1 with a suppressor. Do you prefer burst mode or full auto?"

"I'm a little picky about how my weapons are rigged. I'll go with full auto."

"We were not aware of any senior female FSB operatives in the San Francisco area. Your contact goes by 'Marie.' She doesn't show up in any of our domestic databases. My analysts don't think she's been operating in the States. I'll get you the sign and countersign for the meet and a manual for the vehicle."

"A manual…?

"It has defensive systems. I expect you to be able to use them proficiently. Do you have access to a good range?"

"Out to 200 yards, Sir."

"That is adequate. We have an armorer in California. I'll have him deliver your weapons and the vehicle. He can check you out. Your legend will take a few days longer. It will come by FedEx. He'll check out your route and flag the good spots for fishhooks or interventions if you need to lose pursuit."

"I dislike the standard-issue triggers. I have a Jewell with a light pull and…."

"We don't like them either. I will tell him of your preference."

"What are my Rules of Engagement for the meet?"

"No specific ROEs. That's your call. With that said, defend yourself as needed."

"We don't expect problems, but the Russians might want to track you. That can't be allowed. You are to lose any ticks. Use what level of force you deem necessary to get clear. Your Personal Security Detail will go full lethal to prevent a snatch and grab or if you signal them to do so. Are you good with that?"

"I am. If the Russians try to prevent my egress I may need to use lethal force myself."

"We will plan it that way. Black will be on channel and in control of the security team. Are there any other details?"

"I'm curious about this vehicle, Sir. It sounds like something out of Hollywood. I prefer to be low profile for hot zones."

I chuckled, "You are. It's a plain vanilla Dodge Challenger body, a two door coupe, like a little old lady would drive in California. It started as the R/T Scat Pack model, which as stock was 485 hp. No special tricks and an automatic transmission. The brakes and suspension have been upgraded. The defensive systems don't show."

"I say, old chap, not a bloody Aston Martin?"

"Don't overdo your legend, Raven. It's a boringly American car. We picked that model over the other high performance coupes on the market because normal people can fit in the back seat. It's useful for up to a team of four."

"Interesting."

"It's a three to four hour drive to your meet with the Russians. If you are more than a few minutes late, FSB will probably abort. We don't have the time to do this twice if you intend to wrap this up before the team meeting."

"I won't be late, Sir. What is the status of Goldfarb's meeting?"

"We've gone **Covfefe**, Raven. It's gotten a bit more complex."

"The more complex part sounds like typical Washington, but you lost me on the rest."

"Covfefe. Look it up on the Internet. The meeting has grown a bit. Goldfarb's boss has set up a dedicated operations committee for oversight. You will still have a single controller, me or Goldfarb. Right now, it is me. The committee name is Covfefe."

"Stand by."

Josie and I looked at each other. I muted the phone. "The President must have intervened. We need to get through our action list before then."

"We already knew that. We'll get it done," Josie said. "Don't ask him what, ask him who and when."

"Good plan." I clicked the phone. "You surprised us on that one. Do you know when our meeting out here is scheduled?"

"My guess is a month. I expect it will not be held until after you can complete your assigned items on the list Goldfarb and the President gave you. The first item on the Covfefe agenda will be for you to report on the status of that list. That's all that I can promise you."

"We're good with that."

"I'm guessing the longest lead time for you is with the Russians."

"Probably. I'd guess that they can act a week or two after their agent reports in, assuming she is high level and has access to leadership who can make decisions."

"The last isn't a problem. It is why I wanted good security for your meet. I do not want you to be abducted. The Russian interest level appears to be quite high. Almost too high.

"I didn't tell them what you would offer them, nor do I want to know, but I did make it clear that it is of high value to them and actionable."

"How do you know so much about the Russians, Sir?"

"I have worked the Russian side for most of my career starting as a young Captain out of the Embassy in Moscow during the Cold War. Later, I ran Marine HQ Intel. They know it, and they also know that I've never suggested a back-channel meet to them before."

"Nice of you to share, Sir."

"I was going to tell you. Now you know. Is there anything else?"

"This Covfefe committee. Who exactly does it consist of?"

"Me, Goldfarb, his boss and one or two others. No more. You will be an Ad Hoc member, nonvoting, but there to represent Josie and your team. The committee will meet about once a month. The initial Covfefe meeting is what allowed our getting you better security."

"That is good to know and appreciated, Sir. Can you give me a clue as to why our small team has suddenly been blessed with so much oversight?"

"External events. I will limit my comments to the things the Russians already know, or strongly suspect. There have been two recent *jihadist* attempts to assassinate the President. At least one and possibly two Quds attacks – state sponsored attacks on our homeland. The situation is exacerbated by a pile of dead FBI agents, and the use of advanced American heavy weapons – our own weapons – in the most recent attacks."

"The mortar they used in Monterey…?"

                              John D. Trudel

"The FBI is still trying to get that particular weapon back from the Peoples Republic of California. The attackers fired a Stinger missile at our air assets at Camp David. It missed, failed to explode, and we have it. It was a FIM-92J, Block 1 model. This version can take down drones and resists jamming."

"Does the California National Guard have Stingers?"

"Yes. As with the mortar, the FBI is working on how the attackers got this weapon. Do you have any more questions?"

"Negative."

"Can you come to New York for a short meet if I send a plane for you? Just for an overnight, no longer."

"Why?"

"It may help me get Black on board and I have something for you."

"When?"

"Soon. In the next day or two."

"I think that will work."

"Good. I assume you are fully aware that the Russians and our interests are in alignment only so far as fighting terrorism in general and Islamic *jihad*."

"I am, Sir."

"The most recent attacks on us are coming from Quds, from Iran."

"We agree. Recall the sketches we shared."

"Those are of great interest and most useful. That's not my concern. The Russians and Iran are *allies*. It's rather a big deal to them and FSB can be, ah, impulsive. Does whatever you are doing with them involve Iran?"

"It does not, Sir. Not in any way."

"Good. I will send Black to pick you up if he agrees. I need both you and him to be comfortable with the security arrangements."

"That works. Thank you, Sir."

"Tell you what. We're civilians, a small team. Just call me Mike."

"Yes, Sir."

CHAPTER TWELVE
OPERATIONAL

TSG Headquarters, New York

We'd landed on the roof helipad, but I'd asked for the tour. The young woman, Crystal, who greeted me shrugged. She walked me to the elevator, out on the street, and then back.

"There is not much to see. Nothing fancy, just shops and workout places, but there are several good places to eat. City College is about 20 blocks down. We keep the company aircraft over in NJ at Teterboro. It's about a twenty-five minute cab ride most times if you go by the NJ Turnpike and maybe twice that if you take the Lincoln Tunnel."

"Right," I said. It had been ten minutes by copter.

Coming back up was interesting. TSG had the entire 40th floor, but there was only a tiny plaque in the lobby. *Low profile. I liked that.*

The elevator opened into a closed room. It took a retina scan or a call to get us escorted though the steel door on the opposite wall. She did the former and the door clicked open.

There were three security cameras and two guards. The older one had a Remington 870, both had pistols. They had the look. SpecOps. An alarm was beeping.

"Oh, whoops," the closest guard said. "Are you carrying?"

I nodded, spreading my open hands slowly. "Sig on my right hip."

He pointed to a tray. "Leave weapons and electronic devices here." When I did so, he had me pass through the door again.

I set the alarm off again. Crystal rolled her eyes.

"Sorry."

I had my Gerber knife in an ankle sheath. After Monterey, it was sort of a talisman. With one hand I pulled up my pants leg. With the other, I carefully put it in the tray.

"An 8-inch blade," the younger one said. "Looks like a weapon to me."

"It's a tool with many uses. You can clean toenails with it."

The guards laughed. "You'll fit in here just fine," the one with the shotgun said.

Crystal said, "I'm always setting the damned thing off too, Harry. We're late and he's cool. We came down from the helipad. He wanted a quick tour of the naked city, and so here we are. I haven't badged him in yet. How about we just empty his pockets and call it good?"

"Will you shoot him if he acts up?"

She shrugged, shook her arm, and a derringer magically appeared, pointed at the floor.

Nice move. Very professional, I thought. "Is that a .357?"

"Lord, no. It's a .45 ACP. Subsonic rounds. Same as your Sig most likely. Shooting Mike's visitors in confined spaces was hurting my ears and pissing people off.

"Empty your pockets, slow and easy. While you and Mike are chatting, I'll get you into the system so you don't make our people nervous."

"Roger that," I said. Using one hand, two fingers, I carefully emptied my pockets.

"He's all yours, Crystal." The older guard lowered his shotgun and waved us through.

Mike stood to greet me as I entered his office, smiling with his hand extended. It wasn't what I'd expected. It was very modern inside – chrome and glass like a High Tech company. Outside, it was an older looking brick office building, looking like something out of the '60s. Only the Broadway address was impressive.

"Don't shoot him," Mike said. "I went to a lot of trouble to get him here."

"He made the guards nervous. I'll get him into the system."

Mike laughed. The derringer disappeared and she closed the door behind her with a soft click.

There was a decent view of the Hudson from the smallish windows.

"They're bullet proof, of course. We have ultrasonic oscillators to block laser snoopers. When I have meetings here with buttoned down Fed types, I even put on some Willy Nelson. I got a thank you note once from NSA."

"Not from the FBI?"

"Not yet, but you never know. How was the flight?"

"Surprisingly short. Black got in some stick time. I think you made him happy."

"Hope so. That aircraft is rented, but we have an option to buy it. It's a Citation X, the fastest civilian aircraft made, Mach 0.94. It has enough range for domestic flights and costs less to operate than the Gulfstream. Right now, we are testing how much our pilots and maintenance folks like it. So far, they love it."

We settled into the chairs around his conference table. He offered me a coffee.

"Just ice water. Flying dehydrates me."

"New York makes it worse. I think they suck their local water out of the river, and I know they crap on the sidewalks and piss in the street. It reminds me of Mogadishu. Our water here is imported." Mike poured me a glass, crystal clear and cold.

"I hear the FBI got burned badly."

He nodded and filled me in about the disaster. It was worse than I thought.

He finished by saying, "The FBI is blocked from taking evidence or even getting into the crime scene. Goldfarb told me that you can track objects across time and space, and that you can find out where that mortar came from. He says you have magic. Is that true?"

"Sometimes. You'll get briefed in at the meeting. Josie is a remote viewer, a paranormal."

"You've seen this work?"

"I sure have, across half a century and thousands of miles."

"That's good to know." Mike produced a small bag and set it on the table.

I peered inside. "What is it?"

"Evidence. Keep it close. I'll need it back."

I frowned at him.

"It's an M64A1. It is safe to handle and it weighs 2.5 pounds. It's the sighting unit off the mortar that Quds used in Monterey."

"You are sure it's part of that specific weapon?"

"Positive. I stole it. That's probably a felony."

"Who did you steal it from?"

"I'm not sure. The FBI and California are arguing over ownership. Both sides have their backs up and lawyers out. It's a snake pit down there. The only thing they agree on is keeping the media out."

"Who else knows about this?"

"No one. I gave Goldfarb a quick look at the unit, but no other information. It's better that he doesn't know, I think. Will this let you track the weapon?"

"Yeah."

"If you take it back with you tomorrow morning, how long before we find out where it came from?"

"A few days, maybe a week, but you need to understand how it works. I can give you truth, but not any legal proof that a court would accept. Validation is up to you. This is deep-black *woo woo* tradecraft from the bad old days of the Cold War."

"I've heard the rumors. What else can you tell me?"

"Paranormal viewings were only used in cases where there was no other way to get information. At best, you will get sketches of images and maybe some names and words. Nothing that can be attributed. No sources that can be quoted."

"Who knows this stuff works?"

"Me. Josie. Goldfarb. A few others."

"The Covfefe committee?"

"Yes. Soon. When Goldfarb chooses to disclose."

"Does President Blager know?"

"Officially, no. He never can. Rumors of mysticism and using paranormal viewing could destroy his Presidency."

"Unofficially?"

"He knows. It saved his life. Before that, our remote viewing thwarted an EMP attack that would have devastated America."

"That thing with Durham and the Russian ship? The *Orbleko* or something…?"

"You are well connected to RUMINT, it seems. The *Krasivi Oblako*. She was Russian built, but had been sold to Iran. CNN reported it probably went down with all hands somewhere in the far South Atlantic."

"What did Iran say?"

"Essentially nothing."

"You were there?"

"I was for Durham, Antarctica, and with the President in Monterey. All of which you are not yet, if ever, cleared to know."

"Who can read me in?"

I shrugged. "Possibly Goldfarb, if the President so approves. Not me. If I were you, I'd stay clear. The cluster fuck we have coming down now with Iran making attacks on our homeland with American weapons should be more than enough. I'll give you a sneak peek. My bet is that the Quds weapons are coming from the California National Guard."

"Marvelous. What do you need from me?"

"My agenda is to get briefed for the Russian meet and to pick up my cover documents from you. I'd like two or three Dixie cup identities in addition to the major legend you want me to use. Since I'm coming here periodically, perhaps one of the throwaway Dixie cups could be for a NY city address. If it comes with a concealed carry permit, so much the better."

"We think alike. I've got all that. We own this entire building. They've put your kit in one of our rooms. It has a King sized bed and all the amenities. You can stay here. For your NY Dixie cup, you'll have a New York City apartment in your name, but it's on the other side of town, over on the East Side, and not worth messing with on this trip.

"I have commitments for tonight, but we can have breakfast in the morning. I'll have the copter take you to the airport. Is that acceptable?"

"That's perfect. Thank you."

"Do you want to meet the security team Black is training with?"

"Not yet. He needs to work that chemistry out himself."

"Agreed. I'm staying out of that myself. I'm getting Black type rated in our aircraft and he needs some flight time. Would you mind if he crewed on your flight to CA tomorrow? It's a quick turn that won't impact his running and gunning. We still have two of his team coming back from the Mideast."

"Fine by me. Now I have a question. What is it that you are not telling me?"

Mike blinked. "What are you talking about?"

"You ran me round the barn and through a briar patch of need-to-know compartmentalized information, asking me about events from the past that are unlikely to overlap with our current mission, things I'm not supposed to discuss. I went along."

"I am now your control. Not Goldfarb. Me."

"Yes. So?"

"When we have our Covfefe meeting, I'm going to bring in some of my own team. People we need for support of our current missions. I'm going to bring in Doctor William Giles, the President of Cybertech. They make our secure phones, among other things. His technology allows us to function under the radar."

"I know that. What's your point?"

"My wife is Will's sister. She used to run projects for NSA."

"I agree Cybertech is uniquely qualified. I agree that we need them. I still don't see where this is going."

"Over ten years ago, Colonel John Giles, the founder of Cybertech, vanished. He was abducted in Oregon by Islamic terrorists."

I vaguely remembered the abduction of a High Tech executive. "You are talking about Iron John? He was a SpecOps legend. I met him."

"One and the same. He'd retired and was trying civilian life. John is my wife's father and William Giles' father. I expect both of them, with my support, will want to make finding John, or retrieving his body, part of our mission. This will be on our Covfefe meeting agenda."

"I still don't get it. How does this connect with me and Josie?"

"The person who abducted John Giles is Ahmed Mahmoud Muhammad, aka Nassar Fuad, the same person who showed up on the sketch you gave me, the one Josie made. We've been looking for him for years. So have the Israelis. All the conventional methods of finding him have failed."

I said, "You shot Ahmed. You want to finish the job."

"I want to get John Giles back, or his body. After that we can decide how to best deal with Ahmed. Actually, it might be best to give him to the Israelis. They'd have a celebration and a public hanging. That would be a major blow to radical Islam."

"It sounds to me like this is personal. That makes me nervous."

"For me and my family it is, very much so. But Ahmed is also a national security threat who is tied to Monterey and Quds. He is already part of our mission. We would be ridding the world of a major terrorist."

"You want to structure a top level mission around rescuing an old hero?"

"It is a win/win/win. We are dealing with the Quds attack, eliminating a major terrorist, and, yes, possibly rescuing a friend and family member. The last is a long shot, maybe one in a thousand odds. Either of the first justifies a mission."

Mike was staring at me. Waiting. Finally he said, "Well? Could Josie find him?"

"Possibly. She sees things that normal humans cannot. What you need to understand is that she is fragile. Violence traumatizes her."

"It traumatizes most people...."

"You don't get it. Josie has magical powers, but violence is her kryptonite. After Durham, she was catatonic for months. We almost lost her. She's not an operative you run, Mike. She is an irreplaceable national treasure, one that we need to protect at all costs."

Mike was silent. Finally I said, "Didn't Goldfarb brief you in on that?"

"It didn't come up. At the time we spoke, I didn't really understand what she did. I couldn't believe that her sketch was the same person. It's been a long time...."

"Marvelous."

Mike sighed. "I've not thought about Ahmed or John for years. I still haven't told my wife or Will that we've located Ahmed. They don't know. It's old history."

"**We** didn't locate Ahmed. Josie did."

"Yes."

"You do know that my primary job is protecting Josie? I keep her safe. My job is to keep her operational, to keep her safe, to keep her sane. You surely know that the Quds kill team that kicked the FBI's ass was sent there to get her. That is why I bugged out. Goldfarb left us hanging. He left us exposed in a compromised safe house with only one way out."

"I got it."

"Josie trusts me. She wants us to retire. I keep delaying it...."

"It's personal for you too, isn't it?"

I said, "Bet your ass it is."

Mike looked into my eyes and nodded. "What do you need from me now?"

"I need enough space to finish the assignment that Goldfarb has tasked us with, another week or two. When that's done, we can Covfefe our heads off and try to resolve these issues."

"And the support I promised you for the Russian meet."

"Yes, of course. That's part of it."

"Would you like me to brief you now?"

"If we can get some lunch."

"The lunch part is easy. Your Russian meet has come together, but it's more intense than I expected. The operative they've assigned, code name Marie, is new to us. We don't know much about her."

"What do you know?"

"The only place she showed on the radar was France. A Deputy Minister of the Armed Forces of the French Republic disappeared. Most say he's dead. Some think he defected to Russia. Their current

Minister of the Armed Forces is currently embroiled in a scandal over corruption and security leaks. We think it was getting too hot for 'Marie' over there."

I shrugged. "We didn't expect they'd send a nun. She's FSB. You insisted on a security team and I agreed. Let's focus on my meeting with her. What are you worried about?"

"I don't want you snatched or followed. I think the meeting will be clean, but I want John Black and our team close to make sure you get clear. Just to keep the Russians honest. Are you good with that?"

"I wouldn't have it any other way."

"Good."

Mike buzzed and Crystal came in to take our order. She passed me a folder with several identities and an access pass for the building.

"You can collect your weapons from the guards, Mr. Raven." She looked at Mike. "He had a combat knife; said he used it for cleaning his toenails. Blades make New York police go ape shit."

"True. Note that he's fastidious in his personal grooming and please get him a smaller knife, something street legal, maybe a Kershaw, for his visit here. And put cards with phone numbers for our attorneys and clean up team in his folder...."

Crystal said, "I already have."

Mike looked at me. "I'm sure you know New York is a sanctuary city. Watch your ass. Stay safe, but try not to add to the body count. We're happy to have Chicago lead those stats. It's not the blood – it's the publicity...."

"Right," I said.

CHAPTER THIRTEEN
WET WORK

It had been a good day. Mike briefed me for the Russian meet. Crystal got one of the TSG vehicles checked out and made sure I had her home number, directions, and all the pass codes I'd need to get around.

I'd filled my pockets with what was needed to satisfy my NY Dixie Cup identity. It came with one of the rare New York City carry permits. My cover legend was perfect. I was Brian Casey. No more Raven, not for tonight. I was good to go.

As Casey, I had a background in law enforcement. I had my own business as a bonded courier for high value documents, financial instruments, and, yes, equipment, including weapons. Hence my legal concealed carry permit.

My TSG corporate condo was over on East 72nd, not far from where Marco Ricci lived. He kept his mistress over on East 61st in the 200 block. It was a pleasant night. Josie said he'd be walking the few blocks back without his security detail about 1 AM.

Ricci had gotten lazy and fallen into patterns. He was untouchable. The police wouldn't bother him with his diplomatic immunity. The mob was thankful for his high level connections in Italy and the occasional use of his diplomatic pouches.

This part of New York was free of violent crime. Those in power didn't want their hookers and dealers interfered with. Disputes could be resolved elsewhere. There was a long tradition of dumping the bodies at sea or burying them in garbage dumps over in Jersey.

Jimmy Hoffa was pardoned by Richard Nixon in 1971. It was Nixon's highest profile pardon until that of "Songbird" John McCain became known, half a century later. Hoffa had vanished from Detroit in 1974 after hundreds of millions of dollars of mob money went missing from union coffers.

The FBI claimed Hoffa was buried in a NJ toxic waste garbage dump in a 55-gallon drum. If so, they never found the correct drum. The Hoffa story faded into legend, but the use of NJ garbage dumps and "feeding finks to the fishes" became enshrined in gangster lore.

Riots and protests excepted, drive-bys, muggings, and assassinations needed to stay out of the news. It was bad for business, bad for the mob, and bad for politicians. People could disappear from the West Side if necessary, but you simply didn't leave their bodies there.

I was about to violate that tradition.

Josie picked up immediately when I called her secure phone.

I said, "I'm on the ground in New York and we're still a go. How are things at your end?"

"Amazing. Your friend is getting a workout. His lover is most creative."

"I love it when you talk dirty, but is the time we planned for still good?"

"Ricci leaves around midnight. He has been punctual in the past, but there is a potential problem."

"He might stay at her place for the night?"

"No. He's only done that once over the last year. But if he's late, he might take a cab."

"Explain."

Josie said, "When he walks, he invariably goes down 67th street past the public library and on down towards the river. That's the route we planned for."

"Yes. Our tango then typically hangs a left on York in front of Rockefeller University, just north of the Caspary Auditorium. That's his home turf. The UN is just south of there."

She said, "Yes. So remind me of why you think that place is best."

"There are parked vehicles on the East side of York Avenue. There is a tall fence in front of the University, along with trees, dark places, and no cameras. Locations north of 68th have buildings on that side, including hospitals that are open 24/7. I can loiter and mingle there, but I can't make my move. Too many eyes and cameras."

She said, "If he takes a cab, he won't go that way at all. The cab would take a route to accommodate traffic and one way streets. It would go up 61st toward the park, hang a right on Park Avenue, and then right again to go down 72nd and drop him off in front of his building. That is 1.4 miles and ten minutes."

"You saw that in a viewing?"

"No, Google Earth. My remote viewings still show him taking the route we planned, on foot."

"What's the time if he walks?"

"Forty minutes, typically, plus or minus ten. He takes different routes, but he always comes down 67th at the end."

I said, "Can you give me a heads up when he leaves her apartment?"

"Sure. I'll text you his departure time. If he takes a cab, I'll give you the number. Do you need his description?"

"Negative. This tango stands out. He looks like Tony Soprano from the old TV Series. Five foot ten, 250 pounds plus, black hair, intense, and ready for a heart attack. But you could include what color clothes he is wearing."

"I shall. Anything else?"

"I'm good. You are wonderful. See you tomorrow."

"Stay safe. I miss you. See you soon. Bye." Josie signed off.

I sighed. I didn't want to worry her or draw her near violence, but the truth was that I was so far away from "good" that you couldn't find it on a map.

"We're screwed," would have been more accurate than what I actually told her. The end of 72nd was a dead end up against the river, well lit, with far too many people watching, cameras all over, and no way out. His condo had a guard in the lobby, cameras, and locked down elevators.

Plan A was too tight, both in time and space. Plan B was a hard target, and Plan C – abort the mission – was something I did not want to contemplate. Some days are like that....

Fairmont Hotel, San Francisco, 5 PM

Karlov Petrovich was nervous. His tradecraft was rusty. He wasn't comfortable in the field and this visit lacked official cover. But it was too important to delegate and he didn't trust electronic communications.

Petrovich was dressed in a sublime two-button dark Brioni suit, with a Vivienne Westwood white dress shirt and silk navy tie from Marinella with tiny scarlet dots. He wore black Tod Gommino loafers over charcoal-gray socks.

The knock on the door came precisely on time. First one knock, then three, as agreed.

"*Введите*," Karlov said in Russian. *Enter.*

Agent Marie was wearing a simple white dress, with one string of pearls, matching earrings and a small black purse in her hands. Her right hand was in the purse.

I smiled. I knew it held a weapon. I'd trained her.

"Softly, my little sparrow. All is well."

Marie looked stunned for an instant. Then her training kicked in and she smiled. "Is that really you, Sir? You look so different."

"We are **both** different now, and your English is excellent. May I offer you some Champagne?"

She nodded. I gestured at the small table by the window, then went to the computer desk, the only other flat surface in the room and poured her a glass, plus one for myself. I sat down across from her and held up my glass in a toast.

"To new beginnings."

"New beginnings." Marie smiled and took a sip. "This is quite good."

"There actually **is** American Champagne. Not the swill from California. It's too warm there even though some of their brands do have the legal right to call it that. The best American Champagnes come from cooler places, like New York and Oregon. This is an *Argyle Blanc de Blanc*, Knudsen Vineyard 2011, from Oregon. It's quite good."

"Not legal to call it Champagne, and don't tell the French, but it is indeed. It's excellent." Her smile faded. "I don't think I'll ever be able to return to Paris, Director Petrovich. I will miss that."

"You might be missing your head if you'd lingered, my dear. For you they might bring back the guillotine. The French are an emotional race."

"Thank you for getting me out."

"I am the one who should be thanking you. You did an excellent job in France. It has changed both our lives, hopefully for the better. I was promoted, you know."

"They said you are now a Deputy Director."

"Not exactly. Administratively I report to the Director, but that is a formality. Our orders come from President Putin. I'm smiling at your puzzled look, and I admire your tradecraft."

She was frowning.

"This room has been swept for bugs and neither of us has a cell phone, Marie. It's safe for tonight. This is why I picked this old Hotel, elegance, but with antiquated small rooms and only a basic Internet connection. It opened two weeks *after* the earthquake of 1906 and it's still here. I like that. It sits on top of Nob Hill and has outlasted everything."

Her look turned dubious. "Surely...."

"Neither of us is going to set foot in a Russian Embassy or Consulate, Marie. That is a mistake the American CIA made and President Putin is most insistent that we don't repeat it."

"I don't understand, Sir."

"One of the most counterproductive things the CIA has ever done – perhaps even more foolish than making Brennan, an admitted

Communist and later a Muslim convert, its Director – was putting its operatives in embassies around the world. They started thinking like State Department employees."

"And became corrupted under Hillary and Kerry...."

I shrugged. "That too, but corrupt officials come and go. Failure was built into the structure."

"How?"

"Think about it. CIA agents brought their families along on each two-year rotation, focusing on their next promotion, while the Ambassador, not the Chief of Station, had the final say in what ops they could and could not conduct. It was poisonous."

She nodded slowly. "They've certainly not had many successes of late."

"What would you expect? In an environment controlled by a State Department, diplomacy comes first. Espionage comes a distant second. Depending on the Ambassador, it may not come at all. Paramilitary OPS are pretty much off the table."

She had an odd look on her face. "We are doing the same thing...."

"Putin has noticed that. FSB, and everyone else, is working disinformation through Western News Media. It's totally dysfunctional. Every time an American politician does or does not do something the Russians are blamed. It's become part of their elections and a drum beat in their media. We have PR officers running FSB for political agendas. It's madness."

"American madness...."

"Yes, but it has infected others, including Russia, including some in the FSB. We have many enemies of the state, including the Muslims, the Globalists, and perhaps China who would be happy to see Russia and America pitted against each other."

"Surely they don't expect **us** to fix that?"

"No, my little sparrow. That insanity will be resolved by our own political leaders in the traditional way. I expect the Lubyanka will host new guests before it is over, including some of our own."

"Another Great Purge? A *Yezhovshchina*, like the 1930s?"

"Probably much smaller and much more selective, but who knows? Our job is to avoid that drama entirely. We are going to get some work done while the elephants butt heads."

"What kind of work?"

"Your first mission will be a short one, an important counterterrorism operation. After that, we have a list of other things to explore. Does that interest you?"

Marie took a sip of her Champagne. "I expect we will find out, Sir. Are you going to brief me tonight?"

"No. We are going to have a nice dinner. I'm going to help you set up a meet. After that, you are going to brief me. How does that sound?"

Her smile was radiant. "The restaurant here is famous. How can I pass up an excellent dinner?"

CHAPTER FOURTEEN
IMPROVISE

Park Avenue, New York, 1 AM

Nothing was working. Josie's text said Ricci left his mistress on foot at 12:18 AM, wearing a light blue jacket and tan slacks. He should have arrived at my kill zone, appearing from up 67th at 12:58 AM plus or minus ten minutes.

I'd run my CSRs to ensure I was clean, gotten into the area over an hour early, and put eyeballs on the surrounding few blocks to familiarize myself with the environment and to practice blending in.

Going unnoticed is half the game when you are doing surveillance or waiting to take out a tango. People put out signals – body language, gait, attitude, speech, mannerisms – that can tell you where they're from, what they do, who they are. The second most important lesson from my training was *do **they** fit in.*

If they don't, it's a red flag. Pay attention.

The first most important lesson, of course, was, *do **you** fit in.*

If you don't fit in, the target will spot you and you won't be able to get close enough to do what you need to do. Or a cop will spot you, and you'll have some explaining to do. Or a counter surveillance team will spot you, and the target will then be **you**.

The environment and ambiance tonight was better than I had hoped. It was a dark night, with few people around, little traffic for a city of this size, best of all, no security presence, or even an indication of anyone paying attention.

I had no problem killing time, loitering on York Avenue and watching the intersection of 67th. Most New Yorkers don't care. They go out of their way to mind their own business. They avoid eye contact. Pedestrians avoided me and the vehicles that came by were hurrying somewhere, with few if any passengers and the drivers looking straight ahead.

One problem. *No Ricci.*

I waited, practicing looking inattentive and bored, but, in truth, I knew my mission was going to shit. I could feel it. Something was wrong. My tango had vanished. I was running out of time and out of options.

I'd decided that Plan B was a potential disaster. Hitting Ricci in his nest was a formula for disaster, not just a miss but likely exposure. It would be a dumb move.

I'd have to abort, and that was game over. This was the only shot we were likely to be allowed.

Time crept by. At 1:20 I decided that I had nothing to lose by moving, becoming active. I started down York and finally up 67th. That street was our touchstone.

Ricci always came down 67th at the end. That what Josie said and she was so right it was spooky.

I had a clear view up 67th all the way to First Avenue. Nothing. No traffic and not one pedestrian on either side of the street. I crossed over and started up the left side of 67th, moving slowly. There was no hurry now.

I crossed over First, and reminded myself this was a soft zone, to keep my head in the game. This block had been my number two pick for a hit. It was more secluded, but had one major problem. The egress options were poor.

Across the street was St. Catherine's park, filling most of the block. It had long ago been a church. When that was demolished, it had been replaced by a park, a playground for children, with a running track, handball courts, and the like.

The park would have been good for egress because it extended all the way to 68th, but it closed down at 9 PM. It was surrounded by a tall iron fence and well illuminated. I'd marked it off as a no go.

I kept walking up 67th. It was then I saw him.

It was Ricci, way up the street by the public library, limping along in a light blue jacket, moving slowly. I couldn't tell if it was his back or his left leg, but something was bothering him.

I slipped my gloves on. It was show time.

No wonder he was late. Josie hadn't been kidding about his highly energetic, extremely creative mistress. Ricci had apparently pulled or sprained something. The Italian stallion had apparently been rode hard and put away wet.

It might yet be the death of him if I could just come up with good egress. The park was out. So was the notion of standing over his dead body waiting for the police, or trying to sprint to safety on the streets of the densest and most populous city in the United States.

I looked to my left. The right corner of the building was occupied by a small laundry that looked like it had been there for years. To the left of the shop was the main entrance to the building, a recessed door with an ornate stone façade on both sides.

The door had a buzzer for admittance. I didn't touch it. The door was locked.

It looked like an old apartment building, brown brick. It went up out of sight with small, ornate windows, some of which housed air conditioners. The night was warm and some of the units were straining and rattling. I saw no lights in the building.

That doorway wouldn't solve my egress problem, but I'd be out of sight and the noise would cover the sounds of a struggle. Things were looking up.

To the right of the building was a massive, solid, wooden gate, perhaps eight feet high. It blocked the access to an alley.

Bingo.

The gate was locked. It took me only a few seconds to pick the lock and pop it open. The heavy gate moved freely and I could see all the way through to 66th.

I closed the gate, leaving it unlocked, unlatched, and ajar. Here was my egress.

I positioned myself in the doorway and checked the street. Ricci was halfway down the block, still making slow progress. He was concentrating on walking, not looking around.

Further off in the distance on the other side of the street was a figure, it looked like a woman, going away. Behind me, there was nothing. I didn't even see anyone down on the other side of First Avenue. The coast was clear.

I could hear Ricci approaching even over the rattling air conditioners. The sounds he made were lower. He was panting, breathing hard, and dragging his left foot.

He straightened when I stepped out and opened his mouth to scream. That was when I hit him with my white canister of weapons-grade pepper spray. A two-second blast in the face. I'd read the directions.

It worked as advertised.

Ricci's nascent scream chopped off. He threw his head back with his mouth wide open struggling to breathe. That's when I stuck the nozzle down his throat and let him have the rest of the can.

He went limp. I dropped the canister, held him up by his hair, and dragged him toward the alley. Three long steps and I leaned into the gate, pushing it open.

He was heavy. I had to put my other hand under his arm to support the weight. Then we were inside the alley. Another two staggering steps took us diagonally sideways to the brick wall of the building.

I slammed his head into the wall, then let go and stepped clear. Ricci fell away from me, backwards, straight down.

His head made a sound like a melon when it hit the concrete. Taking care not to step in the blood, I retrieved the spray canister. The street was empty. I returned to the alley and closed the gate behind me, locking it.

I checked my pocket to make sure I still had the plastic baggie I'd used to hold the canister. There were no alarm calls or sounds of pursuit.

I left the canister next to Ricci's body. It didn't contain my prints or DNA, and it would give the police something useful to do.

I removed my cap and jacket putting them in the fanny pack I'd brought, but left my gloves on for the time being. The gate on the other end of the alley opened easily.

Checking 66th, the street was clear in both directions. I walked down to First Avenue, crossed the street, hung a left, and continued up to 68th. My objective was 411 E. 68th, a large building, The Church of St. Catherine of Siena.

The church was open. If I had detected sirens, I would have lingered and lit a candle or two until things settled down, but there was nothing. It was peaceful and serene inside.

I kneeled in one of the rear pews and rested for a few minutes, taking deep breaths and willing my body to relax. On the way out, I dumped my jacket, hat, and gloves into the bin labeled *clothing donations for the poor*. I then walked slowly to my car, which I'd parked in the garage at my new condo a few blocks away.

I didn't go into my condo. The security system meticulously logged such things. It would show I'd visited and left five hours ago. Nor did I run any Counter Surveillance Routes. There was no need for CSRs.

Under my persona, I was a New York native going over to my employer's building to prepare for an early morning departure. If I was stopped, there was nothing to arouse suspicion, nothing that wouldn't check out.

I drove back to TSG headquarters, took a shower, and hit the rack. Tomorrow, I'd have breakfast with Mike and be on my way.

Ricci would no doubt come up at the Covfefe meeting. There was no need to discuss him in the morning. Mike's mind would be on the Russians, as would mine.

CHAPTER FIFTEEN
THE MEET

The Ranch, Mendocino, California, three days later

Josie shook her head, looking puzzled. We'd prepared for a call, but not this one.

I'd been training for the Russian meet, checking out on new weapons, the car, and protocols for working with the security team TSG would provide. She'd been doing viewings of the meeting spot and my expected access and egress routes.

We had both Goldfarb and Mike on my secure phone. They were fixated on the pocket litter that I'd snatched from the spotter who was sitting on our egress out of Monterey. I'd given it to Mike at breakfast when I left New York.

It was no big deal at the time. Now it was. Especially for Goldfarb.

"I didn't interrogate her. It was dark, time was short, and we needed to bug out. I just collected it out of habit. Her car had funny license plates from Oregon as I recall."

Goldfarb said, "Yes. STOP H8."

"Right. Personalized plates."

"Could you ID her?"

"I doubt it. Like I said, it was dark. She was maybe five foot eight or nine and fit. She was quick. Moved like an athlete. I thought it was a man until she started talking on her phone. Who takes calls with the ringer on when you are on a stakeout?"

Mike said, "Eye color? Hair?"

"She had light colored hair and a white jacket. Blonde, I guess. No idea on the eyes."

"The name on her driver's license is Sally Wilder. Comes from a wealthy Portland family. Grandpa was a timber baron, but the family switched to running liberal non-profits when logging shut down. Green jobs, stopping global warming, that sort of thing...."

"If you say so. I don't know. Why don't you ask the FBI about her?

Goldfarb said, "They asked me. She is a person of interest."

"Don't they have her? I left her gift wrapped."

Mike said, "The FBI missed her."

"They didn't put up a perimeter?"

Mike said, "No idea. When I was there, they would not talk about what went wrong."

Goldfarb said, "They went ape shit when I passed them her driver's license and credit cards, like it was a gift from God. They wanted to interrogate **you** as a witness. I told them this came from a confidential source and that we'd get the information for them. Hence this call."

"They don't know where she is?"

"It seems not," Goldfarb said. "If they do, our brothers at the Bureau are not sharing that information. They found her car at the Portland airport in long term parking. A woman matching her driver's license description booked a round trip on Delta to JFK at New York using a Stop Hate, Inc. corporate card. She has not used the return leg of the ticket, and the name she checked in under was that of an employee who'd transferred to Brazil six months ago."

"Stop Hate? I'm more used to VISA or American Express...."

Mike said, "That's the name of the company. What you saw on the license plates is the firm's Internet hash tag, #stopH8. It is Portland-based, but incorporated in New York. I take it that you've not heard of them?"

"I have not."

Goldfarb said, "The Bureau says Stop Hate is part of a new wave of high tech. It does post-Facebook social media bundling. They referred me to an article in *Wired*. Stop Hate is less than a year old, privately-held, venture capital funded, and it has an estimated market valuation of over $100 million. Ms. Sally Wilder is listed as their customer relations manager."

"Do we care?"

"The Bureau does. We might get dragged into this. A major investor is the World Economic Forum, which is, of course, owned by our friend Dr. Claas Vogel."

"What exactly does #stopH8 do that makes them worth all that money?"

Mike said, "It arranges protests and riots. I expect that's why the Bureau got intense when we passed along her information from their disputed crime scene."

Goldfarb said, "There are dozens of radical left groups who do protests, sometimes violently: Black Lives Matter, Antifa, Sharia Foundation, STORM, and on and on. Mostly the groups don't get along with each other, except for sharing the standard talking points."

I said, "Talking points like, '*police are racist, capitalism is oppression, open borders, Muslims are peaceful, climate will kill us*', etc. Is that what you mean?"

"Exactly. Turn on a news channel for details."

"What do you mean by, 'don't get along?'"

Mike said, "Picture mixing a gay rights group with a Sharia law group at a protest or the Black Panthers with a women's rights group and having it turn violent. The results might not be what the client wanted. They might throw bricks at each other instead of through windows."

Josie smiled.

I said, "Those are extreme examples. What's the big deal about Stop Hate?"

Goldfarb said, "Bundling, precise targeting, and effectiveness. If you want to organize a protest in a major city, there is no need to contact a dozen different groups, many of which are under surveillance. You just specify your issue and budget and Stop Hate will take care of getting you the right mix of demonstrators, the right demographics, the best local contacts, etc. For a few dollars more, they will manage your political support, media relations, and PR."

"Is that legal?"

Goldfarb said, "Protests are protected by the First Amendment."

"What about riots and terrorism?"

"Not so much, but Stop Hate has excellent lawyers who are happy to represent their clients. They have an 'event aftermath' package for that."

"Does Stop Hate have connections with Iran or Quds?"

"They don't reveal their customer list. You'd have to ask the FBI."

"Why was Sally in Monterey – or in New York, assuming it was her?"

"You'd have to ask the FBI."

"Who doesn't know shit. This is politics. Do we want to get involved?" Josie was shaking her head, '**No!**'"

Mike said, "For the record, Doctor Goldfarb and I have already discussed this. My vote on that one is a strong, 'no.'"

I said, "Good. Mike is now our control and we both agree with him on this. Why are we discussing this, Doctor? Am I missing something?"

Goldfarb said, "It came up at NSC. Director Johnson expressed gratitude that we'd provided him with the only good lead the Bureau has."

"Sally? A woman whose name I didn't even know? That's his best lead?"

"So he said. The Director is somewhat embarrassed that they were unaware she was there."

"He should be. Why is that our problem?"

"It isn't yet. I want to make sure it stays that way. The President was in the meeting, and I need to get back to him with an honest answer. Before you got to us, got sheep dipped, and were teamed with Josie, you had a reputation of, ah, leaving a trail of broken China…."

"That is not a question."

"Is there something you need to tell me about this woman? If so, now would be a good time."

"I'll try to be more clear, Doctor. I never spoke one word to the woman. She never spoke a single word to me. I neutralized a threat to my team and secured a tango for the support elements that you'd promised were coming to extricate us from a compromised safe house. Until you told me, I'd never heard of #stopH8. Until you told me, I didn't know her name."

"Because you hadn't looked at her license...."

"I hadn't looked, because I didn't give a shit. My focus was on getting Josie clear of a threat, which is to say, doing my job. That's the truth."

"We've left you on a loose rein until our Covfefe meeting, which is pending. President Blager will be at that meeting. If he asks about this, will he get the same answers?"

"He will. It is the truth."

Mike said, "I think we've covered this, Doctor. Is there anything else?"

"No," Goldfarb said. "Josie, do you have anything to add?"

"I do not. I remote viewed a threat to our getting out of a compromised safe house. I thought it was a man, but it turned out to be a woman. Raven dealt with her. We're still alive. That's all I know."

"It was an unfortunate situation," Goldfarb said.

"Again."

"Yes. The lapse was largely my fault. We're getting you better support."

I said, "The TSG support is appreciated. Your cutting us slack is even more appreciated. Thank you."

"Covfefe," Mike said. "In about two weeks."

"Covfefe. See you there."

Two hours later my phone rang again. I looked at the ID. It was Mike.

I said, "Covfefe. That last one was not the call we were expecting."

"No," Mike said. "Do you want to talk about the Russians now?"

"I do. I'm checked out on the vehicle and my new weapons."

"Good. They now want the meet next Sunday at noon at the location we discussed. Can you do that?"

"Will Black and his team be ready?"

"Yes. It will be him plus four. His training went well. Two on the team are sniper qualified. We'll have one covering you during the meet."

"Why did they change the schedule?"

"They didn't say. They are holding this close. I have no additional background on your contact, but they did send us a picture. She will be wearing a white dress with flowers on it, and a sun hat, sort of like a French impressionist painting."

"No other information?"

"Our sources inside the FSB and at the consulate know nothing. They are running this one deep black. The agent's code name is Marie. The FSB has no such agent."

"I've not worked against, much less with, the Russians. Isn't this unusual?"

"Very."

"She must have a control and a support team."

"I expect she does, but we have no information about that either. Would you like me to query the FBI? They are tasked with counter intelligence…."

"I would not."

"I didn't think so."

"The CIA did have a slim file on her time in France. It ends that she was burned and recalled to Moscow. They report the FSB is going through some purges."

"Do you believe that?"

"The purge part, maybe. It's hard to say. There is a lot of noise about Russians. Most of it is our own news media propaganda, sometimes aided by their disinformation. Russians survive by projecting strength. Historically, the most ruthless are the ones who get to rule.

"Ioseb Jughashvili earned the childhood nickname of Soso, a diminutive of Iosif (Joseph). After a long string of revolutionary aliases, *noms de guerre,* he came to power and changed his name to Joe Stalin –

Joe Steel. He used nicknames like 'Man of Steel' to impress the Western news media."

"Did we counter with Superman and comic books?"

"Probably," Mike said. "They are controlling your meet tightly. All that my contact for the meeting provided to me was her picture and some protocols. No context. I'll send you what I got by secure courier."

"What did we give them back?"

"We mirrored them. No bluster, just tit for tat. Your picture and a cover name. We agreed to their protocols, but made them apply to you as well. Stick to your legend. You are an Aussie living in Canada."

"Crikey, Mate. I'm not going to come a gutser! It's just a meeting; we're not going to have a naughty."

"Say what?"

"That's Aussie. You can look it up. Now give me the highlights for the meet, please."

"She will be there early. The pass phrases and countersigns are these."

"I'm ready."

"Here is the meet and greet: You say, *'You are a French vision, but do you have a parasol?'* She says, *'Are you an American?'* You say, *'No. I was just practicing being rude.'*"

"Cute. Got it."

"There is also an alert phrase if surveillance or a threat is noticed."

"Really?"

"Really. They seem a bit nervous."

"Give it to me"

"The alert is, 'Do you think it may rain?' If either of you say that, the meet is over and you are to get clear. There is a countersign if you wish to reschedule."

"Go ahead."

"To reschedule, say, 'It never rains in California.' That means you will both meet at the same place at the same time tomorrow."

"Got it. Was there anything unusual about the protocols?"

"One thing did stand out. They don't want their agent tracked. The protocol warns us that lethal force may be used if their agent is interfered with or followed. That is extreme for a peacetime meet. During the Cold War, we took great pains to not kill each other's agents."

"So if Marie gets arrested, I get shot?"

"I don't think that is their plan. I think they just don't want her followed. They are making a point as well as showing strength."

"Have you shared these protocols with Black and his team?"

"Not yet. I'll send the packet to you and copy it to them."

"We will all have secure phones. Put in a cover sheet saying that the use of force is my call. No shots are to be fired without my authorization. I want three codes, the first to disengage and get clear, the second to allow force as needed to disable pursuit WITHOUT endangering life, and the last is the clearance to go full lethal. Options A, B, and C. Are you okay with that?"

"It's your run, Raven. I won't second guess you."

"Thanks, Mike. Covfefe."

"Covfefe to you as well. Contact me 24/7 if you need anything. I'll see you at the meeting.

CHAPTER SIXTEEN
A WALK IN THE PARK

Fairmont Hotel, San Francisco, next morning

Marie gave the code knock and got the signal to enter. Karlov was standing by the window, impeccably dressed as usual. This time it was a dark pinstripe suit, white shirt, and blue tie.

He pulled her chair back from the small table. "Would you like some tea?"

"*Спасибо..*" *Thank you.*

"I'm coming to like the view," he said as he poured her a cup. "It's at the top of Nob Hill. Did you know that America had an aristocracy just as we had our Czars?"

"That seems odd."

"Railroad barons. Central Pacific Railroad's Big Four – called the Nobs – built mansions here. The word was *nabobs*, from 1850s British slang, those who used their money and influence to corrupt Parliament. The Americans distorted it to Nobs. It was a term of derision."

I smiled, "Some things don't change."

"The Nobs all moved away. The 1906 earthquake and fire destroyed the entire neighborhood, leveled it. This hotel was gutted, but its granite walls saved the structure and so here it is."

"And so here we are."

Karlov smiled. "I have something special for you, Marie, not just a legend, an actual American citizenship. You don't need to use it for the coming meet – and should not – but this will let you burrow deep my little Sparrow.

Even our masters in the Kremlin don't know about it. It will be our little secret. You will have an ice-cold alternate identity."

He handed me an envelope.

"The best covers are layered. Identity theft from a living person always leaves one exposed. It's not really theft; it is more like borrowing. Where did the bills get sent, what about creditors, relatives, friends, enemies, employers, and so forth? No matter how well that ploy is executed, it's not safe, long term."

I nodded. They'd taught us that in the Sparrow school. *It usually didn't matter. Everything is temporary.*

"For the time being, we will stick with your Marie persona. You know that identity inside and out. You were burned in France and we will use that to refine your legend. You are a failed, retired agent, now burned out and cast aside. All our FSB stations can access that information, and we expect it will leak."

"Why do you want it leaked?"

"I want you viewed as a low level FSB operative. A burned out, failed agent suitable only for meetings like we will have Sunday, just a messenger. Marie will appear harmless."

"And Patty? How will she appear?"

"She will not appear. She will not be noticed at all."

I frowned and shook my head. "How can that be?"

"Back during the Cold War, we were unsurpassed at planting moles. We stole America's nuclear weapons, all of them, atomic and hydrogen bombs. In Britain we had Kim Philby and others. Back then, we took identities for our moles off tombstones and it worked. Now there is an intense focus on death certificates and birth certificates that can be authenticated. Everything is networked and archived. You can hack the databases, but that creates more risks."

"Risks we live with. All who serve the motherland know that."

"Yes, we do what we must, but the contents of that envelope make you an authentic American citizen, Marie. This is Hawaii gold. Cherish it. Save it. We will not use it operationally. It will be your safe space. It is not connected to Marie or Russia, not to FSB, not to me."

"Say more, please."

"That envelope contains an official pre-2008 birth certificate, one which was hand-recorded in a paper book at the time and so noted in local newspapers in Hawaii. No matter what happens to Russia or at the FSB, you are an American, Patty Allgrove.

"This will be your deep cover identity. It is one that must be protected. I do not want it used operationally."

"I will put it in a safe place."

"Exactly. Put the Allgrove identity documents into a safe deposit box at a bank and open an account there. You pick the bank. I don't want to know. If anyone asks, I know nothing about Allgrove."

"I understand." *I didn't really.*

"There is a California driver's license for Ms. Allgrove in the envelope too, along with $50,000 in cash. If you make deposits, keep them under $8,000. American banks report deposits of $10,000 or more. It's best to stay well under that limit.

"In a few months I want you to buy Patty Allgrove a house here and get her an American passport. When that's done, I will get you a job with an American company that requires you to travel. It will get you a legal income so you can start reporting taxes."

"What about my Marie identity?"

"It is active. Marie is **Russian**. We will use her persona for your missions. She goes operational Sunday. Our meeting is confirmed. Here are the details."

He handed me a folder.

"Excellent."

"Time is short. I want you to study this now. I set strict protocols for the meet, and you need to understand these fully."

"What is the purpose of this meeting?"

"A prize is offered, something that we have wanted for years, to the point where Russia has offered a $10 Million dollar reward in hard currency or gold. We've had no takers, but this is now suddenly offered to us for free. President Putin thinks it may be too good to be true."

"It might be a trap?"

"It probably is a trap. If so, a price must be paid, one high enough that it will send a signal to our enemies."

"What is this prize?"

"A high-level terrorist who we've been seeking for years, a capitalist billionaire who funds both *jihad* and the New World Order, the Global State that will end Russia's national sovereignty, Dr. Klaus Vogel."

"So why don't we put a bullet in his head or some polonium in his tea?"

"It would be like assassinating a major head of state, an act of war with many possible adverse consequences. World War One was started over an assassination. We do not want to start World War III, a war that would almost certainly lead to a nuclear exchange."

"What actions have we taken?"

"We have had a valid international arrest warrant out for him. We have offered a generous bounty to anyone who delivers him to us, and have applied what political pressure we can. It has not helped."

"A diverse group of countries have Vogel on their terrorist lists, but not the United States or Switzerland. He has dual citizenship with both nations. Both protect him, as does the UN."

"What other options do we have?"

"Until now, we've had none. His personal security is at least as good at Putin's or President Blager's, possibly better. Not only do his host nations use their resources and political influence to shelter him, but he also has first-rate private security. Killing Vogel would be difficult. Arresting him has been impossible"

"What's changed? Why now?"

"A private American source has set up a back channel meeting to discuss it with us. Arresting Vogel is the prize we are offered. It's gotten our attention."

"The Americans are meeting with us to discuss this?"

"There is no official contact, nor is any suggested. A private individual has brokered a meeting. We're told your contact will be from a third party nation. He will be meeting with you as a private Canadian citizen, allegedly without the knowledge or approval of his country or the Americans."

"Do we believe any of that?"

Karlov shrugged. "We believe enough to set up the meeting. Perhaps this contact can convince you it's not a charade. Perhaps he is treacherous, or maybe just a disposable tool sent to test us."

"Interesting."

I took a sip of my tea, and started reading.

The Ranch, a Private Estate near Mendocino

We were doing our normal morning breakfast on the patio, bagels and coffee. It was another beautiful day with full sun and perfect temperature. I'd even seen a whale and her calf close off shore when Raven was off doing his daily workout.

Mendocino had its whale festival in March, a time said to mark when the California Grays left with their calves, going north to Alaska waters for their feeding season. If so, this pair must not have gotten the memo.

My secure phone was buzzing. I looked at the ID. "It's Black. Probably reporting on his training program with the security team Mike set up. I hope he didn't shoot anyone...."

Josie rolled her eyes.

I pushed the button and said, "How's it going, Kid?"

I listened. "Great news. Coming here *today*?" Mike didn't...."

I paused, listening. "No, that's fine. It's a good idea. I'm going to put Josie on too. I want her in the loop."

I looked at Josie and said, "Black and our security team for the meet will be here tonight."

We waited a moment as her secure phone synched and our green lights came on solid.

"I'm here," Josie said.

Black chuckled, "Can you stand visitors? Me, plus five. We can make it in time for dinner...."

She said, "It's fine by me."

I said, "I like your idea. Josie and I can meet the team personally, and they can get down there early to put eyes on the meeting location and access. Showtime for the meet is now Sunday. Do you have approval for this, or have you gone rogue again?"

"Mike's cool. He doesn't have any trouble making decisions. He bought that Citation X. He had it upgraded to the same COM gear as in his Gulfstream and registered to TSG."

"What about Goldfarb?"

"He is not in the loop. Mike said close hold until Covfefe. Are you good with that?"

"Affirmative. Keep it that way."

"Roger that. He wants you to get the secure conference room reserved for that. We need a meeting to brief and plan, and then dinner."

"Can do, but all the meeting prep is making me crazy. The Russians have their knickers knotted. Their protocols are extreme."

"Mike said the same. That's why we're coming early. There are problems. The Russians are tricky and we've never worked with or against them: not you, not me, not any of us, not since the Cold War. Mike doesn't want any unforced rookie errors. I'm bringing shooters plus an expert to give us a briefing and make suggestions."

Josie and I exchanged a look. "*Suggestions?* What the Hell does that mean?"

"There is no hidden agenda. It is your meet. Mike made that clear. Our role is to support you."

"Okay, come ahead. How has your training been going?"

"Good. I'm qualified to co-pilot the Citation X, not just by the FAA, but, more important, by TSG's insurance company. It's a kick to fly."

"What about the rest of your training?"

"I have been having a ball. Running, gunning, and blowing things up. It's catching. Almost as good as flying F-22s and a lot more up close and personal."

"How soon can you get here?"

"We're already in the air. When do you want us?"

"If you can make it here by 1500, I can get us some range time and see if you guys can hit a bull in the ass with a bass fiddle."

"Stand by one."

"Roger."

The phone went dead for just under two minutes. "The team says you're on, but there is a catch."

"Go ahead."

"You provide the Ammo. We are traveling light. If you want a shoot-off, we need .45, .223, and .300 Winchester Magnum."

"What's with the .300 Winchester Magnum?"

"It was Kris Kyle's favorite gun. Snipers love it. You can dial in 1,000 yards, and it shoots like a laser. For shorter ranges, you don't even have to correct. You dial in your 500 yard dope and can hit a target from 100-700 yards without worrying much about making minute adjustments."

"I'd have to be really pissed off to shoot at something that far away. Can you even *see* anything at 1,000 yards?"

"It's not about me, Raven. These guys do head shots at 2,000. If you want to mess with the sniper stuff, we need .300 Magnum and at least a 1,000 meter range. They prefer Hornady ammo."

"No go on the .300 Winchester Magnum and the range here is only 200 yards. The rest isn't a problem."

"Let's do it. These guys love to shoot...."

I said, "Deal. How about the best shooter gets bragging rights and the worst pays for the drinks?"

Black laughed. "That will cost you. We'll be there by 1430. See you soon."

Raven heard them coming up the walk. No one was trying to be quiet. He looked at his watch. 1415, they were early.

It would be a bit crowded on the patio, but they'd fit. Josie had made ice cold lemonade. She had crackers and energy bars and had been looking forward to seeing Black again.

I opened the door.

"You made good time. Hand guns only inside. Weapons freak Josie out."

"Roger that," Black said. "I told them."

"What about knives?" said a short, muscled up White guy.

"Terry was Force Recon. Marines like knives. Never know when you'll need to cut a pastry or stab someone in the throat…."

"*Oohrah*," said a tall, bald, Black man.

Black grinned. "That translates to 'charge.' Mike likes Marines for some reason. Burt and Terry share the same background."

"I know what it means. Come on in."

They lined up on the patio. Black did the introductions.

I pointed at Josie.

"I shoot back, but this lady doesn't do violence. It freaks her out. She sees things. Josie is a National Resource. Among other things, she saved the President's life. My Job #1 is to protect her.

"Your job is to back me up. Putting your bodies in front of Josie to keep her safe is expected. Is that understood?"

There was a chorus of, "Yes, Sir."

Black said, "I briefed them in. So did Mike. They know."

"Good."

Josie smiled and made a gesture that included them all. "Thank you. Black saved our asses in Durham when we were attacked by a *jihadi* kill team that was coming for me. He broke rules, but got us air support. I'm grateful."

They all looked at Black. He shrugged. "It turned to shit. We were all wounded."

I said, "The main thing is we all came back. With your help, that can continue."

Black did the introductions. The two who'd spoken were specialists in close combat, Rudy Rogers, jet black, bald, and six foot four. He looked like an NFL linebacker. Terry Coston, a muscled up white guy just under 6 feet who looked like a weight lifter. Both were former Marine Force Recon.

Pat Barry was the sniper. Six foot two, solidly built, and a former SEAL.

I looked at him, "You're the .300 Win Mag guy?"

He shrugged. "It's a good load. I like the .338 Lupua too. It shoots farther and flatter than a .50 caliber but they don't have adequate suppressors for it. It keeps my spotter awake."

Vinnie Russelle was a little guy who looked even smaller next to Pat. He was Italian looking, 5 foot 9 and wiry, small for an Army Ranger.

"You're his spotter?"

Vinnie shrugged. "I lie there comfortable and Pat shoots at things. Sometimes he hits people. Then I get to write up who it was and explain why we shot the bastard."

They all laughed except for the one who'd not spoken, Millie Seymour. She didn't fit in. Petite, tiny, 5 feet or maybe less, wire rimmed glasses, with intense blue eyes, short white hair, and 68 years old.

She looked like a retired school teacher. She looked like a snack dog standing in the middle of a wolf pack. The weird thing was the body language. The wolves were respectful.

I said, "You're former CIA."

"Technically, I was. I was a liaison to MI6. The Brits operate differently than we do."

"How so?"

"Americans depend on technology. MI6 specializes in human intelligence. Its officers are regarded as the finest recruiters and runners of agents in the business. Far smaller than its American or Russian counterparts, it punches above its weight."

"What is your weapons preference?"

"This one." She touched her head. "I'm like your Josie, I guess. I don't do violence. I see things that others do not. James Bond notwithstanding, there are no licenses to kill at MI6. It prevails on the focused, targeted, native cunning and natural deceptiveness of those who run it."

"Your Brits bungle spectacularly. What about Kim Philby and the rest?"

"That disaster was a MI5 counterintelligence failure. MI6 thought, but could never prove, that Sir Roger Hollis, long the head of MI5, was the Fifth Man in the Philby ring.

"America has suffered larger failures. Our own FBI allowed the CIA to be taken over by the Deep State. Brennan was an *admitted* Communist when he was *hired.* He and FBI Director Comey, a leftist political lackey, politicized our Intel community. The Washington swamp – or sewer of corruption, if you prefer – is still being drained to this day."

I said, "My guess is that your return to Langley was troubled."

She shrugged. "I was happy to retire."

"What exactly do you do now?"

"I run the Watchers. It's a new group Mike set up. We do counter-surveillance, plus a bit of sneak and peek."

I took a deep breath. We had a short time line, and a lot to get done. I could care less about MI6 and old history.

Millie was watching me closely. She had piercing, intelligent eyes. I could sense she saw what was coming.

"I guess we need to cut to the chase, Millie. Why do I care? What can you possibly do for this team that I would deem essential for the OP we have coming next weekend?"

There was instant silence. Total stillness. I looked around at the faces as it lengthened. Josie and Black looked shocked. Our shooters put on poker faces. This did not involve them.

Josie said, "We need to talk."

Black said, "Me too, boss."

Millie held up her hand. "It's a fair question." She looked at me. "Have you studied the meet location and protocols for your adventure with the Russians on Sunday?"

"I've looked at them."

"Have you studied them? Why there? Why those rules? *What are the Russians up to?*"

I repeated, "I've looked at them."

"I will take that as a 'No,' Mr. Raven. You've only just glanced at them, haven't you? No deep critical thought?"

"I've not studied them deeply...."

"Let's go a bit deeper then. Where are you meeting your Russian contact specifically?"

"Golden Gate Park."

"Wrong. Your specific meeting location is the Sweeney Observatory Site. There is no observatory there, not even ruins, just large stones from the foundation. The site was destroyed by the 1906 earthquake.

"The location is on an island, surrounded by Stow Lake. There are only two foot paths across the lake. You will have to walk in and walk out. From wherever you park, you can figure at least 45 minutes each way."

"So?"

"The Russians have set up a perfect trap. Your security detail – she gestured at the men standing and watching her – will be of no use at all."

"Why not?"

"They will stand out as if they had neon strobes on their heads. So will you.

"The meet location is on high ground, called Strawberry Hill. There are a few trees, but it is mostly exposed to where you can see it from the whole island. There is essentially no cover going in or out."

"This is a skilled team. They are expert at using cover and avoiding notice."

"That won't help."

"Why not?"

"Your best access once on the island is across what they call Mother's Meadow. On a Sunday morning, it will be full of young mothers, grandmothers, infants, toddlers, and, of course, other children of all ages."

She ran her eyes over the men surrounding her. "Can you blend in to that?"

No one spoke.

She looked at Barry, the sniper. "Do you want to take a walk in the park on a bright Sunday morning toting a long gun with a silencer?"

Barry shrugged. "I'd make my spotter carry it."

"Screw that," Vinnie said.

"She's got a point, Boss," Black said.

I looked at Millie. "What else?"

"A lot. That would be a longer discussion. In my view, the Russians are acting insane. They appear to totally distrust you. The FSB and their embassies appear to know nothing. The ROEs for the meeting allow lethal force if their agent is followed. Why might they do that?"

"Why, indeed. Do you know?"

"I do not, but I can speculate. I think the agent you are meeting may be someone important, someone high-level. You've offered them bait they can't refuse, but they may be thinking that this is a deception to expose, kill, or arrest their agent."

"Do you have a solution?"

"It's why I'm here. I do have a solution. My Watchers. We've been looking for a good trial run to prove our value to Mike. I think your meeting is a perfect test."

"Who exactly are these Watchers?"

"I will never disclose that. Would you disclose your people?"

"I would not."

"So Mike assured me, which is why I'm here."

"What can you say?"

"Many people have been retired from or quit the Intel community. My Watchers are mostly retired spies, agents, and analysts. They also include young women, bored, or at home raising children. A few are young men who decided they hated working for the government. It varies, but all have been vetted by me for patriotism and good tradecraft.

"My youngest operative is twenty, my oldest is eighty-six. On a mission, some will bring their children or grandchildren along for cover, or perhaps companionship. If we do our jobs right, you will never notice us, nor will our adversaries. If you use us, we have rules that you must agree to."

"Which are?"

"We do not carry weapons. We are civilians, noncombatants. We just watch and report. You do not notice us, or if you do, you pretend not to. If you get into trouble, you do not – not ever – run to us for help.

"We can't save you. We are not warriors, just Watchers. You need to know that."

I looked around the room, meeting each pair of eyes. Finally I said, "Your asses are on the line. What should we do?"

Josie said, "I like this woman. She has a good aura."

Black said, "Mike and I talked. It's your call, but I say we need her."

I looked at the security team. "I need answers. Does this make us safer or not?"

They all said, "Safer," one after the other.

"Good," I said. "I agree. Can we go shooting now?"

"Absolutely," Josie said, "Dinner will be ready at six in the main lodge. Practice up. It would be embarrassing if you shot the Watchers who are trying to keep you from screwing up."

CHAPTER SEVENTEEN
HIGH NOON

Golden Gate Park, 11:35 AM

I paused, and stood quiet for a moment surveying the area after crossing the foot bridge over Stow Lake. All was peaceful. No visible threats and a lot of people around. A few young families, but mostly women and children on blankets in the meadow.

I was the only unaccompanied male in sight. *Great way to blend in, you idiot.* I was breaking too many of the basic rules. I'd used my Raven legend for over five years and had it down cold. This one was brand new. It was not yet embedded in my thinking and mannerisms.

I was Digger Simpson, Aussie born. Aussie mother, Canadian father, now deceased. My father was a Captain killed in Afghanistan at Kandahar Airbase while serving with Canadian Military Intelligence in 2009 by an IED.

It was simple enough legend. I had it memorized, but it wasn't ingrained into my subconscious, textured, or put into context. If I'd been deploying to a foreign post, they'd have me isolated, living my legend for weeks, being grilled by experts.

Now my first test was the real thing. I was going up against a senior Russian FSB agent.

They kept telling me, *"No one is better at spy games than the Russians."* If she started testing me on deep background, I was screwed.

"Who was your third grade teacher? What did she look like? Who did you take to the prom?" *Sorry FSB, you got me on that one. Shoot me in the head, I don't have a clue.*

Screw it. There was no time, and no choice. The meet had to be today. I needed to suck it up and get it done. Josie and I had wanted to go on offense, and we'd finally been released.

Be careful what you wish for.

I spotted agent Marie from a hundred yards out, leaning against a large finished stone that bordered a grassy knoll. She looked like an 19th Century French Impressionist painting. She was watching the clouds, enjoying the gentle breeze.

The day was warm and sunny. She wore a loose white dress showing ample breasts and nice cleavage, but leaving her shoulders covered. She had a wide brimmed hat of some kind, not straw, white cloth. No parasol. That would be out of place.

Marie saw me coming at about fifty yards. I saw her tense and focus. One of her hands dipped into a bag at her feet. She had on practical shoes, also white, some kind of modern high end athletic shoe, not cloth, leather, with both laces and a strap.

Practical footwear. Useful for running or kicking enemies in the balls.

I approached her slowly, keeping my hands in sight, and we went through the pass phrases and counter signs. My part finished with, "... I was just practicing being rude."

She smiled at me. "Practicing, Digger, or rude for real?"

"It's too soon to say, Marie. It might help if you kept your hands in sight. I'm just here to talk, to give you some information."

"You must have issues with women...."

Her English was excellent.

I stood there patiently until she removed her hand. It took her about a minute.

"Thank you," I said. "May I sit?"

"Certainly." She gestured for me to sit on her left. Which kept her right arm free, but left mine close enough for her to encumber my draw.

I sat, leaving about a foot between us. We could both lean against the stone, but it left our heads sticking up over the rim. "Thank you."

"Are you comfortable now? Can we begin?"

"First, I have a question, if I may. A personal concern."

Marie's eyes were violet, darker and deeper than Josie's. She was studying me intently, hanging on my every word. Some men liked for a woman to do that. I wasn't one of them.

She nodded.

"I'm told you represent the Russian State who has insisted on protocols. We have been warned that 'lethal force may be used if you are interfered with.' We agreed to that and made it reciprocal. Is that essentially correct?"

"I believe so."

"About 230 yards out at my five o'clock you have a man with a black beard and a long gun with a suppressor. At present he is looking though his scope at me. Would that be a sufficient level of threat for my side to activate our agreement?"

She blinked. I saw the surprise in her eyes. Then she turned her head and looked in that direction. "You are imagining things. There is no one there."

"That's a great relief to me. Would you mind if I took out my cell phone, called 911, and had the Park Police check it out?"

"Wait." She stood, looked in that direction, took off her hat, and waved it twice in front of her face. "I don't see a thing. If there were anyone there, I'm sure that he's gone now."

I rose and stood next to her, scanning the area. It was an excellent location, shielded on three sides and with a clear view of our meeting place. An easy shot, but he was gone.

Thank you, Millie.

We reseated ourselves. Marie left her hat off. "Who exactly are you, Digger, and who do you work for?"

I wasn't going there. Control the discussion now, or the meet is blown and so are you.

"Does it matter? You know the Americans asked for this meet. You and they have a mutual problem. I've come with information that should allow you to solve it."

"Doctor Claas Vogel, the financial terrorist. He's a monster."

"Yes. My American friends agree with you on that, as do I. Russia has a legal arrest warrant for him and has posted a significant bounty."

"You want the bounty. Our terms call for him to be delivered to us."

"I would be happy to have you deal with Vogel. I do not personally want the bounty, nor can I earn it."

"Why not?"

"I lack the power to deliver Vogel to you. I work for myself. I'm trying to help some American friends who **also** lack the power to deliver Vogel to you. They are trying to help you without exposing themselves. I am trying to help them, which means that I'm also trying to help you. You are not making it easy for me."

"How can you say that?"

"It's easy for me to say. Where do you want me to start?"

There was something different in her eyes, something softer.

She said, "Wherever you wish. Do you suggest that Russia should trust the American government? That would be insane."

"Personally, I think that both the American and the Russian governments are insane. You have been stabbing each other in the backs and threatening each other with nuclear Armageddon ever since 1945.

"Back then, America and Russia mutually saved the world from the Nazis and Japanese fascism. Since then, you have mutually reenergized ancient evil, radical Islam, and unleashed the most corrupt unaccountable bureaucracy in history, the UN."

"I think you need to start somewhere else if you hope to have a productive meeting today."

"How about with your guy set to put a bullet in my head?"

Marie sighed. "No one has tried to harm you, Digger. There are no guns aimed at you."

"Maybe that's not a good starting point either?"

"No. It's not."

"Can we agree that Russia has joint interests with America? Fighting Islamic *jihad* would seem to be at or near the top of that list. You are both suffering major attacks. These are not going away. These terrorists have access to WMDs."

"Perhaps we could agree, in theory and as individuals. I'm not sure it matters."

"How long would groups like ISIS and Al-Qaida and Hamas and Hezbollah last if you and America worked together to totally annihilate them, like you did with Hitler?"

"Not long. I'm not sure that matters either."

"Okay. You try. What can we, you and I, agree about concerning Vogel?"

"We could agree that Russia should take him out."

I nodded. "Yes. We could. We do. What follows from that?"

"Russia has offered a bounty for Vogel, dead or alive. We have an international arrest warrant for him as a financial terrorist. We are told you can help. That interests us."

"That's why I am here. What I can do to help you is limited."

"Will the Americans help us?"

"No. I don't think they can officially. What exactly does Russia want to do with Vogel?"

"Our rulers prefer to take him alive, put him on trial, and execute him. If that is impossible, and so far it has been, I don't think we mind if he dies, so long as it is not by our hand."

I said, "Vogel is a hard target. He has high level political protection in both America and Switzerland, which is where he spends most of his time."

"We know that. Can you get us access to him?"

"Where would you want to target him?"

"Not Switzerland. Not at the UN. America would be acceptable."

"How much notice would you need?"

"It depends. You can forget his enclave, government facilities, or public events."

"Of course."

"If it's an easy snatch and a unique opportunity, at least 48 hours. If it is a structure we would need to penetrate, perhaps a week.

I smiled and nodded. "Excellent."

"You came prepared…?"

"I came hopeful."

I dipped my hand into my left pocket, letting my fingers touch the little Gerber knife with its snap-open razor-sharp blade. I came out with a folded piece of paper, not the knife, and handed it to her.

She hadn't flinched. There were no alarm cries. Perhaps we'd reached a level of *detente*.

I said, "Here are two specific opportunities that might suit your needs. The note lists street addresses, GPS coordinates, dates, best access times, and a few other useful items including guesses about how long Vogel might be there. You will need to do your own research to validate it."

"Is the American government surveilling these locations?"

"Not to my knowledge. America suffers from political correctness and a peacetime mind set. Their intelligence community and law enforcement dares not touch Vogel. I doubt they are paying any attention to him."

Her eyes narrowed. "This man funds most of the terrorism in the world, directly or indirectly. Do you expect me to believe that?"

"I have trouble believing it myself, but that is my opinion. Consider this. Russia **twice** warned America of the Boston Marathon bombers. America ignored your warnings and many other red flags. It treated that major attack, and many others, as criminal activity, not terrorism."

"My superiors will be skeptical."

"They should be. As I said, check it out. Do your own research. I've given you accurate targeting, but it does not come with a guarantee."

"The guarantee could be your life."

"That truly sucks. Unfortunately, it's the nature of our business, isn't it? Do what you think is best."

Marie was silent. She was watching me intently, studying me, and perhaps trying to read my thoughts.

"Is there anything else I can do for you?"

"There is," she said, reaching into her bag. She too came out with a folded piece of paper, not a weapon.

"This is the number for a burner phone. No one will answer, but you can text it. If you discover any indication that we should cancel, any hint, you also should do what **you** think is best. It might save your life."

We nodded at each other. I said, "I hope you get him."

Then I walked off. I did not look back.

CHAPTER EIGHTEEN
EGRESS

Golden Gate Park, 1:45 PM

I paused on the foot bridge over Stow Lake and did a full scan. I saw nothing hostile. I'd done what I could to spot ticks, but the terrain and having only one good egress route – again – prevented my running aggressive CSRs.

I had other options. I exited the park, found a good location, pulled out my secure phone and called Black.

"I'm clear of the park."

"Roger that. Any problems?"

"I'm not sure. What do the Watchers say?"

"Six tangos. The sniper had a spotter. Two others were on the island. Two more were watching the bridges from outside. The one on your end is wearing jeans, a T-shirt with a marijuana leaf, normal height and weight, black hair, wearing sunglasses."

"No one followed me across. No joy on the pot shirt."

Black said, "They probably won't follow on foot. They spotted your vehicle and put a GPS tracker on it."

"Cute. You are sure?"

"Double confirmation. Millie's people plus Josie."

"Do the tangos have eyes on my vehicle now?"

"No. Two teams are now sitting in cars, two to a vehicle, a white Prius with California plates and a blue Kia. Low performance vehicles, but politically correct and common."

"Where?"

"Both are on your side of the park, but neither is close. They seem to be waiting for you to move. They can pick you up if you head out on the 80 or on 101. The 101 is egress route B1 in your GPS, the 80 is egress route C."

"What about the other two tangos?"

"The sniper and his buddy. They took the other route out. They are sitting in a red Corvette with the top down, watching the other foot bridge. That's where your Red Sparrow was headed."

"They do NOT want her followed. It's a good thing we're not."

"Roger that."

"The two tango teams on my side can cover our egress routes B1 and C. The team on the other side has a better shot at the 101. It can clear her, and then get to position and pick me up as I head over the Golden Gate Bridge on the 101. The only routes out of here to the North are over those two Bridges."

"They have them covered. Do you want to egress to the South? You can go down the 101 or 280. The tangos would all be out of position to cover those."

"Negative. Let's stick with the tangos we know."

"Roger that."

"Can you get the rest of the team on this net?"

"I can."

"Do it." I waited for the others to check in and the green light to come on.

Black said, "Scooter One is Vinnie and Pat. Scooter Two is Rudy and Terry."

"Got it. Raven to Scooters. Confirm we are Option B on the Rules of Engagement."

"Scooter One confirms option B."

"Scooter Two confirms option B"

"Black, you remind them what that means."

"We use force, but try not to go full lethal. Stop them, but try hard not to kill them.

"Good summary. Scooters, these tangos might not want to back off. Killing them would compromise our mission, but we cannot and must not lead them to me or Josie. We do whatever it takes to stop them."

Both teams acknowledged.

I said. "Which Scooter has the zapper?"

"Scooter two has the zapper."

"Excellent. Raven to Scooter One. I want you guys to head North on the 101. Up over the Bridge on route B1. Get out and ahead of the action. I want you north of the Robin Williams tunnel. You can't miss it, four lanes going under a mountain."

"We got it." It was Vinnie.

"North of the Tunnel there is an overpass, Wolfback Ridge Road."

"We got it."

"Take that exit and get positioned there to take any ticks off my tail."

"Clarify."

"Shoot the bastards. Disable their vehicles. Take out the engines and tires."

"How many do we expect?"

"Zero to three. Most likely a white Prius, a blue Kia, and a red Corvette. Two tangos in each vehicle. Take them all out, but focus on the vette."

"What if he misses?"

I could hear a faint *bullshit* in the background.

I smiled. "Always have a Plan B. I'll go around again. Wolfback goes into a loop with Cloudview. I'll take them around, and give you another shot at them on the way out."

"Scooter One confirms. Take them all out."

"Correct. Do not spare your ammo. We want to make a point. Kill the vehicles. Try not to hit the occupants."

"Roger that."

"Scooter Two, your job is deception. First go by my vehicle, peel the tracker off the bumper, lose it well to the south, and then head back up north."

"We're only a few blocks away. We can drop your tracker somewhere on the 280 southbound. We'll try to stick it on a vehicle going that way."

"Perfect. With luck, you might pull **all** the tangos off. I'll delay my run until you are headed back North. Call me when you're headed back up."

"Roger that. What do we do then?"

"I want you to work your way back to our route B1. Check in when you are about ten out from the Golden Gate."

"What then?"

"I want Scooter Two positioned on the approach to the bridge. Wait for me to go past and check for ticks. I'll do a slow drive-by, about ten under the speed limit."

"Understood."

"Tuck in behind the tangos, get your zapper out, and give me a count of how many ticks I have."

"Roger that." It was Rudy, the big Black guy.

"I'll try to lose my ticks before I get to you. If it is zero when I come by, and it might be with your diversion, we can all go home."

"Roger that."

Black said, "One more thing. An insurance policy."

I said, "Let's hear it."

"I can be your cut out. Our ultimate priority is to not lead anyone back to you. We are assuming that our adversaries are damned good."

"Affirmative."

"If your James Bond road chase stuff works, and you are sure you are clear, head North to Santa Rosa and CSR your ass off.

"I'll pick you up at the airport. I'll take you home. We'll have someone return your car to Mike's offices in San Fran."

"I like it. See you there. If it all turns to shit, I'll call the abort. In that case, we scatter. We run south or east, not north."

Black says, "That works."

I said, "Does everyone have the abort plan?"

"Black confirms."

"Scooter One confirms."

"Scooter Two confirms."

"Let's get it done." I liked the plan. No one was taking any chances with the Russians.

I'd like it better if it worked. This was our first OP together and Murphy's Law was a bitch.

Fairmont Hotel, San Francisco, 2:30 PM

"How did your meet go?" Karlov said.

I smiled. "Good. It was an overall success, but we have some work to do."

"Will the Americans help?"

"No. Our contact says Vogel is untouchable. He says the Americans are not even watching him. Can that be true?"

"The first part is likely. Americans are soft on terrorists by our standards. The second is possible. Americans are naïve. Your contact is a Canadian?"

"He might be. My focus was on getting Vogel."

"Yes. So how does your contact propose earning our bounty? He needs to deliver Vogel to us."

"He's not a bounty hunter. He doesn't want the bounty. He doesn't want money."

"What does he want?"

"The mutual interest we share is having Russia get Vogel. He wants that. He said his American friends who set up the meeting want that too. They want to help us and he wants to help them. I tend to believe him about that."

"Why does he care?"

"He claims to be helping Americans who want Vogel, but can't take action themselves. He also may have personal reasons. His father was killed by terrorists in Afghanistan."

"That is possible. Vogel's public statements indicate that he hates America more than he hates Russia. He's certainly done them a lot of damage."

"I'm convinced that our source wants Vogel taken down. I believe that part."

"Can we turn him? Will he work for us?"

"He showed no interest in working for us. He delivered something valuable."

I handed Karlov the note and waited for him to read it. He did. *Twice.*

He looked at me, frowning. "This is precisely detailed. Do you believe it?"

"I am inclined to, Sir. He said if we wanted Vogel, he could offer us two opportunities. He claims the Americans don't have either of them under surveillance."

Karlov was frowning. "The first targeting is, ah, unusual. Why would Vogel visit there overnight?"

"I have no idea, Sir. He said we'd need to do our own research to validate what he told us. That he provided information, not guarantees."

"You accepted that?"

"It is what it is, Sir. I told him that the guarantee might be his life. I said we'd need at least 48 hours advance notice for a soft snatch. That one fit."

"I'm not comfortable with this. We will be kidnapping an American citizen on U.S. soil. Some would term that to be an act of war. That's why Russia got a warrant and offered a bounty. That's why we've been stuck for so long."

"I thought Vogel was Swiss?"

"He has dual citizenship."

"Perhaps you could hire a bounty hunter and distance yourself?"

"No. This is too important. If this is real and we fail, Putin would not forgive me."

"Do you want me to handle it, Sir? It's my Intel."

Karlov was silent for a long moment. Finally, he shook his head.

"I won't ask that of you. This calls for muscle and people familiar with the area. I need brute force, not subtlety and brains.

"We have people in the area who can do what's needed. This is right up on the border between Canada and New York. FSB has teams who work that border to move things in and out covertly. The Americans don't scrutinize people going out and the Canadians are loose."

I didn't speak. I waited for the rest.

"We won't fail. My team will kill Vogel if this is a trap. Putin would accept that."

"Yes, Sir." I was still waiting.

"If this fails, we'll blame your Canadian source. He's on his own. No one will protect him. I'll know where to find him."

"What about the protocols we agreed to?"

"We lied. Your source is being followed."

"Yes, Sir."

Digger had said it himself. *"It's the nature of our business, isn't it?"*

I almost felt sorry for him.

CHAPTER NINETEEN
CANNONBALL RUN

Golden Gate Park, 4 PM

My secure phone beeped. It was Scooter Two, Rudy and Terry. "Raven here."

"Sent the tracker south. Heading back up. Estimate bridge in 45. No contact with tangos."

It was Terry. "You let Rudy drive?"

A short laugh. "Makes him feel useful."

"Are you checked out on the zapper?"

"What's to check? Green light. Got it all charged. Push the button. Done deal."

"Did you read the manual?"

"There is no manual, just an email."

"We're the field test. How long does it take to recharge?"

"Two minutes."

"What's the range?"

"Point, don't aim. Like a shotgun. Effective range is fifty yards or less."

"That's the theory. Expect collateral damage, and make sure it's not me. If you engage, warn me. I'll accelerate hard. Don't push the bloody button till I'm a football field away."

"Roger that."

"Advise Scooter One, and give him a tango count before you engage. Call me when you're ten out. I'll see you there."

"Two confirms. See you there."

I clicked off and started my car, letting it idle, thinking about my best route. I'd troll past the park, act stupid, and see if they picked me up. Everything was dense urban crush, but I had some convoluted back alleys plugged into the GPS. I'd lose my ticks there.

Time to get it done.

The blue Kia picked me up on my first pass past the park. It hung about a block back, keeping a few vehicles between us.

I drove around purposefully for some ten minutes, non-aggressive, as if I were looking for something. Through it all, the Kia followed. I tried some gentle switchbacks that would give me a view of parallel surveillance. Nothing.

Just the Kia. How to best shake it for good? It was too dense and there was too much traffic for a high speed evasion, Hollywood style. It was near rush hour – or maybe SF was always that way – and there were a lot of people around. Too many.

I opted for the blind alley. We'd been past one candidate twice, an industrial district with loading docks, large steel bins and the like on both sides. It had a sharp ninety degree bend to the right about half way down, followed by a reverse.

It would do. Sheltered on all sides, cell coverage would be limited. Being Sunday, the businesses were closed.

Inbound, about a block out, I punched my Dodge Challenger hard. It responded like a spurred thoroughbred. Mike claimed zero to 60 in three seconds, and it came close. I left the Kia behind like it was standing still.

Full antiskid breaking and a hard right down the alley and by then I was back on the throttle hard. The Kia was just appearing in my rear view when I hit the ninety degree right, breaking to the max again. Back to the left accelerating and still no Kia.

I braked to a stop, reversed into a sheltered space between the bins, got out, and watched as the Kia sailed by me at full throttle. About then, the driver spotted the brick wall ahead.

He braked frantically, but his ride just wasn't up to it. That was when I took out both rear tires with four Critical Defense rounds from my suppressed Sig .45. The auto-skid for sure didn't know how to handle that.

The Kia switched ends. I thought it was going to roll, but the impact saved them. It hit the wall backwards and the airbags deployed, but it stayed right-side up. I put my last two rounds into the front tires, slapped in a new magazine, and policed my brass.

Time to get out of Dodge, I thought, climbing into my Dodge and pulling out into the alley. Then I paused, looking back in my rearview. The vehicle was trashed. It was smoking and there was a puddle of gas forming under it where its tank had ruptured.

Whoops.

I didn't want to toast the tangos and violate my own ROEs. Fortunately, they didn't want that either. Both doors opened and out came scrambling Russians. *No problem.*

I drove away, thinking and looking, while I ran a series of increasingly aggressive CSRs. I didn't detect anything, but the bridge was a choke point that still needed to be handled. When Scooter Two was in position, I started my run up over the Golden Gate, trolling for ticks.

My secure phone buzzed. It was Terry in Scooter Two.

We are about a mile behind you, behind the Prius. Two tangos on board."

"Do you have a clear shot?"

"In a few seconds. Rudy is hanging behind other traffic."

"Get it done."

I rolled down my window and checked the zapper. Green lights.
"Get me closer."

Rudy punched the gas and we made a rapid approach. At about 50 yards, the tangos saw us. The Prius moved to an open lane, accelerating to block us. I pointed the zapper, and hit the button.

Things happened fast.

"Holy, shit," Rudy said, taking evasive action. Cars were scattering like quail. Most of them were slowing, but not us.

The dashboard lights flickered and the GPS screen went blank. The Prius went dead, as did the all the cars in the right lanes it was passing.

"Is everything still working?"

"Not sure. We still have power and steering."

"They might try to ram us as we go by."

"Roger that."

Rudy tapped the brakes. They were still working. The collateral damage cars seemed to be under control. They were all moving to the right, trying to get on the shoulder.

Rudy drifted left and accelerated hard. Our GPS was rebooting, and the dashboard was operational. We were good.

I put down the zapper and gave the Prius the finger as we flashed. "The right seat guy was waving a gun."

Rudy said, "Damned Russians. Did he try to collude with you? Want to report him to the media?"

"He tried to *collide*. Collude is different, you redneck."

"Black people can't be rednecks."

"So you say. How about we check in with Raven if the phone still works? He'll be overjoyed to hear how we saved his ass."

"Give it a try."

The phone worked. I gave Raven a report, ending it with, "Prius is down. No sign of the red Corvette."

Raven said, "I know where it is."

"Where?"

"Tucked in tight on my rear bumper. They must know about their buddies being down. They're not surveilling, they're stalking me.

"I'm not going to be able to outrun them. Right now there is a lot of traffic, but they'll go active when it thins out."

"Copy that, Raven."

"I need you to alert Scooter One. Tell them to take the 'vette out hard when I draw it by them. I'll call them five out."

Rudy and I exchanged a look. He was twenty over the speed limit and still accelerating.

"Copy that. We're trying to get to you for backup. How fast are you going?"

"I'm tucked in with a pack of traffic. We're doing about the speed limit. If it thins out and I lose my cover, I'll be running flat out. Nothing to lose...."

"Is lethal force authorized?"

There was a long pause. *Too long.*

"Do you copy me, Raven?"

"Standby..."

We waited.

Raven said, "Okay, Guys. Record what I say and relay it to Black and the rest of the team."

"Copy that." I pushed the record sequence. "I'm recording."

"The protocols for the meet I just attended -- *set by the Russians themselves* – specifically allow for the use of lethal force if an agent is interfered with or followed."

"We read the packet."

"I think they want to take me alive. If you can't stop them otherwise, kill them. Option C is authorized on my authority. When I get clear of this threat, we go back to Option B."

"We copy, Raven. Option C is authorized. Call Scooter One when you're five out. They'll be ready. We're coming."

C H A P T E R   T W E N T Y
FULL LETHAL

North of the Robin Williams Tunnel

I'd put both the Scooters on speed dial for my secure phone. We'd have a command net. I was still in bunched up traffic, but it was thinning out.

The Red Corvette was locked in my rearview. I'd teased them a few times. I could out accelerate them, but they might be able to beat me on top speed. It probably didn't matter.

I expected both cars could do over 140 MPH. We'd be road limited, not vehicle limited. At 110, we'd both been airborne much of the time, even on the smooth straight stretch where I'd tested that.

The driver behind me was good. He was comfortable with high speeds. His Vette had been floating worse than my ride and he stayed right with me.

The speed limits in Russia were even higher than in Europe – except for the Autobahn, which famously had no limits. Russia's were typically 150 KPH on good roads, about 90 MPH.

I punched the button. "Raven to Scooters, check in."

"Scooter One is in place. Locked and loaded."

"Scooter Two is rolling. We're about 5 miles past the tunnel."

"Roger that, Scooters. Raven is about 5 minutes from the Wolfback Ridge Road overpass. I'll hit it as fast as I can, but I don't think it will shake my pursuit."

"Scooter One copies." It was Pat, the sniper.

"There is a hundred eighty degree switchback to the left on Wolfback where it wraps back around to Cloudview about half a click in. Not much around there and we'll have to slow considerably. Is that where you're deployed?"

"Affirmative. It's an easy shot."

"That's our kill zone. Do you have armor piercing for your .300 magnum?"

"One up the pipe and the first three in the mag, Raven. Black is here with us. He and Vinnie have M4s. I've got them down by the road on the entry side. Don't need a spotter at that range."

"Raven copies. I'll do what I can to slow the tango and will put up a roadblock after the switchback. I'll be behind my car and shooting low. No fratricide, Scooter One."

"No fratricide. We've set up our angles for crossfire."

"Excellent. I'll give you a call coming off the overpass."

"Scooter One copies."

"Scooter Two copied all that. We'll get there as soon as we can and cover the backdoor. We'll set up about halfway between the overpass and the switchback to seal it off. Will check in when we're in position."

"We have a plan, Scooters. Raven out."

It was bad luck to wish them good luck, but that's what I was hoping for. I felt like we were on the fine line between taking casualties and causing an international incident. It was asking a lot of a team that had only trained together for a few days.

I was two minutes from the overpass doing the speed limit. Show time. Traffic was thin, and the Corvette was hanging about half a mile back with four cars between us. I was coming up on a semi with a triple trailer in the right lane.

It was good cover.

I hit my secure phone. "Scooter One, Raven is two out. It's show time. I'm coming in hot."

"Scooter One copies. Give 'em Hell."

I punched the gas and my tricked out Charger took off like a rocket sled, pushing me back in the seat. I got a glimpse of the Corvette moving to the left lane, as I ducked in front of the semi, watching it fade fast in my rear view.

My speed hit 130 and the overpass was coming up fast. I could see the Vette back in the right lane. He wasn't gaining on me. The semi was fading into the distance and there were no cars between me and the overpass.

I tapped the button that opened up my countermeasures panel. I hit "jammers" twice. That would take out both speed radars and normal cell phones. I placed my finger on the icon that said "smoke." waiting, and then I hit it, immediately breaking hard and moving left, and then right to drift into the off ramp.

The view behind me vanished in a cloud of white that blanketed the entire freeway. I was looking good for the ramp, but was much too fast. Time to see what those oversized disk brakes could do when linked to a Le Mans grade antiskid system. It was supposedly capable of up to 1.4 Gs of deceleration, depending on the road surface.

Fortunately, the ramp was smooth, clean, and even banked a bit the right way. I was leaning hard into the shoulder belts, when I punched the smoke off. The antiskid was cycling frantically and the car shuddered, but I was slowing and more or less under control.

No cross traffic. Thank you, Lord.

I got off the brakes, put on gentle power, blew the stop sign, and drifted left, using the full width of both the ramp and the road, just like I was on a track. I came out pointed the right way with my foot on the gas and my sheet metal still intact.

There was nothing in my rear view when I looked.

I was coming down off the overpass when I saw the Vette again. He'd lost a lot of speed, but he'd made it through the smoke and up the ramp. That was some excellent driving.

"Raven's off the overpass. He's still on me."

"Scooter One copies. We're ready."

I yelled. "Raven's inbound off the ramp."

Vinnie said, "Roger that. I'm on full auto. I'll hose him down."

I gave them a thumbs-up and settled in behind my bipod, looking though my scope up the road. I'd take my first shot well to the left of Vinnie, aiming frontal for the engine block. I should be able to get off two more rounds, one as it passed in front on me, and the last to Vinnie's right.

I relaxed into my shooting mode, taking deep breaths. That's when I saw Raven.

He was coming like a bat out of Hell. He must have been doing well over a hundred. He was on us and by us in a flash. I saw the Vette coming, bright red, and moving fast. I put my crosshairs on the grill, squeezed gently and rode the recoil, shifting to the right.

We were all shooting suppressed, but I still heard Black open up. Three long bursts, maybe six rounds each.

The Vette filled my scope. I estimated the lead, squeezed gently, and saw my round hit just behind the right front wheel well.

I saw glittery objects all over the road. Raven was using his countermeasures. Stainless steel spikes to shred tires.

Vinny opened up then. Short bursts. *Braap Braap Braap.*

I swung more to the right, clearing Vinnie. I could hear Black shooting too. He'd reloaded.

I caught the Vette again in my scope. It was punched full of holes, slowing, and the tire I could see was coming apart. I used that right front tire as my aim point, adjusting just a bit higher and slightly behind.

This time when I fired I was rewarded with an explosion of steam. I'd either cracked the engine block, the cooling system, or both. The Vette's tires were all flat and it was rolling to a stop.

I saw Raven stand up at the right of my field of vision. He'd somehow made it back. He raised an M4 and put four rounds through the windshield.

Double taps. No suppressor. *Bap Bap. Bap Bap.*

I heard Raven yelling. "Cease fire, Scooters. We'll give them a chance to surrender."

The gunfire ceased.

Raven slowly approached the car. Vinnie stood, moved closer, and then kneeled, keeping his M4 leveled at the right door. He had the best position.

Scooter Two magically appeared. It rolled up, stopped well clear, and swung to block the road. Rudy and Terry jumped out, wearing body armor and holding M4s leveled at the tango vehicle. Black was there too, also with an M4 leveled at the Vette.

That surprised me. They must have picked him up somewhere.

Vinnie was about ten feet from the car, Raven the same. I slung my sniper rifle, walked down, and took Vinnie's M4. I aimed it at the Vette and made sure the selector was on auto. Vinnie pulled his side arm and leveled it at the vehicle.

Raven yelled, "Hold your fire, guys. Scooter One and I have clear shots."

"You in the car, if you want to surrender, put your hands up."

A voice came back, "You'll kill us anyway."

Raven said, "Why do you think we were shooting for tires and your engine block? If we wanted to do that, you'd already be dead. Put your hands up."

There was no answer.

Raven said, "I'm not going to risk casualties. Either put your hands up, or we'll toss a grenade in and go home."

"We're Russians. We have diplomatic immunity. You can't arrest us."

"We're not law enforcement. We're not here to arrest you."

There was no answer.

"The protocols for the meet I just attended -- set by you Russians – specifically allow for the use of lethal force if an agent is interfered with or followed. You followed me. You interfered with me. We won't arrest you, but we will kill you. Your choice."

"What happens if we surrender?"

"We are going to tie you up, blindfold you, and give you back to the Russians."

"What Russians?"

Raven said, "I have no idea. I don't give a shit. The lady I met with at the park gave me a number for a burner phone. I'll leave a message that tells them where to find you."

"We surrender."

"Put up your hands, open."

The driver sat up, raising his hands slowly. Then the passenger sat up and raised his left hand. He had blood on his shirt.

Raven said, "Are you fucking with me?"

The driver said, "His arm is broken."

"Okay. You get out. Go around behind the car, keeping your hands up. You help him out. Then I want you both on the ground, spread-eagled. I want to see your hands at all times. Anything goes wrong, you each get two rounds in the head."

The driver looked at Raven. "You were at the meet."

"Your fault, my fault, his fault, nobody's fault, two rounds in the head. Move."

The Russians complied.

Raven slung his rifle. He walked over and stood behind them, his Sig leveled, finger on the trigger. "I need hoods, handcuffs, and duct tape."

"On it," Black said. He'd walked up behind me.

The Russian driver said, "Do you want to know our names?"

Raven said, "Actually, I do not, but we will take your weapons and IDs, just to be tidy."

Vinnie got them secured and put their hoods on. Black collected their weapons and Vinnie got their IDs. We put them next to their car in the shade, face-down, handcuffed, and with their ankles duct taped together.

"My friend is bleeding," the driver said. His voice was muffled.

Raven said, "Good point. Anyone want to bandage him up?"

Black said, "I can."

"Do it."

When Black was done, Raven asked. "Is that better?"

"Is better."

"Good. Have a nice day. If I see either of you again, I will kill you."

We left them there next to the Vette, got into our vehicles, loaded up, and drove off.

CHAPTER TWENTY ONE
RUSSIAN REFLECTIONS

Fairmont Hotel, San Francisco, Golden Gate Suite, Two weeks later

Karlov was optimistic today, almost chatty. His new arrangements were impressive, even luxurious, which was unusual for the FSB.

Something had changed.

Karlov said, "This is larger than some of my Moscow apartments. Fifty nine square meters."

I translated in my head. *Six hundred and forty square feet.* "It's quite nice. The view is amazing. The entire skyline, but what is that odd building?"

Karlov smiled. "A quaintly American distortion of ancient art. The Transamerica Pyramid. This suite came with a telescope. Through it, I can see cars on the Golden Gate Bridge. The Americans named this suite after something on the horizon that is barely perceptible, but still an irresistible focus of attention. I find it a fitting location for a covert OPS base."

"A permanent base?"

"Our long-term mission here is sabotaging American shale oil production to benefit Russia's state-owned energy companies, primarily *Rosneft*, but also *Gazprom*. My legend is as a wealthy financial speculator. Do you know *Rosneft*, the firm?"

I shook my head. "Only the name."

"The *Rosneft* project has been lingering and muddling ever since the Obama administration. Do you recall the Western political drama about politicians allegedly conspiring with Putin, and the infamous 35-page dossier prepared by former British MI6 agent Christopher Steele for Senator McCain as part of a soft coup to discredit and unseat President Trump?"

"Only vaguely, Sir. I was busy with other matters...."

"So you were. The wheels grind slowly, the world goes around, and that operational need has faded for the moment. The interests of Russia and America in the energy sector are not in conflict at present. We're back to doing joint ventures with them.

"It took years and a false-flag company, but we now have a long-term lease on this suite. It was 'use it or lose it' situation, and so here we are, invisible to American counter intelligence, to our own embassies, and even to our brother FSB *spetsnaz* directorates, including Yuri Sapunov's much larger anti-terrorism division."

The energy sector is our cover. It will become part of your legend, but our immediate operational focus is elsewhere."

"We have a new mission?"

"An additional mission. We've been re-tasked to an area of higher urgency: *Counterterrorism.* You have done well, my little sparrow. Moscow is pleased.

"Putin himself will be awarding medals, in secret of course, to you, me, and to the leader of your security detail, Yakov Petrovitch."

"Yakov's team ran into trouble after our meet, did they not?"

Karlov said, "Tell me again about this Digger person you met with. He and his associates were most competent. Yakov says they could have easily killed him and his team. They refrained for some reason, even though our own protocols allowed it."

I shrugged. "Mostly we talked about Vogel. Digger argued that we had common interests with him and those he associated with, specifically in destroying terrorism."

"The meet was arranged by the Americans, and Digger claimed to be Canadian."

"His legend is Canadian, but he deflected questions when I probed. I can't speak to who arranged the meet. We didn't discuss it."

"What common interests did he suggest?"

"Removing Vogel was the focus. Digger gave me the targeting for that."

"What else about common interests?"

"The obvious ones. Digger asked me, '*How long would groups like ISIS and Al-Qaida and Hamas and Hezbollah last if Russia and America worked together to totally annihilate them, as we did with Hitler?*' I told him that was irrelevant to our meeting and shifted the discussion to Vogel."

"What about differences?"

"Digger somehow knew that we had him targeted. He almost aborted our meet. I signaled Yakov to stand down and we got past it."

"Not really. Yakov's team decided it was necessary to follow Digger to protect you."

"In violation of the agreed to protocols?"

"Yakov can be a bit heavy handed at times. Do you know his background?"

I shook my head.

"The Americans have their September 11, 2001. We have our September 1, 2004."

"The Beslan Massacre, the school where Islamic terrorists took over 1,100 people as hostages including 777 children. It ended with the deaths of 334 people, including 186 children."

"Yakov was a young Captain at the time. The terrorists held the school for three days. Our forces attacked on the third day with heavy weapons after explosions rocked the school and children started escaping. We took heavy losses. Most of our officers were killed trying to protect escaping children from gun fire."

"How many did we lose?"

Karlov said, "There are only 10 names on the Special Forces monument in Beslan, but we lost more. The fatalities included all three commanders of the assault group: Colonel Oleg Ilyin, Lieutenant Colonel Dmitry Razumovsky of Vega, and Major Alexander Perov of Alpha. Perov's second-in-command at time was Captain Yakov."

"He took it personally."

"You might say that. President Putin's powers were increased and the purges began after Beslan. Yakov got bloody revenge, some say for his commander, some say for the children. After Beslan, there was a period of several years without suicide attacks in and around Chechnya.

The Americans noticed. In 2008, the American Carnegie Endowment's *Foreign Policy Magazine* named Russia as "the worst place to be a terrorist," particularly highlighting our willingness to prioritize national security over civil rights. There were suggestions that America and Russia could work together."

I said, "Then President Obama was elected...."

Karlov nodded. "True, but what's more relevant now is that the person providing the funding for Beslan is alleged to have been our friend Dr. Vogel, the man we targeted as a result of your meet. It's why I asked you if Digger was a Canadian."

"I don't understand."

"Your targeting said Niagara Falls, New York. It was correct. Vogel was there, and I dispatched Yakov to give this his personal attention. We have him. We got in and out clean, and the Americans have nothing to complain about."

"Because we had a valid arrest warrant for Vogel?"

"We had an arguably legal right to take him, but there is more. Doctor Vogel came anonymously, low profile, under an assumed name, apparently for a love tryst with some woman. He did not bring his personal security detail, just one guard and his driver, who stayed in a separate building. Officially he's still at the UN in New York attending meetings."

"We snatched him and were gone before there was an official alarm?"

"There was no alarm. There still hasn't been one. Just some local news reports of some missing lovers. It was like stealing candy from a baby. We didn't even have to drug him and smuggle him out across the Canadian border."

"Why not?"

"Vogel, as a geriatric billionaire trying to impress a woman young enough to be the granddaughter of one of his early wives, chose to stay in the most luxurious accommodations in the area, the Hilton Niagara Falls – actually in the Falls View Suite itself, so-named for the vista, through floor-to-ceiling windows, of **both** the American and Canadian falls."

"So?"

"That hotel is in Ontario."

"In Canada? How convenient."

"Yakov is personally escorting Vogel to Moscow. We dropped an Aeroflot flight into London International Airport, which is oddly named and little known. It is located in Ontario, the 20th busiest airport in Canada, and officially an entry and exit port.

"The Lubyanka awaits Vogel. Not only do we have him, we can take as long as we wish for his interrogation and execution. Vakov reports that Vogel is already blathering about major terrorist operations planned in the United States and Russia, bartering for his life."

I said, "This is huge."

"It is historically huge, both for Russia and the world. Vogel is involved in virtually every major destabilization or terrorist operation in the world. He provides funding and pulls the strings for world leaders, terrorists, and revolutionaries all over the planet.

"Russia gets the entire take from his interrogation. The value of that is unprecedented."

I said, "This will bring down governments and change the world power balance."

"Correct, and in a major way. Putin told me that you and I share the credit for bringing Vogel down. He said that you and I are in "For Merit to the Fatherland" medals, the highest award Russia has for civilians."

"What of Yakov? He came close to disrupting my meet with Digger, and, according to his own words, even closer to getting his team killed."

Karlov smiled thinly. "You are perceptive, my sparrow. This part is fascinating to me. I'll be interested to see how it all unfolds. Putin is clever like a fox."

"How so?"

"Yakov survived the near annihilation of his team because they all survived. Two are in hospitals and all were shaken up, but no permanent damage was inflicted. For one of our best Alpha teams to be taken down so easily is a valuable learning experience. This will make Russia stronger."

"He gets a medal for that?"

"No. Yakov gets his medal later, despite that, and only **after** he manages to keep the man he loathes – one who was key to killing his commander and a school full of children before his eyes – alive long enough to ring every possible iota of information from him."

Karlov met my eyes. "Don't you think that result deserves a medal?"

I looked down, keeping my silence.

"I need an answer, Marie."

"Yakov is difficult to work with. He is filled with hate. It makes him impulsive."

"I won't dispute that. A broken beer bottle is a better weapon than an intact bottle."

"You've put me into difficult situations, Sir. I was lucky to make it out of France."

"We got you out."

"Sometimes I sense threats. Occasionally the hair goes up on the back of my neck. There are times when I've scrubbed a meet or liquidated a source for reasons I can't fully explain."

"You have an excellent mission sense, Marie. I've not seen better, and I've been doing this for a long time."

"I was sitting there that Sunday in the park, feeling the warm sun on my face, tasting the breeze, doing my job, when Digger causally mentioned that there was a sniper behind him, a sniper he couldn't see, a sniper that he could not have detected during his approach, a sniper who had him targeted for a kill."

"So?"

"I felt a chill. Like someone walking over my grave."

Karlov said, "Yakov was going to blow your meet."

"What I felt was that Yakov was going to get **me** killed by mistake and all because he was angry, filled with hate, and too eager to kill."

"Did this Digger person threaten you?"

"Not at all, Sir. He was polite. He was calm. When I gave Yakov the stand-down and pretended there was no one there, Digger pretended to believe me."

"But he did not?"

"No, Sir, I don't think he did…."

"Your stand-down order saved the meet. It got us the Intel to snatch Vogel."

"It did, Sir. The thing is that if Yakov had pulled the trigger, I have a strong sense that I would not have survived the day myself."

"What are you trying to say, Marie?"

"This isn't France, Sir."

"Could you put that more plainly?"

"If you wish, Sir."

Karlov nodded. "Please do."

"Whoever it is we're dealing with, they are helping us, are they not?"

"They are."

"I don't think we should fuck with them."

CHAPTER TWENTY TWO
COVFEFE HAPPENS

The Ranch, Mendocino, California, Main Lodge, Morning

Goldfarb had come in last night along with Mike. Over dinner, we'd introduced Mike to Josie. He'd brought his wife along, name of Gerry, an interesting woman, scary smart. She had a Phi Beta Kappa in Physics with a Master's Degree. She'd minored in math and had been a Senior Program Manager at NSA, which was how she and Mike had met.

Gerry was the sister of John Giles who ran Cybertech, the geeks who had developed our secure phones. More interesting to me was that her dad was Iron John, a retired Spec OPs Colonel who'd vanished over a decade ago. Her Grandfather on her mother's side was none other than General George S. Patton of WW II fame. That was a lot of Red White and Blue heritage.

Mike had started off with a similar role relative to Gerry as what I had with Josie, trying to keep her safe as a key National Security asset. They'd run into similar issues with terrorists as what Josie and I faced. He'd kept her safe, but they'd lost Iron John along the way.

No one was happy about that. John's likely abductor was an Islamic terrorist we'd encountered ourselves, one Ahmed Mahmoud Muhammad.

The women hit it off well. They would not be attending the Covfefe meeting. I was there giving a command performance, primarily tasked to report on my assignment from Goldfarb and President Blager, but also to be respectful, answer questions, and to not crap on the table. Mike was there as a respected retired Marine General to provide a semblance of accountability. In theory, Mike was filling in for Goldfarb as my control.

There were concerns at the NSC level about our "rogue operations." The Covfefe committee was apparently an effort to show that we earned our keep and would not cause political embarrassment to NSC or the President.

Goldfarb's presence as an ad hoc member of the National Security Council was itself controversial. He was there to advise the President and to de-conflict our OPs with NSC. In effect, the Covfefe committee was an effort by Goldfarb and President Blager to legitimize our mission to the Joint Chiefs and get their needed support for things best not discussed.

Goldfarb and the President were walking a tightrope. At times, we needed to tap Military support on an urgent basis. For that we needed a legitimate existence. To do our jobs, we needed to stay off the books, deep black, lethal, and unaccountable.

The key people we had to convince to trust us were the President's National Security advisor Peter Neumann, a known skeptic of covert OPs, and Admiral Brandon Quigley, the Chairman of the Joint Chiefs of Staff. The Covfefe committee was the President's attempt to ensure oversight and accountability, to have Constitutional compliance without interference or visibility.

The stakes were about as high as they could get.

President Blager kicked the meeting off at 0900, making brief introductions before turning it over to Goldfarb. The room was secure. The cyber geeks – both the President's and Mike's – had checked it twice for bugs. It was intrinsically a secure room with no windows, but no one was taking chances.

Electronic devices of any type were left outside. The Secret Service had the building sealed off. The Ranch's duty team secured the Perimeter. What with three recent assassination attempts on the President, security was taking no chances. There was a pair of Apache helicopters on hot standby at the airport and a flight of F-16s in Klamath Falls.

Goldfarb looked around the room. "Thank you for coming. We have a lot of talent assembled here, hopefully enough to resolve issues so we can move forward.

"This committee was formed to improve coordination of the efforts of a small, deep black antiterrorism team. In direct support of the President, we've been running intelligence gathering operations off the grid. Raven – he gestured at me – is our lead operative. The methods we use are unconventional.

"We've been effective. That has attracted attention of the wrong kind. My operatives have been repeatedly attacked on American soil. This illuminates our need to better coordinate our efforts so we can tap resources to defend our operations and better neutralize the threats we do identify."

Admiral Quigley said, "What is the nature of the threats?"

Goldfarb said, "Primarily Islamic *jihad*. The most recent ones seem to have been linked to Iran. We believe that Quds teams are now operating on America soil."

National Security Advisor Neumann interrupted, "That's speculative, Aaron."

"We deal with the speculative. It's the nature of our work. We're not lawyers and we are not in law enforcement. Our mission is to identify terrorist threats and neutralize them. The two most recent attacks were by Quds affiliated terrorists. You got to see one up close at Camp David. The other was against my assets in Monterey, specifically Raven and one of our researchers."

Goldfarb pointed at me. Heads swiveled. I found myself looking into every pair of eyes in the room.

I said, "They were after me and my assets in Monterey. Had we been there, they would have overwhelmed us. At Camp David the primary target was surely the President, but it was timed to also target the NSC."

"The FBI has legal purview of those attacks," Neumann said.

"The FBI was devastated in Monterey. They lost 11 people, with three wounded, two of them critically. They have now been blocked from the crime scene by the State of California. It's not going well."

"The FBI still has the legal purview," Neumann said.

"No one disputes that, Peter," the President said. "You asked about threats. There is no dispute that Quds is now operating here in America. It's a threat. Raven's team was the first to identify it."

Admiral Quigley said, "Raven mentioned that his team's efforts had been effective. Perhaps we should ask him to expand on that."

The President said, "Would it save time if I *stipulated* that Raven's team saved my life *twice* in Monterey *before* Quds showed up? When I was poisoned, they helped me recover after the doctors lost hope. When I was attacked again, they thwarted it. Dr. Goldfarb put his body between me and a *jihadi* assassin in the process."

Neumann said, "The Secret Service has that responsibility, Sir. It doesn't need to tap DOD resources to do its job."

Goldfarb said, "Like Hell it doesn't. It took air strikes to stop the Camp David attack."

Mike said, speaking for the first time. "For one thing, the FBI does **not** have an *exclusive* authority to investigate crimes. For another, the notion of treating terrorists as criminals severely limits our options. We'd get better results if we'd view them as what they are – Illegal enemy combatants. The Blager Protocol was a good move as was GITMO."

Goldfarb said, "There are a number of groups tasked with our National Security, including the protection of the President and his staff. Responsibilities overlap. Sometimes they conflict. The Covfefe committee was formed in the hope of preventing turf wars so we can concentrate on eliminating terrorists."

"Precisely," The President said. "This is a good discussion."

Admiral Quigley said, "Could the FBI or Secret Service prevent a terrorist ship-based EMP attack on our Homeland with Iranian nuclear weapons?"

Neumann said, "That sounds like your job, Admiral."

"Correct," Quigley said. "It's why I'm here. Let us suppose that there was such an attack, that it was thwarted, and the details can't be discussed here unless the President chooses to read more people in on it, which I do not recommend."

Neumann looked at the President, who said, "We are not going to go there."

"I'd like to get back to the agenda, if I may," Goldfarb said.

"Are there any objections?" the President said.

No one spoke.

"Good," Goldfarb said. "Before the Covfefe team was formed, I was the control for Raven's team. While this was coming together, we left him with a list of seven names of people who were major threats to our national security.

"We'd been purely defensive. This was a test case for offense. Action including lethal force was authorized."

"There were strict constraints," the President said.

"Yes," Goldfarb said. "I'm here to report on the first two names on the list. I'll spare Raven that task, as this is now in the media. Who is the top terrorist in the world? Who has killed the most people? Our candidate is Claas Vogel."

"Vogel is not a terrorist," Neumann said. "He's a philanthropic patron of social causes, a humanitarian respected by both parties."

Goldfarb said, "Vogel buys and sells politicians and governments. His touch is all corrupting and impossible to prove legally. There are a number of nations who **have** branded him as a terrorist and several — Egypt, Israel, and Russia come to mind — that have active international arrest warrants for him, for war crimes, financial terrorism, or both. Russia has a bounty out on him of over $10 million, dead or alive."

Neumann looked at the President. "We can't touch Vogel, Sir. Why are we talking about this?"

The President said, "We're **not** talking about it. Dr. Goldfarb is merely giving us a report. We're listening. I'd like to hear what he has to say."

"Yes, Sir."

"Proceed, Aaron," the President said.

"Vogel has a home in New York and spends a lot of time at the UN. According to a few local Canadian news sources, he apparently had a recent assignation with a woman in Niagara Falls at a resort hotel. He's gone missing.

"The woman was traveling under a false identity. She is being held by the Canada Border Services Agency (CBSA). Vogel had two security guards. They were found tied up in their room. They say that Vogel was abducted by the Russians. The Canadians are holding them as witnesses."

Neumann said, "What do the Russians say?"

"Essentially nothing," Goldfarb said. "The local Embassy says they know nothing about it. Foreign Minister Sergey Lavrov gave a 'no comment,' except to state that Russia has a valid arrest warrant for Vogel. Which is a true statement. They do. We consider their warrant valid."

"What do our Intelligence agencies say?" the President said.

"I have no idea, Sir," Goldfarb said. "Nor do I want to unless it comes up at NSC. If it does, my recommendation would be that we stay out of it. Whatever happened or didn't happen was on Canadian soil."

The President said, "Perhaps the Canadians will sort it out. I guess that takes Vogel off your task list, unless or until he resurfaces."

"Yes, Sir, Goldfarb said. "Does anyone have questions?"

Mike and I shook our heads. No one spoke.

"Good," the President said. "What was the second name?"

"Number two was Marco Ricci. He's an Italian citizen and a UN official. Officially he is Secretary General of UNCTAD, the UN Conference of Trade and Development. He reports to the General Assembly. He's been there for years. He has diplomatic immunity and high level political connections in Italy. He is also untouchable by the United States."

Admiral Quigley said, "Officially a UN Trade official. What is he unofficially?"

"Let me guess," the President said drily. "A Vogel agent?"

Goldfarb said, "We have no proof, but we think he was Vogel's bagman and cut out for some of the recent domestic terrorist acts we've been facing. Now that the FBI is looking into Monterey, perhaps they could validate that. It might help them sort out the most recent attack if they are given purview and track the money.

"I'm here to report that Ricci is off our action list and close that out. There is an article in the **New York Times** that reports he is dead."

Goldfarb stopped talking and looked around the room. No one spoke. He shrugged.

"That concludes my report, Sir. I've crossed off the top two names. That leaves five pending. I'd like Raven to report on their status."

The President said, "The top two. One missing and one dead. What happened to Ricci?"

Goldfarb said, "I'm not sure, Sir. Apparently he was keeping a mistress and chose to walk home through Manhattan in the early morning hours without his security detail. They found his body in an alley not far from the UN. According to the **Times** he fell and hit his head."

The President said, "Were there any signs of foul play?"

"There may have been. The **Times** said there is an active homicide investigation. There is a lot of attention being paid to this case in New York. It's still a sanctuary city, as you know. One of their sources mentioned a person of interest, a woman, but the police wouldn't comment."

"The mistress?"

"No idea, Sir. It's just a rumor. It could have been a mugging. All I know is what's been in the media. I would expect that the Canadian and New York police might be talking because of the Vogel connection, but, if so, it's not been in the news."

"That's my report." Goldfarb looked around the room. "For us, there is no action required for the top two names on our list. Are there any questions?"

No one spoke.

After a long moment, the President said, "Thank you, Aaron. Let's take a break before we hear about the rest."

When I came back in the room, the President and Admiral Quigley were sitting together, having an intense discussion. I hesitated, not wanting to interrupt.

The President waved me in. "We're done. The rest will be right in. How long do you need?"

"Not long, Sir. Maybe ten minutes. It depends on what questions I get, Sir."

Goldfarb entered in time to hear that.

The President looked at him. "That went well. Let's try to keep this part to ten minutes if we can, Aaron. We have other issues to discuss."

"Right." When everyone was seated, Goldfarb pointed at me. "Raven will cover the last five names. It should not take long and we need to keep this rolling."

I stood. "There are three names where action is deemed to be either impossible, imprudent, or both. I think we can deal with those quickly. The first of these is Dunwood Dunbar."

"*The Vice President?*" Neumann sounded horrified.

The President said, "Former Vice President. He resigned. Yes, Dunbar is off the list. Dead horses and all that…."

"Right," I said. "The next name claimed to be a CIA agent with the legend of Smith. That was false. He did wet work for LBJ, decades ago. He is now almost eighty years old, Barton Raymond Blackwood III, an oil speculator from Houston."

The President said, "He's off the list because this is ancient history?"

"No, Sir. He's off our list for two reasons. For one thing, he's in Iran, well connected there and a bit hard to reach, even if we wanted to. The second reason is that we've doubled him, or at least we think we did."

"He's working for us?"

I shrugged. "In theory, Sir. He's not been active since before the Iran deal. Presumably he's keeping his head down and staying out of US jurisdiction."

Goldfarb said, "He's not a problem and might again be useful to us. I just wanted to revisit that."

I said, "Correct. He's off the list, and it's best if everyone in the room forgot they heard that name. If we blow him – and we're not the best about leaks – he's a dead man."

"I concur," the President said. "Forget the name, he's off the list."

"Right," I said. "We have mixed emotions about the last of the three, a Black minister, Reverend Dilbert Jones. He got one of our agents killed. He runs the Trinity Church in Monterey. He was hosting a Black Lives Matter kill team that had you targeted, Mr. President."

"So why isn't he on the list?"

"I think you can thank the late Mr. Ricci, Sir. There was a management dispute. The BLM team was replaced by Islamic *jihadists*. That was a bridge too far for Reverend Jones. He threw them out of his church."

"What happened to the *jihadists*?" the President said.

"We killed them at Monterey," Goldfarb said. "Some at the safe house where they attacked Raven and his team and the rest at the makeshift hospital at the Presidio where they came for you."

I said, "The Reverend is hostile to America, but he has political and media connections. He won't work with Islamists. The current threats out there are from Quds."

"He's off the list, Sir," Goldfarb said.

"Agreed," the President said.

"Good," I said. "That leaves us with two names. Both are hard core *jihadists* at the management level. The first is a Hamas leader, Firouz, who ran kill teams out of the UN. In the Old Persian tradition, he didn't use a surname. He was so heavy-handed that Vogel himself sent him back to Iran.

"The second is Akbar Safdari, a lower level commander. We think he was in charge of the attacks in Durham that targeted me and my team."

Admiral Quigley said, "The ones that left part of the city in flames?"

"Yes, Sir."

"You've been busy," Quigley said.

Goldfarb said, "We've been lucky, Admiral. Hence the Covfefe team."

The President said, "What do you want to do with the last two names?"

I said, "We lack the resources to take direct action, but things have been heating up in Iran. If we make any airstrikes against their nuclear facilities, we can provide GPS coordinates. A smart bomb or two should suffice, Sir."

"Collateral damage," Quigley said. "That should be possible."

"I hope so," I said. "That concludes my presentation. Thank you for your time."

The President said, "Now you know a bit about what this team has been doing, what they have suffered, and what they have accomplished. You know less about how they do their job. That is need-to-know. Suffice it to say that they can get us Intel that we simply cannot obtain from other methods. Their sources and methods must be protected."

Quigley said, "I'd like to make a motion that we report back to the NSC our unanimous commendation of the Covfefe team, and that we thank their operatives for their professionalism, discretion, and service."

"Second," Neumann said.

Goldfarb and I exchanged a look. *Wow. Didn't expect that.*

"Are there any objections?" Goldfarb said. "Hearing none, so moved. With the President's permission, I will report that back to the NSC."

"Granted, with pleasure," the President said. "The Admiral has some issues we must ponder and resolve, concerns from the Chiefs of Staff. Before we get to that, I have a question for Raven personally and I need a candid answer."

All the eyes were on me again. I looked at Goldfarb, who nodded, then back at the President.

"I'm aware of the thankless sacrifices you and your team have endured, Raven, not just recently when you barely missed being annihilated in Monterey, but for years now. I want to know something."

"Sir?"

"What do you want? What can America do to repay your service?"

I knew the answer. Josie and I had discussed it.

"Resurrection, Sir."

The president frowned. "Coming back from the dead? I'm not sure we can do that. You will need to explain."

"After our first major OP, when we prevented the EMP attack, we were devastated. My entire team was wounded, I thought we'd lost Josie, and I blamed myself. We made it through that. We found redemption."

"But...."

"But this is like trying to empty the ocean with a teaspoon. My small team is fighting a planet-wide generational war against *jihad* and other forms of terrorism. It is like fighting an army of a billion zombies. All they know is the Quran and to hate."

I gestured at Admiral Quigley. "Our military faces a different aspect of the same situation. Using our military against terrorists is like swinging a 600 pound flyswatter. It's ineffective and costly.

The military has a full plate of warfighting threats. Rogue states with nuclear weapons. Ambitious rivals with powerful militaries like China and Russia. The new threat we're going to discuss here, I hope, an Iranian military presence here in America with local political support."

Quigley said, "Amen."

The President nodded. "The first two items are on Admiral Quigley's list to discuss here. The last is on my list to reveal. That's the rest of our meeting."

I blinked. "Good."

"I'll ask again what you seek, Raven."

"**Resurrection**. We're good at what we do, Sir. We can win a dozen or a hundred times against the odds, but sooner or later, we'll lose. If we do, America will lose irreplaceable resources. It almost happened in Monterey.

"We were lucky. We slipped out. The FBI wandered into **our** war zone and they paid the price. We live in the dark, but we'll die there if we can't get military help when we need it."

CHAPTER TWENTY THREE
THE BIG PICTURE

The Ranch, Mendocino, California, Main Lodge, Afternoon

Goldfarb had brought in a whiteboard so he could lecture. We were not keeping notes or electronic records.

"Essentially, what we are proposing for Raven's team is an American version of what the Israelis have used since the 1970s, essentially a *Kidon* team. The name comes from the Hebrew word for bayonet, the tip of the spear. The mission is narrow: liquidation, targeted assassinations.

You are probably familiar with this. It's the stuff of legends, featured in books and movies. Check any Daniel Silva novel."

Heads nodded.

"On rare occasions – for example, Operation Orchard in 2007 that took out a nuclear reactor in Syria – *Kidon* has teamed with other elite groups, in that case 69 Squadron and *Sayeret Matkal*, General Staff Reconnaissance, a group that is modeled after Britain's SAS to do deep reconnaissance in hostile territories. The closest thing we have to that is Delta Force.

"*Kidon* does assassinations. They have more generalized teams like *Nevoit*, a special operations team that handles surveillance, interrogation, sabotage, or theft. This is a general outline. Even though Israel is a close ally, there is almost no reliable information available."

Mike said, "We pretend we are at peace and wish it were true. They know they are at war for their survival and wish it was false."

"Essentially correct," Goldfarb said. "The role of *Kidon* is counter terrorist operations almost exclusively, but it can assist Mossad in other capacities. In the case of Operation Orchard, they probably liquidated Muhammad Suleiman, a general and Special Presidential Advisor for Arms Procurement and Strategic Weapons to Syrian president Bashar Al-Assad."

Mike said, "Probably? Who said so?"

"The Iranian press blamed Israel, saying Suleiman was shot by a silenced weapon in the head and neck on a beach at al Rimal al Zahabiyeh resort near Tartous on 1 August 2008. WikiLeaks said that France told the U.S. that Suleiman was probably killed as a result of rivalry within the Syrian government. The Germans had a different view. *Der Spiegel* gave a detailed description of Suleiman's murder as having taken place by rifle shots from a passing yacht and implied that it was linked to his involvement in Al Kibar and an upcoming visit to Tehran."

I had to laugh. "Iran blamed Israel, France blamed the Syrians, and the Germans blamed Iran? These *Kidon* people are damned good at blowing smoke."

Goldfarb said, "It gets better. In 2015, a National Security Agency document leaked by Edward Snowden claimed that Israeli naval commandos were behind Suleiman's killing."

I said, "So no one has a clue. *Beautiful....*"

"Yes," Goldfarb said. "This is a good example of operational success and how hidden and deeply subterranean OPs like this have to be in today's world. If we are not willing and able to operate at that level, with layers of deception, we should not be in the game."

"Can we do that?" the President asked. "It doesn't sound like us."

"We have a proposal."

The President nodded and Mike said, "I think we can. To do it formally and consistently, we'll need cover at the policy level. We'll start with that."

"We already have the Blager Codicil for dealing with Islamic *jihad*. Thank you, General Pershing. It is now embedded into our treaties. Congress quibbled, but has not objected."

"Correct," the President said.

"We have an environment of major threats to our Presidents. President Trump received numerous threats of assassination, both foreign and domestic. President Blager just survived two attempts on his life."

"Three," Goldfarb said. "There were two in Monterey and then one more at Camp David."

"Three, so far," the President said.

"Three attempts on your life," Mike said, "and all from Islamic terrorism. Would it be possible to get a formal Declaration of War against Islamic Terrorism from Congress, Sir?"

The President glanced at Neumann, his National Security Advisor, who was looking unhappy. "What do you think, Peter?"

"We'd have to prepare the public. Your popularity is good. It's a political issue. It probably depends on the polls, how much public support we can get, and how the winds are blowing in Congress. The media would surely go off on one of their diversions to jam it up. I don't favor the idea, Sir."

"Why not?"

Neumann said, "The last time we had a formal Declaration of War from Congress was after Pearl Harbor, Sir. We've never declared war against anything but a Nation State. It's probably just as well. Invading Iraq was not the right way to stop *jihad*."

Goldfarb said, "We've perverted the word 'war' to cover social causes. We've had the War on Poverty, the War on Drugs, and so forth. We've not won one of those fake wars yet.

"Changing the *meaning* of words is an old socialist tactic. We did have the Cold War. It was undeclared, but clearly understood and terrifying. Doctor Strangelove and all that…."

Mike said, "The Israelis manage to run their *Kidon* OPS without formalities. I don't think killing foreign *jihadists* would be an issue. Of that list of seven names, only three were American citizens. We passed on two, and it seems the Russians handled Vogel for us."

Admiral Quigley said, "Domestic terrorism is a problem. We're still rooting out *jihadists* from the military. Floods of them came in when we had open borders. We now have second and third generation terrorists. One saboteur who wants to suicide could take out a warship."

I said, "The Fort Hood terrorist killed thirteen. He was tried and convicted as a criminal, for mass murder, not as a terrorist. He's never been executed, and this despite millions of dollars and years of effort."

The President said, "Would the Joint Chiefs favor treating *jihadists* in the military as terrorists, as illegal enemy combatants?"

Quigley said, "In a heartbeat, Sir. All branches of the services have voiced major concerns."

The President looked at Neumann, "We have an action item for NSC. Let's get it on the agenda, not as a Covfefe matter, but as a military matter and a national security issue. I want this done in a form that gets us a formal legislative approval from Congress to use military tribunals."

"Yes, Sir."

"Back to Covfefe," the President said. "How can we best enable and protect Raven's team?"

Goldfarb made a note on his whiteboard, "**Point one:** accountability. It's accountable **only** to the Covfefe committee under the authority of President Blager. To other parts of the government, it doesn't exist. If someone says '*Kidon*' we talk about Israelis. Our *Kidon* unit is to be dissolved and all records destroyed at the end of the President's tenure in office or when Islamic terrorism is no longer deemed to be a major threat to America."

He looked around the room. No one spoke. He made another note.

"**Point two:** the mission. The primary mission is intelligence and counter terrorism with a special focus on Islamic *jihad*. The *Kidon* unit can also operate in other capacities to assist the National Security needs of POTUS."

There were no comments.

"Good," Goldfarb said. "Here's the one that may get sticky. **Point three:** Support. We need Cyber support, OP SEC, and perhaps some special tools and weapons. Routine needs will be provided by Mike's company, TSG, The Security Group. Access to additional support will be supplied as needed under the authority of the NSC."

"Examples?" Quigley said.

I replied, "We have special secure phones from TSG. We have a small personal security detail, four people, much like Blackwater used to provide in war zones. Military weapons are needed, mostly small arms. We often need to do Cyber research, sometimes hacking…."

"Understood. I have no problem with that."

"Excellent." I said, "I expect it's the additional, non-routine support we need that might be an issue."

"Quigley said, "Are we talking about things like air strikes, missiles, and assault teams on short notice?"

"I'm afraid so."

"On US soil?"

"Yes, Sir. Possibly."

Neumann said, "That's excessive. It's unreasonable. It might be illegal."

Goldfarb said, "Raven's not talking about future speculations. The need has already been demonstrated. Durham. Monterey. Camp David."

"Such situations can be avoided by proper planning…."

Mike shook his head. "Two decades ago, I had a small gunned up Marine Force supporting a key project for President Carson Hale and NSA. We were too thin and we were too late. We lost Iron John to *jihadists* in Oregon.

"TSG has a dog in this fight too. Cybertech was John's company. Today it is our operational support and John's daughter is my wife."

"You are letting personal matters influence your judgment," Neumann said.

"No," Mike said. "I'm saying we need to **kill** terrorists. At times, that might take a major application of force."

"You have law enforcement."

"Bad idea," Goldfarb said. "Bringing in law enforcement pulls them into highly lethal kill zones. It was local police in Durham. It was the FBI in Monterey, and that one is a long way from being over."

Neumann started to speak, but Admiral Quigley held up his hand. "What?"

Quigley said, "A *Kidon* team needs adequate military support. If we don't supply it, they will fail. If they fail, they will be overwhelmed, and they will die. Then the bad guys will prevail and American citizens will die. In some cases – an EMP or bioweapons attack – we are talking about *millions* of casualties and moving America back to a pre-industrial nation."

"Yes." Goldfarb said. "Those are the stakes."

"There are other issues," the President said. "Some of the people on Raven's team are National Treasures. Losing them puts the entire nation at risk. *This team is not expendable.*"

Neumann said, "Sir, you know that the Joint Chiefs…."

"Will shit bricks if tasked with missions like we are discussing," Quigley said.

Neumann opened his mouth, looked at the Admiral, and finally said, "Yes."

The President looked bemused. He was watching the Admiral.

Quigley met his eyes, "He's not overstating that, Mr. President. The Joint Chiefs have concerns. The political history of NSC tends to exacerbate their fears. A tasking like we are discussing is like waving a red flag. I will need some time to get their agreement. We have problems, Sir, and I need to apprise this group, and you, of the sensitivities."

"Is a half hour sufficient?"

"If you want me to take questions, I'd like at least forty-five minutes, Sir."

"Granted." The President looked at Goldfarb. "Are we about done?"

"Almost, Sir. I have one last topic." Goldfarb marked on the whiteboard, and said "**Point four**: Constitutional compliance. This item could get you impeached if we screw it up."

"Go ahead."

"**Point four**: Constitutional compliance. Operations against U.S. citizens to require a Constitutional review and opinion by the Chief Justice, SCOTUS. No notes will be kept."

President Blager looked around the room. "Any comments? Anything to add?"

"It's a start," Quigley said. "We may have to adjust things when we get going."

"That's expected," Goldfarb said.

"No plan survives contact with the enemy," Mike said.

The President said. "The requested policy framework – formally declaring war against terrorism and having military tribunals for terrorists – is beyond the powers of the Executive Branch. It's a needed political discussion, but I see the effort as mostly symbolic."

"Congress would have to take the lead," Neumann said.

"Yes. Let's get that started. Get me a meeting with the House Majority leader and whatever committee heads he deems appropriate."

"Yes, Sir."

The President said, "Correct me if I'm wrong, but even if we **had** such an approval it would not change a thing about how our *Kidon* team was operating."

"Correct," Goldfarb said. "The last spies we executed were the Rosenbergs, back in 1953. It was a mess. Harvard law professor Alan Dershowitz wrote the best summary: The Rosenbergs were 'guilty – and framed.' If we find a traitor, it is better that they just disappear."

"Agreed," the President said. "The effort to clarify the terrorism threat is needed, but it is a political exercise. As such, it has no operational overlap to the Covfefe committee."

"Yes, Sir."

"I would like to extend Doctor Goldfarb's Point four. I want more than Constitutional compliance. I want to inflict some moral certainty in addition to our having a legal fig leaf."

"Sir?"

"I do **not** want this Covfefe team effort to have any resemblance to some of the past disasters our Republic suffered. I will NOT tolerate any use of our intelligence assets to target my political enemies. Nor do I want to see a trail of 'Clinton body bags' piling up behind you. Do you understand me?"

Mike and Goldfarb said, "Yes, Sir."

Then they all looked at me.

"Raven?" the President said.

"I agree, Sir. That's why we took your former Vice President, Mr. Dunbar, off our action list. He was taking money from Vogel to betray America. He's an asshole and he's dangerous, but there would be no end to it if we started targeting all the assholes in Washington. A public trial, if needed, would be better than making him a martyr."

The President blinked.

Goldfarb said drily, "Raven's soft side is coming out, Sir. I think we can thank Josie."

Mike was grinning. "We'll watch. If we see anything getting close to the edge, we'll call a meeting and confer with you first."

"Do that," the President said. "I like the fact that you are working off the books. My administration will not tolerate another Iran/Contra scandal.

"With the exception of whatever concerns the Joint Chiefs may have and the need to get the Chief Justice to agree to Point four, are we okay going forward with the rest of Doctor Goldfarb's points?"

Heads nodded.

"I need to hear yeas or nays."

He got a chorus of yeas. Covfefe was operational.

CHAPTER TWENTY FOUR
GRAVE CONCERNS

The Ranch, Mendocino, California, Main Lodge

Admiral Quigley had taken over Goldfarb's whiteboard. He said he needed to inform us that the Joint Chiefs were less than happy with what he and the President were doing. Our Covfefe committee was less than loved.

"Have you done your homework? Has anyone **not** read the McMaster book about the NSC's purpose, failures, and the consequences, *Dereliction of Duty*? I need a show of hands."

Peter Neumann stuck his hand up. He and the Admiral locked eyes.

The Admiral frowned. "As National Security Advisor, I should think that it's a dereliction of duty on your part to have not read it."

Neumann shrugged. "I read it years ago when I was a serving Army General. It's why I've not been a big fan of the Covfefe team, but I serve the President, as does the NSC. I used to command a tank corps. I understand that getting down into the weeds on these small team issues is something that will not, and should not, appeal to the Joint Chiefs."

I stuck my hand up.

"What's your excuse, Raven?"

"I skimmed the book. The hidden agendas, overblown egos, indifferences to reality, betrayals, and lies turned my stomach. Robert McNamara and Lyndon Johnson made me want to throw up. For what it's worth, I agree that the Joint Chiefs need direct access to the President, just as they had under Eisenhower.

"How the Hell we could put an accountant in charge of a war? It wasn't the Joint Chiefs that failed; it was the insane notion of using a war to 'communicate with the enemy.' I threw the damned book across the room, Admiral."

Quigley shrugged. "McMaster argues the Joint Chiefs should have all resigned."

Mike said, "I don't think it would have made any difference, Sir. Our political leaders, pundits, lawyers, managers, and analysts were psychologically *incapable* of realizing that Hanoi's commitment to revolutionary war made Ho totally indifferent to casualties. They could not wrap their elitist, liberal minds around that reality. Many of them still can't."

The President said, "I liked General Goodpaster's protest to McNamara in the fall of 1964 – 'Sir, you are trying to program the enemy, and that is one thing we must never try to do. We can't do his thinking for him.'

"War is about *killing* the enemy, not *persuading* him. War is horrific and best avoided, but sometimes necessary. Wars can be just, but prolonging one is immoral. UN peacekeepers have never resolved a conflict, Korea being a poster child. Where war gets immoral is getting into one and not ending it as quickly as possible."

Mike said, "Patton got it, Churchill got it, FDR got it, and so did Eisenhower. We have not had a President since who dared speak about killing enemies until you and Trump."

Goldfarb said, "You definitely get it, Sir. That's why we're here."

"I'm starting to. Thanks to Raven, Josie, and you, it finally came to me. When I was dying in that hospital bed in Monterey with all of you working miracles to save me, I swore that if I lived, Islamic terrorism had to stop, that we had to **make** it stop.

"Islamic *jihad* is a generational war and now one with WMDs. Everyone knows that. There are only two examples over the last thousand years where anyone has stopped *jihad* and rolled it back. One was the Crusades and the other was Blackjack Pershing."

"The Blager codicil," Admiral Quigley said.

"Yes."

"Great comments on the McMaster book, incidentally," Quigley said, "even if Raven's copy has bullet holes in it."

There were a few chuckles.

"Like all of us, McMaster is imperfect. He was a legend back in the day, and his focus was on toe to toe war against Russia. The conflict between McMaster and Russia's General Valery Gerasimov was larger than life.

"Both began their careers as junior armor officers. Both were tested in irregular wars against separatists and militant groups. Both had to cope with the rise of disruptive battlefield technologies including drones, precision weapons, and sophisticated new forms of propaganda.

"The two men never met, but they made a career of studying their opponent's moves. It was like Patton and Rommel or Le Carre's fictional Smiley and Karla. Both men had outsize reputations.

"It was American force and resolve pitted against Russian cunning and diversion. For most of that time, we had an overwhelming advantage in conventional forces. Unfortunately, our advantage has been greatly eroded. Our military is depleted. It was shifted from war fighting to social agendas."

Mike said, "Can you give us some examples of Russian cunning and diversion?"

"What we're seeing in Syria and the Ukraine. We dub it as 'hybrid warfare.' It's a combination of traditional military weaponry with powerful non-lethal tools such as cyberwarfare, fake news, and elaborate deception.

"We've forgotten it now, but climate alarmism *started* under Stalin and the old KGB, first as global cooling, then as global warming, and finally as almost anything, from farting cows to exhaling humans. The goal was to deindustrialize the Western Democracies. Remember when Obama was going around saying that Global Warming was more of a danger than ISIS?

Mike said, "I sure do."

"Bad policy, along with socialistic social programs and open borders, drained over a trillion dollars a year out of our economy. America got dragged into regime change efforts that cost American lives. Bad policy depleted, demoralized, and exhausted our military."

Goldfarb said, "$500 million per year went to fund Planned Parenthood. Green jobs wasted more. Both were legal money laundering. Taxpayer money for political donations."

"Right," Quigley said. "To cut to the chase, this is what you need to know. The view from the Joint Chiefs is that we **must** get back to having a significant advantage in our force-on-force warfighting skills. We need new generations of equipment. We need to better maintain and upgrade the equipment we have. We need better training and leadership."

Goldfarb said, "Let me try this, for a one paragraph summary of the Joint Chief's major concern at NSC, where I've been 'embedded,' a source of dismay to some.

"America's true strength lies not in shadowy commando raids or pinprick drone strikes, but in well-equipped land, air, and naval forces working together to clearly demonstrate overwhelming superiority."

Quigley nodded slowly. "I should let you write our white papers, Doctor."

"I would decline. Do you know why?"

"I do. That view leaves no command-level mental space for a Covfefe committee. It discourages high-level military support of small teams like Raven's."

"Exactly."

"How do we fix that?" the President said.

Quigley said, "May I continue just a bit longer with specifics, Sir? This committee deserves to know."

The President nodded.

"The military is more worried about the Russians and the Chinese than they are about Islamic *jihad* or the UN. I could spend days talking about those threats.

"We face missiles that are invisible. America's force projection centers on carrier battle groups that can level a city, sink a fleet, or turn Moscow into a cinder. The problem is that these are blue water ships and not the best resources for keeping narrow straits open."

Goldfarb said, "Invisible missiles?"

"New generation missiles are faster than a speeding bullet. The Russians are already selling Iran short range missiles that run at Mach 3 with depleted uranium warheads, carrier killers. Can we stop them? Maybe, but it's like a knife fight in a telephone booth.

"The Chinese have demonstrated hypersonic ramjets that do Mach 5, roughly 3,800 miles per hour, significantly faster than a high velocity sniper round. That technology, in theory, could get up to Mach 14. The Russians are working on it too.

"Then there are cyber weapons. Do you recall when our warships kept running into large objects like tankers and container ships?"

"Yes, of course. A lot of it was training, experience, and a fleet stretched too thin."

Quigley looked at the President. "Am I cleared to discuss this, Sir?"

He got a nod. "Go ahead. Need-to-know, people. Speculative. Not to be discussed."

"We upgraded our weaponry and navigation systems to GPS. We can fix the position of a ship, aircraft, or smart bomb anywhere on the planet to within inches. But what if the signals are being spoofed? What if we can't trust them?"

Mike said, "We test that in wargames. We jam the GPS signals. We even warn civilian flights when we're doing it."

"We do. The GPS drops out, alarms go off, and pilots can cope by going back to the old systems, Loran, VHF Nav, star sightings, and such. But what if the GPS signals were not jammed? What if they were spoofed instead?"

"Is that possible?"

"It seems so. People were trying to play Pokémon Go on their smart phones in Moscow, but the fake signal, which seemed to center on the Kremlin, relocated anyone nearby to the Vnukovo Airport, 20 miles away."

"Cute," Mike said. "And we're falling behind in conventional weapons as well, I presume?"

"Let's just say it has gotten competitive. The new Russian SU-57 is impressive. Full stealth and 1,200 miles per hour."

"Dear God. Now our national security depends on Pokémon and kids with iPhones?" Goldfarb said incredulously. "Please stop before we go mad, Admiral. We get it. The Joint Chiefs have a lot on their plate. Shit happens and a lot of it has piled up.

"Given that situation, and stipulating that we **do** want the Joint Chiefs to be the dominant presence on the NSC, how can we provide the support we've just agreed to for our *Kidon* teams, for Raven's team?"

"The support that you've just agreed to," the President said softly.

"I can only think of one way, Mr. President: Leadership. We'll have to cunningly bypass the system. "I will *personally* handle the interface between the Covfefe committee and the Joint Chiefs.

"I'll warn them that we will have to tap their resources to supply military lethal force occasionally on short notice. We'll make it a point to NOT discuss any of this at NSC.

"I will not always be able to attend these meetings, Sir. My exec, Captain Peterson, will be my designated alternate. He'll speak with my authority. I'd like to bring him to our next Covfefe committee meeting so we can brief him in and get him up to speed. Since none of this is written down, we'll need to do it in person."

"I know Peterson," Mike said, "The Covfefe committee should definitely meet him, approve this, and get on the same page. We have a lot of eggs in that basket. We might need things like joint training exercises."

"Is everyone agreeable to that?" the President asked. Heads nodded.

"I need a voice vote, Yea or Nay."

And thus it was, with a chorus of Yea votes, that we made peace with the Joint Chiefs.

We broke for fifteen minutes and then it was my turn in the barrel. Goldfarb and Mike had insisted that I lead this discussion. I preferred to work alone. I favored action over talk, and I wasn't good at briefing or convincing people.

I was worse at trying to describe the kind of magic Josie was capable performing, and generally reluctant to try. Even Goldfarb didn't fully understand the capabilities and limitations of Josie's paranormal talents.

The CIA had once fired me with prejudice. It had wanted to try me for treason, but Goldfarb had eased in, faked my death, and revived me under the Raven legend. That part of my life was long gone, buried deep and forgotten.

I took a deep breath, glanced around the room, and said, "We have a situation. They want me to tell you about it."

Goldfarb and Mike exchanged a look.

"This will be new to you," Mike said. "It's worth hearing."

"Proceed," President Blager said.

"My team is built around soft assets that can give America intelligence impossible to obtain by other methods. We can give you information, but not proof. It's how we may have detected the threats that have been alluded to in this meeting a few times. These are, in general, things that we can never discuss."

"The alleged ship-based terrorist attack using EMP weapons?" Admiral Quigley said.

"That sort of thing," I said. "You had some knowledge. Do you care to comment?"

"I do not, but I can share open source news reports. An advanced nuclear powered Russian icebreaker named the *Krasivi Oblako* was sold to Iran. The name means "Beautiful Cloud," incidentally.

The presence and mission of that ship is unknown, but a fog of rumors surrounding it involves an Iranian base in Antarctica, an unusual military deployment, some type of internal power struggle, and a nuclear threat which may have posed danger to the United States."

"So what happened?" Neumann asked.

"Nothing," Quigley said. "There was some kind of an accident and the ship was lost with all hands in the far South Atlantic. International forces, including the Navy, conducted an extensive search, but nothing was ever found. It was like that airliner that disappeared. It's a lonely, dangerous, hostile part of the planet."

"What about the Iranian base in Antarctica?"

"There is such a base," Goldfarb said, "on the north side of the Antarctic continent. They call it *Muhamad Ali Jinnah*. It is on the opposite side of Antarctica from Little America. We have no assets within a thousand miles of it. It is not a military base."

"How do you know?"

Goldfarb said, "Because it can't be. Commercial and military activities are banned on the continent by international treaty."

"Right," Neumann said skeptically. "Anything else?"

"Raven's team saved my life," the President said, "by detecting and preempting grave threats that all our other sources and methods missed."

"I feel like I'm wandering around in the dark," Neumann said.

"Here's how it works," Mike said. "As Raven said, we have abilities to provide valuable information, but never proof. Whatever we see or suspect must be vetted and validated by conventional means. The key concept is trust."

"Trust, but verify," Goldfarb said. "I was the control for this team. Now, with my NSC duties, Mike has replaced me in that role."

"But you don't trust me," Neumann said.

"Trusting you or not trusting you is irrelevant. Think of this as like the Ultra information back in World War II. It was literally the difference between winning or losing the war.

"It is best to not discuss sources and methods, even with friends. The chances of a leak go up exponentially with the number of people involved, and America simply cannot take a chance on that. We dare not risk our sources and we dare not expose our capabilities."

"Who says that?"

"I do," the President said. "The buck stops with me. If you want to be on this team, those are the rules."

Neumann said, "Yes, Sir. Why are we discussing this now? It seems speculative."

"Excellent question," I said. "Up until now, we've run solo. If we found a threat, we'd verify it ourselves. If action was needed, we'd do it ourselves. It worked, but our enemies were getting too close. Hence, after Monterey, Covfefe."

"This isn't speculative, is it?" Quigley said. "You've run into something bigger than you can handle as a small team, haven't you?"

"I'm afraid so, Sir."

CHAPTER TWENTY FIVE
#CALEXIT

Underground UN facility, San Luis Obispo County

*N*assar Fuad was lucky to be alive. Monterey was the closest call he'd had for decades, and now he was being told that the same man was somehow involved. His second in command, Yasir, the Sunni, had been killed. Yasir was no great loss, but that damned Marine General, Mike Mickelson, had apparently turned up again.

Back then, Fuad had been working for Bukhari, now he served Iran. The rules were different and his stature was greatly reduced. Back then, as Colonel Ahmed Mahmoud Muhammad, he'd run low intensity warfare for all of North America. Now he was living like a mole, underground, a yet-to-be-proven minor commander for Quds.

The only reason Fuad was still alive was that Doctor Claas Vogel had intervened on his behalf, persuading Iran he could be of value. Vogel got him out of Bukhari where he was one step ahead of determined Israeli kill teams.

Fuad was being funded and run out of the UN, but something had gone wrong. Fuad needed replacements, supplies, and more funds, but had been unable to reach either Vogel or his control, Marco Ricci. Both had gone dark. His calls and messages were not being returned.

There was a rap on the door. "Enter," I said in Persian.

"I brought you the American, Sir," Rafi said in English.

I have to work with idiots. Rafi was all but useless as a warrior. His skills were lacking, except for speaking good American English. He hesitated at killing and feared his own shadow.

"Put him there," I said, pointing at the wooden chair in front of my desk.

Rafi complied.

I waved dismissingly. "Outside."

"Do you want me to watch him, Sir? Yasir said that he wasn't cleared."

I sighed, eyeing the American we'd been stuck with. He had a pasty complexion, brown eyes, 32, thick horn-rimmed glasses, mostly bald, 5 foot 6, and overweight. He was a misfit, a Silicon Valley geek who'd run technical support for AntiFa from his mom's basement.

"I think I can handle him. Stay for a moment while I decide if it's worth keeping him alive." I looked at the American. The American was sweating despite the coolness of the room. His eyes showed fear and weakness.

"I'm told that you go by the name Wally, that you used to work for Google, and that your technical skills would be useful to us."

"Yes, Mr. Fuad."

"Yes, Commander," I said.

The American repeated my words.

I said, "You were there to provide us with technical support at Monterey, but you were of no use to me at all. You gave us no warning. I lost half my force."

"Commander, it was the FBI. They didn't communicate on any of the police frequencies. They were radio silent until the fighting commenced. Then they communicated, but it was encrypted. I helped Yasir target their command team with our mortar, Sir."

"So you say. Yasir is dead and the mortar is lost."

"Yes, Commander."

I took a deep breath, "We have friends inside the California government. A man from Washington flew in two days after the attack in Monterey. He met with the FBI, took some notes, said little, and disappeared as quickly as he came."

"I'm told that you can identify him, that you had identified him. You were not even present. How can you do that?"

"It was my dongle, Commander."

"*Your what?*"

"Dongle, Commander, a small hardware device that, when plugged into a computer, enables a specific copy-protected program to run. I have one that monitors air traffic. It caught his airplane. That helped me identify who the man was and why he might be of interest to you."

I frowned. "Tell me more about this 'dongle' device."

"It's an ADS-B USB dongle, sir. They cost about $25 off the Internet. More expensive versions are complete ADS-B receivers, but mine is just a basic dongle. I added my own antenna, decoding, mapping, and management software to interface with other tools I have."

"Let's start with what this dongle does. Why does this matter to me?"

"Depending on how high I place my antenna, my unit reports all air traffic in a 200 KM radius."

"What do you mean it reports?"

"It puts a moving blue dot on a map with the Federal Aviation Administration data block, Commander."

"For every airplane in the sky?"

"Yes, Commander."

"Are you sure of this?"

"I'm certain, Commander. It is illegal for any aircraft to fly anywhere in U.S. airspace without transmitting an ADS-B signal. When they transmit this signal, my dongle picks it up."

"Couldn't a pilot turn this off?"

"In theory, perhaps, but in practice, it's not likely. It is a felony to install an ADS-B unit that can be turned off or that doesn't comply with FAA standards in a civilian aircraft. The mechanic would lose his license and be looking at years or decades of prison time. So would the air crew that allowed it to be turned off. If log books were forged, it just adds to the penalties."

I shook my head. "People break the law all the time. We – you and I, right here, right now – are breaking the law. We have just killed quite a few Federal Agents. We're conspiring to kill more and overthrow their government."

Wally turned white. "I didn't kill anyone."

I laughed. "A Federal Prosecutor or Military Tribunal would disagree. To get back to these pilots: Why wouldn't they just turn this ADS-B signal off or unplug it."

"They can't. Having an off switch is illegal. I suppose they could power down their entire navigation system, but that creates other problems, like having to declare an emergency and land as soon as possible."

"So they cut a wire or pull a circuit breaker."

"An aircraft not transmitting the required signal and data block would *immediately* set off alarms in every traffic control facility in the area. If it could not be contacted by radio, fighter aircraft would be scrambled to force it down or shoot it out of the sky, Commander."

"They would actually shoot it down?"

"Absolutely, Commander. Fighters would intercept and direct the violating aircraft to land. Every licensed pilot knows this, is trained in intercept compliance procedures, and knows lethal force may be used."

I nodded slowly. "Now tell me what this ADS-B signal is all about."

"ADS-B is an aircraft *surveillance* system that depends on aircraft reporting their positions both to government ground stations and to other aircraft. It was originally proposed as a lower cost, more accurate replacement for ground radars. Traffic control radars were to be phased out."

"You said, 'were to be.' I presume that means they were not."

"About half of them were. The government saved money, but you are correct. ADS-B was only a partial replacement technology. The Air Force objected. They pointed out that ADS-B was easily vulnerable to a denial of service attack."

"Which would shut down traffic handling?"

"Yes, Commander. Other concerns were raised, but that was the big one."

"For example?"

"As far back as 1999 – long before 9/11 – the question of terrorists using ADS-B signals to steer a small aircraft in front of a jetliner to cause a crash was raised. ADS-B was designed as a traffic avoidance system. Pilots and airlines liked having an in-cockpit traffic display. There were too many near misses.

"The threat raised was that ADS-B created a very precise homing system that allowed it to be used by terrorists as a 'collision assurance system.' These concerns were dismissed."

"Why?"

"I'm not sure, Commander. Perhaps because no one envisioned back then that GPS receivers with a 3 meter or better accuracy were even possible. Today they are common. More likely, because there are more serious threats, bombs on aircraft, SAMs, suicide-bent pilots in the flight deck, sabotage, and so forth."

"Has there ever been a case where an aircraft was brought down by using this ADS-B to force a collision?"

"No, Commander, never one that was reported or claimed."

"What about a case that wasn't reported?"

"Just rumors, Commander. It may have happened, but no one knows."

"When and where?"

"My Antifa brothers disrupted an event in Virginia back in 2017. One of us brought down a police helicopter by crashing a drone into it, killing two cops. No use of GPS or ADS-B was suggested or claimed."

"Charlottesville, with two State Police officers killed in the crash…"

"Yes, that's the one, Commander. We blamed the incident on white supremacists and claimed the crash was an accident."

"But a small drone would be unlikely to be able to hit a jet, or to bring it down if it did?"

"In my opinion, it would not be likely using current technology, Commander."

"So you can track airplanes. How do you know who is inside them?"

"From the data blocks, Commander. My dongle displays everything. The altitude and speed of the aircraft, but also everything about it. The screen on my computer displays the tail number, type, who owns it, and where it is based."

"All of the government records about that particular aircraft?"

"All the FAA records about any US registered aircraft. If it is foreign registered, it reports that and what country, but not as much is displayed."

"The Americans don't encrypt this data?"

"No, Commander. They do not. They are fools."

"You tracked an aircraft that came into Monterey to the Marine General who visited the FBI? And linked this man to me?"

"A retired General. He is a civilian now. Yes, Commander, I did."

"How?"

"The aircraft is owned by a corporation, TSG, The Security Group. I got that from the FAA data block. It was simple to find a list of their officers. General Mike Mickelson is their President and CEO."

"How did you link the General to me?"

"I just did a Google search. It was obvious."

I shook my head. "You are lying."

The American turned white. "Commander, I am telling you the truth. I swear."

"Until now, I've never used the name Nassar Fuad in America. My involvement with the General was years ago and under a different name."

"Yes, Commander. I know that. You were Colonel Ahmed Mahmoud Muhammad of Bukhari Intelligence."

"How did you associate us?"

"Google knows everything. I started searching with the General's name and Bukhari. I found many old records and news reports. It was all public information."

I was stunned. With the Americans and Israelis both hunting me, I'd worked hard to cover my tracks.

"How did you know about Bukhari?"

"Yasir told me. We all know you came from Bukhari, Commander."

With that sentence, I started trusting the American.

It fit. I was a Sunni Muslim, an Arab, while the Iranians were Shiite and Persian. We had united to kill infidels. I was here because of Vogel's influence in Tehran, only because of that.

For now Sunnis and Shiites had a common enemy. When America and Israel were destroyed, we'd be back at each other's throats, just as we had been for a thousand years. The Sunnis were much more numerous, but now Iran had advanced weapons, nukes. The power balance had changed.

"Why do they call you 'Wally'?"

"It was a joke. He's the geeky bald guy in Dilbert, Commander."

I shook my head.

"It's a popular comic strip, Commander."

"Rafi, I want you to get me Major Mahdi."

"Yes, Sir." He was back with the Major in under a minute.

Mahdi said, "You needed me, Sir?"

"Yes. How many Stinger missiles do we have?"

"Two, Sir. I've requested more, but have not gotten a response."

"These will suffice. Wally has a way to target our enemies. You will take your best missile team to Monterey. Wally and Rafi will accompany you and set up their equipment. A jet will be coming to Monterey soon bringing an American General. They can identify it some distance out."

"What are your orders, Sir?"

"I want you to blow that jet out of the sky, Major. If you miss it on the way in, it won't be there long. You'll get another chance when it departs. Do not get close, there will be security."

"Yes, Sir."

"Stay in Monterey as long as is needed, but keep a low profile. Do not communicate except by courier. The Americans watch everything electronic. I want this General dead. Then make your egress, get clear, and come back."

"*Insha'Allah*, the General will die."

"He will, and his death will reflect well on you. Get it done."

The Ranch, Mendocino, California, Main Lodge

I took over Goldfarb's whiteboard.

"We've talked here about how to protect us. Now I have to disclose some of what we can do, some of what makes us **worth** protecting. My information is still firming up, but it's already clear that the action required to handle this threat is far beyond what my small team can do on its own.

"The threat in California is related to the Monterey attack on my team, but not in the way the FBI is looking at it. The issue is larger."

"Much larger," Mike said.

I said, "There is a secret Iranian military base in California. It's well equipped, and there is a substantial force in place. This foreign force is being supported by officials in the California government who favor #CalExit, the notion of having the state of California secede from America."

"Cal Exit is political," Neumann said. "Petitions are being circulated, with support from California's Lieutenant Governor, Hugo Salazar. That's legal, but efforts have been stalled.

If voters agreed to amend the state's constitution, removing text deeming the republic "inseparable" from the US and declaring the US Constitution to be the "law of the land," then a follow-up vote to form their own country would take place."

"It all started when Trump was elected," the President said. "There are reasons these actions are stalled. It's potentially a re-run of the Civil War. My administration and the courts are aware of these plans. We would strongly discourage them."

"Yes, Sir," I said. "In any case, an Iranian base on US soil is not political, it is an invasion. Some of the heavy weapons used in the Monterey attack came from that base."

"How do you know that?"

"Here is one of the weapons from Monterey."

I gestured, and Mike opened his bag. "It's from an M64A1 mortar. It is safe to handle and it weighs 2.5 pounds. It's the sighting unit off the mortar that Quds used in Monterey."

"You are sure it's a part of that specific weapon?" Admiral Quigley asked.

"Positive, Sir. I stole it. That's probably a felony. If you touch this unit, it is probably best to use gloves. We would not want to leave DNA or fingerprints.

"I'm on my way back down there to return it, see if there has been any progress in the situation of the FBI versus the state of California about jurisdiction, and to meet whomever the bureau has put in charge down there."

"Who exactly did you, ah, borrow this from?" the President asked.

Mike said, "That's a good question, Sir. The FBI and California were arguing over ownership and jurisdiction when I was there. I'll return it to the FBI."

I said, "The important thing is that my researchers have been able to determine *where* that mortar came from. It belonged to the California National Guard, but it came from the secret Quds base I mentioned. It is located in a remote area of San Luis Obispo County."

"You are certain of this?" the President said.

"You know the quality of my source, Sir. I believe what I said to be true. I'm hoping that when Mike returns his borrowed item, we can induce the FBI to assert jurisdiction and come up with legal proof."

"Tell us more about that base," the President said.

"The history is cloudy. Mostly what we know is rumors and strange tales. It is reportedly now a UN facility. Originally, it was originally called the 'California Specialized Training Institute' for foreign security forces. Later it became a FEMA agency facility. I'm not sure who has ownership now, but if I had to guess, either the UN or some agency of the State of California."

"What do you know?"

"This is a forward base designed for company strength, about 160-200. Such a force is more than enough to overwhelm a President and his Secret Service detail. My guess is that it was probably involved in the assassination attempts on you as well as on my team.

"The facility has a security fence and guard towers, but the base is mostly underground. It's on a dead-end private road."

"What weapons do they have there?" Quigley asked.

"They had three M224A1 60 MM mortars, but lost one at Monterey. The .50 Cal that was used at Monterey came from there, and they have four more. They also have Stinger missiles, at least two Abrams M1A2 tanks with the 120mm guns, and a dozen or so Humvees.

"They have small arms, ammo, grenades, and body armor, about what a US Army combat company would possess. These were likely sourced from the California National Guard, so we might be able to get an exact count.

"They may have Sarin gas shells for their mortars. The California Guard didn't have any, but they were trying to source these from Syria using the Mexican drug cartels to get them into the country."

I stopped. Everyone was staring at me.

Mike said, "That fits. The US Military does not provision our troops with poison gas rounds, though we do have some in secure storage. WMDs are prohibited under international law. They may be having Syria modify some of our shells."

I said, "Noted."

Admiral Quigley said, "The Joint Chiefs needs to study this, Sir. We're talking about how to respond to a foreign invasion."

Neumann said, "We should get a legal ruling from DOJ. The way this discussion is going, we may be talking about martial law, Mr. President."

I was out of words. "That concludes my presentation. That's all I know. We need validation and an action plan."

"No shit," Goldfarb said.

"I was tasked with reporting on our action items, Sir. We cleared that list. This is new information, just in. I thought we should discuss it."

"You were right on that one," the President said. "Thank you."

I said, "What should we do next?"

Goldfarb said, "Continue doing what you are doing, Raven. I suggest the President needs to prod the FBI to be a bit more independent and aggressive. We need more insight about what is going down in San Luis Obispo."

"Yes," Quigley said. "We need military contingency plans from the Joint Chiefs before anyone prods that nest. We need an assessment and action plans. I don't want to start a war unless we are prepared to finish it."

Neumann said, "A legal opinion from DOJ. If we are considering military action, they will need a plan for how to handle that as well. There will be blowback."

Mike said, "I need to go to Monterey, put eyes on, and return the FBI's evidence before it is officially missed."

I took up my marker and wrote:

- FBI pushes, asserts Federal Crime status
- Quds base research and possibly recon
- Military assessment, action plans, and resource allocation
- DOJ legal assessment and action plan. SCOTUS?
- Monterey eyes on, status update
- Tight hold on all information. Covfefe meets to discuss?

I said, "Any additions, comments, or questions?"

Goldfarb said, "Looks good. Can we get yeas and nays?"

There was a chorus of yeas.

The President said, "I want to stress the need for a tight hold. We do NOT want Congress or the media involved until we know what's going on.

"I will deal with any leaks severely. The last thing I want is to have the media talking about my going insane and planning to invade California."

No one spoke.

The President said, "I will require a verbal acknowledgment on that one."

We all replied, "Yes, Mr. President."

I said, "I'd like to accompany Mike as part of the eyes on."

Goldfarb said, "Mike is now your control. If he approves, I have no objections."

Mike said, "There is a lot of hostile firepower down there. I'd like clear Rules of Engagement. If we need to go defensive, I want approval for lethal force."

I said, "I share that concern. We have personal security, but some military firepower on standby might be prudent. Defensive only. We're not looking for trouble."

The President met my eyes. "I'm not going to put you in harm's way without support. I'll approve that."

"Thank you, Sir."

Mike said, "I'll make sure he doesn't break the china, Sir."

Goldfarb said, "We'd appreciate that, General."

CHAPTER TWENTY SIX
THE FEMALE OF
THE SPECIES...

The Ranch, Mendocino, California, Raven's Suite

Even though I'm a paranormal, I was having trouble reading this woman. She did not reveal much. She was friendly, but inclined towards silence.

I looked at Gerry. "Are you *really* related to General George S. Patton?"

She was an attractive woman, taller than me, perhaps five feet eleven or a bit more. Her brown hair had flecks of gray and those ice blue eyes were intense. She was thin, but still had a nice figure.

"On my mother's side. He was my grandfather. When I met Mike I was divorced and using the Patton name. It's a long story...."

Friendly, responsive, but no details volunteered....

Raven had told me some about her history, a high level NSA analyst whose boss at the agency had been a traitor. *Raven said it had not ended well for him.*

Gerry said, "My expertise is with computers and security. My father John Giles founded Cybertech. When he was abducted, my brother took over. We make your secure phones."

"Having TSG support is making a difference. Raven told me about your dad. We're sorry for your loss. It must have been horrible for you."

"Yes." She looked at me directly. "Mike says you're a witch. That you see things normal people can't."

"Sometimes. We're trying to keep a low profile."

"You must be damn good at what you do. It seems our enemies want you badly. Kill teams in the night. Durham and Monterey…."

"I'm afraid so."

"Mike and I have had similar experiences. As long as there is Islam, there will be *jihad*. It is why we set up TSG as a personal security company. We can never relax our guard."

"Do you have any children?"

"Two. Both are in college under false identities. It is not the America I was used to."

"How do you handle having targets on your backs?"

"It is what it is."

"Bullshit."

Gerry said, "It's a war. Good versus Evil. We make it difficult to kill us. We kill them first. We associate with people like you, people who can do something to end this."

"I hope so. Raven did seem to relax a bit when we got TSG for security."

"What about you? How do you handle it?"

"Not well, I'm afraid. Violence shuts me down. Raven tries to keep it at a distance, but it's always there, lurking in the darkness outside, creeping into my mind. I don't like living like this. It's not just us. They've tried to assassinate the President, you know."

"Three times. Twice here in California and, more recently, at Camp David."

"You know a lot," I said.

"I have need of a good witch. I'm hoping that might be you."

"Why me?

"I know you saved the President. I know you are a remote viewer, a paranormal. I know that the President has declared you a National Treasure."

"Do you even know what a remote viewer is?"

"I know the rumors and legends. I have a good friend at the NRO. She told me an interesting story."

"NRO? I hate all those acronyms…."

"The National Reconnaissance Office. The people who can image a license plate from orbit with satellites in real time, day or night. We spend billions on that technology in order to gain a national edge. Do you know what she told me?"

I shook my head.

"NRO worries about a lot of things, but at the top of their list is nuclear weapons, especially now with Iran, North Korea, and other rogue nations getting nukes and delivery systems. There is a major emphasis on being able to find concealed nuclear sites, especially mobile launchers, silos, and underground bunkers. *Thank you Clinton and Obama....*"

"So?"

"My friend said the Pentagon commissioned a study on how to best locate hidden nukes. It **specifically** compared satellite imagery to paranormal viewing."

"Did paranormal win?"

"No."

"I didn't think so. As you said, we are viewed as witches and warlocks, odd people with tin hats from the twilight zone. Even the Rhine Institute, the ones who *pioneered* extrasensory research, dares not speak the word *paranormal* these days.

"We keep it all highly classified. It's need-to-know and best not discussed. We get labeled as crazy. They had me in a psych ward. Raven had to rescue me."

"You're not crazy. What you do works."

"How do you know?"

"My friend at the NRO told me the Pentagon's study said the results were *comparable*. It surprised me she'd say that."

I smiled. "They were probably just messing with her head."

"Possibly, but I do know one thing. You are a National Treasure, Josie. You are why there is a Covfefe committee. You are why we're here."

"Why are **you** here?"

"I need your help. I need you to find something. You are my only hope."

"What do you want me to find?"

"My father."

The Ranch, Mendocino, California, Main Lodge, Sundown

The President and his entourage had departed for the White House. Admiral Quigley was off to brief the Joint Chiefs, and National Security Advisor Neumann was to get a meeting of the NSC scheduled after they had an action plan.

The mass exodus left me, Goldfarb, and Mike sitting alone in the conference room, looking at each other.

Mike said, "What do you think is going to happen next?"

I said, "We're not authorized actually to do anything, are we?"

"Easy," Goldfarb said. "There are times to think, and times to act. This is the former."

We looked at him for a long moment. Finally, I said, "Why?"

Goldfarb said, "Do you think the Joint Chiefs will tolerate a Quds base in America?"

I shrugged, "Does it matter? I doubt the President will."

Mike said, "It matters. The Chiefs will want action, but it's not their call. NSC is political. I was on NSC staff for a time."

"It's the President's call," I said.

Goldfarb said, "The Chiefs will give him military options. NSC will instruct on implications, costs, and consequences. That's how it works."

He pointed at Mike. "You're the expert on raids and Spec OPs tactics, General. What can be done to quickly eliminate the Quds base in San Luis Obispo?"

"Not much," Mike said.

"Why not?"

"This UN facility is a hardened, self-sufficient, underground facility that has been there since the Cold War. It would probably survive a tactical nuke. They for sure have tanks, heavy weapons, and about 200 first line troops. They have local political support, including from that Hispanic Lt. Governor, the #CalExit guy."

"Hugo Salazar," Goldfarb said. "He's high profile. Well connected."

"Marvelous," Mike said. "They may also have WMDs. Perhaps not shells for their mortars yet, but canisters of Sarin."

I said, "We're authorized to do an eyes on. Does that help?"

Goldfarb said, "In support of the FBI and in Monterey, not San Luis Obispo."

"Without breaking the china," Mike added.

"Josie can get us Intel."

"We'll need that, but you can forget about a raid to take hostages or getting anyone inside the base to report back. This isn't Hollywood."

Goldfarb said, "How would you take it out, Mike?"

"I need Intel. I'd start by isolating the base, but it would take Air Support, tanks, and perhaps a full Brigade, call it 3,000 troops."

"So many?"

Mike shrugged. "If we use force, we'll need to keep it contained and end it quickly. Santa Barbara is 100 miles and LA is 200. The possibility of a few hundred thousand casualties and civil war in California will surely occur to the Joint Chiefs."

Goldfarb was scowling, looking from face to face. The room was silent.

Finally he said, "This does not sound hopeful."

Mike said, "Not to me. Maybe the Joint Chiefs can come up with something better."

After a long moment I said, "Maybe we're looking at this wrong."

"How so?"

"A direct attack is difficult. What if we eliminate the commander instead?"

"Keep talking," Goldfarb said.

"We're clear to gather Intel in Monterey. And we do know one thing. The local commander for Quds is Nassar Fuad, aka, Ahmed Mahmoud Muhammad."

Mike said, "The same *jihadi* who kidnapped my father-in-law, years back. Are you certain?"

I nodded.

"How do you know?"

"Josie. You saw her sketch. You identified the scar on his temple."

Mike nodded. "Yes."

"How does this help us?" Goldfarb said.

"Fuad has a major problem. We severed his command chain."

They were staring at me like I'd just dropped in from Mars or something.

"We reported all that at Covfefe. It was at the top of our action item list. Josie and I were rather proud that we could close it out...."

"*You reported all that?* I must have missed something, Raven," Goldfarb said. "I think perhaps you need to actually talk with us."

"Claas Vogel and Marco Ricci are gone. Why do you think they topped our kill list?"

"They were notoriously evil bastards?" Mike said.

Goldfarb said, "All you said was that they were off your task list for fortuitous reasons. You took no credit."

"Why would I want to take any credit? I'm in enough trouble...."

Mike was smiling. "*You blamed the Russians?*"

"I didn't blame or credit anyone. If you recall, Doctor Goldfarb presented that portion of our report at Covfefe. He handled it delicately and with elegance. He quoted news reports. Everyone seemed to accept those findings."

Mike said, "Vogel was funding that Quds base? Ricci was the control for Fuad?"

"Yes. Absolutely."

"Ricci's dead?"

"He is."

"Vogel's in Moscow enjoying the accommodations of the Lubyanka?"

"Probably. Putin wanted him badly. The Canadians claim the Russians snatched him. The Russians haven't admitted it, much less said **where** they have him, but that's a reasonable assumption. Where else would they interrogate him?"

Goldfarb said, "Fuad must be in a total panic. His team bungled the attempted snatch of you and Josie, killed a bunch of FBI agents by mistake, and attracted attention. He lost some of his key people. He's now lost both his control and his funding?"

"Yes. Pretty much."

Mike was grinning. "And all this is because of a long chain of fortuitous accidents and incidents for which we claim no responsibility whatsoever?"

I shrugged. "Shit happens."

Goldfarb said, "What do you suggest we do now?"

"Like Mike said, we need better Intel. I think we should invite Josie into our meeting and give her some taskings. She can help us."

Mike raised his hand. "I need to expand on that, Sir. I have a confession to make."

"Go ahead."

"I agree that getting rid of the Quds base is a strategic necessity for America, but it's not what got me involved. I have personal interests, Sir."

"Go ahead," Goldfarb said.

"I missed Fuad 15 years ago. So did the Israelis. Fuad kidnapped my father-in-law, Colonel John Giles, Iron John. My wife Gerry, his daughter, is with Josie now. She has the same issues I do. So does her brother, who runs Cybertech, which is a key part of our team."

I said, "You are certain that it was Fuad who kidnapped Iron John?"

"He had a different identity then, but yes, I am. Fuad led the team."

Goldfarb said, "What precisely do you want, Mike?"

"Closure. If Iron John is dead, we need to confirm that and perhaps recover his body. If he's alive, we need to get him back. We need to dispense justice to Fuad."

"How?"

"Not as a criminal. As an illegal enemy combatant, a terrorist. I'd prefer a military tribunal and a hanging, but I'd be happy to put a bullet in his head myself. Along the way, we need to shut down the Quds base. With no funding and Fuad gone, that will be a bit simpler, I expect."

Goldfarb looked at me. "Well?"

"I agree with Mike. Invite the women in. We need better Intel. We need Josie. This is what she does. After we take out Fuad, the rest is easy."

Goldfarb looked at Mike, who shrugged. "The words 'Raven' and 'easy' don't fit together well in sentences, do they?"

"No, they do not. I'm glad you are now his control."

Mike said, "It's a long shot, but a Hell of a lot better than a civil war in California or a major disaster in LA."

Goldfarb sighed. "Invite the ladies in. Let's see if we can end this mess without leaving LA in flames or creating a Constitutional crisis for President Blager."

CHAPTER TWENTY SEVEN
EMPTY ROOMS
AND IRON JOHN

The Ranch, Mendocino, California, Raven's Suite

I heard footsteps coming up the walkway, moving fast. Gerry dipped a hand into her purse.

"Easy," I said. "Weapons shut down my powers. It's just Mike and Raven."

She gave me an odd look. "Okay."

Raven's knock came. *First one, then three.* It was an odd day of the month. "Come in."

The men were both grinning.

"What?"

Raven said, "Goldfarb is still here, but the President and his staff are off to Washington. They have NSC level issues, we have a mission, and your presence is requested, ladies."

Gerry said, "Do we get briefed in first?"

"Sure." Mike said, "The big news is that we have a green light, a tasking to find out what happened to your father."

"Finally. Thank God."

Mike said, "The President has a huge problem, an Iranian forward base on American soil. It's a tough nut to crack, a hard target. The Joint Chiefs are tasked with that.

Raven said, "We convinced Goldfarb that America needed a Plan B. I suggested that it might be easier to remove the base's commander than to remove the base. He happens to be the same man who abducted Gerry's dad."

"Ahmed Mahmoud Muhammad," Gerry said. "He's finally turned up?"

Mike said, "Ahmed now goes by Nassar Fuad, a Saudi. That was one of his old legends. He's working for Iran now."

"He's here? In America?"

Mike handed her my sketch. "Yes."

Gerry studied it for a long moment before she nodded. "I think it is him."

"Why?"

"The scar."

"That's what I think too. You'll recall that I put it there."

Raven said, "Fuad led the team that went after Josie and me in Monterey."

I said, "The sketch is from a remote viewing I did of the attack a few days after it happened."

Raven said, "The President wants the Iranian base taken out. I want Fuad to interrogate. You and Mike want to get your father back, if he's still alive."

"There is an Iranian military base here in California?"

"San Luis Obispo," Raven said. "Underground. We think about 200 troops."

"Quds force. They have heavy weapons and maybe WMDs," Mike said.

"What do the Joint Chiefs want?" Gerry said.

Mike said, "Good question. They are trying to sort that out. The President wants the base gone. The Chiefs are tasked with submitting an action plan that he can approve. Whatever they decide, we have a green light to collect actionable Intel on our own."

I said, "You want me to go all the way back to the beginning with my viewings?"

"I do," Raven said.

"That is a long way back. Events decades old and half a world away."

"Sure, but for starters, let's focus on Fuad. We'll see where that leads."

"It's a good a place as any, I suppose."

"There are many questions. Where is Gerry's dad now? Is he still alive? How did Fuad wind up working for Iran? How did he get here? What traitors here are enabling a foreign base on our soil? And the biggest one is: What can we do about it?"

Mike said, "Raven convinced Goldfarb that Fuad is in deep trouble. Because of Raven's team, Fuad has lost his entire chain of command, including his source of funding."

Gerry said, "Is that true?"

Raven said, "They are isolated and without command guidance, at least for now."

Gerry said, *"You sold Goldfarb on the notion that it is easier for us to demoralize and collapse the base than it is for our military to take it by force? We convince suicidal Islamic fanatics they can't win, and then you and Mike walk in and accept their surrender?"*

No one spoke. They were all looking at me.

I pointed at Raven. "You do know that's insane?"

Gerry said, "It does sound like something the UN would come up with. Religion of peace, reasoned negotiation, and all that bullshit...."

The two men exchanged a look.

Mike said, "It will be messy to take the base by force. Potentially there could be thousands of civilian casualties, possibly a Constitutional crisis and Martial Law. Maybe a civil war in California...."

Raven said, "There are some details we'll need to work out."

Mike said, "Life and death details. We need to get this right."

"Yes."

Raven said. "Goldfarb and the President need options. What do we have to lose?"

Gerry said, "I want to know if my father is still alive."

I said, "Of course you do. I'll start looking."

Raven said, "How should we start?"

I said, "The dining room is excellent here. They just got a load of Dungeness crabs in from Oregon. How about we have a nice dinner and get everyone to slow the Hell down?

"Let me do some remote viewings. I need Raven to help me and I'd like Gerry to sit in and observe. I can do the first one tonight."

Mike said, "You want us to stand down while you get us some actionable Intel?"

"Yes," I said. "Exactly."

"How long?"

"As long as it takes," Gerry said.

"Not long," I said, "Two days, maybe three. I need some time."

"I think we can agree to that," Mike said. "Why not?"

"Sure we can," Raven said. "You can use that time to reposition our support assets. I want to get Black out here. Goldfarb can go hug that FBI guy and cheer him up. We maybe can work it so they get the credit for catching Fuad."

Mike said, "You never know...."

Dinner ran late and I was tired. We didn't do my remote viewing until the next day after breakfast. Gerry was so anxious about her father that it was distracting to me. At Raven's insistence she and Mike went off somewhere with Goldfarb.

Raven arranged the room, locked the door, and we settled in. It seemed to take me a long time to get into my viewing. The part where Iron John was kidnapped in Oregon was traumatic, and then there were many shifts as he was extracted and moved from place to place around the world.

Finally the spatial distortion and disruption settled down. I locked on John and started moving deeper into my viewing, trying to pick up his perceptions as well as what I was seeing. I was suspended in time, viewing events on the other side of the world that had happened long ago.

Then he was in a cell. I didn't know where. They were speaking a foreign language. He seemed to understand it, but I did not. Years passed in the blink of an eye as I tried to shift towards the present.

John's conditions were not harsh. He had a view out the barred window, a toilet, a sink, and a shower. He got medical care. The guards fed him, he was allowed to exercise, and he was well fed, but he was never allowed to mingle with other prisoners.

Occasionally he was put into a van with no windows, blindfolded, and taken to an ornate building, a palace. There he conversed privately with a thin-faced man whom I almost recognized. He had dark hair, big ears, and dressed in dark Western suits, typically blue, and always with a white shirt and a tie.

That was odd. The man was a Muslim, but he dressed as a Westerner. He was a medical doctor, an eye doctor. He'd gone to school in London.

The man and John conversed in English. He had a British accent.

I tried to get a calibration so I could date events. Shifting back in time didn't help. Wherever they were meeting, it was very old. I moved back a century, then two, then ten, and there were always people living in that site. It predated Roman times.

It was in the desert. I didn't see anything I could recognize.

The first time the man showed up was around 2008. I was pretty sure of that. I locked on him. I saw him frequently meeting with Russians. Later in time I viewed him and John talking about the election of Obama and of America's setbacks in Iran.

That information let me eventually fix the location. It was Syria. Damascus, the Presidential Palace, built on a high plateau. The entire plateau of Mount Mezzeh was part of the palace premises. It was surrounded by a security wall and guard watchtowers.

The palace was odd. In front of the building is a large fountain, and the palace itself largely consisted of empty rooms clad in Carrara marble, white with dark veins of grey going through it. It was beautiful, but filled with large, empty rooms.

I'd never seen anything like it. It was creepy.

The palace was heavily fortified. It included the headquarters of the Republican Guard, a hospital where John was occasionally taken, and, yes, a small prison for political prisoners. That was where he was being held.

It was near an air base. In some of my viewings there were military jets going over at low altitude, taking off and landing. In one they were bombing other parts of the city. There were distant explosions and plumes of smoke.

John was totally inaccessible He might as well have been on the dark side of the moon.

The Western looking man was Syria's President, al-Assad. *Bingo.* That was something Raven was interested in. Poison gas shells with Sarin. Syria was estimated to have large stockpiles. He'd showed me a Pentagon memo that said Syria had produced a "ridiculously huge amount" of deadly Sarin gas.

I started easing myself out of the viewing.

I took deep breaths, feeling the sensations coming back. I stretched, flexed my arms and legs and wiggled my fingers. I was warm. I recognized the sensation. Sunlight on my skin.

When I opened my eyes, Raven was watching me. He was smiling.

"What time is it?" I asked.

"Late morning." He came over to me and wiped my face with a cold cloth. "Almost noon. You were gone a long time. Are you okay?"

I nodded.

"What happened?"

"*I found him.* Iron John is alive."

"Where?"

"Syria."

"You are sure?"

"Positive. Give me my notepad. I need to write this down while it's fresh in my mind."

CHAPTER TWENTY EIGHT
BAD SHIT

The Ranch, Mendocino, California, Main Lodge

Mike and I had an agenda. We needed Goldfarb's help.

I said, "We are asking to stand down for two or three days. Josie is doing remote viewings, and getting great Intel. We want time to process it."

Mike said, "After almost two decades she's located my father-in-law, Iron John. He is alive."

"Where is he?"

"Syria."

"Is he in good health?"

"Josie says he is, Sir. She says he's being treated well."

"Is he safe there?"

Mike shrugged. "He's in prison. There is a war going on.

"The unrest in Syria, enflamed by the 2011 Arab Spring protests, grew out of discontent with the Assad government. It escalated to an armed conflict after protests calling for Assad's removal were violently suppressed. The war is, as you know, being fought by a dozen or more factions and countries in the region, including us and Russia. It's a tinderbox."

Goldfarb nodded. "I do know. I will repeat my question. Is John Giles safe?"

"For now he is, but only for as long as Assad stays in power."

"Assad is protecting him?"

"Assad is *imprisoning* him. John is being held in the palace. I suppose that is as safe a place as there is over there."

"How in the Hell did John wind up in Syria? How can he still be alive?"

I said, "That ties into the Quds base that we were discussing at the Covfefe meeting. The connection is the current base commander, one Nassar Fuad. Turns out he is the same person who kidnapped Iron John all those years ago."

Mike said, "At the time Fuad was known as Ahmed Mahmoud Muhammad. He was a Colonel in Bukhari Intelligence. We had issues with them about bioweapons, and he was operating here in the states.

"We broke his operation, but he escaped. We and the Israelis hunted him for years. They had a kill team after him. Almost got him a time or two, but he finally dropped off the radar."

"Do we know how John got to Syria?" Goldfarb persisted.

Mike said, "Only in a general sense, Sir. It has to be Vogel."

"How so?"

Mike said, "I was involved in that part. We almost got Fuad several times, but he made it back to Bukhari. We hit him there, wounding him, but we never found Iron John.

"I think Vogel intervened on Fuad's behalf, persuading Iran he could be of value. Vogel got him out of Bukhari one step ahead of Israeli kill teams."

Goldfarb said, "Fuad went to Iran?"

"Probably," Mike said. "How else could he wind up running a Quds base? My guess is he wasn't there long. I doubt the Iranians trusted him. Why would they? Fuad is a Sunni Arab who worked for a Saddam-like dictator. The Iranians are Islamic fanatics. They are not Arabs, they are Persians. They are not Sunni; they are Shia."

"Was John in Iran?"

I said, "I don't know. I do know he is in Syria."

"How did he get there?"

Mike said, "I think it was the Russians, Sir."

Goldfarb said, "The same Russians who now are now interrogating Vogel in Moscow?"

Mike said, "Similar Russians, Sir. Not the **same** Russians. Recall that was before Putin came to power and before the Arab Spring and *Hijrah* destabilized the entire region by toppling governments. It was Putin who generated the international arrest warrant for Vogel as a terrorist."

Goldfarb nodded. "Whatever differences we have with the Russians, and there are many, our views about supporting Nation States and resisting jihad are in alignment.

I said, "The Russians are allies of Iran, but they are also allies of Syria. They have a lot of clout in both countries, but they are the main sponsor of Syria."

Goldfarb nodded slowly. "You are telling me that no one quite knew what to do with Iron John, so Vogel parked him in Syria? Syria agreed because it was what the Russians wanted?"

I said, "That's my guess, Sir. I don't think either Russia or Iran wanted John's blood on their hands from Fuad's failed mission in America. Bukhari didn't survive the Arab Spring. There was no one left in the region who wanted Fuad."

"Except for Vogel," Mike said.

Goldfarb said, "Aside from the Russians, does Assad have any interest in keeping John there as a prisoner?"

Mike shook his head. "I doubt it. Why would he? Assad is a thug, but he is not a *jihadist* or an Islamist. His interest is staying in power. The Russians are his lifeline. They protect him from us and from Iran because they want a warm water port there."

I said, "Fuad is running the Quds base here. He is the commander, though not an Iranian. We also know that there is one other thing unusual about that base."

Goldfarb actually smiled. "Only one?"

"It's clearly an Iranian base, a Quds base, but it was funded and controlled out of the UN. Vogel was providing the money. Operational control was out of the UN, run by a Vogel lackey, Marco Ricci."

"A command link which is now severed," Goldfarb said.

Mike and I nodded. "Yes."

"Is there some legal pretense that allows the UN such a base here?"

"No idea," I said.

"It's possible," Mike said.

"What do you want of me?" Goldfarb asked.

"Josie has asked for a few days to research these issues. She wants time to do more remote viewings and analysis. She's asked that we stand down. We support her in that."

"I agree," Goldfarb said. "What else?"

I said, "We discussed rogue operations and Kidon teams at our Covfefe meeting, Sir. We had been cleared to take actions, to act versus react. We did take actions, and they were successful. It turned out well. Do you agree?"

"In general, yes, I do."

"As I recall, the two top points of your presentation were:

Point one: accountability. It's accountable only to the Covfefe committee under the authority of President Blager.

Point two: the mission. The primary mission is intelligence and counter terrorism with a special focus on Islamic *jihad*. The *Kidon* unit can also operate in other capacities to assist the National Security needs of POTUS."

Goldfarb nodded. "Who do you want to kill now, Raven?"

"No one, Sir. Not yet. What we would like is for you and Mike to meet with the President and get my team authorized for two actions. One is recovering Iron John. The other is dealing appropriately with Fuad should opportunities present themselves."

Goldfarb said, "There were tight constraints on how you were to operate. There are checks and balances. You need to stay under the radar and in compliance with the Constitution."

"Yes. We agreed to that."

"I'm his control," Mike said. "I'll give you a heads up if we are getting close to the line."

"I'll discuss that with the President and get you a decision," Goldfarb said. "He's bound to ask me. Are you planning to assassinate Fuad?"

He and Mike both looked at me.

I said, "I don't know, Sir. It's too soon to say, but, yes, we are asking for approval to use lethal force on Fuad if deemed necessary."

"Your request is reasonable under the circumstances. I will support it."

"Thank you."

Mike said, "There is one more thing, Sir."

"Yes?"

"When we meet with the President, I've got an issue of my own. Quds is planning to take me out, to blow my plane out of the sky."

Goldfarb said, "Are they now?"

"I need to visit Monterey to assess the FBI's control of the situation. I have some evidence that I need to return to them, you will recall. Our enemies somehow know that. They have a kill team waiting for us in Monterey with Stinger missiles."

Goldfarb raised an eyebrow, staring at me, intense blue eyes, rimless glasses, and all. His intimidating look, one usually reserved for security lapses. At least he didn't fumble with his pipe. He'd dropped that habit after it was revealed to be a weapon.

I wondered vaguely if they let him take his pipe to NSC meetings. Probably not....

He said, "Raven?"

"That Intel came from Josie. I don't think I want to be on Mike's plane."

Goldfarb's smile never touched his eyes. "Do we have a leak?"

"It's possible. We plan to research that."

"Please do. What do you need, Mike?"

"When we're in Washington, I want to return the FBI's evidence and discuss the situation in California with FBI Director Johnson. Hopefully, the Bureau can thwart that attack. It might need some help from the military."

"That sounds like a useful discussion. I expect the President will want to have his National Security Advisor, General Neumann, present."

Mike said, "That seems prudent, Sir."

Goldfarb looked at me again. "It's possible that the Bureau might get bogged down with protocols and legalities."

"Yes, Sir."

"Preemptive lethal force is authorized to protect Mike, as you deem it to be necessary."

"Kill them."

"Only if deemed necessary."

"Try not to hit my airplane," Mike said.

"Or our brothers in the Bureau," Goldfarb added. "No fratricide."

Hernando's Hooch, Simi Valley, California

Outside, the building was distressed brick, sleazy and ominous, something out of 1930s Hollywood film noir. It had small windows and was distinctive mostly for what was missing – there was no gang graffiti, no security bars on the door, and no dealers, hookers, or vagrants anywhere to be found.

My driver Pablo was nervous. I told him to park in the yellow zone by the hydrant, that I'd be about thirty minutes, and that it was safe.

I heard the vehicle locks click as I walked away. He didn't believe me, apparently.

The truth was that no one in their right minds would mess with the people here. The gangs and junkies avoided it, they did their business elsewhere. So did the police, for that matter.

It was dark inside and dimly lit. The doorman looked like an NFL lineman. All muscle and massive, maybe 280 pounds.

"You packing, Governor?" he said.

I nodded. "I've got a permit. You want my piece?"

The doorman looked impressed. Except for law enforcement, carry permits were as rare as virgins or unicorns in California.

"Keep it," he said. "Best don't show a weapon. Last guy that did wound up on a slab. Big mistake. Stupid all around. Lots of pissed off people."

"No, you take it."

I handed him my weapon. We'd already had enough stupid. I could get my gun back on the way out.

I tried to remember how long it had been. It had been a long time, a long road.

Back then, I was new to politics, a young official of the most populous county in America, Los Angeles. Back then, I did the grunt work. I delivered messages, greased the palms, and picked up the goodies. They'd trusted me with the money.

They still did, but these days we had to move it around in semitrailers. The city of angels had treated me well.

I was now the Lieutenant Governor of a powerful sanctuary state, one in the process of seceding from the United States. Things were different. They were better, a lot better, assuming the Muslim morons, union hacks, and greedy gangbangers didn't screw it up.

Next election, I'd be the Governor of California. The fix was in.

"They're in the backroom. Ruby will take you."

He gestured and a statuesque Black woman appeared. She looked like a professional athlete. Tall, fit, and with legs that went on forever. This woman spent a lot of time at the gym.

She flashed a smile. "You're expected, Governor Salizar. Need anything, just ask…"

"Right."

She knocked and then pulled the door open. "Your guest is here, Sir."

There were three men seated around a small table. I recognized El Capo instantly, and was shocked that he'd be here personally. He had at least ten million dollars on his head. Last I looked, he was #2 on the FBI most wanted. Terrorism, mass murder, human trafficking, and, above all, weapons.

It was always about weapons. That was why I was here.

Jesus, I thought. They are taking this seriously.

"Carlos," I said. "Didn't expect you. I'm honored."

Ruby said, "Anyone need anything?"

"Ice water," I said. The rest shook their heads.

"Good to see you, Hugo. Like old times." Carlos gestured. "We need to talk private."

The other two were gone before Ruby was back with my water.

"No interruptions."

"Right." Ruby flashed her smile and was gone, closing the door behind her with a loud thunk.

"You up to speed, Hugo? Muslim cluster fuck in Monterey."

"What the Hell happened?"

"Not sure. The rag heads made a hit on a house there. Iran has a base in San Luis. You know about that?"

"Some." I nodded.

"I have a problem. So do you."

"The Iranians are complaining you shorted them."

"Bullshit. It's their own damn fault. Big plans, but no brains and no balls. Tried to whack the President a few times. Bungled it bad. Bad feelings between the rag heads and our Black Bros along the way. Feds have their backs up. Monterey didn't help."

I said, "What were they after in Monterey?"

"They were looking for an informer or something. I'm not sure. Whoever it was, it was a goose chase with no goose around. The person who led the raid is dead. The house was crawling with FBI agents. Dead bodies all over the place from both sides."

"That's the same story I got. It doesn't make a lot of sense."

"Do you know anything more?"

I shrugged. "Not a lot. I'm staying distant. It's a fight between lawyers. California wants the crime scene, but the Feds claim purview. Our State AG says the Feds will win, but she can tie it up for some time. We're both trying to keep it out of the media."

Carlos looked at me. "Can the Feds impose Martial Law over this?"

"What do you think?"

"I think yes. A pile of dead Federal Agents and an Iranian base on US soil? Why not?"

I nodded. "President Blager might just go for it. The Iranians are puckered tight. They had something big planned, major attacks, but they didn't get the weapons they needed, lost some of what they had, and have now crawled down in their hidey hole whining about needing support."

Carlos said, "We lost contact with them."

"Sure you did. Like I said, the Iranians are panicked. They think their communications are bugged. They won't communicate electronically. I'm the messenger."

"Good to know. Their communications probably **are** bugged. So what's the message?"

"They need their weapons now. They paid for them and they want them."

Carlos sighed. "They owe us money."

"If they don't get the weapons they are expecting, nothing will happen. If nothing happens, the Iranians are toast and you'll get nothing."

"And if they get them, we'll get paid, and the world will be happy...."

"Our part of the world will be. You'll get what you are owed. Iran will attack, people will panic, State opposition leaders will die, and we'll be closer to Cal Exit."

"And you will be Governor...."

"I'll be Governor anyway. Maybe I'll be President of the Sovereign State of California. Most of the UN would recognize that. Blager's enemies in Congress and the media would rejoice. Maybe there will be a coup, who knows? We are off the edge of the map, Carlos."

"Where do they want these weapons? We'd promised to deliver in Monterey."

"You know that won't work, Carlos. Monterey is crawling with Feds."

"They want them delivered to their base in San Luis Obispo. The middle of effing nowhere, over a poor quality two-lane road, and with no cover going in or out."

"So charge them a premium for the risk. You've delivered weapons in war zones. What's the problem?"

"Do you know what the shipment consists of?"

"Weapons." I shrugged. "Guns, bullets, explosives. That's what you do, Carlos."

"Try twenty tons of weapons, going down a shitty road that is washed out in places. We have high explosives, land mines, grenades, five hundred thousand rounds of ammo, and two thousand mortar shells. One kid with a firecracker, much less an FBI sniper with incendiary rounds, and it all goes boom."

"So you lose a convoy. Short the shipment. Use cheap labor. Hire illegals. Why do you care?"

Carlos sighed. "We have WMDs."

"What kind of WMDs?"

"Five tons of Sarin gas. It's safe until you mix it up, and this lot is active and ready to go. Five tons. Do you know anything about Sarin?"

"Not a lot."

"It's an off switch for life. It's colorless, tasteless, and it kills in seconds. It is twenty six times more deadly than cyanide. Breathe it, you die. It touches your skin, you die. You touch anyone who died from it, you die. It's been banned by international law for decades.

"It is so deadly that even the Nazis, who gassed Jews right and left, never used it against the allies. We have more Sarin in this one shipment than Hitler ever did.

"35 mg in a liter of air, one squirt from a spray can, kills a healthy human in about a minute."

I said, "This is bad shit, Carlos."

"Tell me about it. It's here. Sitting in a warehouse in East LA."

"Send it back."

"I can't, Hugo. The other cartels know about it. I had to make special arrangements to transship it. My own people had concerns. Some in the Mexican government know. A few foreign governments know. My suppliers know. No way that this gas is going back into Mexico."

"You can't destroy it?"

"No and I can't leave it there. I need to move it."

I'd never seen that look on his face. *Horror.*

"What should I do?"

"I think you'd better deliver it as soon as you can, my friend. Get it to the Muslims and get clear of it. If this gets out of control, it could ruin us all."

CHAPTER TWENTY NINE
RUSSIA REDUX

Golden Gate Park, 11:45 AM, Sunday

Marie. She was there, my Russian contact, punctual and professional. She looked the same as last time we'd met, an attractive woman poised and relaxed in the bright sunshine.

Marie wore the same loose white dress, showing her ample breasts while leaving her shoulders covered. She had the same wide brimmed hat, not straw, white cloth. A vision from a 1890s French impressionist painter, here before me in the flesh.

She'd brought a parasol. The woman had a sense of humor. Or maybe a sense of nostalgia. The invasion by Muslims had ruined Paris.

Easy, I thought, reminding myself. *"No one is better at spy games than the Russians."*

This time, my back up team was tested. Millie and her watchers. My TSG security teams, Scooter One and Scooter Two. Most important was that Pat Barry, my sniper, had over watch.

Last time it almost got messy. We were green. We'd been lucky.

"Bonjour, Marie," I said.

Her eyes twinkled. "Horrid accent, Digger, but it is good to see you well."

"And you. Last time could have gone badly, you know."

She gestured and I sat down next to her, leaning against the large block of stone, all that was left of the Sweeney Observatory. I slumped, making it a point to keep my head below the top.

Marie said, "No guns this time. Were any of your people harmed?"

"They were not, but it was a near thing."

"We had two injuries. Both are recovering. Thank you for showing restraint."

"Your operatives seemed impulsive. Do I get to ask why?"

She said, "My control offers his apologies. Yes, some of our people were excessive. We appreciated your gift of Claas Vogel."

"Thank you. I will pass that along."

"Putin himself has expressed gratitude. Vogel funded The Beslan Massacre. He is a financial terrorist. We'd like to pay you the bounty and a bonus. You've earned it."

"I don't want money."

"What do you want?"

"My American friends want something more precious."

Marie smiled. "Information…."

"Is Vogel talking?"

"How do you say it? Singing like a bird?"

"Yes."

"His chief interrogator has a personal interest. It may take some time, but we'll get everything he has before Vogel is executed."

"We'd like a share of the take. The West didn't have a warrant, but he did us lasting grievous harm. We want those records and recordings. We want the names of his agents in North America."

"That request was anticipated. I have the authority to tell you it is granted. We suggest that the details would be best handled between the counterintelligence branches of FSB and America's CIA."

"That works."

"No offense intended, Digger. We sense that Canada wants to distance itself."

"None taken," I said. "Canada will never admit that Vogel was taken on their soil."

"I expect not. That was also anticipated. No problem."

I looked at her intently. Then stood and looked around. I saw nothing. I had gotten no alerts. I detected no threats.

"You seem distrustful, Digger. Why is that?"

I settled back down next to her. "We're friends, are we not?"

"Allies, at least." Marie murmured. She had beautiful eyes. Violet eyes. You could lose yourself in those eyes.

I remembered my briefings about the Sparrow schools. The best trained sexual seducers in history, they said. *Eat your heart out Hugh Hefner.*

I hated having to say my next words. It would ruin the mood.

"You almost got my people killed last time. You almost got me killed. Your madman in the red corvette is lucky to be alive. You mentioned being 'excessive,' and I agree. I came close to putting a bullet in his head."

Marie frowned. Her gaze shifted in an instant from seductive to alert. I was watching a cheetah studying possible prey. Sizing it up. An amazing transition.

She said, "Do you have a question?"

"I do. Will there be any disciplinary action for the excesses of your agents? Back during the Cold War there were rules. If we all go around with our fingers on the triggers, I think we can expect unhappy outcomes. Do you want that?"

"The man you speak of is named Yakov Petrovitch. He is not being disciplined, but he has been retasked. He's not fond of the West, he hates terrorists, and he blames your weaknesses for allowing *jihad* to prosper. We should not have used him against you."

I waited, letting the silence lengthen.

"Yakov has a lot of anger. He's been inclined to rages, sometimes endangering our own operatives."

"But you are not going to discipline him?"

"We are not. Mother Russia is a harsher land than your West. We have other ways, perhaps better ways. If you and Yakov were to meet now, he might embrace you."

"I have no idea what you are talking about."

"Yakov's rage stems from The Beslan Massacre. He lost his mentor, his commander, and many of his best friends. He watched innocent young children being slaughtered by *jihadists*. Do you know who funded that attack?"

"Vogel?"

"Correct. Yakov is Vogel's chief interrogator. He is happier than anyone has seen him for years. He's doing an excellent job by all reports."

I was silent for what seemed a long time. Finally, I said, "A man who loves his work."

"Indeed." Marie was no longer watching me. She was looking out across the meadow, lost in her own thoughts.

Finally, she said, "So we had a mutual operation that ended well for all involved?"

What could I say?

"Yes. I suppose it did."

"It's been good working with you, Digger. I think we are done."

I shook my head. "I don't think so."

"Why not?"

"My friends need some help. An elderly American citizen is imprisoned in Syria. He has committed no crimes, and certainly none against them. He has been there for many years, and we need to get him out."

"So?"

"Russia has an excellent relationship with Syria. I expect a simple request from your government could secure our citizen's release."

"It might. Does this citizen have a name?"

"Colonel John Giles, US Army retired."

"What was your citizen doing in Syria?"

"Nothing whatsoever. He was a civilian executive working for a private company here in the states. Islamic terrorists abducted him from the state of Oregon some fifteen years ago."

"How did he get to Syria?"

"We don't know."

"Why do you think this is my problem, Digger? Why do I care?"

Gotta love the Russians. Pragmatists to the core.

"Actually, it's not."

"Good. I'm glad we agree about that."

"It is your opportunity, Marie, not your problem."

"What makes you say that?"

"Do you know the name Ahmed Mahmoud Muhammad?"

She shook her head.

"How about Nassar Fuad?"

"No."

"You've never worked against the Islamists, have you?"

"Not directly."

"You expressed distaste for Claas Vogel about The Beslan Massacre."

"Vogel funded it. He pulled the strings."

"He's an evil man. Do you know who planned the Beslan attack? Who set it up?"

"Someone working for Vogel, I presume. No attackers survived."

"The *jihadists* who were present during the attack died for Allah. But the mastermind who planned it was not there. He survived. Would you like to guess his name?"

"Nassar Fuad?"

"Bingo! You win. That's why you care. That's why FSB cares. That's why Putin cares. It is also, I expect, why Yakov will care after he questions Vogel about Beslan."

"How do you know these things?"

Her first stupid question? Not bloody likely!

It was either stupid, or very clever and subtle. Either she was rattled or was testing me to see if I revealed sources and methods.

Probably it was the latter, a test to see how far I could be trusted with FSB's secrets, a probe to see how much to reveal. The Russians did not like leaks.

"Friends tell me things. Now that you are a friend, I hope you tell me things."

"What do you want?"

"You should interrogate Vogel about Fuad – ask him about *both* names, and be aware that he has used others. Check it out and validate what I told you. After you do, I'd like a copy of those interrogations, both paper and tape."

"Where is this Fuad person?"

"If you ask me nicely, we are going to deliver him to you, neatly wrapped, just as we did with Vogel."

"But this time you want something in exchange?"

"This time we want something *first*. Can you guess what that is?"

"Your missing citizen, the kidnapped Colonel?"

"Correct. His name is John Giles. It will be like the bad old days. We could use the old Checkpoint Charlie, the bridge of spies, just like back in the Cold War. You give us Giles, who we know is alive and currently in good health. We then give you Fuad."

"Alive and in good health?"

"Of course. He might be a bit battered around the edges, but, yes, alive."

Marie shook her head. "You are an interesting man, Digger. You keep surprising me."

"And you, me. Do we have an agreement?"

"Give me a few days. Do you still have that burner phone?"

I nodded.

"This is unusual. It will have to be approved at high levels, perhaps by Putin himself."

"Fair enough."

"Do you have a suggested time line?"

I shrugged. "There are details. Perhaps a week or two for approval, and a month or so for the actual exchange."

"I think that might work. I will call you in a week."

"What happens to Fuad if we say no?"

"Nothing good, I expect, but that is not up to me. There could be consequences in Syria as well, but I don't know. Again, that is not up to me."

Marie nodded. "That's how it works, isn't it?"

"Seems like…."

"I find these conversations with you useful."

"The feeling is mutual. This time, let's hope we both get to go home without any unnecessary drama."

She smiled. "Let's plan on that. Stay safe."

With that I disengaged. I stood, nodded, and, without a word, we walked away in opposite directions.

The ambiance was different this time. There were no problems with my egress. No ticks. I was clean.

I supposed we could view our dialogues as an odd form of *detente*. I hoped it could last long enough for us to get John back.

Scooter Two picked me up when I exited the park and we were off to the airport, running CSRs along the way. I needed to get back to Josie and Goldfarb. I had just promised to deliver an item to the Russians, to deliver something that we did not possess.

I felt like the old Marshal in **High Noon**. The clock was running and the odds were stacked against success. *Tick-tock. Tick-tock.*

CHAPTER THIRTY
RUSSIA REDUX

The Ranch, Mendocino, California, Raven's Suite

It had been a long day.

When I entered, calling ahead and using my key, the sliding door to the patio was open. I could hear Josie and Gerry Mickelson talking and laughing outside. Mike told me that Gerry was a new woman ever since Josie had located her dad.

"I'm back."

"Out here," Josie called.

The women had bonded. That was always dangerous. They were planning something. I could sense it.

"You look exhausted," Josie said. "There is beer in the cooler."

"Russians," I said, shaking my head. "Never a dull moment...."

"He's involved with a beautiful Russian spy. I get to watch them."

Gerry gave her an odd look. "How nice for you...."

I looked in the cooler. IPA, my favorite, ice cold. I poured, watched moisture condense on the frosty glass for a long moment, took a first sip, and nodded. *Perfect.*

"Thank you."

"I need a kiss."

I kissed her gently, glad to be back. It felt good.

"Does he smell like perfume?"

Josie shook her head. "More like a wet dog."

Whatever they were talking about, I did not want to go there. "Where's Mike?"

"Arguing with Goldfarb," Gerry said. "Mike wants to go to Monterey. Goldfarb says to wait. They've been waiting for you to get back."

"The FBI guy flew in," Josie said. "Mike had something he wanted."

"Marvelous." Screw the FBI. I needed to be working on wrapping up Fuad. "I'm supposed to check in?"

Both women nodded. Josie said, "Immediately, if not sooner."

"Great. Notch that up to just short of fucking fantastic."

I took another sip of my beer, easing back in my chair, willing my muscles to relax. I closed my eyes and took a deep breath. When I looked, both women were frowning at me.

"Mike needs your help," Gerry said.

"Did he say that?"

"He's a Marine, Raven. Marines charge for the guns."

She had that one right.

Josie said, "Mike *does* need your help. I did a remote viewing. It was problematic. I'll do another one after you agree to help him and decide what to do."

"Okay," I said. "Here's the deal."

I had two pairs of eyes boring into me like lasers. They had definitely bonded.

"Keep talking," Josie said.

"I'm going to sit here for a minimum of five minutes and savor my beer. Then I'm going to take a hot shower and put on clean clothes. After which I will trot my ass over and help everyone save the world, FBI and all."

"I'll call them," Josie said.

"Thank you. If that's not acceptable, they can send someone over to either scrub my back or shoot me."

Gerry said, "Do you think you can save the FBI?"

"Lady, I don't think God can save the FBI. The words *Charlie Foxtrot* come to mind. Does Mike think *he* can save them?"

Gerry smiled. "I can see why he likes you."

The Ranch, Mendocino, California, Main Lodge

I looked around the room and blinked. There were more people here than I'd expected.

Goldfarb, seated at the head of the table, said, "Good to see you, Raven."

"I've been a bit busy, Sir."

Mike was grinning. "Can we sniff him and see if he smells pretty?"

There was a ripple of laughter.

Goldfarb said, "You know most of those here. I want to introduce Captain Peterson, Admiral Quigley's EO, and Director Roger Johnson of the FBI. The President's national security advisor was unable to attend. I will be returning to Washington to apprise him of the results of this meeting."

"Yes, Sir."

"The purpose of this meeting is narrow. The agenda is how to best preempt or respond to the foreign force in Monterey. Said force is now deemed to be presenting a clear and present danger to the United States by intended use of military force."

In Monterey. The Quds base was not to be mentioned.

I nodded.

"It is agreed that the FBI has purview of the situation on the ground in Monterey."

"I was told that is disputed, Sir."

Mike said, "Purview is disputed by officials of the State of California. It is not disputed within the Federal Government."

Director Johnson said, "The FBI has purview. The Attorney General is meeting with the Governor of California to ensure he understands and complies. If he does not agree, he will be placed under arrest."

Mike said, "We are allowed to observe under specific rules of engagement. Do we have people on the ground?"

I nodded. "We do. Our TSG team will be there tonight."

Mike said, "Excellent. The ROEs are basic. We will observe to give the FBI time to locate and apprehend these illegal enemy combatants. We will not engage them other than to defend ourselves if attacked."

"The *suspected* terrorists," Johnson said. "We have the names and sketches you provided. We can find and apprehend them if they are there."

Mike said, "Once missiles are launched or heavy weapons are fired, it becomes a military matter. We are then allowed to engage."

Captain Peterson spoke for the first time. "The airspace over and around Monterey is Federal. Iranian terrorists targeting US aircraft with military weapons will be deemed to be a foreign attack on America, an act of war.

"The military has responsibility for foreign air threats. Our Marines will be providing your air support. We are adding equipment to Mike's aircraft to ensure you can communicate on their command frequencies."

Mike said, "I've delayed my trip. John Black is qualified on our aircraft. He will be included in the mission briefings with their assigned pilots."

"What happens when Monterey goes hot?""

Peterson said, "We are coordinating with the FAA. If an attack is imminent, a Temporary Flight Restriction, a no fly zone, will be issued from the surface to eighteen thousand feet. It will apply to all aircraft not involved in this mission. Active launch and artillery locations will become free fire zones."

"My people are cleared to engage at that time?"

"They are." Johnson looked like he was sucking on a lemon. "When the TFR goes hot, the FBI will disengage. We will expeditiously clear the area."

Peterson said, "We will provide your ground teams with laser designators to target enemy positions with precision weapons. I presume they are familiar with their use?"

"They are. I expect Mike will be grateful, Captain."

Mike feigned surprise. "You're passing up my offer of transport?"

"I am, but I'll buy you dinner."

Peterson smiled. "He's not crazy."

Goldfarb made an odd sound, perhaps a snort.

"That is debatable, Captain. In any case, I think this concludes our meeting. Any who need to leave are free to go. The rest are invited to dinner. Thank you for your time and support."

CHAPTER THIRTY ONE
BLACK UNLEASHED

Enroute to Monterey, Southbound at 31,000 feet and 400 knots

Captain Peterson was in a rush to get back to DC, but he had been kind enough to give me a ride to Monterey. His aircraft wasn't as state-of-the art as what we had access to, an old DC-9 – the Navy called them C-9s. It was probably older than the kids up front in the cockpit.

The old bird got the job done, but lacked elegance. We were side-by-side in canvas jump seats, my bugout bag and weapons kit were lashed to the deck, and the rear of the airplane was stacked high with cargo. Except for legroom and not having a terrorist sitting next to you, it was worse than riding the airlines.

Peterson looked over at me, "Hated to miss that dinner, Raven, but we do have some sandwiches on board."

"I'll pass. We'll be on the ground soon. My teams haven't eaten yet either."

For some reason, that prompted a smile. "RHIP."

"Huh?"

"*Rank hath its privileges....*"

"The Duke of Wellington said that. He was the commander who defeated Napoleon and changed history. That's the quote people remember."

I said, "It's usually interpreted to justify misconduct."

"These days, yes. That's because the media and schools always leave out the last part. You can't even find it on Internet searches anymore."

He held up the coffee pot. I nodded, waiting for the rest, while he poured. *The media was worthless. What it omitted was often crucial. What it included was often false.*

My long day wasn't over. Instead of Josie, a warm bed, and a nice meal, I'd be in Indian country and exhausted by the time we arrived. This wasn't normal America. It was a sanctuary state with *jihadi* kill teams and hostile officials.

My scooter teams would have been up, active, or driving into position for over 30 hours. It was worse for them.

"… *after it has fulfilled its responsibilities.*"

"Wellington said that?"

Peterson nodded. "It used to be his most famous quotation."

"Did he say what the responsibilities were?"

"That is what prompted my comment. He said, 'To ensure the men were fed before the officers, and the horses before the men.' You are a good leader. You don't have to be out in the field protecting Mike and supporting your men, but you are."

"Thank you."

"I have a second reason for transporting you. The Presidio is in Monterey. We'll be met at the airport. You needed laser designators for your mission. I can supply two."

"That will be adequate. Thank you."

"The Joint Chiefs are wrestling with the other problem. I wanted you to know that."

The Quds base.

"That is a tough one."

"Your team got the Intel that revealed it."

I nodded.

"Do you have any suggestions?"

"Just the obvious. We need to get it right. We'll know more in a few days. We are still collecting Intel."

"I understand." The tone of the engines changed. "We're starting down. Good luck."

"To you, as well."

Monterey, On the Ground, Two Days Later, Afternoon

We'd gotten some much needed rest, Mike was inbound, and we were in place. So far the FBI hadn't found anything. We were guessing.

We'd staked out the area west of the airport. They were using runway 10L, coming in off the ocean and landing to the East, the ILS precision approach. It would continue to function even if the GPS signals were jammed.

There really wasn't any high terrain, except to the East. The airport was at 257 feet, and except for towers and buildings, it was pretty much flat.

I'd positioned myself on the beach. I did not have a view of the airport, but should be able to see Mike's plane on the approach. He'd go right by me. It would be low, 2600 feet and descending, and in easy range of Stingers or even ground fire, especially if the *jihadis* had brought a .50 Cal with them.

It would also be slow. Damned slow. The usual restriction was 200 knots, with a hard speed limit at 250. A sitting duck. Mike had brass balls. So did John Black, he'd be flying because of his Air Force experience in F-22s.

I had Scooter One positioned North of the Approach Path, and Scooter Two South. Both teams had laser designators and .300 Magnum sniper rifles. Their rifles were useless against SAMs and the designators depended on having platforms around to deliver precision ordinance. That was up to the Marines.

I had three radios, one for the Marine command channel, one for listening to the tower, and my Cybertech com unit for my own teams. According to the tower, Mike was inbound.

His aircraft radio call on the Marine frequency was "Mad Man." Not Mad Dog, which was taken. The Marines had a sense of humor, apparently. I was told there would be two escorts, "Hammer One" and "Hammer Two."

I had no idea of the capabilities of those escorts. I also had no idea where the FBI was, but I did know that we could not engage.

Mad Man reported 20 out. Ten minutes. Easy math. I took a deep breath and clicked team COM.

"Raven to Scooters. Showtime in five. Mad Man is twenty out."

Both scooters acknowledged. I put glasses to my eyes. I could see a white speck far out at sea, with a smaller gray speck on each side clear against the setting sun.

"Raven has visual. Scooters go to Marine Com."

I heard two clicks. I put down that radio and picked up my military unit.

"Mad Man, Raven has a visual."

"Roger that." It was Black's voice. "Hot or cold?"

"Cold," I said.

The specs were getting larger. I could see that graceful white Gulfstream sliding down the sky, a bit nose high at its low speed. The escorts were ugly and square, boxy looking, silver gray with big engine pods and double tails.

Air Force A-10s, flown by Marines. Warthogs. At least Black would be familiar with them. He'd escorted them in the sandbox. He now had one tucked tight on each wingtip.

"Still cold?" Black said.

They swept by, and I swung to track them, raised my radio, and was about to speak when all Hell broke loose.

"Hammer One. **Vampire, vampire, vampire.**"

Showers of flares and a storm of metal chaff poured from both A-10s. I knew their jammers were active.

A missile trailing flame and smoke was rising over the city, moving fast, accelerating, tracking Mike's plane.

"Mad Man is rolling right, out and down." Black's voice was calm.

The Gulfstream, no longer graceful, stood on one wingtip, falling like a piano, leaving nothing but vacant air between the A-10s.

"Hammer One. Break and engage."

The A-10s immediately broke hard right and left with showers of chaff and flares trailing them. They went wings vertical pulling high G, presenting big radar profiles and bringing their weapons to bear.

Come play with us, asshole….

"Hammer One, give us a target."

"Painting the launch site." It was Pat Barry, Scooter One's sniper.

I kept my mouth shut. Everyone was doing their jobs.

The answer was immediate. "Hammer One has a lock. Engaging."

Hammer One was almost inverted when his missile came off the rail like a flung knife. The two contrails passed, parallel tracks, incoming and counter fire.

The rising missile was now swerving back and forth, searching. It was moving fast, a bright spot.

"Hammer Two. SAM is not tracking. I have the launch site. Engaging with cannon."

The entire nose of the second A-10 lit up. Its massive 7-barrel 30 millimeter GAU-8 Gatling gun showered a stream of PGU-13/B High Explosive Incendiary (HEI) rounds, 3900 rounds per minute. It was still firing when I lost sight of it.

The A-10s had both dropped out of my field of view. The Gulfstream was gone. I couldn't see a thing except for the rising SAM and empty sky.

Then I did. A bright flash and a rising fireball. A secondary explosion. They'd hit something.

"Raven here. Heads up everyone. There is a second team."

"Scooter One. Negative. We got him." It was Vinney, Pat's spotter.

"Report."

"I just did. Dumb bastard stood up with his launcher. Pat blew his head off."

"Hammer One is turning back toward the airport. Two, form on me. Mad Man, report."

There was no answer.

"Hammer One. Report, Mad Man."

Nothing.

I could hear a noise. It was my radio on the traffic control frequency.

"Monterey tower to Raven. Do you read?"

"Raven here."

"We just had a Gulfstream land. He says he lost COM with you. Says he's good except for a few branches in his landing gear. We are on lockdown. The field is now closed."

I took a deep breath. I picked up my military radio and keyed it.

"Raven to Hammer One. Mad Man landed okay. Good job."

"Roger that. Hammer flight is exiting the area."

The tower was still talking.

"Do you read me? We are shut down here. What are your intentions?"

"Tower, we are also shut down. Tell the Gulfstream the FBI has purview and will be there soon to sort things out."

"Repeat that, Raven?"

"We are shut down and clear. Is the FBI there yet?"

"Affirmative."

"Good. They have purview. Raven out."

Scooter Two was just rolling up. Terry, in the right seat, hopped out.

"We missed the whole thing. Pretty lights in the sky."

"Yeah," I said. "We are done here. Everyone is good. Mike is safe and we don't have time to get tangled up with the FBI."

"Where are we going?"

"Somewhere else. It's time to kick some ass."

Terry grinned. "Works for me...."

CHAPTER THIRTY TWO
HOME AGAIN, GONE AGAIN

The Ranch, Mendocino, California, Raven's Suite

"Honey, I'm home…."

Josie came rushing in off the patio, her face radiant. She wrapped her arms around me and gave me a kiss. "You disappeared."

"You were in the shower. I left you a note."

"*Going to help Mike. Plane is waiting.* It didn't tell me much."

"You were all over me to help him, so I did."

"You've been gone for days."

"Yeah. We got stuck in Monterey."

"What kind of help did he need?"

"People are wound tight down there. Mostly moral support…."

Josie backed off and raised an eyebrow. She was giving me **the look**.

The look! The one all men dreaded. I was getting to know her. She was getting to know me.

"Gerry is worried. She said they are fixing his airplane."

"It's no big deal. He's doing policy stuff with the Bureau."

"What's wrong with the plane?"

"Something technical."

"Bullet holes?"

I shook my head. "It might not even be broken. They want to inspect it."

Josie nodded slowly. "He told Gerry he was fine."

"There you go….."

"I can do a remote viewing. I have a bad feeling…."

That was the problem with loving a paranormal. She sensed something was wrong.

"We need you to do viewings, but not now. Mike is fine. All our people are good."

She studied me for a long moment.

"Please? We need a break from this."

"Okay," she finally said.

"How about a cold beer, we shut down the phones, and lock the door? We are alone at last. Goldfarb is off to DC and Mike is in Monterey."

Her radiant smile was back. "You bet. Be right back."

I heaved a sigh of relief. Violence shut her down. We required clear viewings for what I needed to do next.

Time was running out. I had to deliver Fuad to the Russians soon if we were to have any hope of getting Colonel John Giles out of Syria

Underground UN facility, San Luis Obispo County

"You know who I am, Mr. Fuad," I said.

For a notorious terrorist, the man in front of me didn't look like much. Five foot 10 inches, stocky, typical Mid-Eastern olive complexion, brown eyes and hair. The scar on the man's left temple was unremarkable.

Their world was like that. It was like the Black gangbangers with their tattoos.

If there was anything unusual, it was his age. Other than protected leaders like Bin Laden, *jihadists* didn't live long.

The man said, "You are Hugo Salizar. You are the Lieutenant Governor of California and you owe me weapons."

I shook my head slowly. "You are mistaken, Mr. Fuad. I'm not your weapons supplier. I am your boss, the man whose orders you will follow. I am also your lifeline, your only hope for staying alive."

He stared at me. "Why would you say such crazy things?"

"Your weapons supplier is El Capo. I know him as Carlos. He sent me here to deliver a message."

"El Capo owes me money."

"I doubt it. He says not, but even if he does, it is a matter between you and him. One of no concern to me."

"He has not delivered the weapons I paid him for."

"He says that you contracted to accept them in Monterey. Due to your bungling, he says that area is now swarming with the FBI."

"There are problems in Monterey. It's not my problem. I did not cause it. I now want the weapons delivered to me *here*. El Capo demanded an extra fee. One I have refused to pay."

"That is your problem, Mr. Fuad. Even if true, I expect that recent events make the issues of an extra fee irrelevant. El Capo will want some or most of his money returned."

"What recent events?"

"Mr. Fuad, you sent some of your men with some of the military weapons that have been provided you into Monterey to attack Federal Officers."

"What if I did? It is what we do. It is why you are supporting us. We are here to attack and destabilize America. This has nothing to do with my missing weapons."

"El Capo delivered over half your weapons order to Monterey, as you admit was agreed to. He delivered them to a warehouse that is owned and controlled by one of your entities as was written into your contract with him, a document you signed. He delivered."

"Good. He may now put them back on the trucks and deliver them to me here."

"Actually, he can't."

"Why not?"

"Because, Mr. Fuad, some of the morons you have working for you chose to attack a flight of American military aircraft. Your men fired a stolen Stinger missile from off the roof of the warehouse where your weapons were stored in Monterey."

Fuad blinked. "What?"

"You need to watch the news. The Americans fired back. Does it surprise you that if you shoot at people, they might shoot back?"

"What's your point?"

"Your warehouse is gone. Half your weapons are gone – **after they were delivered as was contracted**. You now owe – actually Iran owes, and I expect they will pay – El Capo a considerable sum of money."

Fuad was staring at me. "What do you want, Mr. Salizar?"

"I would prefer to become Governor of California, or perhaps the President of an independent California. I would prefer to have monuments made for me. I would prefer not to hang for treason."

"What do you want of *me*?"

"I am on my way to Sacramento at the request of the Governor. I need to assure him that you and El Capo have resolved your differences and that your weapons are being satisfactorily delivered. I need to tell him that you have personally assured me that Iran's plans are proceeding despite this setback. I need to tell him that all is well."

Fuad was still staring at me. "Of course all is well, *Insha'Allah*."

"Good. You have four days to get the rest of your shipment here, secure, underground, and out of sight. You will be held accountable if your poison gas is intercepted or lost."

"What exactly do you want me to do?"

"What you agreed to do in the first place. Put together a convoy and take delivery of **your** weapons. Get that damned gas out of my state and into your bunker. Stop making excuses. Who pays for what is between you and El Capo. I don't care."

"El Capo will kill me."

"He might. He may add extra fees. That is between you, Iran, and him."

"You need us."

"We do not need **you**. You know El Capo's rules. Take possession of your Sarin gas, **all** of it, in the next four days. If you fail him, you fail us and you will die. No excuses. Your fault, our fault, no one's fault, it does not matter. You will die."

Fuad said, "You do not want Iran as an enemy."

"Nor do you. If that Sarin gas is not secured in your bunkers in the next four days you will die. Iran will apologize for your bungling and pay El Capo what is owed."

The Ranch, Mendocino, California, Mike's Suite

My secure phone rang. It was Mike. *Thank you, Cybertech.*

"I was hoping you'd call. Raven's back. Are you okay?"

"You bet, now that I'm talking to you."

I smiled into the phone. We'd been married for years, but he still lightened my heart.

"I'll be back to pick you up in the morning. Get packed."

"I *am* packed. It's lonely here."

"I have been trying to reach Raven. He has his phone shut off."

"He'd better *keep* it off. Josie was planning a romantic interlude. She came out of the shower to find a cryptic note saying he was off to help you. She's likely locked their door and piled furniture in front of it."

A chuckle came over the phone. "Seems excessive...."

"Raven vanished. She's been worried."

"Things have been a bit confused down here."

"It's been almost a week. Is he okay?"

"As far as I know. He repositioned his team to San Luis Obispo and then returned to Josie so they can get back to extracting your dad. It just took some time."

"Your office called. His team has been calling them. You and he have been off the grid. They are desperate to reach Black. Your office needs authorization."

"For what?"

"Legends. Raven's team wants identities, licenses, and pocket litter as locals. I don't have the details."

"Call them back, secure. Mark it urgent. Tell them Black's with me. He's busy. Whatever they need, tell my office it is approved. I'll text an authorization for their records."

"Black's with you?"

"With the airplane, actually. He has a rep as a hotshot pilot. I wanted to see him in action. He did great."

"Your airplane is broken."

"They say it's fixed. Final checks in the morning."

"Did something happen?"

"Sure. We landed. Good is when you can walk away. Great is when you can use the airplane again. Black did great."

I laughed. "I'll tell your office. Miss you!"

"Love you. We'll be there by 1100. Meet me at the airport. We'll be home for dinner."

CHAPTER THIRTY THREE
THE HEART OF DARKNESS

Black Bear Diner, Santa Maria, San Luis Obispo County

"Here are your papers."

Pat Barry passed the packets to the rest of the team. They had each arrived separately and were now tucked into a booth at the rear of the restaurant.

Four old friends chatting and having breakfast. Privately, out of view of the security cameras up front and at the doors. We had a cute little Cybertech box that showed a yellow light for audio surveillance and a red one for video. Neither was lit. No one was seated within hearing distance, and there was enough noise from the front of the diner to cover us.

Terry had eyes on the door. He was over watch, sipping coffee, pretending to study the sports section of the local paper. The morning rush was gone, but the place was still half full, offering good cover.

The waitress, Marge, was friendly but not intrusive. This was a good spot for meets, just off the 101 with good access and egress.

All were dressed like locals with faded jeans, wide belts with big buckles, sweatshirts, loose denim jackets, and baseball caps, all suitably distressed. They'd picked up two battered pickup trucks with local plates for cover, and parked their tricked out Dodge Challengers in opposite corners in the back, shielded by trees, out of view of the road.

Rudy and Vinnie were studying their legends carefully. They were going to be the leads. That broke up the scooter teams, but special skills were involved.

"Black's not coming," Pat said. "He's out of play. Raven's inbound. I'll pick him up. I've got operational control until he arrives."

Terry said, "Do we have official cover?"

"Negative. You are civilians. Our friends at the Bureau are unaware, as are the local police. You all have IDs and carry permits. Best to avoid notice and be polite, like boy scouts. If you screw up, go quietly, hunker down, use your phone call, and wait for legal counsel. TSG will get you out, but you'll miss the action."

Rudy said, "ROEs?"

"We have special ROEs. Here is the big one. No one goes anywhere near the Quds base. They have massive force, heavy weapons, sensors, cameras, and the perimeter is likely mined. It is a kill zone. Stay clear. Do not even think about it."

No one spoke.

"I need a verbal acknowledgement on that one guys."

"If we can't touch the base, what are we doing here?" Terry said.

"Raven will give you a brief on that when he arrives. I'm here to brief you on what we are NOT doing. We are not going anywhere near that base."

They were all looking at me. Terry said, "Why not?"

"Orders. Raven was clear. That base is the heart of darkness. The military is evaluating options for how best to take it out. We are not to touch it. Others have that job. Understood?"

They all acknowledged.

"Good," I said. "As for rules of engagement, until we go hot, avoid situations, avoid lethal force, and play nice. If someone confronts you, back away if you can."

Terry said, "If we can't?"

"If it is law enforcement, get his ID and do what he says. Try not to get into hassles with civilians. If you can't do that, try to avoid shooting them. If it's Quds, and we may have contact, do what you need to do."

"Kill them?"

"Lethal force is allowed for self-defense or to complete the mission."

Vinnie said, "I need more clarity on that one, Pat. What about the drug cartels?"

"It's situational," Pat said. "Has to be. If a *jihadi* or gangbanger comes at you with a weapon, you can kill him. If it's a sentry who might put up an alarm, you might not have to. An unarmed sentry or scout with a radio might need killing to protect the team."

"I can live with that," Vinnie said.

"Verbals?"

They all acknowledged.

"The ROEs will loosen up when Raven arrives."

There were smiles and nods.

"Okay," I said. "We know what the mission isn't. Raven will flesh up what it is when he gets here. Basically, if all goes to plan, we are going to snatch a High Value Target for Raven to extract. To do that, we need two truck drivers. Vinnie and Rudy are our leads"

Rudy said, "Why me?"

"A Black guy fits in better, plus you speak Farsi and Arabic. If you get close, you will have contact with *jihadists*."

"I can't drive a truck."

"Sure you can. Check your legend. You'll be driving a pickup going in. You have a California CDL that says you are good for semis up to double long."

Vinnie said, "I can drive a truck."

"You also speak Spanish. There are drug cartels involved, so that might be useful."

"I. Can. Not. Drive. A. Big. Assed. Truck." Rudy said. "Do you want me to say that in Farsi, *kemosabe*?

Terry said, "It's the bloody details that get people killed, isn't it?"

"*Oh, Ye of little faith*…. Raven has a plan."

"If it's a simple grab and go, why do we need truck drivers?" Terry said.

"Good question," I said. "We don't need *real* truck drivers. We just need *fake* truck drivers. Rudy is perfect for the role."

Vinnie said, "Because he can't drive for shit?"

I shook my head. "No, because of his friendly, can-do attitude, and he looks like a truck driver out of a bad-assed Hollywood movie."

They were all looking at me quizzically.

"I'm tempted to say, *bullshit*," Terry said.

"Here's the deal, guys. We've got good Intel."

I had their attention. They all leaned in a bit. That's when I passed them the sketch. They each studied it carefully. Then I held out my hand and took it back.

"That is our target, the main man at the off-limits Iranian base. He goes by a variety of names, most recently Nassar Fuad. You've never seen him of course."

"Seen who?" Rudy said.

"Right. We can't take Fuad there, so we're getting him to come to us."

"Why would he do that?"

"He's contracted with the drug cartels for weapons. Bad move. It led to disputes of the kind that lead to semitrailers full of contraband and a long trail of dead bodies."

"And we drive the semitrailers?"

"Fuad is not running a truck driving school. His weapons are down in LA, he needs them at his base, and it's his problem to get them there quickly. If he doesn't get that done, the cartels will kill him."

"We *pretend* to drive the semitrailers?"

"Bingo. The trucks and his weapons are in LA, but Fuad is here. His ability to travel is limited. He has to hire truck drivers, he has to hire them locally, and he has to do it quickly. He's desperate. He's in trouble."

Terry said, "He's got a bunch of people at the base. Why can't he use them?"

I smiled. "Want to guess?"

"Because they can't drive big trucks?"

"That's likely true, but even better, because they don't have licenses to drive big trucks in the Peoples Republic of California. You all have CDLs. Probably not one in a thousand Americans has a Commercial Driver's License."

"Fake licenses."

"That's a detail. The point is that Fuad is desperate to get his weapons moved. He's not going to spend time being fussy. Tomorrow at 1400 hours there is a meeting here in town to hire drivers. It will pay well, so there will probably be a lot of applicants."

Vinnie said, "Even though the drivers chosen might get whacked after their run?"

"There could be a high mortality rate for the real drivers. We don't care. No one is asking you to make a career of this, just to be good fakes."

Rudy said, "We just have to be good enough to get hired?"

"All you have to do is be good enough fakes to be in the final pick. When it gets down to the last dozen or so, Raven is betting that Fuad will personally make the final selections."

"Okay, so we get a finalist into the contest, and he sees Fuad. What then?"

"We cuff him, bag him, give him to Raven, and we go home and tell stories about it."

"How do we do that?" Rudy said.

I shrugged. "You are all good at telling stories."

"No, the first part. The snatch. Taking Fuad alive from a group that is likely to be hostile, armed, and pissed off about seeing their paycheck disappear with a bag over his head."

"Right, the exciting part. That's what Raven will explain. I expect it will be something that we're good at, too."

Terry said, "Do we get to know what that is?"

"Something we're good at?" Vinnie said. "I want to hear that, too."

"We **improvise**. Raven will explain the details...."

"I can't wait," Rudy said.

They were all smiling. I noted that. It made me feel good. Maybe I was getting better at motivational speeches.

CHAPTER THIRTY FOUR
TOGETHER

The Ranch, Mendocino, California, Raven's Suite, Late Afternoon

I lay there feeling the breeze and watching Josie sleep, thinking about how lucky I was. Not because of her powers, because of her inner beauty. She was turned away from me, the sunlight slanting across her face and bringing out the highlights in her long brown hair.

She was a gentle soul who sensed the world in ways beyond mere mortals. She could see wondrous beauty and rare events others missed, but she could also sense the horrors and monsters that lurked in dark places or hid behind smiling faces and layers of deceit.

I wanted to stay here, to stay with her, to touch her and hold her, but I dared not. Josie was safe and my team was in harm's way.

She had found evil. We'd hunted it down and the gloves were off. We finally had permission to act. I needed to preempt it before it came for us, for her, again.

Be careful what you wish for.

I had to leave now. I eased myself out of bed slowly, silently sliding out from under the sheets.

"Don't you dare!"

Stealth doesn't help much against a paranormal. I slumped back into bed and turned to face her.

"You're leaving again."

I shrugged. What could I say?

"Don't you **dare** sneak off and leave me here without saying goodbye. You were gone for days."

"I came back to you, Babe. I'll always come back. You know that."

"Of **course** I know that."

"I'm sorry I left you in the shower, but I had a ride to catch."

"That's an excuse." Her voice was a notch softer.

"It's true. You know what I do."

"I know why you left. You knew I was safe and went off to save Mike. Gerry and I asked you to help, but I didn't expect you'd vanish."

"Others saved him. I watched. Black was magnificent."

"Actually, you made a difference."

I looked at her, into her eyes. Clear blue with golden flecks, those eyes could see and sense across time and space.

"It's what I do, Raven. *I see things.* You know that."

I sure did.

"The probability lines shifted. You went to Monterey and the future changed. Mike and Black changed from being a smoking hole in the ground to alive and unharmed."

I didn't speak. I waited.

"In this world, the one that exists now, Gerry was worried. Mike said it was a normal trip, but she *knew* he was going into danger, into a trap."

"Yes." *He knew that. Gerry somehow sensed it.*

"Mike finally called. She asked if anything happened. He said, 'We landed.' That's all he said. She laughed and it was over."

"They did land. Some minor damage to the airplane, I think."

"That was **after** the shift. In the previous reality, the world where you stayed with me and *didn't* go to Monterey, we had a wonderful night, the best since we met."

"I wanted to stay."

"You have no idea how it felt to me. I was expecting something like the honeymoon we've never had, a fulfilled dream. I was happy. Can you understand that?"

I nodded.

"When I climbed out of the tub, you were gone. You didn't even say goodbye. My world went dark. I felt like I'd been left standing at the altar, like I'd been jilted."

"I'm sorry we missed that night, Babe."

"I'm not."

I blinked. *Huh?*

"I'm not angry that you left. I'm **hurt** that you blindsided me."

I shook my head. She had seemed angry.

"You had to go. Because you did, there was a different outcome down in Monterey. There was a different future."

"In what way?"

"In the old future, the one where you stayed with me, Mike was killed."

I took a deep breath.

Josie said, "I was angry because you upset my plans, but it could have been a lot worse. Our friends could be dead. We could be blaming each other for that."

She was silent for a long moment.

"That might-have-been future got worse as time progressed. California in flames, civil war, and more…."

"What can I do, Babe? If I don't go do my job, I put people and things I love at risk. If I do, I abandon the person I love most and bring violence into our lives."

"You're missing the point. Together, we can thwart evil. Separately, we won't survive."

We had talked about that a lot when we first met. It seemed like eons ago. She was right, of course. "I know that."

"Do you really?"

"Yes. I was used to working alone, being alone. It was how I'd survived. It's different with you. I would have died at Natanz. You would have died at Durham. Together, we survived."

"We did, but my powers come with a price. I think the Gods are trying to teach me lessons that I failed to learn a millennia ago. We **have** to work together. I dare not ignore that."

"What do you want me to do?"

"Love me. Trust me. Bond with me."

"I do. I'm trying."

"Try harder. Leave me when you must, but **warn** me before you do. Talk to me. Trust me to understand. Be patient when I'm selfish."

"You're not selfish."

"It is selfish to expect reality to be what it isn't. We can nudge the outcomes a little, you and I, but there will always be good versus evil. There will be pain. It's built into our universe."

"What should we do, you and me?"

"Work together more closely. Communicate. Share. You need to be you and I need to be me, but we have to work as a team.

"Remember when I was dying and you sent me a black rose?"

I nodded.

"Hold that memory, Raven. Together we can survive. Alone, we will perish."

"I believe you."

"It's not enough to believe, you must **know**." Josie's eyes were pleading. "We've lived that out before. You know that, Raven. A long time ago, I was a Celtic Priestess. We died in 56 BC when Roman soldiers under Gaius Julius Caesar destroyed my temple."

"I do know."

"You **died** defending me. We lost our civilization and all we loved."

"I don't remember past lives, but I **do** know. Your mentor Kaimi told me as well."

"You remember, but with my powers I still **see** these things. In ancient times, there were warrior/priestess teams. Today, there are not. That might be why Kaimi came to help us."

"Not sure I'd want to see that stuff, Babe. Back then, we lost. I failed to save you."

"Maybe I failed to save **you**. It is two sides of the same coin. That's how it works."

"Today's enemies are more powerful. It could happen again."

"They've worked hard to erase our history, culture, and institutional memory. It **will** happen again if we don't combine, if we don't trust completely, if we don't work in harmony. *We need to do better*."

"I was wrong, Josie. I should never have left without warning you."

"Thank you." She touched my cheek. "Together?"

"Together! I promise."

"I know you have to leave now. A nexus is forming, I sense it."

"I need to be on the ground in San Luis Obispo County with my team and a plan before noon."

"Arrange transport. I need to do a remote viewing before you leave."

"You got it. I'll tell Goldfarb what we need and make my call backs. Mike's coming here for Gerry in the morning, but that's too late and he has a different mission."

Josie said, "So does Goldfarb. We are on our own, but it doesn't matter. We know what needs to be done. Goldfarb and Mike will cut you slack. I will help guide you."

"Thank you."

"Keep me involved. I hate violence, but I don't want to lose you."

"I promise."

"Together."

"Yes."

Santa Maria Airport, Mid-morning

They'd loaned us the conference room. We watched the Citation land. Raven hopped out immediately, but the crew stayed on board.

Pat went out to meet him. Raven came in carrying a small tote bag. He sat in the middle, his back against the wall.

I said, "You've all eaten? Pat briefed you?"

They nodded.

"We have more support and a change of plan." I proceeded to spread the printout of a Google map on the table.

"I'll give you copies. Key on Highway 101. It's central to our mission."

"We are south. Santa Maria. Other than the meeting tomorrow, there is no action planned here. You have good access to 101, from here, from the diner, and from the meeting."

I tapped the map to emphasize each of my points.

"Slightly north, you see San Luis Obispo, the town, on the coast. It has an airport with good access to 101. We'll reposition the aircraft. That airport will be our extraction point."

I looked around. "Got it?"

They all nodded.

"You all know about the Quds base. It is off limits. It's being watched. DOD has drones up. We will have a real-time feed."

"On the way there is Atascadero. Small town, not much there, no suitable airport, but an intersection of 101 to Highway 41, a lonely road going east into the boonies. Out that way it gets desolate. Out there is where we'll interdict and do the snatch."

I looked around. "Verbals, please."

They all said, "Yes."

"You know our target and have seen his sketch? He's the base commander."

Again a chorus, "Yes."

"We want to take him alive. Here's the new plan. Two of you, our lead drivers, will stick with the original plan. You are Team Alpha. The rest of us, Team Beta, will do the snatch."

I looked at Pat. "Did you bring your Barrett .50 Cal? I want to borrow your .300 Win Mag."

He nodded.

"I need a sniper, so I'm taking Pat. I'll spot for him. Vinnie, being able to recognize trucks, gets to stay here and impress everyone."

"I go with you two?" Terry said.

"Affirmative. Team Beta is me, Pat, and Terry. I've brought more weapons. We'll need to gun up. Take one of the old trucks, Terry. You'll be our blocker."

Vinnie and Rudy were looking uncomfortable.

Vinnie said, "We're on our own?"

"Correct. You are the fake drivers, Team Alpha. Act independently, like you don't know each other. Stay low key, like you need the jobs."

Rudy said, "You *do* know I can't drive big assed trucks."

I said, "You don't have to. Just fake it and look cool. Let Vinnie do most of the talking."

"Vinnie talking is *not* the part I'm worried about. What changed?"

"We lucked out. Better Intel and support. If things go as planned, I'll text you with an ETA for the extraction point. When you get my ETA text, Team Alpha can fade away."

Vinnie said, "ROEs?"

"Our extraction flight will be waiting at San Luis Obispo airport with a hot clearance. Meet us there. Whatever force or subterfuge is needed to discourage pursuit is authorized. You will be cleared though the gate."

Rudy said, "What if you miss?"

"You carry on and try to make the final cut. Stick with the original plan. Team Beta will try to get back in time to assist."

"And if you don't?" Vinnie said.

"Then something went wrong at our end. If you don't get my text, then it's up to Team Alpha to complete the mission. If the package shows up, make the snatch, get to the airport with the package, and get the Hell out of Dodge. Do not wait for us."

"What if we can't make the snatch or the package doesn't show?"

"Get clear. Live to fight another day."

I was getting intense looks, but no one spoke.

"You have your secure COMs. Text me if details come up. This OP should be easy."

"How easy?" Pat said.

"Like farting though a silk rag. Questions?"

"If it all goes to shit?"

"Standard rules. Scatter. Get clear. Get out. Communicate when you can. I'll text ABORT to set that off. If I'm down, Pat will. Team Beta, expect a firefight when we interdict."

"Anything else?"

There were no more questions.

"Good luck. Pat and Terry, we'll take two vehicles. Stay under the speed limit. We will brief when we get to the interdict point."

I looked at Rudy and Vinnie. "Stay cool, Team Alpha. The driver selection meeting starts at 1400. You can expect my ETA text before it kicks off."

With that, Team Beta stood. We left, moving casually, as if we had not a care in the world.

We did not look back. That was bad luck.

CHAPTER THIRTY FIVE
KILL ZONE

San Luis Obispo County, California, Highway 41, Afternoon

This was the place. It was perfect, a blind curve to the east, a narrow canyon, and a straight run going west.

I figured we were about a forty minute drive from the Quds base. Close enough, but not too close. Well outside their perimeter. I had Pat stop, jumped out, and waved Terry down.

"We'll do it here. Go back a hundred yards or so. Find a spot where you can stash the truck out of sight. I want a good view from the hill to the south, and a place where the road is restricted, necked down. I want a choke point."

Terry said, "We're talking roadblock?"

"Probably. You're the blocker, so get set up. We'll double back and brief you."

I looked at Pat. "Go with him and take your Barrett. I want you to have a good over watch point. I've got antitank mines, Claymores, C4, and other goodies in the back. Help Terry get them into his truck."

Pat said, "AT mines?"

"They have several hundred people at that Quds base, including heavy weapons, APCs and Abrams Tanks. Whatever comes our way, we need to be ready."

"Nasty things to leave around…."

"For sure. Rig them with command detonators in addition to pressure plates. We don't want to leave unexploded ordinance."

"You said this was going to be easy, *like farting though a silk rag*. Are you still saying that?"

"Hope so. No harm in being ready, is there? Help Terry prepare a kill zone."

Terry laughed and turned his truck around. They loaded up and rolled away. We had not seen any traffic for the last thirty minutes and we had some time.

Pat's car was one of TSG's geeked-up Dodge Challengers. I slid behind the wheel, fired it up, put my gadgets on the seat, and started going down my check list.

No cell phone service, *check*. We didn't need it and the bad guys might.

I fired my iPad up, put the antenna on the dash, and punched in the codes. Sure enough, a clear picture of the Quds base, in HD and with GPS coordinates. Actually, two of them, split screen.

Perfect. Satellite feed, *check*.

The military had two drones up. One was focused on the main gate and the road in front. The other was scanning the camp. Nothing was moving except for the people at the gate and in the guard towers.

Eight guards that I could see. The ones at the gate had AKs. Those in the towers had belted machine guns. I'd seen bases in Iraq that were not that gunned up.

Our drones were unarmed. Surveillance was all the Joint Chiefs had authorized.

Now to try my Cybertech phone. It was supposed to communicate anywhere, and we needed that now. I called Josie and waited for the secure light to turn green.

It did. Secure COMs, *check*. Everything was working.

Josie answered on the first ring. "You're early. Are you in place?"

"Almost. I have eyes on, but we're still setting up. It looks like the base is on alert."

"Fuad is terrified. The drug cartels and State are furious over his weapons shipment being bungled. They'll kill him if he doesn't get it off the street."

"Unfortunately we need him alive."

"Yes."

"Is he coming?"

"Absolutely. They are leaving in about five minutes."

"What are the logistics?"

"You want the good news or the bad news?"

"Good first."

"Fuad is definitely attending the meeting. There are two vehicles in the convoy taking him to Santa Maria to vet the drivers. Fuad goes, looks, returns to the base, and his people make the delivery."

"Sounds easy."

"It's not. Here's the bad news.

This is his hand-picked personal security detail. The first vehicle is an armored-up Humvee with a .50 caliber and four of his elite guards. It is one of our late models. It will be hard to stop with IEDs or gunfire. The second vehicle will be Fuad in a Mercedes limo, also armored, with a driver and a bodyguard."

"Armored how?"

"The standard package. It will stop .223s and pistols."

I was proud of Josie. She'd done her homework. Her powers were strong. Trying to view the coming violence would have traumatized her, and might have shut her down. She'd avoided viewing that so she could get me the information that I needed to know.

Each time, we worked a little better together. Now I needed to do my part.

"Where will Fuad be sitting in the limo?"

"Right rear, strapped in," Josie said. "You did hear me about his personal security?"

"I did. He has a lot."

"Can you deal with it?"

"Yes, but we're outgunned."

"They'll probably be moving fast. Figure 60 MPH or better. The mission brief he gave ordered the first vehicle to punch through if anyone tries to stop them. If it can't, Fuad turns back to the base and a larger force is dispatched to meet him."

"How large?"

"That's the bad news. Fuad is on a ten-minute check-in schedule. If he misses, they send out a twelve person relief force, including an APC and a gun truck with a mortar crew."

"So after we snatch him, they'll be chasing us?"

"Like the hounds of Hell. Can you handle that?"

"No, but we should be able to outrun them. Incidentally, if they do catch us, Fuad is dead. This is nuts. You're talking about a small war."

"Fuad doesn't care. He didn't care when they hit the FBI in Monterey. It gets worse."

"Go ahead."

"If Fuad calls for help, he gets whatever he asks for. They could send the entire base. They have 200 people there, tanks too."

"That could get interesting."

I was silent for a long moment, thinking. This level of force was going to come as a big shock to Terry and Pat. The silk rag had just turned into a steel cage.

Finally Josie asked, "What are your intentions?"

I smiled and said, "Honorable, Ma'am. Always."

"Not funny."

"We don't want to kill Fuad. That would be too easy."

"It would also end any chance we have to get Gerry's dad back."

"Yes, it would."

"What are you planning to do?"

"Here's the deal. We're going to go for the snatch. Our only chance is hit hard and run like Hell. If this goes down quickly, we can easily outrun a relief force, especially one with big trucks and APCs. If they tie us up, we're screwed."

"If you get killed out there, I'm never going to forgive you."

"It would be an embarrassment. That's why I need you to do something else for me. Call Mike, tell him what's going down, and say that I'm asking for help."

"What kind of help?"

"Military. A pair of Navy A-10s saved his ass in Monterey. They landed there and were being provisioned at the Presidio. I have no idea whose control they are under, but Mike will know. Ask him to send them if he can, and to call Admiral Quigley if he must."

"That is one of the craziest most half-assed plans I've ever heard of."

"I disagree. The 'run like Hell' part is totally sane. It is historically well-tested."

Josie said, "That part might actually work. I'm talking about the rest."

"Durham was crazy. Saving Mike at Monterey was crazy. This plan is only moderately demented. People get medals for doing stuff like this. Ask Mike about his raid into Bukhari."

I heard a deep sigh. "Be careful, my love."

"Always."

Onboard the TSG Gulfstream, 39,000 Feet, Northbound

Gerry pulled the secure phone out of her purse and held it up. "It's Josie."

I nodded. "I love those phones. Cybertech's technology is amazing, totally secure. It can access signals though our onboard COM gear. Fully compatible. Seamless."

"I'm surprised she's calling."

"Me too...."

Gerry picked it up, waited for the secure light, and listened.

"Yes. We're in the air, heading for New York. We're going home."

A few seconds passed.

"Raven's *not with you*? I'm surprised...."

"He's where? With our TSG team? How...?"

"He's what? When?"

"How did...?"

"Yes, we know about the base and Fuad. It is off-limits...."

"Oh my God, yes. Mike's right here. He's sitting next to me. I'll get him to pick up."

Gerry's face was white.

She turned to me. "Pick up your phone. **Now!** Patch into her call. Raven's in trouble. We have a situation...."

CHAPTER THIRTY SIX
THINGS GET MESSY

San Luis Obispo County, California, Highway 41

We'd prepared the battlefield and everyone – all three of us – was in position. Fuad and company were maybe five or ten minutes out and coming fast.

I would see the lead Humvee first, coming in off the blind curve to the east, down into the narrow canyon, coming out on a straight run going west. We were all on the south side of the road, with me to the east, Rudy just over a hundred yards to the west with his M4 and the detonator for our explosives and mines. Pat, our sniper, was on the high ground, in-between, over watching us both, about 200 out with his big Barrett .50 Cal.

My guys were pros. They didn't complain about our tactical situation, though they were fully aware that it sucked. I'd explained to them that our only chance was to take out all the opposition quickly, save Fuad himself, of course.

We needed that one alive. If we had only one man left, his job was to extract Fuad.

They all knew that, of course, but I had to make sure they knew it in every fiber of their being. *This was kill-or-die.* A good commander would have avoided getting his troops into such a situation – think Custer and Indians – but it was what it was.

Sure, Custer was outnumbered. Any history book will tell you that. But what the historians missed, I guess it was embarrassing, was that the Indians had vastly superior weapons, state-of-the-art repeating rifles. Custer's men had Civil War era single-shot breech loaders.

It gets down to how much accurate fire you can put on target. We'd engage at point blank range for our long guns. Accuracy would be good. The problem was that our rate of fire was going to be low.

Pat might able to get off 5-10 aimed shots a minute, at best. No way that I could match that, not with an unfamiliar bolt action weapon. I'd be lucky to do one or two. The Iranians we faced had modern automatic weapons with fire rates of at least 600 rounds per minute and maybe twice that.

Raven's last stand? I hoped not.

In a prolonged fight, we'd lose. We only had two weapons that could penetrate their armored vehicles, the Barrett, and Pat's beloved .300 Winchester Magnum that I'd borrowed. Rounds from our M4s and handguns would not penetrate.

All they had to do was delay us and pin us down until their relief force arrived. Worse, if we let them get too close, say within 50 yards, they'd be hosing us full auto.

The odds for us would get worse, not better, at close range. We had to eliminate all the defensive fire before we went for the snatch.

When Fuad's convoy came down the chute into our kill zone, we'd have only a minute or so to react and engage.

I'd let the Humvee pass and try to take out the driver. Pat was my back up. His backup was Rudy and the explosives.

My shot was the signal to hit them with everything we had. If I didn't shoot, we'd let them pass, abort the mission, and live to fight another day. Hopeful theory.

I was hunkered down in position with my Barrett ready, one up the pipe and my scope dialed in. At this range, I couldn't miss, or so I thought. I couldn't see Rudy, but I had a good view of Raven and an excellent view of the kill zone.

Raven was looking east, up towards the blind curve. I saw him tense and then I saw the Humvee. It was in desert camouflage and had a .50 Cal machine gun on top, with the gunner protected by plates of armor.

The vehicle's weapon was pointed forward. The gunner was looking down the road, searching for threats. It was moving fast. Damned fast.

Raven swiveled to track it as the Humvee passed him, but he didn't fire. Something was wrong. The Humvee passed me and I saw the problem.

Raven didn't have a shot. The rear of the Humvee was solid armor. No window.

Nothing I could do about that. I was not going to fire first. I put my crosshairs on the driver's window and swung left to give a good lead.

That was a mistake.

Someone in the vehicle must have gotten a glint off my glass. The gunner was swiveling his weapon toward me. Time seemed to stop.

I had only a few seconds to live. Long enough to get one shot off.

I stayed with the target I had. Then the gunner's head exploded in a spray of red, followed by the sharp bark of my .300 Magnum. Thank you, Raven.

The pressure was off and the driver was mine. I took a deep breath, held it, and squeezed, riding the recoil of my Barrett. I thought I got a hit, but it was a tough shot what with the angles and the Humvee moving so fast.

I worked the action and came back on target. The driver's window was shattered. He was slumped in his harness. His right seat buddy was leaning over doing the steering and the Humvee had not slowed. If anything, it was going faster.

I fired again, lower, center mass, though the broken window, aiming just over the vehicle's armor. That one was a solid hit, through the driver and into the helper.

I worked to reacquire. I needed to finish that target. I needed to stop that vehicle.

And then I didn't….

A huge fireball engulfed the Humvee. It came out the other side trailing flames and smoke. Then it hit another mine. That one lifted it into the air, flipping it on its side.

Rudy opened up with his M4. He was putting short bursts through the open hatch under the .50 Cal on the now exposed roof of the Humvee.

Some were tracer. I could see them clearly. Those high-velocity .223 rounds could not penetrate the armor, but they sure could bounce around inside.

I shifted targets to the Mercedes. It was breaking frantically, trying to avoid the carnage ahead. It made a bootleg turn and reversed direction, running for home.

I saw the windshield shatter and heard the sharp blast of my Magnum. Raven was slow, but he could shoot.

Time to help him out. I put my round through the driver's side, low, at the bottom of what had been the windshield, but was now an empty hole.

The Mercedes was coming almost straight on. As fast as I could work the action, I put two more into the engine block. Easy shots. Mortally wounded, it slowed to a stop with steam and black smoke oozing out from under the hood.

I saw Raven running flat out toward the Mercedes. He'd dropped my rifle and was firing short bursts from an M4, shooting from the hip at a dead run, not aimed, three-round bursts, suppression fire. *Blaap Blaap Blaap.*

I didn't dare fire at the passenger side. My rounds would punch right through and we needed Fuad alive.

Raven was close. He dropped his M4 on its sling and pitched a grenade in through what had been the windshield, followed by another. The vehicle filled with white smoke.

CS gas. Nasty stuff.

The right rear door popped open and Fuad rolled out. He was doubled up coughing, but holding a weapon. Raven came up and kicked him in the head.

Fuad still had a grip on his pistol. Raven smashed him with the butt of his M4.

Fuad went limp. It was over.

We were about ten minutes out from the kill zone when the radio call came in.

"Hammer Lead to Raven, can you read?"

I pulled my Military COM out. Pat was driving. We had Fuad wrapped and tied in the trunk, and Rudy was running rear guard about a hundred yards behind us in his old truck.

Good news.

Before I could answer, he called again. "Hammer Lead to Raven, check in."

"Raven's here."

A chuckle came over the command channel. "Hammer's a flight of two, loaded for bear. Are you in trouble again?"

I had to smile. "Not sure, Hammer. We're about ten minutes west of the cluster of burned out vehicles on Highway 41. Can you see the kill zone?"

"Affirmative. Hammer has eyes on. Nothing moving."

"We left it that way, Hammer. We are on egress. Do you see any pursuit?"

"Negative."

"Check to the east, Hammer."

"Stand by, Raven."

Several minutes passed. "Hammer to Raven, you have pursuit east of the kill zone. Four vehicles. An APC in the lead, a gun truck, and two Humvees with guns on top."

"Raven to Hammer. We expected that."

"Hammer Flight requests permission to engage."

He's asking me?

A more powerful transmitter broke in, 'Hammer Control to Raven, what do you need?"

"Stand by." I thought for a minute. "Hammer Control, let the convoy get to the kill zone, then smoke the lead vehicle. If they turn back, let them go."

"Hammer Control to Raven, 'Let them go?' Please repeat."

"Raven to Control. Affirmative. If they turn back, let them go. If they press on or fire on your birds, kill them all."

"Control to Raven. Let them go. If they press on or engage us, kill them."

"Affirmative."

"Hammer Control to Hammer Lead, did you get that?"

"Lead to Control, we are cleared to engage if they pass the kill zone or fire on us."

"Control to Hammer Lead. Affirmative. We confirm that."

"Hammer Lead to Control, they are coming up on the kill zone now. They are not slowing. Hammer Flight is engaging now. Follow me in Hammer Two."

Lead was already firing. I heard his big gun pounding away before the transmission cut off.

"You smoked him, boss. APC is burning. Secondary explosions. We did not take any fire."

There was a slight pause, then, "Lead to Hammer Two. The convoy stopped. Let's tease them again. Give them a low fly-by. I'll cover you."

"Two to Lead. Rolling in now."

About a minute passed. "Lead to Hammer Control. Target convoy did not fire. They are turning back."

"Control to Raven, you need anything else?"

"Negative. Follow them home if you have fuel, and thanks for the help."

"Our pleasure, Raven. Any time. Control out."

So far, so good, I thought. *What am I missing?*

I put down my military COM and pulled out my secure phone, sending a text to Vinnie and Terry, my fake truck drivers.

"Egress ETA 1415. Go to identity B when CLR. Respond."

Vinnie came right back, "Outta here."

Twenty three seconds later, Terry sent, "Moving."

They were heads up and rolling, I thought. *What else?*

It's the details that kill you. I sent a text to Mike.

"Need GITMO landing clearance. Isolate one HVT."

That was probably redundant.

The pilot would have a flight plan in for air traffic control, but I was hoping to avoid protocols and excessive scrutiny. A civilian plane invited questions. Mike could smooth that.

Pat was holding ten over the limit. "We'll be at the airport in twenty."

"Right," I said. "You and Rudy do cleanup. Get clear, go back to the Ranch, and take some down time. Vinnie and Terry are going with me."

He grinned. "They didn't get to be fake truck drivers."

"Not to worry. I'm going to give them a shot at being fake Federal Marshals."

CHAPTER THIRTY SEVEN
HIGH PUCKER AND HUMIDITY

GITMO, Evening

I'd gotten Mike's text back, "GITMO set. Check in when you can. No rush."

He had prepared the way for us. We even had executive rooms with king sized beds and showers booked. The Captain who greeted us said that they usually went to visiting elected officials. Fortunately, none were here or expected anytime in the near future.

We had tucked Fuad into one of the high security isolation cells at the old Camp 7. He was now officially "Prisoner C." He'd be parked there in isolation until orders came through channels to transfer him or Hell froze over, whichever came first.

Then I checked in with Josie and assured her that we were all fine. I asked her to do one remote viewing, a low stress one, and told her I'll call in the morning.

She sounded great. For the first time in a long time, she wasn't worried for me. All her senses were showing low threat, both for her and for me. Evil seemed to be occupied with other issues, at least for a time.

I took a hot shower, shut everything down, told the operator "no calls," put a "do not disturb" sign on the door, taped the curtains to the wall with duct tape to keep out the light, and slept like a baby for twelve hours.

Rudy was the first thing I saw in the dining hall. A six foot four inch, jet black, bald, badass sporting a Federal Marshal's uniform, neatly pressed, at a table over in the corner. He looked impressive.

"May I sit with you, Marshal?"

"Bout time you crawled your ass out of bed. You missed breakfast, but if you ask nice they can get you *huevos rancheros*. Love that Mexican food. Navy coffee, but not bad…."

The truth was I'd almost missed lunch. I sat down next to him and a steward took my double order, plus back coffee, and an OJ.

Rudy waited until I'd finished my first cup. "Hear tell you learned to work Pat's rifle."

"Just in time, too," I said. "Where's Terry?"

"With our package. Apparently he's asking for you."

"Really?"

Rudy shrugged. "Terry said that he was. He didn't say a word to me."

"Must be your bedside manner…."

"Reckon so. Do we have a plan?"

Rudy wasn't big for small talk. I smiled, enjoying my first taste of the *huevos*. They were excellent.

"I think Mike wants us to chill a bit and let things settle. Figure we'll probably be here overnight, and back to the ranch in the morning."

"Works for me. California is freaking crazy."

'I noticed that. Pass the word to Terry. I'll go see the package after I've checked in with Mike and Josie."

I walked around outside to make my calls. The base was an ugly place with scrub vegetation, no beaches, and bad vibes. It was like a slum, one with fences, barbed wire, and guards.

For all practical purposes, GITMO didn't have a climate. Guantanamo Bay Naval Base was muggy and cloudy. Through the entire summer, humidity ran 90% to 97%. Even the winters had over

60%. Over the course of the year, the temperature varied from 69°F to 92°F and was rarely below 65°F or above 94°F. It pushed the limits of "muggy" to the max.

Josie's viewing had gotten me the information that I was hoping for.

"Great news. Thanks. You rock, Babe."

"When will you be home?"

"Soon. I'll try to get them to have a Covfefe meeting out there and wrap this up. Figure maybe two or three days."

"Miss you."

"Love you. I'm coming, Babe. The worst is over."

I hung up and called Mike. He picked up on the first ring. "How's GITMO?"

"Warm, humid, and a good warm water training base for the Navy. It's an excellent place for a prison, but not the best for a duty station."

"I was there as a Lieutenant. Some things don't change."

"We have the Quds base commander, Fuad."

"Good job. Intact?"

"Affirmative. Has the situation eased any in California?"

"Some. The FBI has purview. The CA governor is back pedaling, privately. Your recent adventures on the highway from Hell went unnoticed by the media. The Joint Chiefs remain at high pucker. They want options."

"I'm hoping we can offer some. Thanks for the air support, by the way. It was superb."

"I'll pass that along."

"How's Goldfarb?"

"Happy that you and I survived. He's mostly working the Joint Chief's concerns."

"We smoked some *jihadists*. Is there any pushback?"

"Sure." Mike laughed. "Most I've spoken with wonder why you let them go."

"What about you?"

"I'm more interested in Fuad. Why did you deliver him to GITMO?"

"The Russians want him. We can swap him for your Father-in-Law."

"I know that. My question remains…."

"How much time can you buy me before we have a Covfefe meeting to discuss this?"

"Two or three days, maybe a week. Why are you dodging my question?"

"You'll see. Three days is good. Are we still covering the Quds base with drones?"

"24/7, satellite too. We have a thin perimeter up around the base, a tripwire, about a mile out."

"Can you have them keep that distance?"

"Affirmative. Do you want them to back off more?"

"No, that's good. Watch the grounds and guard stations. Call me if something changes."

"Anything else?"

"I remember your Bukhari raid. Do you still have good connections at Fort Detrick?"

"I do."

"Have them get a decontamination team to San Luis Obispo, and make sure Goldfarb so informs the NSC. Fuad was playing with Sarin gas."

"I was afraid of that. What are your intentions?"

"One more overnight here. Can you site the Covfefe meeting at the Ranch?"

"Yes."

"Okay. How about we return to the ranch and I send your plane back tomorrow?"

"Works for me."

"Thanks, Mike. Raven out."

I checked in with Terry. He said, "Fuad wants to talk with you."

"Why?"

"No idea. He keeps asking for the guy who captured him."

"Might as well check it out. Give me a water bottle. I'll go in and play nice cop."

"You never know...."

I handed Terry my weapons, he opened the door, and I entered. Fuad was wearing the signature GITMO orange jump suit. He was secured to the floor with an ankle chain, sitting, leaning against the wall facing the door, watching me, his brown eyes alert.

I thought back, recalling Josie's sketch. The scar on his left temple was faint, but distinctive.

"Hello," I said in Arabic.

He replied, "*As-salāmu alaykum.*"

Peace be upon you.

Good luck with that, I thought.

I shifted to English. "You have invaded my country. What do you want?"

"I am not Iranian." Fuad had just a tinge of a British accent. "I'm not even *Shiite*, I am *Sunni*."

"Even if so, why do I care?"

"You speak our language. You know our customs. Guests are honored."

"So?"

"I am a guest, not an invader. I was invited here."

"You are a guest of Iranians, Quds force, who are invaders. That makes you an invader."

Fuad shook his head slowly. "You are mistaken."

I waited, curious to see where he was going with this.

"The Iranians are guests. They were invited here. They are not invaders. Their presence here is legal under international law, and I am part of their party. My presence here is legal. I have not broken any of your laws."

"None of this is my concern. I'm not a lawyer."

"America claims to be a country of laws, a country that treats all fairly under the law."

This was getting bizarre. "Do you have anything else you want to say?"

"Do you not care about your own laws, about international law?"

"Again, this doesn't concern me. I expect your documents will be checked and your identity verified, but I have no involvement in that. If you claim American citizenship or have a visa, mention it to someone who cares."

"I'm not an American citizen, nor do I have a visa."

"Seems to be a problem for you, doesn't it? That would tend to make you an illegal enemy combatant. As such, you have no protection under U.S. law or the Geneva Convention."

"I'm a guest of your country. The Iranians are guests of your country. We are protected."

I took a deep breath and was turning to leave, when he said. "I can prove it."

"Stand up."

He did, looking me in the eye.

"How?"

Beads of sweat were forming on Fuad's forehead. "I don't understand."

"How can you **prove** you have a right to an armed presence here in America?"

"My Iranian hosts were invited here. America invited us and provided our weapons."

I was getting tired of this. "Prove it."

"Top officials of your nation and the state of California invited Iran here. Your own Vice President is at our base. The Governor of California has visited us there."

"That's nonsense. The Vice President is in Washington DC."

"Vice President Duncan Dunbar, a military veteran, is at our base. I spoke with him yesterday."

"Not likely, and, in any case, Dunbar is not our Vice President. He resigned some time ago."

"He has been staying at our base since he resigned. He is there now. At the time that Iran was invited to America, he was your Vice President."

It could be true. I had no idea.

"When did the Governor last visit you?"

"A few days ago. I spoke with him, Governor Hugo Salizar."

"Salizar is not the Governor. He is the Lieutenant Governor."

"You split hairs. The Governor of California is retiring. In a few months Mr. Salizar will be the Governor, if not the President of an independent nation. That is in your news. Everyone knows."

"You have a vivid imagination, Mr. Fuad. I'm sure someone may be interested in what you are saying. Unfortunately, I'm not that person."

"Who are you?" Fuad demanded.

"A miracle. A mystery to myself," I replied, turning and putting my hand on the door.

"What?"

"George Foreman, a boxer, said that. I've always liked the saying."

"What is your name?"

"That's even harder to know...."

The door closed behind me with a thud.

CHAPTER THIRTY EIGHT
DEAD BIRDS

Westbound out of GITMO, Next Morning, 38,000 Feet

It was good to be heading home. I was looking forward to seeing Josie and actually having a night with her uninterrupted. Fuad was tucked away and my team was safe. I was ready for some down time in a terrific location, a safe space.

Then my secure phone started vibrating. It was Mike. I picked it up and waited for the green light to come on. "Good morning! It's been too long since we talked."

That would be **yesterday**. I was hoping he'd take my hint.

"So how is GITMO treating you?"

He did not. Mike's tone was brusque. This was not a social call.

"No one shot at us. Mission accomplished. Right now, we are in the air heading home. What's up?"

"Dead birds...."

He left the words hanging, waiting for a response.

I finally said, "I have no idea what you are talking about."

"The Hell you don't. How did you know?"

"I know many things. How did I know what?"

"You asked me to call you if anything unusual happened at the Quds base."

"I did."

"Dead birds. How did you know?"

"I still have no idea what you are talking about."

"We noticed it when the sun rose and we got the overhead views. There are dead birds littering the grounds. Mostly crows, I'm told, dozens of them. Several vultures, a few hawks and at least one Eagle. They said it was a Bald Eagle."

"I think you have me confused with the Audubon society. The Bald Eagle may be a problem. It's a protected species."

"Damn it, Raven, how did you **know**?"

Actually, I'd never thought about the wildlife. "What else do you see?"

"Nothing."

"Nothing at all? It's a massive base."

"The structures are untouched, but there is no movement. The guard towers are empty. We have days of tapes and they've never been unattended. No sign of the gate guards either."

"Interesting."

"Did you cause this?"

"Absolutely not."

"Did you know?"

"Know what? That WMDs are dangerous? Sure."

"Don't screw with me. We talked about this. You dodged my questions. Why?"

"We are talking about a toxic mix of Islamic fanatics with a hoard of weapons, including weapons of mass destruction. An invasion force inside of a sanctuary state, one that is on the brink of Civil War. What did you think could come out of that?"

"Nothing good," Mike said.

I said, "Correct. Of course, there was a high probability that things could go wrong. Of course, we saw that. It was just a matter of time, and a question of how bad it might be. What you're seeing is a positive outcome. They had a breach. So sad, too bad."

"They're all dead?"

"Unless they can breathe Sarin gas."

"You saw this coming?"

"Sure, as one possibility. It's what we do, what Josie does. You're upset about some dead birds? The alternative might have been a major terrorist attack with WMDs."

"I'm upset that **you** didn't tell **me** this was coming. Why not?"

"For a number of reasons. Do you want a list? I was a bit busy trying to keep my team alive, it didn't pose a threat, and it hadn't happened. Iran just lost a Quds base. Be happy."

There was a long silence.

"Think about it," I said. "We were **ordered** to stay clear. We already have puckered assholes all the way to the NSC and beyond, and you think we should make an unwanted, speculative, unverifiable prediction of the bad guys suffering a self-inflicted disaster? A prediction that was not actionable, but one that would draw extreme attention and focus on the sources and methods that we intensively DO NOT want to have discussed at all."

"You do have a point."

"Damn right I do. We'd be bugs under a microscope. It would provoke discussions that would be impossible to ignore, even for the President."

"I'm your control. You need to communicate."

"You should be thanking me. The pressure would be unrelenting and inexorable. At best, it would potentially expose our sources and methods. Hell, they might even blame us for letting this happen."

"It would put Josie at risk? Is that your concern?"

"Along with everything else, yes. Josie comes first. She is a national treasure. Protecting her is national policy.

"My prime directive has **always** been to protect Josie first. It's my job. I will never knowingly do **anything** that puts her at risk. Goldfarb set it up that way. President Blager agreed. I thought you did as well."

"I did," Mike said.

"Good. Then this entire discussion is nuts. Understand this: I'll **never** expose Josie. Not under any circumstances."

"We have to say something."

"Why? Do you suggest chatting with people and doing PR is part of our mission?"

"I do not. What do you suggest we do?"

"Covfefe when we can. Keep our mouths shut and our heads down. Stay as far from this as possible."

"Continue."

"You now have a breach officially reported. One involving Sarin gas, a banned WMD."

"So it seems."

"We have organizations that investigate such things, like the FBI. We have organizations that protect our national security, like the DOD. Turn **them** loose. Let them find facts. Have them do their jobs. Can you suggest that approach to Goldfarb and the President?"

"I can," Mike said.

"Good. May I make one more suggestion?"

"Can I stop you?"

"Probably not."

"Go ahead."

"Seal the area. Recommend they send teams in as quickly as possible with full biohazard protection, Class 4. Include forensics as an integral, independent part of the first teams in. Have them wired to photo, tape, and document everything. Bag the bodies. Get all the records, computers, phones, with a pristine legal trail of evidence to the White House and NSC.

"Get copies of those records to the President. At every step have multiple eyes and ears on this. Checks and balances. Every watcher gets watched."

Mike said, "That is extreme. It is unprecedented. That is not going to fly. People will say such an overreaction is paranoid, dysfunctional, and unnecessary."

"They will. You, Goldfarb, the NSC, and the President must resist such people. We need this exposed and investigated, not covered up."

"Why?"

"I'll give you a hypothetical. Not an answer, a challenge."

"Okay."

"A what if...."

"Go ahead."

"What if President Blager could **prove** that America has been invaded by a foreign military force with Weapons of Mass Destruction? What if he could **prove** they were aided by high level officials of the Federal Government and the State of California? What if the bodies of some of those traitors were found in this Iranian base, killed by a malfunction of their own weapons?"

"A total shit storm."

"Correct. This is something that a deep black team like ours should avoid like the plague. It is not our mission. This is political."

"It is more than that. Nothing like this has happened before. It is literally unimaginable."

"I agree. So don't imagine it. Ask the NSC and DOJ to send in teams to investigate, document, and then prosecute. Get **them** to report, take action, and suggest things. And keep us as distant as you can from this."

"You are an interesting man to work with, Raven."

"I'll take that as a compliment. I've just had a resurrection. I'm trying to do the right thing and to have what I love survive the coming storm. What do you plan to do, Mike?"

"Marines are fearless, but this one scares the shit out of me. It is so far over my pay grade I have problems imagining what's coming down. I'm going to bounce your suggestion up to Goldfarb and ask him to inform President Blager and the NSC."

"Good plan. You will make his day."

"I can tell you one thing, before I do. Your expectations are unrealistic."

"In what way?"

"Did you hear the one about the young boy who was telling his father about his plans and dreams?"

"No."

"The boy says, '*When I grow up, I want to be a liberal.*' You know what the dad says?"

I said, "Something unprintable?"

"No. He says, '*Son, you can do one or the other, but you can't do both.*' Think about that. We can try to stay out of this or we can push it upstairs, but do you really think we can do both?"

"Pushing this up the chain is the best hope we have to stay out of this."

"How so?"

"Neither Goldfarb nor the President wants us to be exposed. The Joint Chiefs own this issue. The last thing they want is to have outsiders involved."

"What about the FBI?"

"They'll love it. The FBI needs to show that, despite appearances, they are competent. They like publicity."

"I suppose we can try." Mike sounded dubious.

"You got all over my ass for not communicating with you. Now you don't want to inform your chain of command?"

"I give up. I'll call Goldfarb. But if we have to turn your airplane around and head it for DC instead of back to Josie, we are going have two very pissed off women."

"That one is easy, Mike."

"Do tell."

"Don't make the damned phone call until after I'm on the ground. I assure you I will **not** be answering my phone for at least 48 hours."

Mike laughed. "You have a deal. Good luck."

"To you as well, my friend...."

I punched my phone off. Then I took the battery out.

EPILOGUE
BRIDGE OF SPIES

West Berlin, Late Evening, Three Months Later

It was dark, raining hard, with a thick fog forming. My jacket was waterproof, but cold water was dripping into my eyes and down my neck. I could see the far end of the bridge, barely, the lights reflecting off the wet asphalt.

Nothing was moving. Behind us, elements of an American armored division had blocked off the road with barricades and tanks. Presumably, the Russians were doing the same at the other end. I'd seen lights through the fog as they positioned.

I was freezing my ass off. "How ever did we pick this place for an exchange? Why did the Germans allow Russian and American troops to block off this bridge?"

"Where would you prefer?" Goldfarb murmured.

"Maybe Checkpoint Chonhar in the Crimea, or on a ship off of Syria....?"

"The location is symbolic: Neutral ground in Western Europe. Putin and President Blager picked it."

Mike said, "This is about the superpowers posturing, sending a signal. The big dogs barked. The Germans and NATO acquiesced. We can expect the media and UN to go ape shit."

I looked at Mike, "So why am I here?"

"Goldfarb and the President wanted you to be a part of history, Raven. I expect your Russian spy and her handler are standing in the rain somewhere out there in the dark at the other end, looking our way."

I brushed water off my face. "I think Marie has better sense."

Goldfarb, looking like something out a 1960s John *le Carré* novel in his black trench coat, goatee, and rimless glasses, shook his head. "You don't know the Russians. She's over there along with her handler, the legendary Karlov Petrovich himself. Putin will have insisted."

Mike said, "You can bet on it."

Goldfarb said, "Checkpoint Charlie is long gone, but the Glienicke Bridge is part of the fabric of our diplomacy with the Russian Bear. It is mostly a tangled history fraught with missteps and setbacks, but one that allowed us to both survive the Cold War. This exchange signals a new policy."

Mike said, "We need you to be able to keep meeting with Marie without killing each other. America cut the FSB out entirely when the President bounced this up to the State Department. They could interpret that as a betrayal."

"The Russians tend to take all failures to comply as betrayals, don't they?"

"Karlov would take this one personally. You don't want that."

Goldfarb added, "FSB does not make for a good enemy, Raven. This way the Russians also get a win. Petrovich may well become the next head of the FSB. Marie gets forgiveness for the diplomatic disaster she caused in France. Putin gets respect."

"They must have really wanted to get their hands on Fuad."

"You have no idea," Mike said. "Russians distrust everything, but they love their children. The Beslan massacre was worse for them than 9-11 was for us. It wasn't just the body count – the full power of the Russian state, including their elite forces, had failed to protect helpless children. Worse yet was common knowledge that it could happen again."

Goldfarb said, "Do you know the history of where we are standing? Or the significance of the fact that Putin has made this exchange into a signal of high level policy?"

I shook my head.

He pointed down the bridge. "The **last** of the World War II meetings between the 'Big Three' heads of State was held at the other end of this bridge, in Potsdam, from July 17 to August 2, 1945. By then, Stalin was the only one left standing.

"We'd used nuclear weapons. The Russians had spies inside our Atom bomb program who stole our designs. The next big war would be a nuclear exchange.

"FDR was dead, replaced by Truman. Churchill was replaced on July 26, by Prime Minister Attlee, in the middle of the meeting. Both were in way over their heads, and the public was war-weary. It left Stalin able to exploit a leadership vacuum.

"Truman wanted free elections in Eastern Europe, but Stalin said 'no.' General Patton, the only strong leader in the West who opposed Russia, was soon dead, some said assassinated. The results of the meeting in Potsdam directly led to the Cold War, the Korean War, and the Berlin Wall. It set the next four decades of history."

Mike said, "The Glienicke Bridge has been used for four prisoner exchanges. Tonight, number five, is the first one since 1962."

Goldfarb said, "The Cold War was a scary time, Doctor Strangelove and all that. The Russians only respect strength, and we were nose to nose, toe to toe. One push of the button and the world would become a cinder as thousands of warheads rained down."

"Then came Ronald Reagan," I said.

"Correct," Mike said. "Things got safer for a time, until Obama, the Arab Spring, and the rise of radical Islam. Now it is dangerous again, WMDs and all. That's your history lesson. The world before Obama and ascendant radical Islam came from here, from Potsdam."

"I don't think you finished my lesson."

"It's never finished, Raven."

"Never," Goldfarb said. "The rise of radical Islam was facilitated by a witches' brew of anarchists, socialists, Globalists, Communists, Satanists, and others including puppet masters like Doctor Claas Vogel, who is now enjoying the pleasures of the Lubyanka prison."

Mike said, "What Russia and we have in common is a desire for nation states, and the power to do something about it. This exchange sends a signal to the world, especially to Iran."

"There are now two sides, and they have to choose one?"

"Exactly," Goldfarb said. "Two sides willing to use force and radical Islam caught in the middle. Blager might someday get a peace prize."

Mike was looking down the bridge with binoculars. A solitary figure was striding toward us. The figure stopped halfway, waiting.

"It's him," Mike said. "Iron John."

"Would you like to take the next step?" Goldfarb said.

"Sure."

"Get your package. Send him off."

I hauled Fuad out of the van, yanked him to his feet, and pulled his hood off, pointing down the bridge. "Looks like I don't get to kill you after all. You are being exchanged."

He looked confused. "I'm free?"

"It's up to you. Start walking. Go slow. When you pass the man on the bridge, keep walking. He'll come to us. You will be welcomed at the other end."

Fuad smiled, "Americans are weak. I knew you'd let me go."

"Just walk," I said.

I watched as John approached and Fuad disappeared into the fog.

FACTOIDS AND FANTASIES

Long ago and far away (metaphorically), my nonfiction book *Engines of Prosperity* included a prescient mid-90s quote from Dr. Alvin Toffler, the futurist, *"The sophistication for deception is increasing at a greater rate than the technology for verification. This means the end of truth."*

In today's world, there is a lot of truth in fiction, and a lot of fiction in truth. It is hard to discern which is which, and even harder to verify. There are still First Amendment rights, but truth becomes buried under spin, propaganda and plausible lies. *"Truth is the new hate speech."*

Orwell warned us of this. It is becoming obvious that there are no First Amendment rights or national borders in cyberspace. The Deep State cyber firms have few limits on their behavior.

Raven's Run, featuring terrorists with Iranian nukes, came out before the Obama/Kerry "Iran Deal." It gave Iran a path to nuclear weapons and massive funding (~ $150 Billion) for terrorism. Iran is still chanting "Death to America," a goal which is embedded in their Constitution.

Privacy Wars predicted the NSA and IRS scandals. I am not the only novelist to have done so.

These days, people are going back and reading books like *1984*. *Soft Target* had the notion of a virtual Congress, and several pundits have since suggested that America might be better off with an "iCongress" than the one located in Washington. [**Note:** This has nothing to do with repealing any Amendments. The notion was that a return to how Congress worked in the early years – spending most of its time at home with constituents, versus inside the beltway with lobbyists – worked a lot better. Cyber technology could allow this and make us safer.]

My view is that the best fiction is NOT reality, but it is an image of reality. Consider books like *1984*, or any of the works from major authors like Tom Clancy, Brad Thor, Michael Crichton, and Vince Flynn, among others. Their novels resonate with truth.

In a world where news resembles propaganda, novelists are again becoming the canaries in the coalmine. History tends to repeat. The names Rushdie, Solzhenitsyn, and Lorca come to mind.

ADS-B

This is the future of aviation infrastructure worldwide. It is accepted by the large airlines. By law, aircraft will not be legal to fly in "controlled airspace" without having approved equipment onboard and operational.

The cost of upgrading an aircraft to comply for instrument flight is significant. The minimum is perhaps $5,000-$10,000 for a small aircraft and $50,000-$200,000 for a "legacy" turbine.

Terrorists have it easier. I was astonished when a clever neighbor geek, Mark, proudly invited me over to show me his "dongle," a $25 USB device that displayed all the data for aircraft within a hundred mile circle. It caused me to do the research for this novel.

This technology is a two-edged sword that could be used for good or evil. I was careful to construct my novel in a way that took *more* than ADS-B alone to kill an aircraft, as I have no desire to aid terrorists.

Overlaid on this major infrastructure change is that the US Government plans to "privatize" air traffic control, to turn it over to a private monopoly, thus clouding the accountability for costs, problems, safety, and national security issues.

Some think of this agenda as ObamaCare for airplanes, or perhaps like the Post Office. *You can keep your airplane if you like your airplane.* Passenger delays come from congestion and bureaucracy at the top 50 airports and neither of these is likely to improve that situation.

My guess is that ADS-B will prevail. A lot of money will then be spent to encrypt it and make it secure. I doubt that air traffic control will be privatized in the US.

Islam is Ascendant

The world is in flames. The Arab Spring became the Islamic Winter, and only recently is the rest of the world starting to respond. The FBI says there are ISIS cells in every state.

Global *jihad* has not yet been "declared." Instead, we see terrorism and migration *jihad* — *Hijrah*. Islamic terrorism is the new normal in Europe. London and Paris have fallen.

Jihad is acknowledged as an obligation at least as important as the Five Pillars of Islam. There is, however, a moral obligation to tell your enemy that you intend to attack when you have decided to do so.

The Greater *Jihad* (*Jihad al-Akbar*) is to make Islam "pure." It is an ideology, one of Theocratic socialism, Sharia Law, submission, conquest, and slavery. The Lesser *Jihad* (*Jihad al-Asghar*) is the requirement to defend and extend Islam until the entire world acknowledges the rule of Allah. Today we see the lesser. It is working. Corollaries, supported by texts in the Quran and the Hadiths, are that non-believers who are exposed to the Truth and fail to comply must be eliminated, but temporary measures include *dhimmitude* (paying the *jizya*, stepping off the sidewalk to allow a Muslim to pass) and enslavement.

This Lesser *Jihad* is **not** less important than the Greater. It is the offensive game. It need not require military action. It can be practiced not only by the arm, but also by the tongue, the heart, and the purse. But slaying an infidel does guarantee you a place in Paradise, and a higher level with larger numbers of infidels killed. A famous Turkish massacre was marked by the extraction of the living fetus from pregnant women so that there could be credit for two infidels killed.

The astonishing spread of Islam in its first century was due to the sword. There was a hiatus after the defeat at Vienna when Western technology (more advanced weapons) made battle inadvisable. The nuclear weapon will be the great Equalizer, and allow *jihad* to proceed.

The only option the West has to derail this juggernaut is to demonstrate that the Allah of Islam is powerless. That will be difficult, since Islam has had so many successes in the recent decades.

Remote Viewing

The Intelligence Community had a number of active remote viewing programs during the Cold War, including *Grill Flame and* the famously prescient viewings of the Russian Typhoon ballistic missile nuclear submarine (SSBN) mentioned in my novel ***Raven's Run***. These paranormal programs were officially terminated some time ago.

In the historic aftermath of Hillary losing a rigged election, the Obama/Brennan CIA in January 2017 *outed my fictional character Josie, the remote viewer*. The Central Intelligence Agency released **13 million pages** of declassified documents detailing the agency's **1,864 investigations** into the use of psychic powers.

These documents were posted on the CIA website the week Trump took office. The earliest one I saw there dated from about 1941. None were recent and the highest activity was at the peak of the Cold War. Hours after Trump's inauguration, this trove disappeared. *Poof.*

Any who place confidence in their cyber security and wish to research such things are welcome to try the link below **at their own risk**. Me, I stopped looking and scrubbed my "lab rat" computer when the new documents disappeared.

https://www.cia.gov/library/readingroom/search/site/psychic

Iran and North Korea

Mark Steyn and others have written widely on the increasing conflict between Western nation-states and fundamentalist Islam. Steyn's ***America Alone*** and Samuel P. Huntington's earlier ***The Clash of Civilizations*** discuss this.

The Secret War with Iran, by Ronen Bergman, is also recommended. Gorka's ***Defeating Jihad*** is excellent. The classic book about North Korea is ***This Kind of War***, by General T. R. Fehrenbach.

Before Jimmy Carter, Iran was one of our best allies in the region. Now the Islamic Republic of Iran (though not its people) is an implacable enemy of America, a growing power, and a deadly threat. The same holds with North Korea, a nation which we have technically been at war with since 1950.

Thanks to foolish decisions by liberal politicians, both these implacable enemies now have (or soon will have) nuclear weapons and delivery systems.

What about those Celts?

The Celts are perhaps the best example of an entire culture being erased by conquest and genocide. They are not quite prehistoric, but they are protohistoric. Their own history has been erased, but shards survive based on Roman and Greek writers.

The book that my characters mention is a tough read, but a 2015 BBC TV series ***The Celts*** is entertaining. If you study this, consider the similarities to the Soros/Obama/Clinton "Arab Spring" that has done an excellent job of erasing Western Culture.

Obama's objective was "Fundamental Transformation" and he has largely succeeded. ***The Manchurian President*** by Arron Klein reveals the agreements Obama made with anti-American groups to enlist their support. For the most part, he kept those agreements.

Not with a Bang, but a Whimper?

I have worked in the Mideast. Muslims are the best hosts in the world. They live in a harsh land, and they treat their guests well. The book ***Lone Survivor*** is an incredible testimonial to this.

The history of Islam is one of conquest. The Lesser *Jihad* is constant against outsiders. Islam is a religion of the sword. It is built on conquest, beheadings, and enslavement. ISIS with its brutal beheadings and atrocities is using the old methods. It is as relentless, bloody, and horrific as were the conquerors of 700 AD.

Islam is an ideology of conquest, a total system of government and law with a religious component. It is a form of Theocratic Socialism, just as the Nazis were National socialists; Communists are International socialists, etc. Few Western leaders have understood that, with Thomas Jefferson and Churchill being exceptions.

Fundamental to Islam is Sharia Law, a belief that takes precedence over freedom and laws, national constitutions, and certainly over the Judeo Christian ethic and absolute codes of conduct like the Ten Commandments.

Islam rolled out of the Holy Land in the 8th Century and quickly conquered two thirds of the world. It took the West some 400 years to fight back — longer than the United States has existed. We seem to be in the process of repeating this bloody cycle.

The Crusades to push Islam back did not, and could not, come from inside the conquered territories. It came from the bloody edge of what remained and was at risk.

In **Raven's Run**, my characters thwarted a state-sponsored nuclear EMP attack by Islamic terrorists. In **Raven's Redemption** that huge threat remains, but offstage. In both novels, they fight the Lesser *Jihad*.

In this novel, we see a secret Iranian military base in one of our "sanctuary states." That moves us into the next phase, the Greater *Jihad*.

About the Author

John D Trudel has authored two nonfiction books and six Thriller novels: ***God's House, Privacy Wars, Soft Target, Raven's Run, Raven's Redemption, and this book.*** He graduated from Georgia Tech and Kansas State, had a long career in high technology, wrote columns for several national magazines, and lives in Oregon and Arizona.

As an inventor and an instrument rated multiengine pilot, he has long loved aviation and technology. John had a pilot's license before he had a driver's license. He built and flew his own radio-controlled aircraft before they were called "drones" and programmed computers before PCs existed.

His popular Freedom Writers blog was selected by a Radio Host as one of the "top 8 in the Northwest." It has a mix of information about both real world events and novels. http://blog.johntrudel.com

John's first five novels all won National awards. Two were finalists for the prestigious Eric Hoffer award. Privacy Wars predicted the NSA and IRS scandals, winning three Awards in the process and gleaning many media interviews.

Details, links, interviews, and video trailers are posted on John's website. The first chapters of his novels are there too, free. https://www.johntrudel.com/

Dr. Jerry Pournelle, the world famous SF writer and Star Wars scientist, described Raven's Run as a "Thriller on the bleeding edge of reality." General Paul Vallely, an expert on geopolitics, said of Raven's Redemption, "These things are already happening."

I would appreciate you writing a brief review on Amazon.com of any of my books that you have read. My author's site has links that help lead you and show you how.

**THANK YOU FOR YOUR
INTEREST AND SUPPORT**